Praise for Jill McGown's Inspector Lloyd and Judy Hill mysteries

"A plot Dame Agatha Christie would have much admired ... An ingenious puzzle ... A smashing finale with a solution that is both right and inevitable."
—*The Washington Post*

"Low-key and engrossing, and pleasantly English."
—*Chicago Tribune*

"A murder so baffling it might even have stumped Agatha Christie's Miss Marple ... A lively, entertaining mystery."
—*The Philadelphia Inquirer*

"Ingenious, stylish, and distinguished ... A talented new author."
—*Mystery News*

By Jill McGown
Published by Fawcett Books:

AN EVIL HOUR
GONE TO HER DEATH*
MURDER AT THE OLD VICARAGE*
MURDER MOVIE*
MURDER . . . NOW AND THEN*
THE MURDERS OF MRS. AUSTIN AND MRS. BEALE*
THE OTHER WOMAN*
A PERFECT MATCH*
RECORD OF SIN
A SHRED OF EVIDENCE*
THE STALKING HORSE

MURDER . . .
NOW AND
THEN

Jill McGown

FAWCETT CREST • NEW YORK

A Fawcett Crest Book
Published by Ballantine Books
Copyright © 1993 by Jill McGown

http://www.randomhouse.com

Library of Congress Catalog Card Number: 93-25496

ISBN 0-449-22311-6

This edition published by arrangement with St. Martin's Press, Inc.

Manufactured in the United States of America

First Ballantine Books Edition: March 1995

10 9 8 7 6 5

CHAPTER ONE

Now: Wednesday, 1 April A.M. . . .

MAX SCOTT LOOKED AT THE PEOPLE MILLING ABOUT THE reception area, and an old joke came to him: *Man to wife: "Do you know they say that the man at number seventeen has had every woman in the street but one?" Wife to husband: "Is that right? I wonder which one?"* And he smiled, despite the way he was feeling, because he had had every woman in the room but one.

Not as proud a boast as it might seem; of the dozens of people there, only four were women, and one of them was Catherine.

He and Catherine had married twelve and a half years ago on her eighteenth birthday, in a blaze of publicity as adverse as you might expect so soon after Valerie's death. Eighteen years his junior, almost fragile-looking, fair, pretty—once Max wouldn't have believed that he could ever look at his young wife with something less than love in his heart. God knew, he had done his share—more than his share—of accommodating Catherine's hang-ups. But just getting her here had been like dragging a dog to the vet, and it was the overreaction, the self-dramatization, that had made him lose patience with her. Catherine, with whom he had once been prepared to take infinite pains, was a child no longer, and simply had to grow up.

Now that he was actually going to meet Victor Holyoak, Max was having to fight down the butterflies that he could feel making an uncharacteristic bid for freedom in his stomach. Almost fifty, and this was the first time that he could recall the experience. It was Catherine's nervousness communicating itself to him, he supposed.

She *was* nervous—terribly nervous, and he could have been and should have been more understanding last night, he thought, with a stab of guilt. Catherine had seen him through the worst moments of his life, and looking at her now, she was so like the little girl he had met all those years ago that he felt like a monster. She had never doubted him, not once. And it was thanks to Catherine that he was here at all, if thanks were in order. On the whole he thought they might be, despite the cataclysmic row they had had about the whole business.

But he couldn't go to her, not now. She was too uptight about it all for him to say the sort of thing he wanted to say, ought to say, with all these people around. He would make it up to her when it was all over. He caught himself being pointed out to someone by Anna Worthing, Victor Holyoak's PR woman, and gave a mock bow towards her.

In the meantime, he had some brazening-out to do.

"And that's Max Scott," said Anna to Detective Chief Inspector Lloyd, who was quizzing her on the people present. "He's the new general manager."

Max stood alone, watching the gathering with a faintly amused look as the local dignitaries pointedly stood with their backs to him. He was tall, his brown hair greying at the temples. Not conventionally good-looking; his face was a touch too long for that. The twinkle in his eyes, his light, casual clothes—obvious in amongst all the grey suits—signalled his refusal to take himself or anyone else seriously, though Anna knew that he was undoubtedly taking today rather more seriously than he wanted people to know.

"He doesn't seem exactly popular," said Lloyd.

"Well . . . no," said Anna. Surely he must know about Max? It would appear not, she thought, as Lloyd looked at her with puzzled interest. She didn't enlighten him. Far be it from her to give information to a policeman, even if all he would have to do was look in his own files.

He looked round. "The famous Victor Holyoak isn't here yet, I take it?"

He was Welsh, she realized. Lloyd was, now she came to think of it, a Welsh name, but she hadn't noticed his accent until now. She shook her head. "Not yet," she said. "He'll be here soon, I expect." She looked at her watch for the umpteenth time, anxiety tugging at her.

"Don't worry," said Lloyd. "I understand the minister's running very late himself."

It wasn't the minister's arrival that Anna was worried about, but she appreciated the moral support. Lloyd was quite nice, she supposed, a little grudgingly. For a policeman. She would have said that the chances of her finding any law enforcement officer attractive would have been nil, and it was difficult to see where the attraction lay, exactly. He was balding, for a start. But at least he was letting it happen, rather than combing strands of hair over the scalp. The remaining hair was very dark, short and wavy. Black eyebrows, very blue eyes. A nice smile.

"Is there a Mrs. Scott?" he asked, in apparent innocence.

Presumably he really didn't know, thought Anna. "Yes," she said. "That's her, over there. The one in the coat." She nodded over to where Catherine sat close to the doorway, trying to melt into the background, and very nearly succeeding. She was what dress designers used to call petite. Which meant that she was the same height as Anna but a stone lighter, and a size smaller. And she had an almost childlike air, something which Anna always found intensely irritating, but men found attractive. Today, she looked scared to death, Anna noted with impatience, though what she had to be scared of, God knew. She didn't know she was born, in Anna's opinion, and any problems she had were of her own making.

Lloyd raised his eyebrows when he saw her, a little surprised. "She's very young," he said.

"Not as young as she looks," said Anna tartly. Catherine was just two years younger than she was herself, but if you listened to Victor, you would swear that Anna was old enough to be her mother. It was high time Catherine grew up, in Anna's opinion, and she had uncharacteristically given Max the benefit of that opinion. He had agreed, which was something. But she wished she had kept her mouth shut, all the same, because Max and Catherine didn't seem to be on speaking terms, and she had caused that.

"That's Zelda Driver sitting beside her," she went on, trying not to think about what was really worrying her. "The blonde

3

with the earrings. She owned the business until Holyoak International bought her out."

"Oh, I know Zelda," said Lloyd, with a smile. "I suppose I should be talking to her if I want to know about everyone."

Anna smiled back. Zelda would know more about the people present than they did themselves, she was sure.

"Who are the couple sitting with them?" he asked. "Sorry to be such a pest—if I'd known I was coming I'd have done some homework."

"It's no trouble," said Anna. "Rule, their name is. They're both doctors—they run a practice together. It's thanks to them that we've got a cabinet minister here to do the honours."

Her instinctive reaction on seeing the Rules had been to take to her and not to him, despite the fact that he was really quite handsome; dark, very short, well-groomed hair, expensively dressed, quietly spoken. She hadn't even spoken to him, but she was used to summing up men in an instant, and he had failed to pass the test. Something ungenerous about the mouth, something humourless about the eyes. Mouths and eyes; that was what she went by. Geraldine Rule, on the other hand, was the sort of woman Anna wished she was; tall, slim, trim. Her brown hair curled softly and naturally, and she wore as little make-up as her clear skin needed.

Catherine Scott said something to the others at the table, her eyes on Anna as she spoke. Anna looked back again at Max, who smiled at her reassuringly. But she felt far from reassured.

"Then he's a fraud," said Catherine Scott. "Passing himself off as the devoted husband."

Geraldine Rule didn't let her expression slip when Catherine spoke, but it really didn't do to get all moralistic with your doctor sitting across the table from you, she thought. They were discussing Victor Holyoak, and Zelda's supposition that Anna Worthing was his mistress.

"Oh, Catherine," said Zelda. She laughed, a husky smoker's laugh. Zelda had dramatic, almost gypsy-like looks, with brown eyes, pink lips, dangling earrings and blonde, dye-assisted hair. She was coming up to fifty, and her earthy approach to life had only increased with the passing years. "Surely you can't blame him?" she said. "I mean, with his wife being—"

"Now, Zelda," said Charles, his mock warning sounding genuine enough to startle Geraldine a little. She turned back to look at her husband as he carried on. "You don't know what the situation is with Holyoak and Anna Worthing—and neither does anyone else."

"So you actually believe that he's built a penthouse flat upstairs as a courtesy to visiting businessmen?" asked Zelda.

"It's quite usual, you know," said Charles.

"And—incidentally—for his own use when he's working late and doesn't want to disturb his poor sick wife by going home," said Zelda. "It's obvious what it's for, Charles."

Catherine stood up and walked away with an abruptness that made three pairs of eyebrows rise.

Charles sighed. "Zelda—you'd look for intrigue in a monastery," he said.

A good place to start, if you asked Geraldine. She was glad of Zelda's mildly malicious conversation; she had not been looking forward to today, and the nonstop gossip was taking the heat out of it a little.

Max and Catherine had arrived barely speaking to one another, which did rather leave Max out in the cold, since none of the civic dignitaries wanted to have much to do with him. The cold-shouldering did not extend to Catherine, who had been seen as an innocent abroad at the time, and who still managed to retain that air. But now that she had left their table, she too was alone, standing by the wall, almost as if she needed its support. Max had taken root at the other side of the room, trying hard to look relaxed and debonair; Catherine, on the other hand, was managing to make drinking a gin and tonic look like she was wringing a handkerchief.

"And what do you suppose is going on between Catherine and Max?" Geraldine said mischievously to Charles, not wanting the gossip to stop. "You told me only yesterday that they were rock solid."

Charles sighed. "Just because they seem to have had some sort of row does not mean their marriage is falling apart," he said. "This must be difficult for them both."

Geraldine glanced curiously at him. They usually both enjoyed a little domestic strife; they had none of their own.

"The social outcasts returning to the fold?" said Zelda. "It wouldn't be happening at all if I had my way. It's Jimmy's business, and I don't want Max Scott running it."

Charles glanced at her. "Jimmy is dead, Zelda," he said gently. Her husband had died years ago; Zelda had never quite got over his untimely end. "It isn't his business any more. It's Holyoak's. And Max has been helping you run it for years. Tim didn't want the job—you have to accept that."

"Tim has thrown away everything his father worked for," said Zelda. "But it didn't have to be Max. I *have* worked with Max for years, you're right. So I know him. I'm the personnel director in this brave new world—so why does my opinion of the personnel count for nothing?" She dropped her voice. "I told Holyoak all about Max," she said. "He said it wasn't the company's concern."

"Zelda!" Charles closed his eyes briefly. "No one knows what happened to Valerie—you'll get done for slander one of these days." He glanced round, but there was no one within earshot.

"I'm not talking about what happened to Valerie," said Zelda. "Of course Max had nothing to do with that. Max was doing something much more in character than murdering his wife, whatever the police thought." She leant closer to Charles. "And *that's* what I warned Holyoak about. Because Max Scott can't keep his hands off women. He's been through the entire office staff. It wouldn't be so bad, but they still think he's God's gift even when they're handing in their notices 'for personal reasons.' Well, I don't think someone like that should be running the business."

"He's changed, Zelda."

"He has not changed! He had to change when he married Catherine because no one would have anything to do with him then. But as soon as memories faded, he was at it again, Charles, make no mistake. And he's at it again now, whatever you think. But this time he'll come a cropper, if he's not careful."

Geraldine had had to listen to this running argument for too long to be remotely interested. She looked round the room, at where Anna Worthing stood with one of the policemen, and caught the look that passed across the room between her and Catherine. For two people who barely knew one another, that

6

look was definitely out of place. Zelda had no need to go to a monastery to find intrigue. The air was thick with it.

"Anyway," said Charles. "If you ask me Max is the right person to be running the business now that it's been expanded. He's been asked to do it, and he's agreed, that's all."

"The right person?" queried Zelda. "Someone who couldn't even keep his own business afloat? Someone who only stayed out of jail because a pregnant teenager gave him an alibi?"

Charles was shocked, as he was meant to be. Zelda had a nice line in shocking people, and despite their many years of friendship, it was Charles whom she could shock most regularly. And this long-delayed snippet of gossip certainly wasn't going to shock Geraldine, as Zelda well knew.

"What on earth makes you think that Catherine was pregnant?" asked Charles.

"I don't think it. I know." Zelda glanced an apology at Geraldine, then looked back at Charles. "I thought you'd know all about it," she said.

Charles shook his head, looking bewildered. "Why would I know?" he asked. "What happened to the baby?"

"What do you suppose happened to it? You're a doctor, aren't you?"

Charles sighed. "Zelda, you're making this up—or you've got the wrong end of the stick."

Zelda wasn't at all put out. "I know him," she said calmly. "He specializes in vulnerable women—and to hell with the consequences." She looked at Anna Worthing over Geraldine's shoulder. "And I can imagine who put in a good word for him with Holyoak," she said. "She isn't exactly secure in her new job, is she? Right up Max's street."

"I don't deny what Max used to be like," Charles said. "But he settled down with Catherine, and just because they seem to be having some sort of row, you jump to conclusions. Just like everyone has about Holyoak himself, come to that. He has a sick wife and an attractive female colleague, so they must be having an affair."

"An attractive female colleague that he only put on the payroll six months ago," Zelda said drily. "But whose rent he's been paying for years in Holland."

"Rumour. You don't know that any of that's true."

"I know that she knows nothing at all about the job she's

7

supposed to be doing. Holyoak must go through her lines with her every morning—you try asking her a question that isn't in the script and see what happens."

"Of course she's his mistress, Charles," said Geraldine, turning once more to look at the object of the gossip. "She doesn't have any background in this sort of work—she doesn't have any background at all, that anyone can find. How else would she get that sort of job? And it's only natural for the man to want female company."

Charles looked up sharply. "It may be natural," he said. "It's not obligatory."

"Oh, come off it!" said Zelda. "Men whose wives are perfectly capable of satisfying them look round for someone else—why in the world wouldn't he?"

"Perhaps he meant it when he said he would take her in sickness and in health, and would forsake all others," said Charles.

Geraldine shook her head in wonderment, and looked back at her husband. "Charles—has it never even crossed your mind to sleep with another woman?" she asked.

"No," he said simply.

No. She thought not. Some women would have been reassured by that. But Geraldine wasn't.

"I think I'll go and see if Catherine's all right," said Zelda, getting up from the table.

Charles waited until she was out of earshot before he spoke. "Why did Zelda think I'd know about Catherine's supposedly being pregnant?" he asked.

Geraldine couldn't see that it mattered now. "She's forgotten we weren't in the same practice in those days," she said. "She assumed you'd have known at the time."

"She really *was* pregnant?"

"Yes. Three months. I arranged for a termination."

"Oh."

One syllable. One syllable that said all the things that had been said too many times before. Catherine had had a baby, and had thrown it away.

"You can't blame her, Gerry," he said.

Yes she could.

"She was seventeen," he said. "Max was under suspicion of murder."

8

"I heard all the good reasons at the time," she said.

"And agreed with them, or you wouldn't have arranged for the termination," he said.

Oh, yes. She had agreed.

Judy Hill ran her hands through the short brown hair that she hadn't even had time to wash yet. Getting Lloyd ready for his big moment had been worse than trying to get a five-year-old ready to be a pageboy. She flopped down on Lloyd's big armchair, and smiled.

Election fever was at its pitch at this midpoint in the campaign; a minister of the Crown was in Stansfield to open what used to be Driver Security's big new factory, and Detective Chief Inspector Lloyd was hopefully now present at the opening ceremony, representing the chief super, who had been called away at the last moment. He had grumbled loudly about this extra burden, while secretly being tickled to death. Not about the honour of representing Stansfield's finest—Lloyd already knew he *was* Stansfield's finest—not about meeting a cabinet minister, for which breed he had no time at all, and certainly not about liaising, as he had had to do, with Special Branch, whose entire establishment he dismissed with a snort at every opportunity.

No. But Stansfield was a marginal seat, and Stansfield was news. The TV cameras would be there, and Lloyd's only previous flirtation with the medium had been attended by technical gremlins. This time, if the viewing millions were to catch a glimpse of him, he would be at his best. Not that they were likely to interview him, but there was an outside chance that he would be seen, and he had been determined to look his best, which preparations had included shaving twice—you could see the five o'clock shadow last time—and agonizing over which tie to wear. None of them, Judy had suggested, Lloyd's taste in ties being something that she did her best to overlook. In the end, he wore one that she had bought him.

Detective Sergeant Finch would be there too, watching out for would-be saboteurs; Judy had had to take a week's leave due to her, and had thus escaped Cabinet Minister duty, for which she was truly grateful. She was going to enjoy her solitude, as she headed across the tiny entrance hall to a little piece of heaven.

Lloyd's devastated bathroom might not have represented paradise to many people, but it did to Judy. Despite the damp towels and the splashes, the abandoned shaving gear, the opened bottles and the cold bath water in whose depths lurked the now squidgy soap, Lloyd's bathroom, unlike her own, had the inestimable advantage of efficient plumbing. By the time she had tidied up the mess, the water would be piping hot again, and she was going to make the most of it.

Zelda had joined Catherine, keeping up a running commentary on the others present, but Catherine wasn't listening, and didn't even pretend that she was, as she watched the door, and the big gates across the compound. Zelda had tried hard to calm her down, but even her comforting, gossipy, undemanding presence had done nothing to make Catherine feel any less afraid, and her heart was hammering as Victor Holyoak's limousine drew up outside and its occupants got out. The glass doors, each with the discreet logo of a stylized oak tree, slid open automatically at their approach.

Blood pounded in her ears as she watched the group of people move from the front door through to the reception area, then turned to look at Max, her eyes fixed on his face as he saw Victor Holyoak for the first time. She watched his mouth falling open in disbelief, felt a dull pain in her chest as the tension became unbearable. Zelda's arm came round her as she asked what was wrong, but Catherine couldn't speak, couldn't even move, until Max finally tore his gaze away to look slowly back at her. The eye contact broke the spell, and she pulled free of Zelda, making for the rear of the building, pushing through the knots of people, running through the corridors to the fire exit. She could hear Zelda calling her name, then feet coming down the corridor.

But it wasn't Zelda's high heels. It was Max. Max, running after her, catching her up. She felt him grab her wrist as she pushed down the panic bar, and they tumbled out into the cool dampness of the April morning.

"Oh, no, you don't," he said, his voice just a whisper, as he dragged her round to face him. "What the hell's going on, Catherine?" He pushed her hard against the wall, knocking the breath from her body. "Answer me!" he shouted.

His face was white; he shook with anger. For the first time

10

in her life, she was afraid of him, and she tried to struggle free from his one-fisted grip.

He pulled her back. "Don't dare run away again," he said. "No wonder you didn't know how to tell me, you little——" He slapped her face hard in lieu of a word bad enough to call her.

She stared at him in shock. It was as if he had turned into someone else, not the man she had known and loved for fifteen years.

"Tell me!" He shook her. "What have you done?" His hand came down again and again, stinging against her face. "Tell me!" he demanded over and over with each slap.

Catherine closed her eyes against the anger.

"God help me," Max shouted, "I'm getting the truth out of you if I have to beat you black and blue!"

"That's what you think, mate," said a voice.

Catherine opened her eyes to see a young man with fair curly hair striding towards them.

"Are you all right, love?" he asked, as he arrived.

Catherine nodded briefly.

"Who the hell are you?" Max demanded, still breathless, still holding on to her.

"Detective Sergeant Finch, Stansfield CID." Finch showed Max his ID. "Let's cool it, mate—all right? Let the lady go."

Max looked as though he might start on the policeman, but he swallowed hard, and let her go.

"That's better," said Finch. "Now—name and address."

"What the hell for?"

"Because I'm asking you for it!" shouted Finch. "And if you refuse to give me it, I'll have you down the nick in no time flat—all right?"

"Max Scott," he said, through his teeth. "Seventeen Garrick Drive. This is my wife, and this is a private matter."

"Then maybe you should try talking about it, whatever it is."

"I can't very well do that with you standing there," Max said, his voice still a low, almost whispered monotone.

Finch looked at Catherine, who nodded.

Finch backed off a little. "All right," he said. "But I've warned you—keep your hands to yourself. And you call us if you need us, love," he added to Catherine. He walked off, back to wherever he had come from.

As soon as he was out of sight, Max pushed her bodily through the open fire door back into the building, his anger unabated. "You and I are going back in there," he said, his hands gripping her arms.

She shook her head.

"Oh, yes," he said. "We'll see this thing through. Then I'm getting you home."

She found herself being propelled back along the corridor to the reception, his hand clamped around her wrist like a handcuff. His fingers dug into her as he took another deep breath, and pushed his way back into the room through the gathering, his grip on her growing even tighter as Victor Holyoak's speech began.

"I had a very special reason for wanting to move not only back to Britain, where I belong, but to Stansfield . . ."

The voice came to her in waves of nausea and giddiness; fading away, coming back.

". . . already had a toehold with the admirable operation set up by Jimmy Driver and carried on so ably by his widow, in which I had the foresight to buy shares . . ."

Blackness gathered at the corners of her vision, and she seemed to float away from it all.

". . . may come as news to some of you that my new general manager's wife Catherine is in fact my stepdaughter who has sadly been estranged from her family, but now . . ."

Catherine heard the startled applause; she saw the stunned look on Zelda's face. Her body weight tore her hand from Max's grasp as she fell to the floor.

Holyoak's eyes had been on his stepdaughter as he spoke; he broke off as she slipped to the ground, then walked over, pushing through the crowd that had immediately gathered round her.

"Get out of the way!" he shouted. "How do you expect her to breathe?"

Geraldine Rule was pushing through from the other side; Holyoak watched as she knelt down. Catherine hadn't looked well—he'd noticed that when he came in, before she'd had to rush out of the room. And her cheeks were flushed; she had probably been sick. She had always been highly strung, and she was bound to be nervous.

"It's all right," said Geraldine, helping her into a sitting position, and pushing her head down. "She's only fainted."

Holyoak nodded. He had known that it would be an ordeal for her, and hadn't expected her to come to the opening, but Scott had presumably insisted.

Geraldine helped her to her feet. There was a brief hiatus while everyone expected Scott to come to her, but he didn't. He just stood tight lipped and unmoving, and watched while Charles Rule went to help.

"Here," Holyoak said, digging in his pocket for his keys. "Take her up to my apartment."

He wanted to go with her, but he couldn't; the minister would be here at any moment. Perhaps he shouldn't have put the extra pressure on her that he had; he might have misjudged that. But she had to accept her responsibilities, and if that was the only way to make her understand, then so be it. She knew that there was no need to put herself through all of this.

He looked across to where Scott stood, and frowned. He had deliberately avoided meeting him before today, but he had promoted him in the face of fierce opposition from Zelda Driver. He was virtually running the place anyway, so it was a reasonable move, from a business standpoint, and no skin off his nose. He had told Catherine what her husband was doing behind her back; that had made very little impression on her. He hadn't understood that at the time, but he did now. He watched as the two doctors Rule helped the semiconscious Catherine out of the room, and still her husband took no notice of her. Matters had clearly come to a head.

He knew why, and so did Catherine.

Charles, his arm round Catherine's waist, pressed the button with P on it. Presumably that was the penthouse. Catherine hadn't meant to attend at all, according to Zelda. And she had been seeing Gerry about menstruation problems; it might be that time of the month. Or perhaps she was pregnant again, he thought, still brooding about what Zelda had said. He looked at the angry red marks on Catherine's face, frowning a little, as the lift rose, and the doors opened on to a small landing. He and Gerry stepped out, with Catherine more or less walking under her own steam. But Charles still had to hold on to her as Gerry unlocked the flat door, which admitted them directly to the sitting room of the large flat; high-tech, shiny, tastefully furnished, with a low ceiling and no visible lighting.

He helped her to take off her coat as Gerry briskly opened the bedroom door, and ushered their patient in. Charles waited in the sitting room as the door closed.

She had been pregnant when she came to Stansfield. Max had always sworn that he had not been having an affair with Catherine when they were in London, whatever Valerie had thought. Charles had believed him, had honestly thought that seducing seventeen-year-old girls was something at which even Max would have drawn the line. But the police had been very anxious to find the other woman about whom Valerie had been so upset, and whose existence Max had strenuously and uselessly denied; Catherine's turning up had confirmed it, as far as they were concerned. Max had got Zelda to put her up, and had continued to deny any involvement with the girl, practically until the day he married her.

Charles had known that there had been rather more to it than a simple working relationship, but he had believed that Max had for once kept his baser instincts in check, and that avoiding the temptation had been a factor in his decision to move away from London. But Max had been running away from a problem, and it had run after him. In the end, he had married it, if only to put an end to the gossip. But angry though he was about what he had learned, Charles knew that Max genuinely loved Catherine; he couldn't believe that he had hit her, but that was what those marks looked like, and it was hard to see what else could have caused them.

It had happened, if it had happened, after Holyoak had appeared, but before he made his startling announcement, upon which Catherine had fainted. And Max, who treated all women with something approaching reverence, hadn't made a move towards her. It was hard to imagine what in the world Catherine could have done or said to him to produce a violent reaction, but Charles supposed it had something to do with another woman, as Zelda had heavily hinted.

Charles admired Max's success with women; he always had. There was nothing obvious about it; no heavy chat-up lines, no quiet dinners for two with wine being ladled into the targeted female. Max was always just the way he came, and the way Max came was something that a great many people found very attractive, including Charles. But of course Max was always at ease with women, unlike Charles, who had never really understood what made them tick. "The same things that make you and me tick," Max used to tell him, but Charles had never found that, and Max had tempted more than one girl away from him as a result.

"The trick," he had told Charles once, "is not to make a pass. Make her feel entirely comfortable with you, and chances are she'll make the first move. Then all you have to do is make sure that she's glad she did."

Charles supposed that that was how it happened with him and Gerry, but there had been nothing calculated about it. They had known one another since their first year in medical school, and he hadn't felt shy with her as he had with other girls. And it was true to say that she had felt comfortable with him, and that she had made the first move. She had married him, so presumably she had been glad that she had, but he didn't suppose that Max had been referring to the long term when he had said that.

Gerry came out again, and crossed the room. "Water," she said, opening another door to reveal the even more high-tech kitchen.

Charles followed Gerry in, watching as she got a glass from one of the cupboards and filled it. They weren't ordinary taps that you turned and the water came out; Charles wouldn't have had a clue how to make them work. "Is she all right?" he asked.

"Yes, of course," said Gerry.

He hesitated before he asked his next question, because he didn't want confirmation of what he suspected. "Did you see those marks on her face?" he asked.

Gerry indicated by a movement of her head that she had, and looked at him, concerned. "Surely Max didn't hit her," she said, but it was obvious that she too thought that he must have done.

Charles shrugged. He had never known Max to get angry with a woman, never mind to the extent of physical violence. But the marks were there, and he had practically dragged Catherine back into the reception. Gerry walked past him with the glass of water, and the bedroom door closed again.

15

She had asked him about other women, and his reply had been wholly and unequivocally true. Women had never been that important to Charles; his physical relationship with Gerry was, he supposed, satisfactory, but from the moment they had sanctioned it by marriage it had taken place with a view to procreation, and all too soon had become technical and intense as Gerry tried desperately to conceive.

How like Max to have fathered a child without even trying. Charles had always had to work at everything; at his studies, at the practice, at his marriage, at making the right contacts and building up the private patient lists, at attempting to impregnate his wife.

It was his fault, if blame came into it. A low sperm count. Some men got very upset if they were told that; they felt it reflected on their manhood. Charles didn't. His manhood wasn't something to which he ever gave much thought. And, if truth were told, he wished they had been told that it was simply impossible for him to father a child, because then that would have been that. As it was, the possibility was there, if just one of the little buggers made it through when Gerry was at her most receptively fertile. For years now they had made love according to temperature charts and ovulation periods, with Gerry lying flat on her back without moving as soon as the act was completed so as not to lose whatever meagre sperm he had managed to produce. It had become a clinical exercise; almost a chore. Just a means to an end.

It was par for the course that Charles had had to work hard for everything that he had achieved or hoped to achieve, doing whatever was necessary to keep things going, to ensure that the Jag stayed in the garage and the detached farmhouse and the private clinic remained out of the building society's reach, that no hint of scandal or even disapproval ever touched him. And Max, who had never given a toss about personal advancement, or what anyone thought of him, always seemed to have had it all handed to him on a plate, and usually didn't want it.

Charles himself had handed Max his original job at Driver's on a plate, all these years ago. He hadn't wanted it. And now it would appear that he was the stepson-in-law of one of the richest men in Europe, and from his totally uncharacteristic behaviour towards Catherine, Charles presumed that he didn't want that either. And he hadn't wanted the baby that his seventeen-year-old mistress had been carrying.

Charles sighed. Max was a difficult man to defend.

In a flat in a London tower-block, Dave Bannister opened another can of beer and switched on the TV for the schools programmes. Some of them were quite interesting. In the afternoon, it would be the racing. He didn't have a bet on; he didn't get his Giro until tomorrow.

His wife was working in the supermarket, and would be until eight o'clock. They opened from eight till eight every day except Sunday, when they opened from ten till five, and she worked all the overtime she could get. The kids went to their gran's after school; he was alone all day and didn't even get fed until after nine. So all he could do was watch the racing, and see whether he would have won or lost. He had never been a big betting man; just a couple of quid now and then. Her money got paid straight into the bank, so he had to rely on subs from her, and she'd run out too, or so she said.

Relying on a woman. If only he could have stayed in the force, of course, they would have been all right, and it had been his own fault, he supposed, that he had finally had to give it up. But he had only got in fifteen of his thirty years, and that had made money more than scarce, with the mortgage to pay.

He had had a job with a security firm, but that went bust; he had set up a private detective agency, and that had been worse than being on the dole. Then various other ex-copper jobs, none paying much and all, one way or another, crumbling to dust.

He had done a few labouring jobs and even a temporary clerical post, but that hadn't brought in enough to make it worth his while. He was better off getting benefit, though God knew it didn't exactly let you live the life of Riley.

They had had to give up the house, and it had been so long since he had paid rent on this place that they were threatening eviction. He and Jackie had constant rows—always about money. They tried not to, but cooped up in this midair flat with three kids was hardly a way of staying cool. And now there was nothing in the way of work. Every night, Jackie would bring home the evening paper, and he would see the vacancies section shrink from the night before. People didn't even bother to reply.

One of his contacts from the old days had offered him a job as a minder; at first Bannister had told him where to stick it, and Jackie had begged him not to change his mind. It would be crooked for a start. And could he take being ordered around by scum like that? Being treated no better than a pit-bull? Besides, he wasn't that far off forty, and the problem which had caused his resignation from the job would hardly stand up to the sort of punishment minders sometimes received. She was right; he knew she was right. But he had an obligation to her and the kids, and he was failing in it.

He knew how to keep out of trouble, as long as it wasn't out of his league. And this job was small time. So now he was considering it. One step further down the career ladder. Story of his life, that was.

It was the scar Lloyd remembered, not the man. A scar, running from just under the left ear almost to the corner of his mouth. An irregular pale line through the grey, formally trimmed beard. Lloyd had seen it before. The beard hadn't been grey then. He looked away quickly as Holyoak's eyes met his across the room. Even that was familiar; he had done that before.

"The minister's here," said Anna Worthing, as the official car pulled up outside, and she moved slightly closer to Lloyd, almost as if for protection. Lloyd checked the impulse to put his arm round her, and brought his thoughts firmly back to the here and now, the tangible and real. A moment's *déjà vu*, that was all.

He saw the nervous glance she gave as Holyoak and the reception party moved towards the glass doors to meet their guest of honour, and laughed. "He won't eat you," he said.

"I know." She smiled. "But he's important."

"So what's your job?" Lloyd asked.

She looked a little uncomfortable as she answered. "I'm in public relations," she said.

It sounded like a lie, but for the life of him Lloyd couldn't imagine what reason she would have for lying. It was, he supposed, a hazard of his at times antisocial occupation. You couldn't simply make small talk if half your life was spent interviewing suspects. "It'll all go without a hitch," he assured her, employing more Welshness than was necessary in his accent. "You'll see. If the sniffer dogs say there aren't any bombs, I'm quite happy to take their word for it."

She cast one last look towards the foyer, across which had been hung an outsize white ribbon. A pair of gold scissors lay on a small table. "It's not bombs I'm worried about," she said, looking up at Lloyd.

This pleased him, since most of the ladies of his acquaintance were colleagues, and virtually as tall as he was; his lack of height had over the years been joined by a lack of hair, and both these inadequacies were less noticeable when someone had to look up at him. "Don't worry about him," he said. "He's not important. None of them is. They're all just candidates in a general election."

But she wasn't impressed by this piece of wisdom. "He's important enough to have armed police crawling all over the building," she said.

Lloyd sighed. "That's just a sign of the times," he pointed out. "Not of his importance."

"He's a *cabinet minister*," she said.

"Not until he *and* his party are re-elected," Lloyd said in a stage whisper. "Maybe not even then. He might find himself on the backbenches. But Holyoak's quite a big wheel himself, isn't he? Back in Amsterdam or wherever?"

"Not just there," she said, a note of irritation finding its way through her general nervousness. "I'd forgotten how cut off Britain is. Everyone in Europe knows Victor Holyoak. The papers here might not find him newsworthy, but they do abroad, believe me."

Lloyd accepted the rebuke with a smile. "Well then," he said. "You don't get the jitters just because he walks into a room, do you?"

"Not always," she said, with a half-smile. Then it went, and the little worried frown that Lloyd found very attractive came back. "But this is very important to him," she said.

The minister walked towards the open doors followed by the sitting MP, two bodyguards, two TV news cameras, and a staggering number of press photographers, interested in the election, not—as the girl had pointed out—in some entrepreneur of whom their readers had never heard. Stansfield, with its marginal status, had become the place to be seen, and to be seen to care about very deeply, in the three-week scramble to Election Day.

"Is there a collective noun, do you think?" mused Lloyd. "A snap of photographers?"

"An exposure of photographers," she said.

Nice, he thought, and gave her an interested glance, but she wasn't looking at him. She was almost on tiptoe, anxiously watching progress as the ministerial party was met by Holyoak and Max Scott, the man who was so remarkably uninterested in his wife's health. Lloyd amused himself for a moment or two by playing Spot the Special Branch, as the minister began his speech. His remarks were short and to the point, time having become ever more pressing, and soon Lloyd and the girl were clapping with the others as the ribbon fell to the ground and the air shuddered to fifty cameras clicking at once and a small electrical storm of flash-bulbs.

A photo opportunity. That's what they called this sort of thing these days. A piece of stage-managed bonhomie to show the electorate what great guys they all were. Sometimes they patted puppies, sometimes they visited old people's homes, and sometimes, especially in a marginal constituency with rising unemployment, they opened factories. Since the election had been announced, Stansfield had been invaded by every charismatic and not so charismatic member of parliament the parties could lay their hands on. This one was relatively young, reasonably dynamic, and almost handsome—the jewel in the government's crown—and he always got national news coverage. Holyoak was lucky to have got him.

The Rules re-entered unobtrusively after the official ceremony finished; Holyoak and Zelda Driver immediately went over to them. Scott didn't. Zelda took the keys, and went off to the lift; Scott remained where he was.

"Holyoak's stepdaughter did know he was going to make this announcement, did she?" he said, as the crush of people began to organize itself into groups to which the minister could be introduced while casting furtive glances at the clock.

"Oh, of course," said Anna. "I think she just got a bit overemotional, that's all."

Lloyd and Anna had inadvertently become a group; the min-

20

ister met them, had a sip of wine, and then he and his media circus moved on to the next port of call.

Lunch was in the boardroom, an impressively large and imposing room off the foyer. They filed in, and Lloyd was agreeably surprised to find himself seated next to Anna Worthing, and at the opposite end of the long table from Holyoak.

"Holyoak won't actually be running this place himself?" he asked, over the soup.

"No. That'll be Max Scott's job," she said. "But Holyoak UK's head office will be based here—for the moment it's housed in this building, but a prestige building is being designed. And this factory will be just the first of Holyoak UK's acquisitions. Holyoak Security will be the flagship company."

Lloyd raised his eyebrows a little at the idea, and the self-conscious quoting from some PR pamphlet.

"This is just the start," she said. She looked round the boardroom, and at the portrait of the firm's founder. "When the factory's in full production, it'll employ up to two thousand people. And he'll build more, in other areas. He wants Holyoak Security to be the biggest manufacturer of state-of-the-art security systems in Europe."

"So I'm told," said Lloyd. He felt, and sounded, more than a little sceptical. "Up to" two thousand people could actually mean any number under two thousand, after all.

"Another non-believer," she said.

"How many has it actually taken on so far?" Lloyd asked, his voice dry. "Apart from the ones already employed by Driver's?"

"A hundred and fifty, since the expansion," she replied.

More than Lloyd had thought, he conceded. "Not bad, I suppose," he said. "But it's still a long way from two thousand." He smiled. "And a very long way from Mr. Holyoak's goal," he added.

"Victor Holyoak started out with nothing," she said. "His wife had a dreadful stroke about twenty years ago. He looked after her and his stepdaughter—making himself a millionaire at the same time. If he wants something, he gets it. If he says he'll do something, he does it. He never gives up, he never lets himself be sidetracked—whatever his goal is, he achieves it. He's a household name in Europe. Do you know how many people Holyoak Industries employs altogether—how many facets of life Holyoak products enhance and improve?"

"No," said Lloyd, smiling. "But you can switch off the PR machine. I'm just a policeman."

"Sorry," she said, flushing slightly, which Lloyd found even more attractive. "It's just that no one seems to believe in him here. And they should. He does what he says he'll do."

"Perhaps they've heard one too many promises," said Lloyd.

"He never goes back on his word," she said, looking across at Holyoak and Scott, who were in conversation with two local councillors.

Scott looked edgy; he wasn't actually taking part in the small talk. Perhaps he was belatedly worrying about his wife, thought Lloyd.

"Victor Holyoak doesn't want vast complexes churning out a product none of the employees gives a damn about," Anna carried on as the lamb arrived. "That's why he invests in smaller businesses in smaller towns where they need the work."

Because the rates are cheaper where they need the work, thought Lloyd. And they work for lower wages and waive their right to trade unions. And you can buy into going concerns for a song, and add them to the bewildering number of companies you already own, snuffing out their identity if they work, and their existence if they don't.

But he didn't voice the thought; policemen weren't allowed to have public politics and Holyoak Industries had built the new factory, and increased the labour force, so they must be reasonably serious about Stansfield at any rate. Besides, the food was surprisingly good for in-house catering. And he had no wish to offend his companion; he liked her. She must have learned all the PR hand-outs by heart, he thought, with a private smile. Every now and then she would speak in her own voice, but mostly it was pamphletese. There was something touching about that. And odd; she was obviously bright, and yet she seemed to be doing a job of which she had no real or personal knowledge.

Lloyd turned his attention back to the beard, unable to rid himself of his absurd notion about it. "The Holyoaks," he said to the girl, leaning towards her so as not to be overheard. "Do they live in Stansfield?"

"He moved to Stansfield about three months ago," she said. "His wife came over first—she wanted to be with her daughter, and ... well ... no one was sure how much time she had left."

"And until three months ago he lived in Holland?" he asked.

"Yes." She looked up at him, a quick frown crossing her brow. "Why?"

He didn't answer, and contented himself with chat about this and that until the pudding arrived. Then, he thought, it might be safe to try again.

"Have you worked for Mr. Holyoak long?" he asked.

There was a moment's hesitation before she answered. "Six months," she said.

"You won't know him all that well then," Lloyd said.

She turned, her eyes almost angry. "I'm sure you've done your homework on that," she said.

Lloyd smiled a little uncertainly, not knowing at all what she meant. All he knew was that he had seen that scar before. It was a long time ago; at least, it wasn't in the recent past. He could hardly explain what was really bothering him, because it didn't make any sense.

"Where did he live when he was in Britain before?" he asked.

"I'm not all that certain," she said. "I think he lived in Hertfordshire." This last piece of information was delivered with unmistakable defiance.

"You wouldn't know how he ... ?" Lloyd ran a finger from his ear to his chin.

"Are all these questions in the line of duty?"

"No. Idle curiosity." She was beginning to get very irritated, and he really didn't want to irritate her. He liked her. But he had to get to the bottom of the scar. "I just feel as if I've seen him somewhere before," he said.

"You might have seen him around," she said, a little doubtfully. "Though he has rather kept himself to himself since he's been here."

"Probably," said Lloyd. But he had never seen Holyoak around, he was sure of that.

"Oh, you mean Anna!" Holyoak's voice carried down the table, and Lloyd's companion looked up quickly, apprehensively.

23

"Oh, Anna represented me in the early stages of negotiation," Holyoak said. "But her forte is PR—and nobody does it better—isn't that right, Max?" he asked.

Scott smiled and nodded, but the tension was tangible. Something was going on, and Lloyd's curiosity was doubled, as he glanced at Anna's anxious face.

After lunch, the assembly moved back into the foyer, and Lloyd felt a little deserted as Anna moved round, keeping an unobtrusive eye on the young women who came round constantly with jugs of beer, bottles of spirits, wine, soft drinks, even coffee. Good coffee, Lloyd discovered, but not too many of his fellow guests would have found that out. Someone should be standing outside with a breathalyser, he thought, as practically everyone present took full advantage of Holyoak's generosity. Every now and then Anna Worthing would smile across at him, and he would feel ridiculously pleased that she had. But mostly, she was involved in what she was doing, and so was he.

He was watching Holyoak. He was watching him as he moved around the room, as he ate and drank, as he chatted to his guests. Lloyd felt like a child, fascinated by some nonconformity, knowing that he shouldn't stare. But he knew that scar. He knew that it ran through a beard, knew that that beard was old-fashioned, formal and clipped, Edwardian style. He frowned. It was that beard, and that scar. And one thing was certain. The absurdity which he hadn't put into words, not even in his own head, now wouldn't be denied. Lloyd had never seen Holyoak before; he would swear to that on a stack of PACE handbooks. But he had seen his beard and scar before.

And they were on the wrong face.

CHAPTER TWO

Then: December, fifteen years ago . . .

MAX REACHED OUT A HAND TO PUT ON THE RADIO. HE didn't much like music when he was driving, but tonight sleet was slicing across his windscreen, and the visibility was poor. He wanted some company, as he drove at a steady fifty, peering through the freezing rain at the signs leading him to the motorway.

"Follow the signs for the A something-or-other," his client had told him, entirely seriously, "and you can't go wrong. You go through an underpass, and that brings you out on the slip-road to the motorway."

Max, who had come the pretty way during the clear cold sunlight of the chill November day, had wanted to get home as early as possible, given that his appointment had dragged on until nine o'clock at night and that he had a very early start in the morning, what with the wedding and the ad that he wanted to get into Monday's paper. He had no girl for the office now that Susan had left. They had a tendency to do that if he got involved with them; once the affair had run its course, they would vanish. And getting involved with them was something Max seemed quite unable to avoid. He liked women. Genuinely liked them, not just going to bed with them. But that was the best bit, of course.

The problem was that they did have this tendency to see sex and love as one entity. The partings were almost always amicable, but for some reason they involved leaving the office as well as ending the affair. So he was often left in the lurch. A more sensible man might have thought of employing a grey-haired spinster to overcome this disability, but no one had ever accused Max of being sensible. Besides, he would rather enjoy enlivening the social life of a grey-haired spinster, he suspected. But he employed the likely looking ones, and was rarely disappointed. And even when he was, he still lost them to bigger companies who could pay much more than he could. One way or another, keeping staff wasn't easy.

He had, of course, followed the signs for the wrong A something-or-other, and had finally given up trying to find the motorway in favour of actually getting home. He was only now confident that he was at least heading towards London. And he didn't switch on the radio, because he saw the girl.

She stood by the road, the horizontal sleet flying into her face, her head uncovered, holding out a hopeful thumb to the traffic that thundered past her. Max would normally have thundered past too; picking up hitchhikers of either sex was not something he normally did. But she looked very young . . . he turned his head as he passed, and sighed. He couldn't just abandon her to her fate.

He signalled left and slowed to a stop, looking over his shoulder. She hadn't seen him stop; he still had time to change his mind. But if she was as young as she looked, she could be in danger. If he drove on, anything could happen to her. At least if he picked her up, he wouldn't be reading about her in the papers.

There was no traffic behind him; he put the car in reverse, and shot backwards towards her, then stopped, still a little way in front of her, so that she would make the decision. He watched in the driving mirror as without hesitation she ran towards the car, the big leather bag over her shoulder making it awkward for her to move. He leant across and unlocked the passenger door.

The bag was thrown on to the back seat. "Thanks," she said.

He drove on for a few moments without speaking; neither did she.

"You know," he said eventually, "hitching isn't a very sensible way to get about."

He felt rather than saw her shrug as he kept his eyes on the road ahead. She could be anybody, Max, he told himself. For all you know she'll whip out a knife and steal your wallet. He sneaked a look at her. Her hair was dripping on to her face; she looked cold and tired and miserable. He turned the heater on full.

"Where are you going?" he asked.

"Wherever you're going."

He ran a calming hand over his chin. Max, Max. What have you done? You've picked up a runaway. He had to make a decision, now. Take her with him, or throw her out, now. He looked at the weather, and looked again at her. He couldn't. "Am I going to find myself in trouble for picking you up?" he asked.

"No," she said.

"But for all I know you could be an absconder from an approved school."

"I'm not. Where *are* you going?"

"London," he said.

"Fine."

"Camberwell."

"Fine."

Max sighed. "It's not really fine, is it?" he asked. "I mean— where are you going to go when you get there?"

A shrug.

"*Are* you running away?" he asked.

"How do you mean 'running away'?"

The weather grew worse on the exposed road, and Max slowed down. "I suppose," he said, "that I mean have you left wherever you have just been without telling anyone you were going?"

She thought about that for a moment. "Don't you ever leave wherever you've been without telling anyone you're going?" she asked.

It was Max's turn to think about his move. "I think," he said slowly and truthfully, "that I only do it if I don't intend to be away for more than a few minutes."

"Then I'm running away."

He smiled, despite the dread forming deep within his soul that he had made a pretty dumb move when he had stopped for her. "What from?" he asked.

A shrug.

He saw a roadside café in the distance, and glanced at her. She might have been on the run for days. She might need some food. But the longer she had been missing, the more likely it was that someone was looking for her. If the police stopped them—what would she say? She might say he'd abducted her, anything. Oh, what the hell. He'd got her now; he was responsible for her. "Are you hungry?" he asked.

"No."

Well, he didn't have to risk that. That was something. "Do you want music?" he asked. "There's a radio."

"No."

She could have done with someone teaching her to say please and thank you wherever she had spent her time until now. Max drove on into worsening conditions, his back beginning to ache. How had he managed to get himself into this? All the other drivers ahead of him had driven on, sensible fellows that they were. They hadn't been daft enough to pick her up. Oh, but what if? She was too young to have been left on the side of the road. Max couldn't have lived with himself if he'd driven on and then read that something awful had happened to her.

He entertained gloomy visions of what he might well find himself reading next morning. "Police are anxious to interview the driver of a car seen . . ." He glanced at her.

She was asleep. Her hair was drying out now; it was much fairer than he had thought. She was very pretty; beautiful, really. The heater had sucked all the air out of the car, which was now filled with the smell of her damp clothes. But he left it turned up high. She looked about six years old, asleep like that.

Oh, God. That was a point. How old was she? If she was a minor, he really ought not to be assisting her flight. He wasn't what you'd call an expert on adolescent females; he could give you a reasonably accurate assessment on women between twenty-five and forty, but she was in her teens, and that was as close as he could get. Maybe he should take her home. Valerie would be better at this sort of thing than he was. But somehow the thought of arriving home with a runaway teenager in tow filled him with even more dread than the thought of being suspected of abduction. The sensible thing to do was to take her straight to the police, wasn't it? That's what he would do.

But he looked at her again. If she had wanted to go to the police, she would have done. She was bright enough. She had

28

trusted him enough to go to sleep—he couldn't do that to her. It might even be the police she was running from. He'd be an accessory then, to whatever she had done. At the very least he would get done for harbouring a fugitive from justice.

A petrol station; he glanced at the fuel gauge and signalled, pulling in at the pump as smoothly as he could. The last thing he needed would be to run out of petrol. She didn't stir. An attendant came, startling Max, who had just got used to serving himself with petrol. He resisted the temptation to drive away again, and wound down the window. "Fill the tank, please," he said.

The attendant smiled indulgently at the sleeping figure. "Someone's had a busy day," he said, unhooking the nozzle. "Your daughter, is it?"

"Yes," Max heard his own voice say.

Her eyes shot open. Max smiled nervously at her. Please God, make her keep her mouth shut. Please. I was being a Good Samaritan. I wasn't passing by on the other side. Please, please, make her keep her mouth shut.

The cap was screwed back on, and he paid the attendant, remembering to tip him, but not too much. He didn't want anyone to have any reason at all to remember him, to give his description to the police, and he tried not to look as though he was sweating with apprehension as he fired the engine, and drove out of the lights of the garage, back on to the dark road.

"Why did you say I was your daughter?" she asked, right on cue.

"What was I supposed to say? No, it's not my daughter, it's a kid I picked up in Buckinghamshire?"

"I'm not a pick-up. And I'm not a kid. And it wasn't Buckinghamshire. It was Hertfordshire."

"I meant picked up as in gave a lift to. How old are you, anyway?"

"I was sixteen last week."

"Sure," muttered Max.

"It's the truth! Do you want to see my birth certificate?"

Could it be the truth? Could it be that God was smiling on him for his good deed, and hadn't really sent him a thirteen-year-old compulsive liar who was going to land him in prison for years? Of course it wasn't the truth. Max sighed heavily.

"Look," he said. "I can't just drop you off in the middle of London. I think I should take you to the police."

"No," she said, with something like panic, and made as if to open the door of the moving car.

"All right, all right!" he shouted. "Forget the police."

She relaxed a little. "So you'll just let me out when we get there?" she said.

"No," he said.

"Why not?"

"Because even if you *were* sixteen last week, which I very much doubt, London is a big city, with big-city vices."

"I'll go to an hotel."

"Hotels cost money."

"I've got money."

Max looked at her. "Oh, yes?"

"Yes! Do you want to see it, too?"

"No," he said. "And I don't think I want to know how you came by it, either." Probably by robbing Good Samaritans, he thought, as his day of reckoning neared, and city landmarks began to appear, lit up against the dark sky. "What sort of hotel?" he asked.

"Any."

He pulled the car up as soon as he could, turning to face her. "Do you know London at all?" he asked.

"Not really."

He closed his eyes. "Right," he said. "Well—London has got every conceivable kind of hotel. From ones that cost more a night than I earn in a week to ones that Al Capone would think twice about entering. Now—I know one that's clean and pleasant, and not terribly expensive."

Her eyes narrowed a little. "All right," she said, her voice full of suspicion. "It'll do."

He pulled out, and began making his way through the late-evening traffic, sparse now; he made good progress through the wet streets, on some of which still hung the tattered, sodden remains of the Silver Jubilee bunting. "But even a not very expensive hotel is expensive if you don't have much money," he said.

"I've got enough money," she said.

Thank God, he thought as he finally saw the hotel, in a terraced row of similar hotels, most of which he would not have recommended. But this one was all right. Max parked on double yellow lines in a side street, and got out of the car to be met with an accusing look over the roof as he straightened up.

"What are you getting out for?" she asked.

"Because you may or may not be sixteen," said Max, "but you look about thirteen. And I don't think that they will feel entirely happy about giving you a room without an evidently adult person sanctioning your request."

She looked at him for a long moment. "And what relationship are we going to be this time?" she asked. "Uncle and niece?"

Max leant over the roof of the car, despite its clammy dampness. "Have you any idea how lucky you are?" he asked. "You could have been picked up by someone who raped and murdered you. But you weren't. You were picked up by me. I was already hours late getting home, and I'm being best man at someone's wedding tomorrow morning—back out in the sticks somewhere. I have to go into the office before I leave, so I have to be up very early. Notwithstanding all of that, I stopped and gave you a lift because I couldn't bear to think of what might happen if I didn't. I brought you here in one piece, and I've found you somewhere that's clean and comfortable and respectable to spend the night. I would now like to give myself the peace of mind of knowing that you've actually booked in to it, and you're not going to sleep on a park bench."

"And all you want is to come in with me?" she asked, her voice still suspicious.

"My dear girl, I don't want to come in with you at all! I want to go home and go to bed. With my wife. Who will by now think that I have been involved in a multiple pile up. But I don't think you'll get very far on your own. Try, by all means." He made as if to get back in the car.

"All right," she conceded. "You can come in with me."

"Good," he said. "And now perhaps I've earned the right to know your name?"

She hesitated.

"Your *nom de guerre*, at least," he said.

"Catherine Barnes," she told him. "It's my real name," she added, grudgingly.

"Max Scott." He smiled. "That's my real name, too," he said.

31

They shook hands over the roof of the car, and for the first time, she smiled at him.

Detective Sergeant Lloyd looked through the binoculars from his vantage point on the ship-like balcony of a thirties cinema turned bingo hall. A residential area, quiet and peaceful on this cold, wet London night, lay directly below. But it had cars cruising at all hours of the day and night, according to the residents, who were tired of picking their way through the French letters as they took the short cut across the waste ground to the tube station.

Ten thirty. Normal people were just thinking of leaving the pub. Some would go home to bed, some would carry on drinking at nightclubs, and some would indeed go cruising the streets looking for some action. All of these activities seemed preferable to freezing to death while directing Operation Kerbcrawl.

A couple of girls appeared, strolling up and down the damp pavement, leaning against the wall, occasionally chatting to one another. Their breath, like his, steamed in the night air. Unlike him, they were not wearing two pullovers and an overcoat and scarf. Kids, both of them, half naked, and half frozen.

He thought of Linda, then. Three years old, and cheeky with it. How did you know where they would end up? These girls had been three years old, once. And not all that long ago by the look of it. They didn't all come from stereotypically deprived backgrounds. Some of them simply fetched up in London, homeless, jobless, shiftless. They could see no easier, no quicker, or perhaps simply no other way of making money.

He was getting depressed. Perhaps because he *would* rather be here than at home. Home wasn't much fun at the moment. Barbara didn't like it in London. They had been here five years now, and she liked it no better than she had to start with. Still, things would improve when he got promotion, which shouldn't be too far off. Peter could get his bike, the one that Lloyd had marked down for future purchase when the intended recipient was three weeks old. He was almost seven now, and he was tucked up in bed like all right-thinking people. Not that Lloyd would have been tucked up in bed if he had been home; he would have been pottering about until the small hours doing nothing in particular. But right now, bed seemed a very good place to be. Though not, perhaps, his own.

WPC Judy Russell's eyes caught his, and he almost blushed. Perhaps she could read minds; he wouldn't be surprised at anything that went on behind that liquid brown gaze. She had been in the job for almost two years; she was good. Good CID material—he ought to get her on to a detective course now that her probationary period was almost up. But that wasn't the extent of his interest in her; she knew that, and responded to it despite herself. Whatever it was, it had been there since the day they'd met, and it was still there.

He had asked her out for the evening a few weeks after she had arrived; he had never done anything like that before, and had been as nervous as a kitten all evening, expecting Barbara to jump out at him from behind lampposts. In the end, he had told her he was married, and she had told him that there was nothing doing. He hadn't tried again, but he had thought about it. Often.

She was taking a turn at watching the street; she looked cold, as she sipped coffee from a flask. She offered it to him, and he shook his head, his eyes glancing down at her black-stockinged legs and regulation shoes. Great levellers, uniforms. In civvies, Judy Russell's legs were something to write—

"Punter," Judy said, into the radio, ditching her coffee, as a car turned into the street.

They all tensed up; all the people who waited out of sight on the balcony, the four in the unmarked van parked off the road, and the two who displayed their wares on the road. But the car drove past at a normal speed, and went on its way.

"A waste of good coffee," observed Lloyd, as he stood everyone down.

She smiled. "It wasn't good."

"That's why I didn't have any."

More girls had come to join the first two; each had her own space, violation of which led to the odd scuffle, but nothing too noisy. Eventually, the cars were coming thick and slow, their drivers weighing up what was on offer. Lloyd watched until he had seen enough to state for certain that business was being transacted.

"Russell, Horton, left stairs," said Lloyd. "Maidley and Simpson right. When I say go, go. Don't forget the drivers are

33

committing an offence too. Names and addresses. Put the fear of God into them."

"Don't worry," said Judy.

One of the cars drove off with its prize, but the other girls were still negotiating. "Go," said Lloyd quietly, into the radio, and looked through the binoculars to watch the operation. It was quick, it was efficient. The car drivers who tried to get away were unable to do so by the unmarked van which was suddenly blocking the road one way, and the very obvious police van which had swung in from the other end, its doors open ready to receive the girls. One girl got away, outrunning Horton, who was sorely in need of fitness training. The others were rounded up neatly and efficiently. The men were warned that they might receive a summons, the girls arrested, cautioned, and taken to the van, some unwillingly, in which event they had to be manhandled in.

This was a street-cleaning exercise; the girls would be fined, the punters possibly summoned in vague terms that wouldn't mean too much to their wives. With luck, the operation might rescue some under-age kid from a life on the streets, but probably not. They would drift up west, and get into the clutches of the real villains that the Vice Squad tried to mop up. By that time, it would probably be too late. For the moment, the whole thing was simply a public nuisance, and the spot raids which would take place over the next eighteen months nothing but a sop to the public, and a lot of cold legwork and time-consuming paperwork.

God, he was getting depressed. And he had another dozen or more nights like this to look forward to. "A street-cleaning task force" was how his motley crew was described. Designed to scare away the punters and make the girls less willing to walk the streets. Fat chance. He looked at his list, and picked up the binoculars and tripod, getting ready to move the show on to its next venue.

He met Judy and Horton at the bottom of the stairs, as the others made their way to the van. Horton was out of breath still, and bleeding from a scratch inflicted in the scuffle. Judy was inspecting the damage and passing him fit.

"You want to lose some of that," said Lloyd, prodding his midriff with the tripod. "Sedgwick Terrace next," he said.

Horton swore mildly as he turned to go.

"Something bothering you, Horton?" Lloyd asked testily.

Horton turned back. "What's the point, Sarge?" he asked. "We do this all night, and we know that all these girls'll be back on the street tomorrow night. *This* street!" He stamped the frosty ground in emphasis.

Lloyd looked at him. "Then maybe we should come back here tomorrow night and do it all again," he said.

Horton sighed, his breath streaming into the light from the street lamp. "We're never *going* to clean up the streets," he pointed out. "You know it, I know it, and they know it. We can do this over the next eighteen months, or eighteen years, and it'll make no difference! So what's the point?"

"The people who live here don't like it. And they have every right to expect us to stop it, or at the very least curb it," said Lloyd, slipping the binoculars into their case, and handing them and the tripod to Horton. "Just get that stuff into the van, Horton," he said. "And stop moaning." He was angry at Horton for articulating his own feelings; it wasn't very fair.

Horton went off to the van, and Judy's eyes rested on Lloyd's for a second longer than was required in a colleague-to-colleague situation, as his DI would have it.

"Don't just stand there!" he shouted. "We've got work to do."

Charles Rule didn't really want the drink that was being thrust into his hands. His head already felt as though it belonged to someone else, and he knew that he had lost count of the drinks a long time ago. He was a doctor; he knew from research rather than experience what effect this was going to have on him in the morning. He wasn't a drinker of any note.

And he was marrying Gerry tomorrow. He closed his eyes, but the room seemed to sway alarmingly, and he opened them again, taking a swig from the glass.

"Go on," said Phil, also a doctor, also pissed out of his mind.

Charles frowned. "Go on with what?" he asked, burping.

"This Max bloke. Go on."

"Oh, Max. Yes. Max—well, he was acshully . . . ack—he was my brother's friend in the first place. He's a coupla years older than . . . anyway. He and I got . . . you know . . ."

"Pissed," supplied Phil to gales of laughter.

"No ... got ..."

"The same girl pregnant."

"We got ... whassaword? You know. Anyway—we got talking—that's it. And we ... we ... and we were both—we were both ... er ..."

"Queer."

"Stoned out of your minds," said Phil.

"... quite keen on acting," finished Charles. "We joined an amateur thingy."

Phil looked at him unsteadily. "You?" he said.

Charles nodded. "I played Iago once," he said. "And ... er ... you know. Thingy."

"Get on. Thingy? Did you really? I saw Olivier's Thingy once ..."

"Max was good—he could've been a professional. But he never ... he was an accountant. Is. Is an accountant." He smiled. "You should see him with women. You should. Women. He ... he can have any woman he wants. He's got ... er ..."

"Oh, God," groaned the barman.

Several ever more lewd suggestions were made as to what it might be that Max had got, until the barman had had enough, and they were sent out into the cold, rainy night, shouting through the streets of Stansfield, telling one another dirty jokes to which no one could remember the punch line.

The last thing Charles remembered was throwing up all over the road, and knowing that Gerry would kill him.

"Oh, Christ."

Three o'clock in the sodding morning, and the temperature dropping rapidly, making the wet roads freeze ... one more and she would have packed it in. And now what seemed like half the Metropolitan police force was leaping out of the woodwork, running across the street, rounding them up, going through all the rigmarole of arrest, and handing them on to be bundled into the van that stood waiting to receive them. It had been scary the first time it had happened to her; now she knew what to expect, and the routine wasn't so bad.

One of them was having trouble with his radio aerial, and couldn't make himself heard above the general confusion. Then, in one of those rare and precious moments, a temporary lull sent his words ringing through the street. "I can't get this bloody thing to stay up!" he shouted, to no one in particular.

"That's always your problem!" shouted a female voice, and the remark was followed by ribald laughter, mostly from the girls, but some from the cops too. The target of the humour looked embarrassed as the girls crowded round the back of the van; a younger one came to his rescue. She knew him; he'd picked her up before.

"Calm down, calm down, girls. Just get in, ladies, one at a time. There's room for you all . . . you too, Annabel," he said, fielding her as she made a less than committed bid for freedom.

"Get off me!" she shouted, and was helped up and into the van by a thrust of his hand under her crotch. She felt an expert finger slip under her G-string and into her, and she spun round in the door, breaking the heel of her shoe as she did, to look into the arrogant handsome face that smiled up at her.

"Sorry, love," he said. "My hand slipped."

She was in just the right position to kick him under the chin and break his jaw. His neck, even. His smile faded, but he didn't move. And she would have done it, if a WPC hadn't placed herself firmly between her and him.

"OK, Annabel—get in the van and sit down." Her eyes were fixed on the other cop, not her. *"Now,"* she said, still not looking at her.

And with the finality of that word, she subsided, hooking one diamond-patterned leg over the other, morosely examining the gold-coloured heel that hung off her shoe.

The policewoman turned then to look at her. "I don't know who you're showing off for, Annabel," she said briskly. "Both feet on the floor, if you don't mind."

She pulled off the ruined shoe, and complied sulkily, pulling the thin material of her dress back over her black stocking tops. Her name wasn't Annabel. It was Anna. She'd added the rest to make it more suitable. And she actually spelt it with a capital B in the middle, two Ls and an E, but none of these cretins ever spelt it right on the charge sheet. Through the open door, she could hear the low voices.

"Thanks, Jude. I owe you one."

"That's the second time your hand's slipped tonight, Dave," the girl's voice said.

"Cold night, Jude—my hands are numb." Then a laugh. "You'll make someone a wonderful sergeant one day, sweetheart, but until then—keep your nose out, all right?"

Anna reached into her bag for cigarettes, but the packet was empty. "Anyone got a fag?" she asked.

"No smoking," said the driver.

"Oh, come on!"

"No smoking." He twisted round in his seat. "It smells bad enough with the cheap perfume. No smoking."

Anna blew out her cheeks. "Fuck you then," she said.

"Some other time, love. I'm driving."

No laughter this time. Partly because you didn't laugh at cop jokes, and partly because it possibly wasn't a joke. Bloody hypocrites, the lot of them.

They were joined by a couple of uniforms, pushed out at the station, searched for drugs, and charged. Great. That was all she needed. A bloody fine. She was trying to get a flat. She'd have to live there too, to start with, but living on the premises would be better than doing it in the back of the punter's car, then getting picked up and herded into a van like cattle, only to go back to a squat she shared with two of the other girls, and God knew who or what else.

Her dream was to have her own flat, *and* working premises. Her own flat, where she could live the way she wanted to live, and never have to let anyone in that she didn't want to let in. She'd been made offers by sleazy little pimps, but she wasn't turning over half her earnings to anyone. She'd do it on her own, and she reckoned she could afford the rent on one flat. But she needed key money—everyone was out for what they could get, and key money might be illegal, but it was a fact of life. She almost had enough; she had been hoping that the bloke might accept what she had if she threw in a few inducements. But now it would all be going to the bloody courts. It was far from being her first offence.

She saw the cop whose head she had so nearly kicked in, and she still wanted to do it. But there was another way to get her own back. A way that might make them drop the charges. She turned to the sergeant who was booking her.

"I want to make a complaint," she said.

* * *

38

"And she ran off last night?"

Victor Holyoak nodded. He was talking to a private detective, one of several that he had briefed. She had rung that morning; she was in London, she was safe, and she wasn't coming back, she had said, and had hung up.

He had had to tell Margaret, of course. If he had thought for one moment that he could have got Catherine back before Margaret came out of hospital, he wouldn't have told her. But Catherine wasn't half as guileless as she appeared; she wouldn't be easy to find. He had thought that Margaret would insist on the police being brought in, but it had been surprisingly easy to talk her out of it. They would have wanted to know what had happened to his face; the whole thing would have become even more of a disaster than it already was.

Margaret had accepted that; she had always accepted that his way of life was hazardous, and that the less the police knew of it the better. She had surprised him the day she had agreed to marry him; she could always surprise him, even now.

"What was she wearing, Mr. Holyoak, do you know?"

He had no idea. "I'm sorry," he said. "I don't know what she was wearing, but she will almost certainly be wearing something different by now."

"Well—perhaps your wife could tell me—"

"My wife is in hospital," he said.

"Oh—I'm sorry. Nothing serious, I hope."

"Not really," he said. "But my wife is paralysed, you see. Minor illnesses can be dangerous—the doctor thought she should be under supervision."

The man nodded sympathetically. "Do you know why Catherine should have run off?" he asked carefully.

Oh, yes. He knew all right. But he wasn't about to tell him or anyone else. Holyoak pointed to his stitched and dressed face. "She unfortunately witnessed this," he said.

"Ah, yes. I was going to ask . . ."

"A dissatisfied customer," said Holyoak. "I answered the door, and . . ." He shrugged.

The man looked a little startled. "What business are you in, Mr. Holyoak?" he asked.

He might well want to know. "I run a finance company," Holyoak said. That was true; that was the legitimate arm of his business. "Some people don't think they should have to pay

39

back loans." That was true too, but they didn't usually take cut-throat razors to you as a result. Holyoak's business, and how he came by his current looks, were not fit subjects to discuss with even private detectives to whom he was paying enormous sums to ensure confidentiality.

"Have you reported the attack to the police?" he asked suspiciously.

The others had respected his privacy; Holyoak might have to get heavy with this one. "No," he said. "I accept these things as an occupational hazard."

This one's a bit iffy, said the detective's look. But that was all right; he had always been a bit iffy, but he wasn't going to have the police getting curious about him at this late stage. If that was too rich for the private eye's blood, he'd better turn down the work now before he was in too deep.

"Is that why you don't want to involve the police in Catherine's disappearance?" he asked.

"Is that a problem for you?" asked Holyoak, his voice deceptively polite.

The man shook his head. "None of my business," he said.

"Good." Holyoak relaxed a little.

"So you were badly hurt, and she just took off?"

Holyoak sighed. "No. She called an ambulance, and waited for it to come. But when I got back from hospital, she wasn't here. I went to bed, and this morning I realized that she hadn't come back. Then I got the call from London."

"Did she see your attacker?"

"No."

"So you don't think she's in any danger—I mean, she couldn't identify him?"

"She didn't see him, and it wouldn't matter if she had, because I know who did it," said Holyoak.

"This is a very nice place," he said, looking round the extremely comfortable sitting room in which they were talking. "My guess is that she'll not want to fend for herself for too long."

"Your guesses don't interest me," Holyoak said.

But yes, he had done well for himself. He had had the house built for his wife, who now had to use a wheelchair; everything was within reach. He had a full-time nurse. He had a Daimler and a chauffeur. But Catherine had chosen to run away just when he was in danger of losing it all; perhaps the lure that the detective guessed would bring her back wouldn't be there for much longer. He had a lot of thinking to do, and this joker had better not be a time-waster.

"Do you get on with your stepdaughter as a rule?"

Victor had had enough. "What's that got to do with it?" he asked.

"I . . . I thought that if she was frightened by what happened—"

"Don't think," Holyoak said, his voice quiet.

The man looked at him, his eyes widening slightly.

"Catherine wasn't frightened," Holyoak went on. "She disapproves of me, of what I do. She was ashamed, maybe, but not frightened. And I just want you to find her, not psychoanalyse her. Whether or not she can cope with my lifestyle is something her mother and I have to worry about—not you." He leant forward, and the other man shrank back. "I'm employing you to find her with minimum fuss and maximum efficiency. Don't think. Just look."

The man licked his lips slightly, nodding. "Just trying to get the picture," he said hastily. "No offence. I just meant that if you and she don't exactly . . . hit it off, well—she'll probably just stay somewhere until her mother's back."

"Didn't you hear what I just said?" asked Holyoak.

"Yes—but . . ."

"Find her and you'll be banking more than you've ever banked at one go in your life. Start 'just thinking' instead of doing what you're being paid to do, start poking your nose into my business—and *you* won't have a business any more. Got it?" He stood up. "And if you don't want the job, then you've just wasted an hour of my time. I could get very angry about that."

"No—no. I want the job. I'm not wasting your time. Did your stepdaughter have any money on her?" he asked, swiftly getting back to impersonal questions.

Holyoak nodded. "I expect so," he said. He sat down again. "She usually does."

"And she took clothes, you said."

He nodded again.

"Do you have a photograph?"

Holyoak had sorted out photographs that morning; he had

41

chosen the ones taken on her sixteenth birthday, and handed the last one to the detective. "If you find her, you report back to me," he told him, as he had told the others. "You make no contact with her."

He nodded, and took the photograph. "London's a big place," he said.

"Use your head," Holyoak said. "Use your wallet. Use muscle if it helps jog any memories, but don't let the police get interested, and don't let her out of your sight if you do find her."

London was a big place. But she'd be found. Sooner or later, she would turn up somewhere. She couldn't just disappear.

Saturday, mid-morning. Grey, overcast, but dry, thus far. Geraldine stepped from the car, taking her father's arm. Her matron of honour held up the creamy folds of material clear of last night's puddles as they picked their way through the cars which had spilled over from the church's tiny car park on to the pathway.

A white wedding. A cream wedding, at any rate. It was supposed to be her big day, but Geraldine had never cared for all the razzmatazz of church weddings. Charles was the one who wanted it this way, who wanted the bridesmaids and the confetti and the picture of them cutting the cake, who wanted top hats and morning suits and a reception in an hotel that cost the earth.

And it was her father who was having to pay for it all, of course, because she and Charles couldn't afford it. They were saving every penny for the practice. Not that her father minded in the least. What he hadn't liked was Charles's and Geraldine's habit of holidaying together, and going off for the occasional weekend together, as they had done for the last four years. Despite the fact that she was now a qualified doctor, her father tended to regard her still as his little girl, and this was what he had wanted, just like Charles, who had never seemed too keen on their premarital forays.

Charles had been planning this since he and Geraldine had met, practically. She smiled. He was a great man for plans, was Charles. As soon as they had saved enough, he had said, they would marry, and they would set up a practice in Stansfield. She wanted all of that; she just hadn't wanted this.

42

And more than anything, she wanted a baby. But she hadn't told Charles that yet.

She stood in the doorway of the church, with her dress being arranged, and smiled at her father, trying very hard to make herself feel romantic. In truth, she just felt a little silly in her bridal gown, with flowers braided through her long hair. Her father had had *tears* in his eyes when she came downstairs. Because she was wearing an off-white dress. This was what it amounted to.

The inner door opened, the vicar nodded to the organist, and "Here Comes the Bride" heralded her entrance. She felt sillier than ever, not looking right or left, but staring straight ahead at the back of Charles's head, at the soft dark brown hair that had curled down over his collar, but which was shorter this morning than it had been since she had met him.

He turned. His face was pale, his eyes distinctly red-rimmed and dark-circled. As she got closer, she could see the perspiration darkening the hair behind his ears. She saw the fabled Max Scott for the first time; she had heard about him as long as she had known Charles. He was attractive, and clearly didn't have a hangover, as he gave her an amused glance. He was hanging on to Charles for dear life. Poor Charles. They must have got him drunk last night; he must feel like death. She could imagine him dragging himself to the barber so as not to offend her father with the length of his hair, climbing into his unfamiliar hired clothes, with an even less familiar hangover; now he was standing there, probably praying that he wouldn't faint.

He could faint if he liked. He could fall asleep if he liked. The sheer effort of will that it must have taken for him to be here was what brought a loving tear to her eye, and he could be sick all over her cream bridal gown for all she cared. She wouldn't mind.

She loved him.

"I'm a married man with two children, and I'm falling in love with you. Is this going to be a problem?"

"Yes," said Judy firmly, to her half-pint of lager.

The West End pub was warm, with a smattering of conversation and quiet background music as it waited for the Saturday lunchtime crowd to arrive. Lloyd's foot had rested against hers under the table; now, he drew it away.

"Why did you agree to come for a drink with me, then?" he asked.

"Because," Judy solemnly told her lager, "I can't pretend that nothing's happening between us. I wanted to see you."

"You'd find that easier if you looked at me," he said, his voice gentle.

She loved his voice. Slowly, she raised her eyes from the glass to his face; the Celtic colouring, the dark wavy hair that fell untidily over his brow, the blue eyes looking directly back into hers.

"That's better," he said, smiling.

She didn't smile back. She didn't feel like smiling. So many of them were crass and stupid; so many of them were anti-women, and the odd one, God help her, was like Dave, the one who carried out routine indecent assaults on prostitutes, and had got away with it. Judy hadn't seen the incident; she had put two and two together, but she hadn't witnessed it, and she could only report what she had seen and heard. They only asked her about Annabel; she had answered them, and hadn't volunteered any other information. Even sergeants were supposed to turn a blind eye to anything short of full-scale corruption; one PC shopping another was unthinkable. Sometimes she hated the whole police force, from the commissioner down. Because they had all taken Bannister's word against Annabel's.

Lloyd wasn't like any of them. But if she wasn't careful, she'd be like them soon. Bannister had interpreted her silence as a personal favour. She had had a long chat with Annabel, in the hope of persuading her to give up life on the streets; it hadn't been successful.

The pub began to fill up, and people sat down at the next table, noisily organizing who was having what.

"Do you want that drink?" Lloyd asked.

She shrugged.

"Then let's go somewhere else."

"Where?"

Lloyd stood up, and bent down towards her. "I don't care," he whispered. "I just don't want to carry on this conversation in a pub."

She followed him out into the diamond-hard air, and they walked through the streets, not saying anything at all. Buses shuddered, Big Ben chimed, taxi engines chattered as they waited at the lights. The smell of a dozen different national dishes wafted out of the restaurants as they passed.

"No money," said Lloyd.

"No appetite," said Judy.

"I know," he said, grabbing her hand, running with her, jumping on to the open platform of a not yet phased-out Routemaster, pushing her upstairs ahead of him, to the empty upper deck, where he pulled her down into a seat. The bus groaned as it pulled out from the stop, and car horns sounded.

Judy stared at him. "Well?" she said.

"Well. We're on the top deck of a bus."

"Where's it going?"

He grinned. "Who cares? We'll get another one back when we've been." He turned as the conductor laboured up the stairs, his girth making the task only just this side possible.

"Fares, please," he said, in a deep West Indian baritone.

"Two to the terminus," said Lloyd. "Thank you."

The machine spat out the tickets, and the conductor stayed where he was.

"Thank you," Lloyd said again, a little more loudly, rather as though he were talking to a hard-of-hearing butler.

The conductor didn't move, and Judy's mouth began to twitch. She didn't really know how Lloyd was likely to react to being laughed at; she gave him a sideways look, to find him winking at her. Then he literally fell on top of her as the bus swung round a seemingly endless bend to the right.

The conductor made his way down once the anticipated hazard of being wedged in the stairway had passed, and the bus had made it round the bend. But Lloyd stayed where he was.

"Get off me," Judy said, but there was a lack of authority in her tone.

He smiled, and kissed her. She kissed him back, and he smiled again.

"More," he said.

Oh, such a kiss. They emerged from it eventually, and Lloyd sat back. "How much of a problem?" he asked.

"Too much." She sighed. "I thought you wanted to be somewhere we could carry on a conversation."

45

"Only so that I could say what was on my mind. I think I just did."

"No, Lloyd. It wouldn't be right."

"Not on the top deck of a bus in broad daylight, no."

Judy closed her eyes. "Not anywhere," she said.

"I . . . I can't stop thinking about you," he said. "And when we were working last night, I got the impression . . ."

He left the rest of the sentence to her. Judy stared straight ahead as the bus made its way through unfamiliar streets, praying that it would stop and pick up a chain-smoker, but it just swept past all the stops. Had he known it would do this? She wouldn't be surprised. She could hardly tell him he had got the wrong impression, because he hadn't. "I'm sorry," was all she came up with in the end.

"What harm would it do?" he asked.

In different circumstances, perhaps none. She even had access to a flat, and she wanted nothing more than to go there with him, but she wouldn't. Not because it was Michael's flat; some girls might have had qualms of conscience about using their boyfriend's flat for such a purpose, but she wouldn't. Michael was the first and only man whose bed she had shared, but their relationship was fluid; he was away on one of his long business trips, and he wouldn't be going without, of that she was quite certain. He made no secret of it.

And it wasn't because Lloyd was married. Or because he had two small children. She could imagine circumstances in which she might well ignore all the moral objections for a bit of fun that would harm no one.

But she knew how she felt about Lloyd, and that added up to a great deal of potential harm all round. People would get hurt. *She* would get hurt. There was no way she could compete with a wife and two children, and she wasn't getting into a destructive relationship of that kind. Self-preservation was the strongest drive of all, and her fear of the consequences outweighed everything else.

"You're married," she said softly, getting up. "Forget it, Lloyd. Please."

She made her way downstairs, travelling on the platform until the conductor rang the bell for the next stop. Lloyd didn't follow her down, and she headed for the Underground, not daring to look back at the bus.

Coward, she told herself, as she got her ticket. Coward, said the doors as they closed. Coward, said the wheels, taking her back to her nice safe mum and dad. Coward, coward, coward.

Saturday evening. Catherine looked up sharply when she heard the knock at the hotel door, and might not have answered it, had she not realized that it had one of those peephole things.

She looked through it to see Max Scott, and her lips went into a straight line. She should have known he was too good to be true. Reluctantly, she opened the door a little.

"How are you?" he asked.

She didn't answer.

"I . . . I may have a proposition to put to you," he said.

"You don't say," she said dully.

The look that she had got to know quite well during their journey to London crossed his face. "I want," he said slowly, "to talk to you. That's all."

Why, though? He'd given her a lift, that was all. Catherine felt certain that other hitchers didn't acquire their drivers for the rest of their lives. He was just trying it on.

"Oh, yeah?" she said.

"Look—what I am thinking of doing requires a great deal of trust on my part," he said. "Do you think there's any chance of a modicum of trust on yours?"

He'd been as good as his word so far, she thought, and reluctantly opened the door to admit him.

"You must be joking," he said. "Come down to the lobby, where there are people. People who can swear in court, if necessary, that I remained at all times at least four feet away from you." He turned, and went back towards the stairs.

Catherine looked round the little room, and picked up her bag, in which she had everything that she deemed essential, and which she was not going to let out of her sight. Then she followed him down to the lobby.

He walked over to the small table near the door at which there were two upright chairs. "Sit," he said.

Catherine sat.

He sat.

Nothing was said.

"What?" said Catherine, eventually.

"Do you swear to me that you are sixteen years old?"

"Why?"

"Because it's against the law to employ someone under sixteen," he said.

She delved into the bag for her birth certificate, and handed it to him.

He smiled. "You were sixteen last week," he said, then frowned a little. "Have you left school?" he asked.

"Yes." She had now.

"Fine," he said, then looked at her again, the way he did. "Am I likely to have the police round looking for you?"

She shrugged.

"I'll have to tell them, if I do."

"They won't find me."

"Have you broken the law?"

"No."

He looked at her with every bit as much suspicion as she felt about him, then carried on. "Well, I've got a vacancy for a ... well, I would have called it a Girl Friday in the ad, but that's a bit ... well, anyway. Someone to do a bit of typing, answer the phone when I'm not there, keep the files in order—that sort of thing."

"I can't type."

"No ... well. Maybe I could run to ... an evening class. Or something."

She thought about it. "Why are you doing this?" she asked suspiciously.

He smiled. "That's what I keep asking myself," he said. "I think it's because I don't like the alternatives on offer to you. Your money won't last for ever, and ... well, runaways are prey to a lot of very unsavoury characters."

"What's it to you?"

He shrugged. "Nothing, I suppose. But there you are. That's the offer. I can't pay very much, but it'll be what other sixteen-year-olds are getting."

Catherine thought about that, and its implications. "Would you pay me in cash?" she asked. "No forms, or anything like that?"

His eyebrows rose, and then he mulled the idea over for a few moments. "It would save me money," he said. "But it's illegal. You wouldn't be properly insured, you wouldn't get state

48

sickness benefit if you were ill . . . and I'd be in deep trouble if I got found out."

"But will you?"

He seemed to be going to refuse; if he had, she would have turned down his offer. But in the end, he nodded. "OK," he said.

"I'll take it," she said.

"Good." He smiled. "I've done you a little plan of how to get to the office from here—it's just a few streets away. And you will have to look for somewhere else to live, of course. You might be able to find somewhere to share—"

"No," she said. "I'll find something on my own."

"Rent is high in London."

She nodded.

"It's up to you," he said, and stood up. "Till Monday then," he said, and held out his hand.

For the second time, Catherine shook it. For the second time, she remembered her manners. "Thanks," she said, and, for the second time, she smiled.

But for the first time, she had lied to him.

Night shift again. And having to face Judy Russell; Bannister didn't think he could take it. She had had to rescue him from a girl who didn't come up to his shoulder; he had frozen, when he saw the sheer rage on Annabel's face. Russell knew it, and he knew it. And the little whore had the nerve to make a complaint, and that had put him in hock to Russell again. Bannister pulled on his uniform jacket, his face grim.

"What's up, Dave? Russell been giving you a ticking off again?"

He grabbed the speaker by the lapel and pushed him against the metal lockers, rocking them. Someone grabbed him from behind before he hit him.

"Come on, Dave!" said the arbitrator. "It was just a joke."

He turned. Horton. Bloody Horton. He'd got him into this. He should have been getting the women into the van, but the fat sod was too busy letting them make a fool of him.

"Sorry," said the first, whose lapel he still grasped. "I didn't mean anything by it."

Bannister let him go, and shook off Horton's restraining arm. The others, robbed of their entertainment, began to drift

49

out to get their instructions for the evening; Horton stayed behind.

"Come on—we'll be late."

A cheap little street-walker showing him up. Making a complaint about him. Bannister slammed the locker door, which merely opened again. He locked it, and followed Horton out.

She'd be sorry. He'd bide his time, but she'd be sorry she messed with him.

CHAPTER THREE

Now: Wednesday, 1 April, P.M. . . .

"SHE'S FINE," SAID CHARLES RULE. "I'VE JUST CHECKED on her again. She wants to be left alone for a little while."

Holyoak nodded, and thanked Charles and Geraldine for their part in bringing the minister to his opening day, and for their professional services with regard to his stepdaughter.

Geraldine was Margaret's doctor; her prognosis in his wife's regard was not optimistic. But Margaret had known that; that was why she agreed to come back to Britain, though the travelling hadn't helped her. To Stansfield, to be where Catherine was. And Catherine had been to see her. But only once.

Holyoak had always kept an eye on Catherine, from a distance. He had tried anonymously to buy his way into Driver's several times, to be met with resistance from Zelda. He had acquired some shares, but nothing to give him any kind of control. But the recession had weakened both the company and her resolve, and he had finally bought her out. A move dictated by the heart and not the head, but he would make it work. Margaret's health had grown steadily worse, and he had judged the time right to move back. He had done it for Margaret, not for her ungrateful daughter.

He had known what Catherine's reaction would have been if he had done it all openly, so he had sent Anna ahead, to put all the pieces in place before he came himself.

"I suppose you think it's odd that I haven't gone up to Catherine," he said. "But she and"—with difficulty, he used the man's first name—"Max seem to have had some sort of . . ."

51

"Yes," said Geraldine.

"I think perhaps I shouldn't interfere," he said.

Geraldine gave a brittle smile. "That's what Charles says," she said. "Isn't it, Charles?"

"Well—husband and wife, you know," said Charles.

"Has he even asked how she is?" said Holyoak.

Charles Rule got out of answering as they were interrupted by the man Holyoak had come to think of as Anna's policeman, so much of her time had he monopolized.

"I'd better be off, Mr. Holyoak," he said. "Thank you very much—I'm glad we weren't needed."

Holyoak had to see the man off the premises; he nodded an apology to the Rules, and forced a smile as he followed Chief Inspector Lloyd to the lift.

"I'm going to speak to Max," said Gerry, making to get up from the table. "Find out what's going on."

Charles caught her arm, and shook his head. "Even if we're right, it's none of our business," he said.

"You sound like those people who live next door to battered children," she said.

"She was hardly"—Charles realized that the words were carrying—"battered," he continued, lowering his voice. "And you said she denied it anyway. Whatever's going on, I'd rather it wasn't discussed here."

"I'm worried about her. I don't want Max going home with her in this mood—I've never seen him this angry."

Charles sighed. "I have," he said. "Once or twice." It took a lot to rouse easy-going Max to anger, but it wasn't totally unheard of. Hitting a woman was. "But it'll blow over, whatever it is," Charles said, more confidently than he felt. "It's probably something to do with this business about her stepfather." He looked at Gerry, watching for her reaction when he asked the question he was about to ask. "You didn't know, did you?" he said.

"Know what?"

"That Holyoak was Catherine's stepfather?"

She looked uncomfortable. "Why would I have known?" she asked, asking another question instead of answering his.

"You treat her mother," he said. "I thought . . ."

"Oh," she said. With relief. "No. I didn't know."

"Do you think Max knew?" he asked. "Before Holyoak made the announcement?"

"I . . . I don't know. He must have done, surely."

"It might explain why he's behaving like this," said Charles.

"It doesn't explain what happened before he made the announcement," said Gerry. "And he has to have hit her, Charles," she added, in a low voice. "Whatever she says. What else could those marks be? And it worries me. I've never seen him like this—neither have you, or Zelda—"

Charles dismissed her fears with an impatient wave of his hand. "You're getting as bad as she is," he said. "Why don't you just pop over and ask him if he's going to murder this wife too?"

"Really, Charles—"

"Well, that's what you're thinking, isn't it? No one's ever seen him like this—except maybe Valerie?"

"I didn't say that!" She flushed slightly, and tried to rise again. "I'm going to have it out with him," she said.

Charles increased the pressure on her arm. "Sit down, Gerry," he said. "I won't allow you to make a scene in here."

She sat down again, and he relaxed a little.

"You speak to him then," she said.

Charles didn't want to speak to him, but his behaviour really · was so remarkable that someone ought to say something, he supposed. He finished his wine, and took another glass from one of the girls. "All right," he said.

Max stood on his own, looking out of the window at the darkening sky.

"Don't you think you should go see how Catherine is?" Charles asked.

"With two doctors and Zelda attending her, she would seem to be being adequately looked after," said Max, not turning round.

"People are talking about it," Charles said.

"Oh, and that's the worst thing that can possibly happen, isn't it, Charles? People talking. My God, how will I ever get over the shame of it?"

Charles drank some wine before he spoke. He really didn't want a scene, but Max was spoiling for a row, and if he wanted one, he'd damned well get one if he wasn't careful.

53

"You did know, did you?" he asked. "About Holyoak being Catherine's stepfather?"

"Oh, yes," said Max, his voice low and angry. "I knew. I found out yesterday."

Ah. Charles could see that could have led to marital discord. But it didn't really explain the way he had behaved today. Hitting her? Ignoring her when she fainted? "Don't you even want to know how she is?" he asked.

"She fainted. She'll get over it."

"I think you could be showing a little more concern."

Max turned to look at him. "Why?" he asked. "Is she ill?"

"Well, she has been seeing Gerry for some time . . ."

"She's always had trouble with that! It's hardly life-threatening."

"Always?" said Charles, emboldened, perhaps, by the extra glass of wine which he had now almost finished, stung by Max's attitude, and angry. Very angry. "Or just since the abortion?"

Max stared at him. "What the hell are you talking about?" he said.

Lloyd let himself into the flat, throwing his coat over the telephone table. It wasn't enough to have one phone these days. He'd got one in the hall, one in the sitting room, and one in the bedroom. The flat wasn't the size of twopence; Judy made fun of him about that. Judy came out to meet him, picked up his coat and hung it up tidily on the coat rack.

"It went on long enough," she grumbled, kissing him. "This was supposed to be a day off. How did it go?"

"Well—it was all a bit odd," he said.

"Oh?" She stood aside as he headed for the kitchen. "How?"

"He announced some sort of reunion with his estranged stepdaughter, who promptly fainted dead away," said Lloyd, surveying the fridge. "Lamp chops?" he asked.

"Lovely," she said. "I'll make them, if you like."

"No, thanks," he said, with a grin.

Judy and food were virtual strangers to one another. She could cook breakfast, and did a fair steak and chips, but there her talent, and her appetite, seemed to end. She ate if there was food going, but if there wasn't, she didn't seem to bother.

Lloyd looked at his waistband, and wished that he was like that.

"So then what happened?" she asked, coming into the kitchen. "Don't leave me in suspense."

"Her husband took no notice of her at all," said Lloyd, lighting the grill.

"When?" she asked, frowning.

"When she fainted. Totally ignored her."

Her eyebrows rose. "Fancy," she said. "So—what's the story?"

"There's more," said Lloyd. "Finch tells me that before all that happened, he saw Mr. Scott—that's the husband—laying into Mrs. Scott round the back of the office block. He had to sort him out. She's a lot younger than him, incidentally." He selected two lamb chops each, and placed them on the grill pan.

"Well? Stop being so annoying! What was it all about?"

Lloyd pulled out the salad drawer and took out mushrooms and tomatoes. "I don't know," he said.

"You mean all that was going on and you didn't stick your nose in?" she asked incredulously.

This was it. The moment he had been putting off. "No," he said. "Because something odder than that happened."

His recollection had an unreality about it that bothered him. He was seeing the beard and the scar, but the face wasn't clear. He just knew it wasn't Holyoak's face. And he remembered looking *away*, just as he had today, as though he shouldn't have been looking at all.

He knew why he'd looked away today, but why would he have done so before? *Had* he done so before? Was the whole thing a figment of his imagination? If so, when had it lodged itself there? Just today? Then why the feeling that it had happened a long time ago?

"What?" she demanded.

He knew what her reaction would be. But he had to tell someone, and Judy was the only person in the world that he could tell. Even if she was looking at him the way she was looking at him now, as he related his strange experience.

"The wrong *face*?" she repeated.

He nodded, pouring cold boiled rice into sizzling oil in the pan. He wondered if he should get a wok.

55

"Lloyd—"

She didn't say whatever she had been going to say. If she had been going to say anything. Just saying his name more in sorrow than in hysterical laughter was enough, really.

He stoically made her dinner. Why, he wasn't sure. She was supposed to be sympathizing, understanding. But no one had ever told her that, unfortunately.

"So," she said. "What do you think? He lends the beard and scar out? Perhaps someone stole it—perhaps *he* stole it. He could be the leader of a gang of international beard thieves. Maybe it was false—did you try to pull it off?"

"Very funny," said Lloyd.

"Any funnier than thinking he has a *doppelgänger*?"

"It can't be a *doppelgänger*," Lloyd said seriously. "Or it would have had the same face."

"*Don't,*" she said, looking uncomfortable.

"I tell you," he said. "I've seen that beard and scar before. And it—"

"Yes—don't say it again, Lloyd, please. Perhaps you just saw someone else once who—"

"Who had a beard and a scar exactly like his? What do you suppose the odds are against that?" he asked. "It's a very particular kind of beard and it hasn't been fashionable since Edwardian times."

"Then you saw *him*! He's changed, that's all. You said yourself it seemed like a long time ago."

"Yes. Ten, fifteen years ago. It was London. I'm sure it was London." That had come to him on the way home. The feeling that accompanied the half memory was London. A feeling of not being very happy, of the world lying heavy on his shoulders. He'd only really felt like that in London. By the time he and Barbara had come back to Stansfield, they had known the marriage was over; it had just been a matter of playing out the last act.

"Well—he probably had a business in London." Judy looked at him. "Maybe he's got a twin," she said.

"With exactly the same beard, and exactly the same razor scar?" He put in the mushrooms and the tomatoes, and turned the chops.

"A *razor* scar?"

Lloyd shrugged. "It looked like one," he said. "On both of his faces," he added.

"Don't keep saying that!" she said. "Why would someone like him have a razor scar?"

"I don't know," said Lloyd, putting in a dash of Worcester sauce. He grinned. "It's a mystery," he said, in a stage whisper.

Judy filled the kettle. "I'm surprised you didn't ask him," she said. "Good afternoon, Mr. Holyoak, who slashed your face with a razor?"

"I tried to find out," he said. "But the girl didn't know how he'd come by the scar." He put plates in the oven.

"What girl?"

"The one he's supposed to be having an affair with, according to Zelda Driver," he said, with a grin.

"Oh, that woman should be put down!"

Lloyd laughed. "Heart of gold," he said. "It seems that Holyoak's wife is an invalid—Zelda excuses him on those grounds."

"You do realize she's told half the town about us?" asked Judy.

"No one takes any notice," said Lloyd. "It's all guesswork, anyway."

"It's good guesswork. We could do with her in CID."

They were eating when she returned to the subject of Victor Holyoak, as he knew she would.

"It could be a twin," she said. "You read about it. Twins separated from birth, one in Australia and one in Manchester. Breaking their legs at the same moment. Or giving birth on the same day."

"Getting into razor fights and receiving the same injury?" asked Lloyd.

"Mm." She frowned, then returned to her lamb chop. "I'm being infected by you," she said. "You saw him, that's all. A few years ago. He's changed—people do." She grinned, and tapped what he still liked to think of as his receding hairline, though in truth it had receded practically to the back of his head. "Look at you," she said.

He stuck his tongue out at her.

Geraldine found Zelda sitting alone, and joined her; Max and Charles were deep in conversation, and Holyoak was busy. She hoped Charles was finding out what had been going on with Max and Catherine; she had hoped he might calm Max down a little, but his presence seemed to be having the opposite effect.

Zelda gossiped about the ones who had left, including the policeman who had been so taken with Anna Worthing. He, it seemed—according to Zelda—had been having an affair for years with a married colleague, who had left her husband as a result. How Zelda knew the intimate details of everyone's life Geraldine didn't know, but it was always good fun to listen. She never believed a word of it.

Now Zelda began to look round for likely targets among those who remained, and her eye fell on Max and Charles; the conversation seemed to be getting a little heated. "Surely Charles isn't *arguing* with Max?" she said. "I always thought that Max could do no wrong in your husband's eyes."

"I think Max shocked him a little," said Geraldine. "Not going up to Catherine."

"Perhaps he's discovering that his idol has feet of clay," said Zelda. "At last."

Geraldine had known Zelda all her life; she wasn't offended. Charles had always hero-worshipped Max; Geraldine had heard all about him before she ever met him, which was on her wedding day, when he was Charles's best man. Max's feet of clay were obvious to everyone but Charles. She watched as Holyoak saw off another group of guests, seeing him glance at his watch.

"I think I'll pop up to see Catherine, and tell her it's just friends down here, if she wants to come down," said Zelda.

"Good idea," said Geraldine. "I'm just going to tear these two away, anyway. Victor must be shattered." She smiled as she realized he had heard her.

"No!" he said, with forced bonhomie. "No, not at all. It's a party. I want you to enjoy yourselves for as long as you like."

Geraldine wasn't enjoying herself; neither was he. Catherine obviously wasn't, and Zelda was only enjoying being able to gossip aloud about everyone now that they had all gone. Max and Charles were having a public row, something that she wouldn't have believed possible. But then she would have thought that Max hitting a woman was impossible, too. Anything, it seemed, was possible now.

After a few moments, Zelda reappeared with the intelligence that Catherine had already left.

"What?" Victor turned away from Geraldine to look at Zelda.

"She was probably too embarrassed to come back in here," Geraldine suggested. "People feel like that about fainting—it's silly, but they do." Too scared of her husband would be more to the point, but she thought there was little point in worrying Victor more than he already was.

"Yes," he said. "Probably. You must excuse me, Geraldine," he said. "Do you have the keys, Zelda?" he asked. "And perhaps you could play hostess to our guests? I have to have a word with Anna."

He went to where Anna Worthing was standing alone, and led her firmly out to the lift, just as Max pushed past Charles, and headed for where Geraldine sat with Zelda.

"Where are these keys?" he said to Zelda, his face pale and angrier than ever. "I want to talk to Catherine."

"Catherine's gone," said Zelda.

He gave a short sigh. "Then I'm going too," he said.

"It's time we all left," Geraldine said quickly.

Zelda walked towards the lift. "I quite agree," she said, pressing the button to recall it.

Geraldine couldn't let Max go home to Catherine in this mood, though she wasn't at all sure how she could stop him. She would have to say she wanted to make a house-call on Catherine. No one spoke in the lift, not even Zelda, as it took them to the basement, and they walked into the cavernous car park. But only Charles and Zelda's cars remained, where their three cars had been parked side by side.

"She's taken the bloody car!" said Max.

"We'll give you a lift," Geraldine said, her relief almost audible in her tone. The words had no sooner been uttered than Charles's pager bleeped.

"Sorry," he said. "I'll have to go and find a phone."

"I'll come with you, Zelda," Max said. "I want a word with you, anyway." His tone was less than friendly.

"Do you mind if I join you?" Geraldine asked, using her original excuse. "I'd like to see how Catherine is."

Charles sighed loudly, and went back into the lift as the others got into Zelda's car, the doors banging. Geraldine sat in front with Zelda; Max was in the back.

Zelda didn't start the car. "What did you want to talk to me about?" she asked.

"I want to talk to you about rumour-mongering, Zelda," he said. "Charles tells me that you're saying Catherine was three months pregnant when she came here—that she had an abortion! What put that idea into your head, for God's sake?"

Oh my God, thought Geraldine, Charles had told him. Charles, who had visions of lawsuits if he so much as gave someone else's patient a sticking plaster, had *told* him? Geraldine couldn't believe it.

Max was staring at her, at the reaction that had entirely given the game away. "Is it true?" he whispered.

"I can't discuss Catherine's medical history," said Geraldine.

"It is true," he said, stunned. "She had an abortion? But when?" Then his brow cleared, and he turned to Zelda, who had been keeping well out of the dilemma into which she had unwittingly thrust Geraldine. "You sent her away on that course," he said. "That's the only time we've been apart since she came here."

Zelda twisted round to look at Max. "Don't you pretend you would have wanted her to have it," she warned him. "If the police had found out that she was pregnant, they would never have left you alone! You don't deserve her, Max. The way you behave is quite reprehensible at times."

Geraldine took her cue from Zelda. "While we're on the subject of your behaviour," she said, "did you *hit* Catherine this morning?"

The question sounded ludicrous, and Zelda's mouth opened as she stared at Geraldine.

"If being given a lift home means that I have to submit to interrogation, I'd just as soon walk," he said, opening the car door.

"You'll stay where you are," Zelda said quietly. "And answer Geraldine's question."

To Geraldine's surprise, Max closed the door again and subsided in the back seat. She looked at Zelda, but Zelda wasn't taking her eyes off Max.

"I slapped her," he muttered. "All right?"

"Max?" said Zelda, disbelievingly. "Why?"

"Because I was very angry with her."

Geraldine shook her head. "But Max," she said. "You've never hit a wom—" She broke off. Charles was right, though she had denied it, hadn't really believed what she was indeed thinking. What if that was what Max did when he was very angry? What if laid-back, easy-going Max got violent on the rare occasions that he did become very angry?

"Just take me home," he said.

Zelda shook her head. "I'll take you anywhere else you want," she said. "But I won't take you home. Not while you're in this mood."

Victor hadn't spoken once they had got into the flat that had been the subject of so much eyebrow raising; Anna knew better than to speak to him. Catherine had done it again. She had done another disappearing trick, and it would somehow all be Anna's fault. She had known she was in trouble as soon as he had whisked her away from the stragglers.

Chief Inspector Lloyd had sought her out to say goodbye to her and to tell her that it had been a successful day, and that she needn't have worried. Victor had been a lot less complimentary. The frustration that lay just skin deep surfaced when he was under stress, and that weakness was something that Victor couldn't afford to let anyone see but Anna. Catherine, as usual, had pushed the needle to overload.

He hadn't started yet, but he would. Anna had borne the brunt of his wrath many times before, and it was never in the heat of the moment. Victor always got himself under control first; it was more menacing that way. He even took a shower, still without saying one word to her other than the unflattering assessment of her performance as his public relations manager, to which he had entertained her on their way up. Now, he came out of the bathroom, tying his bathrobe, walked to the door and touched the bank of switches that closed the curtains, and brought on concealed lighting, hidden above the low ceiling. He switched the television on to the news, then crouched down beside the video, picking up a brand-new tape.

He tried to loosen some cellophane with his thumbnail, and gave up. Then he caught a bit between finger and thumb and pulled, finding himself with half an inch of the stuff clinging to his hand and the tape still *virgo intacta*. He picked at the tiny hole until he got a sizeable chunk of cellophane, but the rest remained welded to the tape. He hacked away at it, and finally succeeded, scattering the bits all over the floor as he inserted the tape with a sigh of relief.

It was funny, but nothing in the world would have induced Anna to laugh. All it was doing was making him look foolish, which made matters worse; all he was doing was making her wait. She hoped it was Catherine who had really made him angry, and not her. But Max had *promised*; he wouldn't have told him.

He started recording as the news came on. About five minutes into the election special, their item appeared. A shot of the minister getting out of the car, then one of him talking to Victor. She could see herself in the background with Chief Inspector Lloyd. A few words about the end of the recession being in sight, then the minister shaking hands with her; she was female and under forty, so they'd chosen that clip, of course. Then the minister cutting the ribbon, then on to the Leader of the Opposition at a children's hospital.

He switched off again, and ran the tape back to the beginning of the item on Holyoak International, playing it, looking at his watch. "Eighteen seconds," he said. "All these photographers, cameramen. Sound men. For eighteen seconds." He switched off, and looked at her. "Holyoak isn't news here," he said. "But it will be. And you've got a great deal to learn about public relations."

Anna almost sighed with relief. She had told him she would be no good. She was grateful to Victor for the job, but today had merely confirmed what she had been afraid of all along. She had hoped that he would have reconsidered, but she should have known better. She had never known Victor to change his mind about anything, but she had another go.

"Victor, I can't do it," she said. "I don't know the first thing about corporate identity and marketing and stuff like that!"

"That, I'm afraid, is all too obvious." He got up and sat in the armchair. "In fact, people think you must be my mistress."

"You can't blame them," she said. What else would they think about this place? she thought, though she didn't say it. And grabbing her and bringing her up here would just add fuel to the flames of the gossip.

"I don't blame them. I blame you."

"I've not had any training, Victor," she said. "It's obvious I don't know what I'm doing. Oh, I'm just so much excess baggage," she said angrily. "And they know it! They've started publishing things, Victor."

"Who have started publishing things? Some German scandal-sheets? What do they know?"

"They know I've known you a lot longer than six months. They think we're having an affair—and issuing denials doesn't make it any better. If they start digging into my past, where does that leave me?"

"It's of no interest to me where it leaves you," he said. "You've let me down, Anna."

"No," she said, alarmed, shaking her head. "Victor—I've done my best! I'm just not good at it! That's what I'm trying to explain to you. I read all these things you gave me—I even learned them off by—"

"Be quiet!"

Anna stopped.

"I'm not talking about your pathetic attempt to do a real job I'm talking about Max Scott."

Oh, God. Her relief had been premature, as Victor had intended it to be. Max had told him. The bastard. The rotten bastard. He promised. He *promised*. She swallowed hard. "I'm sorry," she said, prepared to defend herself to the last ditch, but this time she had misbehaved, and she knew it. "I thought—"

"I am not interested in what you thought. I told you a very long time ago not to 'think' anything. I warned you never to let me down again. You betrayed my trust, Anna. Again. No one does that twice."

Her mouth was dry.

"However," he said.

It was the most beautiful word she had ever heard.

"Your very betrayal has earned you a reprieve. Your intimacies with Mr. Scott have proved useful. You will remain in my employment—but not, I hasten to add, as my public relations manager. I will be terminating that appointment tomorrow morning."

She didn't understand what the hell he meant, and she didn't care. She had to sit and listen while he told her quietly and unpleasantly what he thought of her, but that was nothing new. It used to hurt; now she knew that it was probably no more than the truth, it didn't any more.

"Keys," he said, when he had finished.

She went into her bag, and handed him her set of keys to the penthouse flat.

"Tell him the arrangement is at an end," he said. "You will not see him again."

She nodded, and decided she could speak again. "I'm really much better at what I do best," she said.

He raised his eyebrows, and explained then, quickly, concisely, and brutally, why she couldn't continue in her old job, what the PR job had all been about, and what he expected of her in her new job.

And not since that night in the police van had Anna felt so violated.

Catherine huddled into her coat for security, rather than warmth, as she sat in the dark. She had come to her decision; she wouldn't be going home. Not tonight. She couldn't. She was afraid; she seemed to have been afraid for months. Ever since she had known what was going to happen. She had been afraid to tell Max, because of what she had done at the time; she had just let it all roll on, let it happen, putting off the dreadful moment.

But it wasn't until this morning that she had been afraid of Max himself. She hadn't ever expected that. But he desperately wanted an explanation, and the only one she could give him was quite inadequate.

Even if she could work out what in the world she could say to him, it wouldn't work, because he would be in no mood to listen. He felt betrayed, and small wonder. She could have put an end to all the speculation, all the innuendo, all the police questioning, and the cold-shouldering. She had tried to help the only way she could, but it had only made matters worse; he had been grateful for that once, but now he knew the truth, and he hated her for it. She could have proved Max's innocence, and she hadn't, it was as simple as that.

Except that it wasn't as simple as that. If only Max hadn't seen her stepfather that night, none of this would have happened.

Her mind was filled with images; of Max, white faced with

anger, of Zelda, anxious and puzzled. Why hadn't Catherine told her? Why was she so afraid? Of Geraldine, briskly examining her, asking about the red marks on her face, so obvious against her pale skin. It wasn't Max's fault; they mustn't blame Max. It was her own fault.

And she had fainted, when all that fear had got too much; lying on the bed in that low-ceilinged, beige and cream room, she had had to look at the situation logically. Max might never forgive her, whatever she did, whatever she said; the hurt could have gone too deep. Unless . . . at the back of her mind had been the hope, the single, almost indecipherable hope that she could get him back.

And she was going to try.

Max's interrogation by Geraldine and Zelda had been punctuated at one point by the sound of high-heeled shoes clicking down the stairway; a few moments later, Anna Worthing's Porsche had backed out from behind the stair wall, and she had driven noisily out.

Zelda had refused to start the car until Max had assured them that he wasn't going home; Charles hadn't reappeared, and Max had finally asked to be dropped at the estate where Anna had her flat. It was a five-minute journey from the factory, but it was almost nine o'clock when he at last heard footsteps on the stair.

He pushed himself away from the wall as Anna made her way up towards him. She looked terrible; her face was drawn with fatigue and worry, her eyes dark and dull as she came up to him. "What the hell are you doing here?" she asked, the words slurring.

"I needed somewhere to go," he said. "I couldn't go home. I thought you'd be here—I saw you leave."

She frowned, and fumbled with the key in the lock as she opened the door. "I didn't see you," she said. "I thought it must have been you at the door."

He frowned. "What door?" he said.

"The door," she said. "The flat door. Victor's door."

She had had a great deal to drink. Max followed her into the flat. "Did you drive in that condition?" he asked.

"Yes," she said, throwing the keys down on the table. "I drove in this condition. Wasn't that wicked of me?"

She went straight to the table where she kept the drinks, and held the bottle up in enquiry.

He shook his head. He had never found solace in alcohol, and by the look of Anna as she tossed back the brandy she had poured herself, she wasn't finding much either.

"Why couldn't you go home?" she asked. "And why did you behave as though your wife wasn't there when she fainted?"

"Because I knew why she'd fainted," he said.

Anna frowned. "Why?"

"She was scared to death," he said.

"What of?"

"Me. And Zelda wouldn't take me home. She and Geraldine thought I might kill her—I make a habit of that, you know." He sank down on to the sofa. "I don't know what to do, Anna."

Anna stared at him, still frowning. "Why didn't you use your own car? You've not been drinking."

He sighed. "It's a long story," he said.

"You had a row last night?" she asked, pouring herself another brandy, joining him on the sofa.

"Yes," said Max. How like Catherine to think that if she didn't tell him that Holyoak was her stepfather, the problem would just go away. That bit at least made sense. None of the rest of it did.

"Victor's told her about us," she said.

"It doesn't matter," said Max, and watched her for a moment as she drank. "What's that all about?" he asked, touching the glass as he spoke.

"Victor." She looked over the rim of the glass at him. "I told him to stuff his job tonight." She drank some more. "And I think perhaps I wasn't very clever," she said.

For a moment, Max's own insurmountable problems took a back seat as he became intrigued by hers. If problems *were* insurmountable, then all you could do was leave them alone. Hers must be easier to handle. "Why did you do that?" he asked. "You were singing his praises to that policeman."

"Well, I'm not now." She poured herself another hefty measure, lifting her glass in a sardonic toast. "Don't you think you should ring your wife or something?" she asked. "This isn't like you, Max."

66

Max didn't know what to do. He didn't think he had the courage. He didn't understand what was happening. He felt as though he didn't know her any more.

"She was in a bad way, Max," she said. "And you just abandoned her. That's not like you. I wouldn't like to think I'd caused that."

"You didn't," he said. "It had nothing to do with you." He drew the phone towards him, dialling the number, waiting long enough for her to come from the other end of the street. "Did you get into trouble because of me?" he asked Anna, as the phone rang out.

"Not really," she said. "It was my own fault."

She would have gone to Zelda's, he supposed. He must have frightened her so badly, and he . . . He bent his head, then looked up at Anna, who was filling her glass again already. "She's not there," he said, hanging up.

"Well, let's hope she's not gone to make it up with stepdaddy," said Anna. She smiled, without a trace of humour, and joined him on the sofa again, bringing the bottle with her this time. "In view of what happened last time she walked in on him," she added.

"He's got someone with him?" said Max.

"Oh, yes," she said. "He got rid of me fast enough." She took another swig of brandy. "His wife's as good as dead, I suppose. And this is someone whose reputation Victor has to protect at all costs. It doesn't matter what people say about me."

He smiled, just when he had thought that nothing would ever make him smile again. "The last I heard you were denying that you had ever had any relationship with Holyoak," he said.

"Fuck that," she said.

Max had never heard her swear. Not even the mildest of oaths. "The relationship?" he asked. "Or the denial of it?"

"Both."

Max was quite used to women crying on his shoulder; he seemed to attract it. She had problems too, and he much preferred someone else's for the moment. "I'm sorry," he said. "You've been with him a long time."

"He set me up. He'd set his own mother up if it got him what he wanted. He's a psycho, Max," she said seriously.

"Only I think I'm the only person who really knows that." Then she shook her head. "No," she said. "Someone else knows. I shouldn't have done what I—" She broke off. "I think I've lost my job, Max," she said, her voice small.

Once again, Max took refuge in someone else's problems. He was so much better with them, even if he didn't understand a word of them. He thought she had handed in her notice; now it looked as though she had been sacked. He felt guilty about that. "How did he set you up?" he asked.

She took another fortifying gulp of brandy before she spoke. "His wife got much worse, and she wanted to be with Catherine, for them to be a family again." More brandy. "And he said he wanted me to come here and . . ." She waved her hand as she tried to remember the language that she had only recently begun to speak again, and which was deserting her now that she was drunk. "You know . . . represent him. But I hadn't got to say which company it was," she said. "So that Catherine didn't try to put a spoke in it before it was finalized."

Max nodded, remembering the secret negotiations about which he and Catherine had laughed. Hard to believe now that they had ever laughed.

"Your wife's the only person who's ever got the better of him—you know that?"

Max said nothing; he watched her drink, and listened.

"And then when he went public with it, he said he wanted me to be his public relations manager. It was a proper job, he said. He was the one who kept saying that he wanted me to have a proper job. This . . . this public relations thing. And . . . and . . . I was frightened I wouldn't be able to do it."

She gave a little, unconvincing half laugh. "But I needn't have worried about not being able to do it, because the whole thing was just bullshit. Bull . . . shit," she repeated, leaving a long space between the words. "All of it. But now he's met someone. And no one must know. So I'm reprieved." She blinked.

Max frowned. She hadn't lost her job?

"Catherine was right, and I was wrong. He's a Grade A dyed-in-the-wool bastard. I mean—I knew he was, all along. But I thought—"

She was very close to tears. Max's arms were round her.

"A bastard," she repeated. "I was all right the way I was!

He didn't have to tell me that I could have a real job, and a real life. He wants people to think *I'm* his mistress."

Max had taken liberties with the opposite sex in his time, but he'd never had the brass neck to get his ex-mistress to act as decoy for his new one.

"You mean he ditched you, but you were supposed to carry on as though he hadn't?"

She closed her eyes in frustration. "I'm *not* his mistress, Max. I never have been. He wants people to think I *am*. He wants to give the so-called journalists something to get their teeth into. That'll keep them happy, and then they won't dig about in his dustbin." She finished the brandy and reached down for the bottle again. "Well, fuck that!" she said, and poured another, even larger, measure. "Fuck that, and fuck him."

"I—I don't quite understand," Max began. But she was crying now, the words tumbling out, and he gave up trying to understand.

"I believed him," she said. "He said I'd done a good job. I deserved it." She leant closer to him, her eyes barely focusing. "I was set up," she said. "D'you see?"

No. Max wasn't following much of this; the alcohol and the hurt didn't allow for a very coherent telling of the story.

"His wife's dying, so he needs me." She stopped, and looked bleakly at him before downing what was in her glass, and pouring herself another with utmost care.

She was drinking far too much and far too fast; Max felt he ought to try to stop her, but he didn't know how. He was beginning, just, to understand, remembering what Catherine had said last night. Victor was using Anna to cover up his homosexuality, just as he had used his wife. That was what had upset Catherine so much all those years ago. Anna didn't seem to know that that was why the secrecy; Max thought it best to leave it that way.

"I *know* I'm just paid to do what he wants," she shouted, moving her arm in an expansive gesture that at least got rid of some of the alcohol from her glass, "but I don't—" She broke off. "I thought we were friends," she said, quietly. "That's the relationship I thought we had. I know the sort of things he does, but he doesn't do them to me, and I thought we were friends. I thought that was why he took me with him in the first place."

"Why *did* he take you with him?" Max asked, mystified by the whole thing. "What did you do?"

She shrugged. "This and that." Her eyes grew misty. "But he did take me," she said. She looked at him, pointing an unsteady finger. "I want you to understand," she said. "I'd have done it. I'd have covered for him. But I think I blew it."

Max felt as though he was the one who had consumed vast quantities of brandy.

"I'm glad he's got someone—it wasn't natural, before." She smiled. "Maybe she gave him permission," she said. "Bitch. She's always got me into trouble."

"Who?"

"Who do you think? Your wife."

She was pretty good at getting him into trouble too, he thought. But perhaps the abortion explained a lot of things. And the anger was subsiding now; he was simply bewildered.

"He was good to me. He's always been good to me. He's done really terrible things, you know. But not to me. He was good to me. So I'd have done it. But he shouldn't have set me up. So I told him to stuff his job up his . . ."

She was crying; Max kissed away the tears, comforting her and himself at one and the same time. She returned his kisses through brandy-laden sobs, and he couldn't work out if she hated or loved Victor Holyoak, but he supposed it hardly mattered; the distress was much the same, whichever. Her mouth touched his in a tiny kiss before she drew back and wiped the tears with her hand.

"Will you come to bed with me?" she asked, her face wet and streaked with tears, her eyes glazed, her nose red.

He had had more alluring invitations, but none had been more nakedly vulnerable to a rebuff, and none had been more welcome. If ever he had needed the comfort of a woman's body, he needed it now. He needed the respite, the relaxation. Then he would be able to think clearly. But he wasn't sure Anna could provide him with that, as he found tissues, and handed them to her, helping her up from the sofa.

The bottle came with her, but even stoned out of her mind Anna was the best partner he had ever had. So it wasn't until some little time later, in his post-coital calm, that he realized

70

what must really have happened, and what, in her inebriated and largely incomprehensible ramblings, Anna had actually told him.

Judy was having a hard time making Lloyd concentrate. He was supposed to be playing Scrabble with her, but his mind was miles away.

It wasn't ordinary Scrabble. In this version, the more suggestive or downright rude the word, the more points you got. Judy had devised it to even things up, because he always won the straight game. This way she was in with a chance because he was too polite to put some words down even if he saw the opportunity. A word carried no extra points at all, even if it covered two treble word squares, contained the Q, and used up all your letters, it if did not have a sexual or vulgar connotation. The bonuses ranged from five to thirty points, and any word described as "taboo" in Lloyd's dictionary of slang got an extra fifty.

She put down an arbitrary collection of letters. "It's mildly rude," she said. "The score plus ten."

"You've made that one up," he said.

"No, I haven't! Shakespeare used it."

"Now I know you've made it up," he said. "How would you know?" He smiled, but then the smile faded.

"What?" she asked, a touch apprehensively. She had grown used to that look during the evening.

"The face," he said slowly, frowning. "I could see *it*, but it couldn't see me. I *knew* it couldn't see me."

This was beginning to get to her. "Lloyd," she said sternly, "I don't know what silly game you're playing, but if you don't stop it, I'm going home. Play your word."

"It's true," he protested, examining his letters, and putting down MOTHER on the T of her PHAT. "Extra fifty," he said.

"Rubbish!"

"It's a frequently used shorthand form of a taboo word," he said.

"It's an abbreviation, or it's innocuous," she said. "So either you can't have it, or you get no bonus."

"It's not an abbreviation. It's a word in its own right, used in a vulgar context. Thirty points," he bartered.

"Ten. They wouldn't bleep it out on the telly."

71

"Oh, yes they would. They did. Remember? In that film we watched at New Year."

So they had. "All right," she said. "Twenty." Twenty was all right. She would still win. He still had two tiles, and she was left with s, e, m and n, which she put down proudly round the e of MOTHER. "Seven," she said. "Plus a bonus of five. And I'm out. What are you left with?"

"An A and a D," he said.

She totted up the scores, deducted the spare points from his, and added them to hers. She had won by three points.

"You cheated," he pointed out, as she announced the score. "Phat is not a word."

She smiled. "Neither it is," she said, clearing the board. "But I can add up quicker than you."

"You could have had phantoms," he mused. "That would have got you more points, even without a bonus."

"I wouldn't have been out." The truth was that she hadn't seen it.

"And it would have been very topical," he said. "Since I seem to have been seeing them. Do you think phantoms have different faces from their flesh and blood counterparts?"

Judy put the letters back in their bag, folded the board, and put the box away tidily. "I'm making coffee," she announced, and escaped into the kitchen, where the crockery from dinner was draining. She stayed in there, drying it needlessly, for it had been dry for some time, putting it away. She ground coffee, and hoped that she had remembered how to use his new percolator. Serve him right if she'd done it wrong. She put everything on a tray, and opened the kitchen door.

"I'll bring the coffee in if you promise to stop going on about ghosts," she called through.

He smiled as she came in with the coffee things, and set them down.

"He's still alive," he said. "So it couldn't have been a phantom Victor. Or could it?" he asked, dropping his voice melodramatically. "Perhaps we all have ghosts *even before we die*."

Her arms were bare; the tiny fair hairs rose visibly at the thought, and Lloyd laughed at her.

"I spy a little streak of superstition running through all that good common sense," he said.

"Don't be silly," she said, sitting on the floor beside the coffee table. "Anyway—if you could see him and he couldn't see you, doesn't that make you the ghost?"

Lloyd thought about that. "Maybe it was a premonition," he said. "I could see him at some future time. That's why he couldn't see me."

Judy felt distinctly uncomfortable. "A premonition of what?" she asked, trying to sound dismissive, and failing.

Lloyd grinned. "Unnatural death," he whispered dramatically, leaning down towards her. "What else? His face looked different . . . I looked away. It's obvious, Watson. Violent death had altered his features . . ."

"Lloyd, if you don't stop this right now, I'll . . ."

"But you don't believe in all that, do you?" he laughed. "Second sight and premonitions. Telepathy. You're supposed to be giving me a nice rational explanation of it all."

He held out his hand, and she joined him on the sofa, reluctantly permitting him to give her a cuddle.

"I don't trust you," she complained. "I never know when you're serious." Her eye fell on the newspaper that he had left abandoned on the sofa. She automatically picked it up to fold it, getting up to put it where he theoretically kept his newspapers. That was when she saw the date.

She folded the paper a second time. "You rotten sod!" she said, setting about him with it.

"What?" he laughed, arms up to protect himself. "What have I done?"

"You know perfectly well what you've done!" She gave him a final smack, and thrust the paper into his hands. "April the first," she said. "Very funny." She sat on the floor again.

Lloyd smiled at her. "It's not an April Fool," he said. "I really did see him." Then the smile disappeared again, and when he spoke, it was no longer in the teasing tones he'd been using to try to scare her. It was in a voice that sent a genuine shiver up Judy's spine. "He was a long way away," he said slowly. "But I could see him quite clearly."

Judy swallowed. She didn't want to hear this. She didn't want to know.

He frowned, concentrating, like a mind-reader at a seaside show. "I was close. Really close. But *he* wasn't. He was a long way away. I *know* he was."

"Don't, Lloyd!"

73

He snapped out of his reverie, and grinned. "I never realized I could *scare* the pants off you," he said. "Or I'd have done it years ago." He leant down, his face close to hers, his voice low and creepy and very, very Welsh. "Perhaps you're right," he said. "Perhaps I *am* a ghost. There are a lot of ghosts in Wales, you know. Mining disasters always have ghosts." His eyes widened as he reached out to her. "Perhaps I'm the Phantom of the Pithead, come to have his evil way—"

"Stop it," she said, pushing him away, and scrambling to her feet. "Or I'm going home."

He didn't stop it, but she didn't go home.

Bannister went a yard or so down the unlit ramp up from the underground car park, and pulled himself on to the wall that was only a foot high on the ramp side and six feet high on the other, dropping down, crouching low as he ran towards the offices while the camera's back was turned. The building was in darkness save for a light at the top, which was the penthouse flat, he presumed.

The flat lights were on some sort of time switch, Annabel had said, so that it looked as though it was occupied, since it was empty for so much of the time. He didn't imagine that that was true; perhaps the whole thing had been a pack of lies. But he didn't think it had been; she had wanted him to get into the flat. She wanted to embarrass Holyoak; he wanted a little more than that out of it. He was taking a risk, but it was worth it.

There was a security camera on the main entrance and exit, and a swivel camera on the roof of the office block. But the sweep of the rooftop camera didn't take in the exit from the underground staff car park; by entering there, and keeping an eye on the high camera, it was possible, Annabel had said, to reach the office block without being picked up on the video. Once there, clinging to the wall kept you out of range. He was there; he assumed that the lack of activity meant that he had indeed arrived there undetected.

Bannister looked round, and picked up a half-brick left by the recent construction, swinging it hard against one of the windows, twice. It didn't break the glass, it didn't bring security, and it set off no alarm. She had said it wouldn't, but he had had to be sure; he didn't trust her, even if she was mad at Holyoak, and drinking faster than a sailor on shore-leave. A

74

successful breaking of the toughened glass would set off an alarm in security, but as long as he didn't break in he would be all right. She had said he wouldn't have to break in, and so far, things had been how she said they would be; he was beginning to feel more confidence in her.

In the darkness, he could hear the radio that was keeping the security men company; he kept an eye on the security office, the only other light, as he slipped round the corner of the building, and found the metal ladder that ran up the back, with access to a balcony with a fire door.

Silently up the ladder, in his trainers, stepping down on to the balcony. The fire door was open; Annabel had said it would be. That was what had made him doubt her story about the lights; if there was some sort of security system on the flat itself, an open door would trigger it once the system was set, and if the system wasn't set, then Holyoak was in residence.

Warily, he moved the blind to one side, and slipped into the kitchen. The door was closed; no light showed underneath, and he turned the handle slowly, opening it to find a sitting room, lit only by the light spilling from the half-open door directly opposite.

A jacket lay across the sofa, an expensive wallet sticking out of the inside pocket. Bannister smiled, and pulled it out, extracting the wad of notes, and letting the wallet fall to the floor. All the doors off the main room were shut, except the one opposite; he moved silently across the carpet towards the light. From somewhere behind him he could hear a low, rhythmic sound which he recognized, and couldn't quite pin down, and which stopped as he looked round the door, into the room.

But everything stopped as he looked into the room. His brain, his muscles, his heart seemed to stop; he couldn't hear, or move, or think. He could only see, until the unplaced but somehow comforting noise began again, its very familiarity returning his other senses to him and allowing him to move again.

CHAPTER FOUR

Then: Fourteen years ago . . .

ZELDA LOOKED EVEN MORE DRAMATIC AND FLAMBOYANT than usual in her funeral outfit; she was being comforted by her son and Gerry and Jimmy's parents, so Charles didn't feel the need to go to her.

It had been a shock, even to Charles, though he had advised Jimmy on more than one occasion to modify his lifestyle. He never had, of course. He had smoked cigarettes and drunk beer and eaten pie and chips while working a ten-hour day at the factory, and then taken work home with him. All the same, he hadn't reached forty; if his lack of exercise and dodgy diet and overwork had been going to kill him, Charles would have expected it to have had the decency to wait a decade or two.

And even when he had had the heart attack, Charles had expected him to make it. But he had had another in the hospital, and try as they had, they hadn't been able to save him.

Zelda was shattered; she had hidden her reaction under a veneer of life-goes-on toughness, but that hadn't fooled anyone, and had crumbled away when Tim had arrived home from boarding school. Charles had been there, trying to make Zelda take something to help her sleep, when he had come in. The wordless reunion with her son had touched something, and the unnatural control had snapped.

Tim, never that close to his workaholic father, had taken over in a way that belied his fifteen years, and had reported to Charles that his mother had cried herself to sleep, and had slept for twelve hours. It was Tim who had made the funeral arrangements, Tim who had seen to the business of death.

Spring had merged into a wet early summer; it had rained nonstop throughout the burial service. Charles was glad that he didn't have to comfort Zelda; it was hard to know what to say. You weren't supposed to be burying your husband when you were thirty-five; that was something in the future, something you'd have to do when you were old, and you had had your life together.

Jimmy hadn't had his life at all. And he had had such plans for the business, which was already employing more people than any other single employer in Stansfield apart from Mitchell Engineering, and had weathered inflation and recession without a single redundancy so far. He had been clever, and resourceful, and he had known when the time was right to do everything. So how could he have lost his sense of timing so badly? How? Thirty-nine years old, and a heart attack killed him. Old men survived heart attacks. New-born babies survived heart attacks. Jimmy had been fit, and strong . . . such warnings as Charles had given him had been of the "those things will kill you" type. Even Charles himself hadn't taken them all that seriously.

Charles looked again at Zelda, at the grief, and he knew he had let her down. He had let Jimmy down. He hadn't seen it coming; he couldn't let himself off the hook by saying that he had. And in amongst the shock and the grief, there was real worry about the business; Zelda had only ever been involved in the personnel side, the pastoral care of their employees. She couldn't make the sort of financial deals that Jimmy had made; she didn't understand that side of it.

Two ideas came to Charles, as he stood by Jimmy Driver's grave. Not in a sudden flash of inspiration; his own sense of loss was too great for that. All he felt as the coffin was lowered was that he had lost a friend; a lively, vital man who had altered his corner of the world by his presence.

But until then, Charles had seen himself as a healer of the sick. It was in that moment that he saw that that was wrong; so many of life's ills were preventable that in a strong, civilized, rich country there was no excuse for young men's healthy hearts becoming diseased. His half-hearted attempts to alter Jimmy's suicidal regime would be whole-hearted from now on. He was there to keep men well, not to help bury them. Gerry joined him, and they walked away. He turned to say a last silent farewell, and seek Jimmy's forgiveness.

Zelda was on her own by the graveside as everyone melted away to stand by the rain-soaked cars, waiting for her. To do what? To start her life on her own? To carry on the business? Jimmy's mother and father stood together, closer to the grave than the others, but still a respectful distance away. They had never liked Zelda much; she was too flashy, too dramatic for their taste. Jimmy had loved her, and had provided for her; Zelda wouldn't be in financial need, whatever she chose to do.

But she had employees. Employees who depended on her for their livelihoods, and Zelda wasn't going to sell out; she had told Charles that. She needed help that Tim was too young to give, and that the firm's accountant was probably too old to give. He was coming up to retirement, and he didn't understand the new technology that was revolutionizing not only the security systems field in which they operated, but the running of the business itself. Zelda needed someone who could take over the financial side, someone who could take on suppliers and customers, someone who understood money, and today's business world. Someone she could trust not to cheat her.

And perhaps Charles knew just the man.

Max watched Catherine covertly as she picked up the calendar, and tore off the previous month. It was June, already; where did the time go? She had been with him seven months; in some ways it seemed like she had been there for ever. She had picked up the office work quickly, and she had gone religiously to the typing classes. She made him coffee in the morning, and tea in the afternoon. His correspondence went out on time, balance sheets and profit and loss accounts got filed away, the office looked immaculate.

But it wasn't working, and if Max hadn't noticed before, he was being forced to now. Because in another way, it seemed as if she had come into his life just yesterday. He kept waiting for the novelty to wear off, for his awareness of her to become dulled, for the pleasure he felt at just seeing her there to become simply an acceptance of her presence.

He had no illusions about himself; he had had brief affairs with several of the girls who had worked for him, and several more who hadn't. They had been meaningless, at any rate to him. He needed variety, that was all. And he had always been attractive to women, though he couldn't honestly say why. He didn't work at it much; it was just the case. Some men might have settled for just one, but he had found himself unable to do that. And he knew only too well that this was, however diverting and enjoyable, a major flaw in his character.

It had occurred to him, at Charles's wedding, that if he couldn't bring himself to employ a spinster of sixty, he could bring himself to employ a kid. Which was how he had thought of Catherine, then. A kid, in whom he had no interest. It was what she had been. Shy, young even for her sixteen years. But he had looked forward to that Monday morning like a child anticipating a birthday treat, and that feeling had never left him. She was always in the office before him; every day, his heart would give a little skip as he opened the door, just in case she wasn't there.

She smiled at him as she caught him looking at her, and sat down at her desk. He looked away, and read Charles's letter again, more for something to do than because he wanted to read it again.

Zelda Driver, a friend of Charles and Geraldine's, had lost her husband earlier in the year, and needed someone to advise her on the financial side. Her chief accountant had been doing the job, but he was due to retire early next year. Perhaps Max might be interested.

No. Max wasn't interested, but Charles would try to persuade him. Charles knew what shape his business was in; he and Geraldine had been to visit. A house in Stansfield would hardly cost anything compared to London, the letter said. If you sold yours, you'd have money in the bank, or only need a seventy-five per cent mortgage, it said. But no. No, he didn't fancy Stansfield.

Valerie wouldn't want to move away from London, he told himself.

Yes, she would, said the perverse voice in his head. She would if it meant a steady income and lower outgoings.

All right then, *he* didn't want to leave London.

Why not? Because he liked crawling to work through traffic jams in order to have nothing to do when he got there? Because he wanted to pay through the nose for a partitioned-off

79

corner of someone else's office in an unattractive side street in an already unfashionable and rapidly deteriorating part of the city?

No. Because of Catherine.

Why? Why because of Catherine?

My God, if this was a conscience, he was glad he hadn't developed one before now. Because, he told it, Catherine was a little girl adrift in a big city. She needed him.

Not really, said the voice, as once again Max lifted his eyes from the paper to look at her. Six months had wrought a change in Catherine. Having a job, a flat, responsibilities, having to organize her own affairs, had made her grow up fast. And there had always been something about Catherine, something about the eyes, that had known all there was to know. She could get another job now, without too much trouble. Certainly by the time he actually went, which obviously wouldn't be until at least the end of the year.

He didn't want to go. But it did make economic sense, and he was tired of working for himself, of watching the income dwindle, of not knowing for certain that there would be any income.

So what was stopping him?

He didn't want to leave Catherine, that was the truth of it. And he had known the truth, really, from the moment he had picked her up in the rain. All that stuff about saving her from sin was hogwash. He had fallen in love on the road to London that night. Which was why he had gone looking for her at the hotel, why he had taken her on, not knowing the first thing about her, and why he hadn't looked at another woman since she had been with him.

It had never happened to him before, and it had taken him a long time to recognize the signs. Extra-marital relationships were part and parcel of Max's life, and he had never, in truth, given them a moment's thought. But a roll in the hay was one thing; falling deeply in love with a sixteen-year-old girl was quite another.

It wouldn't do.

Charles was telling him that the job was his, if he wanted it. Zelda remembered him from the wedding; Max didn't remember her, but he, as usual, had made a favourable impression. She was quite happy to go on what she had seen and Charles's character reference. There would be an interview, of course, but Max could be assured that that would be just a formality. It made sense economically; it made even more sense emotionally. He had no option; he had to go. He'd talk to Valerie tonight. But first things first. If Catherine was going to get another job, she had to have an employment record.

"I think it's time we put your employment on an official basis," he said.

Her face fell. "Why?" she asked. "It's working out all right, isn't it?"

"Yes," he said. "Of course it is. But it isn't something you can do for ever, not really." He smiled. "Well, I understand that some building-site workers can, but you can't."

She knew that, really. And she reluctantly nodded agreement. Good. That was one problem solved.

"And now we'll slow the tempo, with the Commodores . . ."

The big doors leading on to the car park of the police section house were open to the overcast, humid August night as Sergeant Compton's retirement party got into full swing.

Judy danced with one of the probationers; he had been all right when his gyrations, executed with considerably more enthusiasm than technique, had been at a safe distance, but now that the disc jockey had deemed it time to let the sweating dancers get their breath back, she was being shuffled awkwardly round the floor while he sang to her that she was three times a lady, off key.

Lloyd was there, but he hadn't asked her to dance. He was deep in conversation with the inspector, and seemed to be unaware of her presence. Sid Compton, in whose honour the evening had been arranged, was sitting with a crowd of men, drinking. Not many people were dancing, so her choice of partner was limited.

Valiantly, she made it to the end of whatever dance it was that her partner was doing. They parted company on the dance floor as the disco once again belted out the sort of music that she really liked. No chance of Lloyd liking it, of course, but still he didn't even look at her.

She had moved in with Michael in May—or, to be more exact, she had moved in without him while he was off somewhere exciting. It had been nice, being there when he came home. He was nice; she enjoyed being with him. Her parents would have preferred them to have got married, but Judy was fighting shy of that; Michael had asked her more than once. She had known him since she was eighteen; she had wanted to be with him, and now she was. She could be with him now, instead of at this dreary party.

She gathered that Dave Bannister's outstretched hand and jerk of the head was intended as an invitation; her instinct was to refuse, but she wanted to dance. She wanted to show Lloyd she didn't need him to have a good time. So she followed Bannister on to the floor, throwing herself into an energetic interpretation of the disco number that drowned out any chance of conversation. He could really dance; she followed his movements, and they found an unexpected rapport as they moved together. Their few fellow dancers began to watch, hands clapping in time to the music as Bannister postured and hip-swivelled with the best of them, taking her along with him. Without a pause, the Bee Gees turned into John Travolta; by this time they were dancing to an audience. They finished to a cheer and a round of applause, collapsing on to one another.

"Never knew you had it in you, Jude," he said.

She smiled, out of breath, perspiration trickling from her hair down her temple. "I did," she replied, wiping away the sweat, glancing across at Lloyd, but he was still talking to the inspector, oblivious to what was going on around him.

"Well, this is a summer night, so what else should I play but . . ." said the DJ.

"I need a beer," said Bannister as the music started. "Can I get you one?"

"No, thanks," she said.

"Right," he said. "Oh—and I've repaid one of the favours. All right?"

Judy frowned. "By *dancing* with me?" she said, laughing.

He smiled too. "No!" he said. "You know what I mean." And he went off, disappearing into the crush of people round the makeshift bar.

She didn't know what he meant. Judy stood irresolutely in the middle of the floor, half wanting to go after him to find out what he did mean, half wanting to run away. She compromised, and made her way through the drinkers to the window, and out into the slightly fresher air, walking round the building, out of sight. She needed to be alone, to work out why Lloyd's indifference had made her angry enough to do a spot of exhibition disco-dancing with Bannister, of all people. She would let Bannister's enigmatic remark go for the moment. She leant against the bicycle railing, and through the impromptu community singing from inside the building, she heard footsteps coming up behind her. Oh, God, not Dave Bannister, please.

"If that was to make me jealous, it worked."

Lloyd. He had been watching. She closed her eyes, and didn't turn round. "Of course it wasn't," she said. To make him notice her, maybe. It hadn't occurred to her that he would be jealous.

"Oh, of course not. You thought I'd enjoy seeing you carrying on like that."

She let out a gasp, half amused, half disbelieving. "Carrying on?" she repeated. "I was dancing. I like dancing, and he's a good dancer."

"I've never been much of a dancer," he said.

No. She could have guessed that.

"You're pretty good, I'd say."

She shrugged a little. "It depends who you're dancing with," she said.

There was a silence before he spoke. "Yes," he said, at last. "It does, doesn't it?"

He was probably the most annoying man she had ever met, she thought. "Don't start all that again, Lloyd," she implored him, still with her back to him.

"You want me to," he said, as his footsteps came closer. "The floor show was for my benefit. Don't pretend it wasn't."

She swallowed. Oh God. It hadn't been deliberate, not really. Bannister had just been there—how was she to know that they would hit it off on a dance floor in a way that they never had anywhere else, nor were ever likely to? But she had hoped that Lloyd had been watching, and he had.

He joined her at the railing, as though they were passengers on a cruise, looking out at the Caribbean rather than the car park.

She turned to him. "I didn't mean to make you—"

He was kissing her; she was kissing him. She pulled away, shaking her head. "This is silly," she said.

He smiled. "What's wrong with being silly now and again?" he asked.

"Because it wouldn't stop at kissing," she said.

"I should hope not."

"I've told you," she said. "Twice."

"I'm married. I know. I don't need to be told."

"Well then."

He looked at her. "I had to be here tonight," he said. "I work with the man. I've worked with him for five years. You didn't have to come. You hardly know him."

"Oh—I'm supposed to arrange my social engagements round yours, is that it?" she asked indignantly.

"You did arrange your social engagements round mine," he pointed out. "And I tried to behave as though you weren't there," he went on. "But you didn't like that, did you?"

Her face flushed. "So I'm making all the running? It has nothing to do with you?"

"No," he said. "You feel exactly the same way that I do, only you won't admit it."

She gave a reluctant smile. "You're a good actor," she said. "I really thought you hadn't even noticed me."

"I'd notice you in Wembley Stadium on Cup Final day," he said.

She sighed. There was a long silence, which Lloyd eventually broke.

"Had we but world enough, and time, This coyness, Lady, were no crime . . ."

"What?"

"Andrew Marvell," he said.

"Who?"

"Who? What did they teach you at school?"

She smiled at his mock horror. "Do you know the rest?" she asked.

"Oh, yes." He put his arms round her waist, and began the poem again. From inside a muffled cacophony of sound rose as the community singers tried to hit the high note at the end of the song, drowning out the music. Another ballad drifted soulfully through the night air and then faded into nothingness as Judy heard only Lloyd's voice.

". . . And you should if you please refuse Till the conversion of the Jews . . ."

She rested her head on his shoulder; his lips brushed her ear as he spoke. It was a nice feeling. She loved his voice. She had never heard him speaking verse; right now, she never wanted him to stop. Even if he did probably have a poem for every occasion. Even if he was enjoying the sound of his own voice as much as she was.

"... *then worms shall try That long preserved virginity: And your quaint honour turn to dust, And into ashes all my lust.*" He lifted her head from his shoulders, and smiled. "*The grave's a fine and private place, But none I think do there embrace.*" He kissed her.

But she couldn't let this go on. She broke away from him. "I haven't preserved my virginity," she smiled. "And barring accidents, we're a long way from the grave."

"You have no soul," he said.

"I like it," she assured him.

"Oh, good. I'll tell Andrew when I see him." He smiled again. "It's not finished," he said.

"Yes it is." She turned away, her back to him, looking over at the vehicles in the car park.

"No, Judy." He came closer, his voice low. "It isn't. And we both know it isn't. It's only beginning. You know that, too."

"It mustn't happen, Lloyd," she said.

"But that's just it. It must. One day. So why not sooner rather than later?"

She closed her eyes and gave a short sigh. "There's no must about it," she said, reminding herself of her mother.

"Oh, but there is. Because we've both wanted it for a very long time."

"I know," she said, her voice small.

"At least you're not denying it," he said.

She shook her head. "But I'm denying that we're under some sort of obligation," she said.

"I think we are," he said.

She turned her head to give him a disbelieving look.

He smiled. "Don't look like that!" he said. "I *do* think we are. I think we owe it to one another."

"What about your wife? Don't you owe her anything?"

He nodded. "Yes," he said. "Don't you think I've tried to tell myself it's wrong? But it doesn't feel wrong. It just

85

doesn't. It seems right, and inevitable, and . . . I love you," he said. "It's as simple as that, really."

Simple. That was the whole problem. Love was anything but simple. "That doesn't make it right," she said, turning her back on him again.

His arms came round her waist, his lips touching the back of her neck. "It's the natural step to take," he said. "That's what Marvell was talking about."

"Marvell was trying to get *her* into bed. Of course he said it was the natural step to take."

"Are you saying it isn't?" His voice was amused. "The most fundamental and basic of all human activity isn't natural?"

"Human beings aren't fundamental and basic! They have feelings, and emotions. They make promises. Was he married with two children?"

He let her go. "I don't know," he said.

There was silence then. She hadn't meant to hurt him. She hadn't meant to get herself into this in the first place. Or perhaps she had. She wasn't sure about anything any more.

"Anything I say will sound corny," he said. "Or callous." He paused. "I sound like a chiropodist," he said.

Judy laughed. He could always make her laugh.

"But we have found something," he went on. "And it doesn't concern my wife and children. It concerns you, and me, and no one else."

She twisted round in his arms and drew him closer to her, not just letting things happen any more; she was making them happen, the consequences of her actions no longer an issue. She didn't know how the situation would resolve itself, and right now she didn't care.

"Listen," he whispered, after long, increasingly passionate embraces. "I've got the key to one of the lad's rooms."

The music came back from wherever it had gone, and cold reality washed over Judy as she stood quite still, his hair still twined round her fingers.

"Nobody will know," he assured her. "We can go up the back stairs. It's quite safe. As long as we go now before they start coming out to their cars."

"Bannister," she said, her voice barely a whisper.

"Well, yes—he's going home for the weekend."

She pushed him away from her. "You arranged this in advance? With *Bannister*, of all people?"

"Oh, come on, Judy! It wasn't like that!"

"Not much, it wasn't!"

"It wasn't. He was going to be away, and I didn't fancy driving all the way home after I'd had a drink. It's a coincidence, that's all." He put his arms round her again.

"No," she said, twisting out of his embrace.

"It's the truth!" he protested. "I didn't even know if you'd be here!"

She was walking, then running, to her car, pulling the keys from her bag. She had to get out of here, get out of this. A moment ago she would have gone anywhere with him. Anywhere but Dave bloody Bannister's room in the section house, the key doubtless handed over with a wink and a nudge. How dare he. How *dare* he?

She got into the car and slammed the door as he arrived at the passenger side. He knocked on the window, then they both realized at once that the door wasn't locked. He was quicker than she, but she doubted if she would have locked him out anyway, and her attempt to reach the door first had been halfhearted.

He got in, and sat down with a sigh. "I'm sorry," he said, pushing his hair back from his forehead, smoothing it down.

But he did that when he was angry, not when he was sorry; she didn't speak.

"I just wanted us to have somewhere to go if . . ." He finished the sentence with a shrug.

"If you got lucky," she supplied.

"Yes, all right," he said defiantly. "If I got lucky." He took her hand. "And I did," he said.

She pulled her hand away. "How dare you bring Dave Bannister into this?" she demanded.

"He doesn't know about us!"

"How the hell do you think I knew who it was?"

He sighed again. "All right, it was a mistake. I'm sorry. I just thought you'd prefer it to any of the alternatives, that's all."

"I'd *prefer* it? I'd prefer that creep to know my private business?"

"Yes! I didn't know you thought he was a creep. You

seemed to be getting on with him very well on the dance floor."

"Oh, for God's—"

"And I thought you'd prefer it to booking into some sleazy hotel or parking in a layby somewhere. They don't seem quite you."

"You were very sure I'd come across," she said.

Lloyd shook his head. "I hoped it might happen," he said. "That's all. And the choice *is* limited," he pointed out, "when you're married, as you never cease to remind me that I am."

Yes. Yes, he was. He was married, and she would get hurt. She was getting hurt already.

"And the damage, if it exists, has been done," he went on. "He's going to think we used the room whether we do or not."

She sighed. That was true. They probably all thought that that was where they were now. But it wasn't her reputation that was worrying her.

"So we might as well use it." He smiled at her. "No point in letting it go to waste," he said.

But the room would be going to waste. Her automatic distaste of the deal with Bannister had saved her from making a dreadful mistake; the whole thing was too difficult and too dangerous, and much too likely to end in tears.

"Lloyd, I don't want to get involved with you," she said, wearily.

"For God's sake, Judy, you *are* involved with me."

"All right, if you're going to quibble over words. I don't want to have sex with you—is that plain enough?"

He nodded. "It's plain enough," he said. "But you're not a very good liar." He took her hand. "Come on Judy," he said, putting his arm round her. "I was wrong, but it's done now. And we can't go on like this." He smiled again. "It's too frustrating," he said.

He was kissing her again. And he was right. It couldn't go on. It mustn't go on. She pulled away from him. "I'm not going to break up your marriage, Lloyd," she said quietly.

He looked genuinely startled. "Who's talking about breaking up marriages?" he said, giving her a hug. "This is quite separate. I told you. It doesn't concern anyone else."

"Now who's lying?" she asked miserably.

His eyes held hers for a moment, then he let her go, and opened the car door. "Don't think I've given up," he said.

She locked the door this time, and waited until the physical and emotional turmoil had calmed down a little before she tried to take stock of her situation. Irrelevances crowded out the important issues. She was lucky the car hadn't been stolen, forgetting to lock it like that. She must remember to post that letter that still sat on the shelf. Come to that, it was time she gave the car a good clean outside and in. She took out cigarettes and lit one, inhaling deeply, trying not to cry.

The survival instinct had triumphed again; she had weathered his most determined assault on her sensibilities yet. But cowardice had always been her trump card, and she had played it. She stubbed out the cigarette, and drove out of the car park, feeling indescribably guilty as she headed the car towards home, and it wasn't because she had so very nearly been unfaithful to Michael.

It was because she hadn't.

Anna had a maid now. An old pro, long past her best; she knew much better than Anna did how to vet the punters, and she didn't let the iffy ones past the door. Anna looked after her; she paid her as well as she could, and she always got her a taxi to take her home. It didn't matter how much experience of the streets you had, London was a place to be wary of, if you lived in the sort of areas they lived in. One policeman driving about in a Panda car was the sum total of the security, if you were lucky. She saw her into her minicab now, and waved as it roared away into the early hours of the sultry October morning, going back into the flat.

She was earning more now that she had a proper room to do the business in; you could charge more. And she had been given lots of sound advice about looking at their clothes and their watches, and estimating how much they could and would pay for extras. She closed the door of the bedroom, all made ready for tomorrow night's trade.

She didn't sleep in there. She slept on the sofa bed in the room that the clients weren't allowed into. During the day, it was her sitting room, and she could pretend that she was somewhere else altogether. But if business kept improving, she might be able to afford the rent on somewhere to live. Somewhere respectable. Then she would be like the others, and get to go home after work.

She fell asleep quickly; she always did. It was about nine thirty when she heard the knocking at the door, and woke to brilliant sunshine. She didn't lock the street door during the day, or she was woken continually by meter-readers and others who wanted access to the building. But she didn't expect anyone to come knocking at her door, not today. She pulled on her dressing-gown, and stumbled sleepily out into the long, narrow hallway.

She unlocked the door, and opened it to see someone's back view. A cop's back view, sweat staining his shirt. A visit from the police usually meant that they wanted information. One of the girls might have been attacked. That was a constant worry for Anna; she didn't mind talking to cops about that.

He turned, and when she saw who it was, she tried to shut the door again, but he was too quick for her. He pushed his way in. He shut the door.

"Hello, Annabel," he said, putting the chain in place. "You should use that, you know," he said. "You never know who's going to come calling."

She backed away from the handsome, smiling face.

"You caused me a lot of grief, Annabel," he said.

Her heart was pounding as he walked slowly towards her; he must be able to hear it. She backed away. They hadn't even believed her, for Christ's sake. They'd taken his side.

"You shouldn't be so sensitive, Annabel. Not in your business." He stopped walking, and looked at her. "You know your problem?" he asked. "You've got too much brain for this job, and not enough sense."

She couldn't speak.

"Did you think I wouldn't find you?" he asked. "It took me a while, but I got here." He smiled. "And I wanted the heat to die down." He looked round. "You live on the premises," he said. "The other tenants go home when they call it a night, don't they? There's no one here but you and me, Annabel."

She looked round desperately, as though an escape route might materialize.

"Shout for help, why don't you?"

She was still backing away from him as he advanced on her, but she knew that there was nowhere to go.

"Let's go for a picnic," said Geraldine, as she finished her cereal.

Charles looked up from the letter he was reading. "It's October," he said, as though that was an answer.

"I know it's October. But we've both got the day off, and that never happens, so let's go for a picnic. It's a lovely day."

"It's still October."

Geraldine laughed. "It's hotter than it was in July," she pointed out. "It's the hottest October day in London for nearly twenty years—they just said so."

"We're not in London. And it's Tuesday." He went back to trying to read his letter.

"What's that got to do with it?" asked Geraldine.

Charles put the letter aside. "People don't go for picnics on a Tuesday," he said.

Geraldine started clearing away the breakfast things. "They do if Tuesday is the one day they both happen to be free," she said.

"But you go for picnics on a Sunday," he argued.

"It could be pouring on Sunday." She dropped the shells of Charles's boiled eggs in the pedal bin. "It's warm and sunny today."

"But we haven't planned anything." He picked up his letter again.

Geraldine ran water into the basin. "What's to plan? I'll make a few sandwiches, and we've got cans of stuff in the fridge—that's the whole point of a picnic, isn't it?" She opened the fridge door as she spoke. "There's a bottle of wine in there too," she said.

"But we don't know where we're going."

Geraldine closed the fridge. "My God, Charles—every sentence you've uttered has started with a but! It's just a picnic—you don't have to book! There are lovely places round here. All these old villages—I don't think I've even been to Byford for about five years. Is the castle still open in October?"

"I don't know. So let's do it properly, when we can plan our route." He held up the letter. "Max," he said. "He's going to come and talk to Zelda, and Valerie's all for it. So I expect he will come."

Geraldine took the letter. It would be nice if Max and Valerie came to live in Stansfield. She and Charles had other friends, of course, but they had all married much earlier than they had, and had young families now; they didn't have much opportunity to go out for meals and things the way they used to.

One day she and Charles might be a family. They were trying; they had been trying all along. Geraldine had come off the pill before they were married. But it wasn't happening; they had gone for tests, and were waiting for the results.

Charles wasn't as bothered about it as she was; he still wanted them to set up a practice together, and thought that a baby might make that difficult. But he'd be just as pleased as she would be if she got pregnant, she knew he would be. And a baby wouldn't interfere with his plans. He was doing well with private patients; they could afford a nanny. He had plans for a clinic, for regular checks on people's blood pressure and other vital functions. Get them when they're well and keep them that way, he said.

She hardly ever bought red meat these days. Chicken and fish. She didn't use as much butter as she had ... well, if she were to be honest, she used rather more than Charles knew she did. Sauces weren't sauces without butter. She brightened a little. It was a long time since she'd had a dinner party. She gave Charles back the letter, and hoped that the Scotts would come. It could be fun.

Then she looked out at the Indian summer day, and sighed. Charles jogged every morning these days; he had been out in it, at least. But there was obviously to be no picnic.

Victor Holyoak got out of the car and pulled his shirt away from his back where it stuck to his skin. He walked down the deserted, unkempt street, counting door-numbers when there were any. He stopped outside an old building with a neglected frontage and weeds sprouting up in the tiny space that separated it from the pavement. This must be it.

At last, Catherine's name had turned up on an official form, and one of his private detectives had detected it. He took a breath of warm fresh air, since it seemed there would be precious little of that inside, and walked up to the front door.

My God. Every doorbell had a more outlandish name written above it than the one before, and a less than cryptic message to the caller. Surely she hadn't ...

The front door was open, anyway. He pushed it further open, and walked into the hallway. Stairs went up on his left, and he checked the piece of paper for the number of her flat.

His foot was on the bottom step when he heard the woman crying out, and he raced upstairs to where the cries were coming from, praying that he would be on time as they grew ever more frightened.

"No! Don't! Don't! No, *no*!"

The last word was screamed over and over in sheer panic, and Holyoak was at the door, which jammed itself against a chain. He shoulder-charged it, breaking the chain, and ran into the flat, following the direction of the terrified screaming, along the hallway, and burst through into the room.

A girl lay half-clothed on the floor, curled into a ball for protection. A shirt-sleeved police officer crouched over her, his truncheon raised. Holyoak seized him by the arm, forcing it behind him, making him drop the weapon, then pushed him headlong into the wall. On impact, he bent over, both hands clutching his head, swaying slightly.

Holyoak looked round, and saw his helmet lying on the bed. "You should keep that on," he advised him, thrusting it at him as he straightened up. He kicked the truncheon to his feet. "Pick that up and get out," he said, his voice quiet.

The policeman did as he was told, and fled.

Holyoak went to the girl, checking her for serious injury before lifting her on to the bed settee, where she sobbed in his arms until she had no more tears. She was thoroughly scared, but not too badly hurt. The injuries were superficial; she wouldn't look too good for a couple of days, but she was all right.

She begged him, almost as frightened as she had been before he'd arrived, not to report Bannister, for such was his name. Or he would come after her again. Reporting him was the last thing on Holyoak's mind, but he didn't tell her that. He promised her that he wouldn't, and in return made her promise not to tell the "stuck-up bitch across the landing," for such was her description of Catherine, that he'd been there.

He had to handle this very carefully; he wanted to work out his strategy. He had more pressing worries than Catherine's retrieval; now that he knew where she was, that could wait until his other difficulties were sorted out. A possible solution to one of his problems had dawned as Annabel had told him how she had let herself in for Bannister's retribution; now, he had to work everything out without distractions.

He would need Annabel's co-operation; he gave her money in return for her keeping a weather eye out for Catherine. He gave her a number to ring if she had to contact him, told her he would be back. He believed he could trust her, but the money was a test. If she and his money had disappeared by the time he returned, he might have to think again.

Annabel had assured him that Catherine wasn't on the game; indeed, she would have laughed, if she could have with a split lip, at the very idea.

Candlelight, soft music playing. Catherine had never been out to dinner; it was a special treat for her birthday.

Max had picked her up from the flat, and hadn't stopped talking about her choice of accommodation until they had got to the restaurant. It was cheap, she had pointed out. It was a bedsit, and therefore not what her fellow tenants wanted; they, she had discovered, needed to have a waiting room, like doctors. She had supposed they would, once she had thought about it. She didn't have much to do with them, but in a way it was comforting to know that all these people were around in the middle of the night.

Max had continued to be horrified, but he had at least stopped going on about it now. He had bought her a present; she unwrapped it at the table, and smiled as she saw the little pendant. He got up to do up the clasp, and sat down again, his dark brows drawn together in a query.

"It's lovely," she said.

The meal was wonderful, Max was wonderful. Until he cleared his throat. He always did that when he had something bad to tell her, like losing a client or having to wait for her wages.

She looked apprehensively at him.

"Catherine—" he began, and looked down at his biscuits and cheese.

She waited. She knew she wasn't going to want to hear it, so the longer he took the better.

"I'm thinking of giving up the office," he said in a rush.

"What?"

94

He sighed. "It isn't paying," he said.

"Will you be working from home?" She supposed his wife could do what she did; she would be out of a job.

He shook his head. "I'm packing it all in," he said. "I've got the offer of another job, and I'm told it's as good as mine already. I'm going to tell them I'm available."

Catherine took that in. Well, she could get another job too. It was a shame, but it hadn't been too difficult to see it coming.

"It means leaving London," he said.

Her eyes widened. No. *No.* "But—but . . . where are you going?" she asked, trying desperately not to cry.

"A place called Stansfield." He cut up a piece of cheese with no intention of eating it. "I'll be chief accountant at a factory there," he said. "But we've got weeks to sort things out. I don't start until February—and I've still got to meet the woman who runs the place." He smiled. "Maybe she'll change her mind when she interviews me," he said.

They drank the coffee in silence, and he ran her back to the flat, insisting on coming in with her to make sure that she didn't run into any of the passing trade.

She loved Max. He had never asked her after that first time in the car what had made her run away; he had never tried to find out about her. He could have taken advantage of her, financially or any other way, and he hadn't. She made him coffee, and wondered if she should make her feelings clear.

She hadn't known many men; her benchmark was her stepfather, and now she knew how different Max was. Victor Holyoak was a wheeler-dealer, who made money and lost money and made it again. She doubted very much if any of his activities were lawful. His money didn't go into the bank, like other people's. It went into safety deposit boxes, and antiques and paintings. And everyone thought how wonderful he was, how devoted to her mother, but that wasn't true. He was a fraud through and through.

Max didn't really care about money, except when he couldn't meet his mortgage. He had taken a risk just stopping to pick her up that night; he had given her a job, and security. He had been a friend, someone she could talk to, someone she felt more at home with than she had ever felt.

Max had his faults; he wasn't a paragon of virtue—far from

it. His office was a couple of rooms in a building full of similar tiny enterprises, and when she had started work, Max had good-naturedly put up with a lot of teasing from the other people, jokes which suggested that she was the latest in a long line, and by far the youngest. A lot of would-be witty remarks about cradle-snatching, even one about jail-bait that she had not been meant to overhear.

She was quite certain that his Don Juan reputation was deserved, but he had never been anything but a gentleman as far as she was concerned. And the jokes had altered in character during her time at his office; now, the emphasis was on his recent good conduct. The office was closed up at five thirty, and remained closed. The office, it seemed, was Max's preferred site of operations, and had been in use long into the evening in the past. He had changed; the evidence suggested that her presence had changed him.

But she loved him; she didn't want to change him. And if that was what he wanted, if that would stop him leaving . . .

The headlights that lit the frosty cobbles, and which Dave Bannister expected to sweep past him as he walked through the narrow lane, didn't; instead, the car slowed to walking pace and was now moving along beside him. He had just come off duty; he was having to walk home, hunched inside his leather jacket, his ears burning with the freezing wind that howled through the darkness of the alley. His car was off the road, and it was going to cost an arm and a leg to get it through its MOT. He didn't need jokes, not tonight.

The Daimler pulled in, its front wheel on the tiny strip of pavement, blocking his way. Bannister turned to find the rear passenger door opening into his path, and a man stepping out, ensuring that he couldn't go that way either. In the dim light from the inside of the car, he couldn't make out the man's features, but his mind instantly logged a police description of what he could see. Medium height, bare headed, dark overcoat, dark gloves, brown trousers, lace-up shoes. It was expensive gear. His eyes flicked towards the car, but there was no one with him except the driver, who was thin and weedy, and sat behind the wheel, staring straight ahead, hearing nothing, seeing nothing.

The passenger walked beyond the car door, beyond the light,

coming closer to where Bannister stood. He was completely in shadow now, and Bannister turned his attention to the Daimler; the colour, the model, the personalized number plate.

"Good evening, Mr. Bannister."

The voice was quiet, but it carried in the confines of the arched alleyway. Bannister watched warily as the figure walked into the pool of light thrown up by the car's headlamps on the white-painted wall, and automatically catalogued the features. Light brown hair, mid to late thirties, powerful build, bearded with facial scarring.

Christ. It was the guy from Annabel's. Bannister tensed up, ready to defend himself.

The man smiled. "No need for that, Mr. Bannister," he said. "I'm sure we can conduct ourselves in a civilized fashion."

Bannister frowned. "What do you want?" he asked.

"It strikes me that your attitude to your duties as an upholder of the law is, shall we say, flexible? I think I could use your services, Mr. Bannister."

Bannister leant back against the wing of the Daimler. So that's what it was. He gave Annabel a hiding, so he must be for sale. Well, he wasn't. "I don't take bribes," he said.

"I wasn't offering one. But if you don't co-operate with me, I will persuade Annabel to press charges."

Blackmail. A smoothie who thought he could intimidate him with his flash car and expensive tailoring. No chance. He smiled, shaking his head. "Whores get knocked about by their pimps all the time. I'll say you did it yourself when you couldn't bribe me, and now you're trying to stitch me up. Let's see who they believe. Me or a couple of slags."

"But I'm not her pimp, Mr. Bannister," he said, his voice still quiet, well modulated. "My name, for the record, is Victor Holyoak. I've never been involved with the police in any way. You can check."

Not so good, if he didn't have a record. But Annabel had a deep distrust of authority, of police, of courts, of anything that smacked of officialdom. Her one departure from form had got her into trouble; he'd scared the hell out of her, and she wasn't about to repeat the experience. "You'll never get that little whore into court," he said.

"Oh, yes I will." The statement was unequivocal. "And I wouldn't like to be defending you." He stepped closer, his

97

shoes making a soft scrunching sound on the frosty pavement. "She's already made one complaint against you, she can identify you, she has an eye witness, and the bruises to show for it."

Holyoak wasn't about to stick his neck out for Annabel, and Bannister knew it. And if she still had bruises, it wasn't from what he'd done to her. "Good," he said. "I hope they're bad for business."

Holyoak tutted as he gave a brief nod in the direction of the driver. "I had expected remorse," he said.

The car's headlamps were extinguished; in the sudden, disorienting darkness Bannister felt the other man's fists slamming into him, forcing the breath from his body; he doubled up, sinking to the ground as his legs gave way. On his hands and knees, retching with the effort of trying to breathe, he was completely helpless as Holyoak stood over him.

"I advise you to think again about co-operating with me, Mr. Bannister."

He was breathing again, if the agonizing, uncontrollable gulps of icy air which his lungs immediately coughed out could be called breathing. But he wasn't for sale. "Get stuffed," he said, with difficulty.

Holyoak grasped his jacket collar, almost strangling him, and wrenched him to his feet with one hand, while landing vicious body blows with the other, over and over and over again, until Bannister knew no more about it.

He came round jammed into a sitting position between the wheel of the car and the wall, his legs sprawled out in front of him. His head swam, and he sank into near unconsciousness again until a strategically placed kick forced his eyes wide open with pain and shock.

"Get up," said a disembodied voice from above him.

The headlights were switched on again, the full glare two inches from his face.

"Now."

His eyes screwed tight shut once more, he heard his own voice rasp out through the double agony. "The headlight," he croaked. "Put . . . put it out."

"Get up if you don't like it."

He couldn't get up. But he had to get away from the light. One hand on the rough surface of the wall, the other clasping the front tyre of the car, Bannister tried to move, but it was too difficult; he dropped his head again.

"I said get up. Unless you want some more."

Oh, God, no. He dragged himself into a crouching position, but there were long moments before he could haul himself out of the beam of light, slumping exhausted over the bonnet of the car, his chest heaving. He opened his eyes, but he could see nothing but a wall of light.

"If you're going to throw up, get off my car."

Fighting the nausea, Bannister straightened up, trying to blink away the blindness, staggering a little. He put a hand out to steady himself, finding the car roof.

"I need you fit for duty after Christmas. That's why you can still stand up. You'll do what I tell you, or you'll never stand up unaided again."

Eventually, the kaleidoscope of light began to fade, resolving itself into the colour-stained image of the bearded man, backlit by the reflection of the headlamps. He hadn't even broken sweat.

"You can continue to refuse to co-operate with me, of course. But if you do, you won't be fit for duty or anything else." He moved towards the car. "Except to stand trial—and Annabel will go to court whether she likes it or not, believe me." He opened the rear door of the Daimler.

Bannister believed him. And Annabel would have bruises, if bruises were required.

"Get in."

Through the swathes of purple and green, Bannister felt his way along the car, his hands on the cold metal, groaning as his battered body was pushed in.

The car fired and drove off as soon as they were both seated, the driver behaving for all the world as though his employer had stopped to give Bannister a lift.

The Christmas party. Sitting with his colleagues in a pub, wearing a party hat, smoking a cigar he didn't like and didn't want, watching them all get legless, wasn't Lloyd's idea of fun. But Judy was there.

They had weathered the non-happening at Sid Compton's leaving party quite well, considering. They didn't often have a lot to do with one another in the normal way at work, task-force raids excepted. When their paths had crossed again, she had apologized, and thereafter their working life had gone on as though nothing at all had happened, much to his relief. No embarrassed silences, no awkwardness.

But that just made it worse, in a way. If she had compounded her perverse behaviour by trying to put him in the wrong, he could perhaps have told himself that she was just a tease who got her fun that way. But she wasn't, and he knew it. She had meant to go through with it; his bright idea of borrowing a room had blown it. He wondered if Andrew Marvell had had better luck.

He was going before the promotions board in the New Year; if he was successful, and there was no reason why he shouldn't be, he would be moving on. Before, he had worried about that, but now he thought that it might be easier when they weren't actually working at the same station. It was, after all, the thought of one of her colleagues knowing that had given her cold feet, and the ever-present possibility of their superiors finding out. He'd get in touch with her once he was in his new post. He wasn't going to lose her.

He was startled when she joined him at his table, which he realized had been deserted while he had been staring into his pint and his future. He smiled at the tiny policeman's helmet which perched on the top of her head. "Trust you to get that one," he said.

She looked puzzled, then realized what he was talking about, and smiled too, removing it. Then came the reason for her unexpected presence at his table. "I thought you ought to know," she began.

No one ever thought you ought to know that you'd won the Irish Sweep; this wasn't going to be good.

"Michael's firm is sending him back to Nottingham," she said. "He'll be based there instead of in London. It won't be for about six months," she said. "But I'll be going with him." There was a tiny pause before she carried on. "We're getting married before we go," she said. "The date isn't fixed yet."

What was she expecting him to say? It was a moment or two before he could say anything at all. When he did, it was that he hoped they would be very happy.

And perhaps they would.

CHAPTER FIVE

Now: Thursday, 2 April, A.M. . . .

ANNA HAD FINALLY SUCCUMBED TO HER ALCOHOL IN-
take; her eyes had opened once or twice when Max had tried
to waken her, but there had been no conscious thought involved. She had been murmuring, but what she had been saying had consisted mostly of incomprehensible obscenities
about Victor Holyoak.

Now, there wasn't even that.

Max lifted his clothes from the floor where he had dropped
them in his hurry to divest himself of them, and hung them
neatly over the chair. He took another look at the unconscious
Anna, and went out into the living room, through to the
kitchen, where he made himself coffee, and sat down. And that
was when the full realization of everything that had happened
came crashing down on him, unstoppably, unbearably.

He had been operating on some primitive level of self-
preservation until he had stopped having something to do; now,
his hand shook uncontrollably as he tried to lift the mug to his
lips. Coffee wasn't the right thing, not if he wanted to calm
down. It just made people jumpier than they were in the first
place. He poured it away, and went back into the bedroom.

Anna still didn't stir, as he got back into bed beside her. She
was what he needed; it had worked before, and it would again,
if only she would wake up. But gentle shaking failed to produce more than a snuffling little snore as she turned over. The
alcohol had worked for her, he thought, in the end. She wasn't
quivering like a leaf, jumping at her own shadow. She was

oblivious to everything. He had never tried it; maybe it would work for him, even if she hadn't left much. How much would he need to reach oblivion? Probably not a lot.

He used her glass; he shivered as he drank. He had never liked the taste of alcohol.

Two o'clock in the morning, and all was far from well. Charles wondered what town criers had actually said when things hadn't been as they should be.

Gerry would get over it, in time. It was, after all, her own fault. But she still hadn't come back upstairs. The crying had stopped, at least the audible crying. He sat up, suddenly frightened by the silence, but in that moment he heard her come upstairs, and he lay back, deeply relieved. Her tread was slow, like an old person's, and she didn't come back in to the bedroom. After a few moments, he heard the guest-room door close.

He hadn't really been surprised when she hadn't come home; he had rung Zelda, and got no reply. As eleven o'clock approached, he had rung again, but there was still no one there. He hadn't waited up. She had come home just after midnight.

"Where have you been?" he had asked, putting down the book he had been trying to read, as she had come to bed.

"With Zelda," she had said, and had stopped undressing as she had spoken. "We were worried about Catherine."

"I'm sure he isn't going to murder her in her bed," he had said.

"What in God's name made you tell him about the abortion?" Geraldine had demanded.

Charles could feel again the cold wave of realization that had swept over him with her words. "He didn't know?" he had said, horrified at the thought that he had betrayed a medical confidence.

"No! Catherine made Zelda promise not to tell him. He was angry enough as it was without finding that out as well."

He should be grateful to her, not angry, in Charles's opinion. The discovery that Catherine was having his child would rather have given the lie to Max's insistence that they were no more than employer and employee, and that would have made that whole dreadful episode drag on even longer than it had.

Gerry had begun undressing then, picking up her nightdress,

102

stopping in the act of slipping it on over her head. "Why were you so angry about it anyway?" she had said.

Charles sighed, as he recalled every sentence that had led to the inevitable. He had wanted to leave all this until tomorrow, but the conversation had moved inexorably towards it, and he had been powerless to stop it. "I thought he'd sent her to you. All the doctors in Stansfield to choose from, and he'd sent her to you. I thought it was a lousy thing to do."

If only things had ended there, he might still have waited, at least until the morning, when daylight would bring with it the common sense that seemed to desert human beings when the sun went down, before saying what he had to say. But far from it; his reason for berating Max had touched Gerry, and her baffled irritation with him had softened into a smile of apology, of gratitude, even.

She had put her hand on his where it lay on the covers, and had given it a little squeeze. "Thank you," she had said. "But no one sent her. We were the only doctors she knew. She chose me because I was a woman, that's all."

Then she had got into bed. Leaving her nightdress lying on the duvet. "She didn't know we were desperate to have a baby," she had said, kissing him gently on the cheek, moving closer to him.

He had shifted away from her. "Gerry," he had said. "I've been meaning to . . . well, talk to you. Because we really can't let this dominate our lives for much longer."

She had frowned, puzzled. "Let what dominate our lives?" she had asked, and it had been an innocent question. Trying to have a baby was so much a part of her life that it was as if he had been telling her that she mustn't let breathing become too important to her.

"Having a baby," he had said, with as much patience as he had been able to muster. "You're forty-two, Gerry." He had turned to face her, taking her hand. "A baby would have been fine once," he had said.

"A baby would be fine now," she had said, smiling, though he had been able to see the tears already bright in her eyes. "It might happen, Charles. If it doesn't . . . well, at least we'll have tried."

"But there are too many things to go wrong."

"What?"

"There would be a higher risk of miscarriage, of the baby's being damaged—you couldn't take that kind of disappointment—it's become too important to you."

"I could. I know—for God's sake, Charles—I *know* the pitfalls! I'd be prepared for them. And most births are perfectly all right, even with older women!"

"But some aren't." He had clasped her hand tighter, more for his own sake than for hers. "Look—I know I wasn't too keen on the idea, but perhaps we could try to adopt."

She had pulled her hand from his then. "Oh, no," she had said. "No. You talked me out of that a long time ago, Charles. And you know as well as I do that they'd say we're too old now!"

He knew they were too old; it was why he had been prepared to suggest it, because if she had taken him up on it, it would never have happened. And it had provided him with an opening for the rest of the reasoned argument that he had been working on all evening.

"We are too old," he had said. "A childless couple, in their forties—they'd say that we were too old to start having to cope with nighttime feeds and dirty nappies, because we *are*, Gerry. We're too old."

"No! They say it keeps you young, having a—"

"We're too used to being a couple. Sleepless nights, nappies, babysitters . . . we couldn't adjust to all that, not now."

"Yes—oh, yes, we could. We *could*. It—"

"All right," he had said. "We'll go to an agency. If they say we can adopt, we'll do that. Fair?"

She had been shaking her head all the time, blinking away the tears. *"No,"* she had said. "No. It isn't fair. Not now. If I have a baby now, then I want it to be *my* baby!"

But not necessarily his. In his solitude, Charles faced the reasons for his decision.

He thought again of Gerry's familiarity with Victor's penthouse flat; that had set up a suspicion that he had pushed away. Not with Victor, he had thought. Surely not Victor? But all doubt had been dispelled by the conversation that he had overheard between Victor and Anna Worthing. No wonder she had been so keen to convince him that Anna was Victor's mistress; that, apparently, was the idea. But Anna had clearly been unwilling to play ball.

He hadn't questioned Victor about it; for one thing, it had been obvious that Anna Worthing must still be in the flat, though Victor had chosen to pretend that they were alone, pressing him to stay, even. For another, there was little point. Charles knew why Gerry had done it; she was quite prepared to have someone else's baby, and let him believe that he was the father. He doubted if Victor was aware of his entirely perfunctory role. It wasn't the first time she had done it, and he had kept his counsel then; she never knew that he had found out. But this would be the last time, he had promised himself that.

Charles's own deviation from acceptable social behaviour was one he preferred not to think about, but he had been forced to, as he had listened to the furious Anna Worthing. Zelda was right about her and Max, of course, and Victor had been far from pleased by their behaviour.

But it was when Anna had begun shouting at Holyoak about her being used as a decoy for his own amorous adventures that alarm bells had started to ring; Charles had interrupted before any names were bandied about, and had given Victor no inkling that he had overheard.

"The risk of my making you pregnant may be minimal," he had told Gerry. "But I'll be taking precautions from now on, so there will be no risk at all."

If she had a baby now, she couldn't pretend that it was his, and he knew Gerry well enough this time round to know that that would ensure that she would never put him in this position again. She wouldn't cheat on him, not if she couldn't disguise it.

Gerry loved him; she would never take the risk of losing him, and he knew it. Her infidelities had been prompted by an overwhelming desire to have a baby, and nothing more. But it had to stop. The scandal could be ruinous.

She had stared at him, the tears falling, running down her face.

"I'm sorry," he had said. "But I'm only thinking of you. So that's the way it's going to be."

And she had got out of bed, pulled on her dressing-gown, and left the room.

She was upset, of course she was. A baby was the be-all and end-all of her life. It was the first real row they had ever had, and he hoped very much that it would be the last. He liked things the way they were. She would get over it; there weren't many husbands who would behave as well as he had over such lapses. But he still couldn't sleep, even though he had averted potential disaster. He wished he had kept his mouth shut about the abortion, for one thing.

Dawn was breaking as he finally felt his eyelids grow heavier, and his burdens, for a few snatched moments, just a little lighter.

Judy's eyes opened as light filled the room through the half-open blinds that they had never got round to closing when Lloyd had cornered her in the moonlit bedroom in his attempts to scare her witless.

Half-past six, she noted, before closing her eyes again. Half-past six on almost her last day off, but that was all right, because she was in Lloyd's flat, and that was always a little like being on holiday. She glanced at him as he slept, and smiled. He *had* scared her last night with all his talk of *doppelgängers* and premonitions. She had almost believed him about Victor Holyoak and his two faces.

She *had* believed him, she admitted to herself. Lloyd could do that; he had always been able to make her believe whatever he wanted her to believe. That he was happy when he was miserable, that he was indifferent when he was hurt. That he was hurt when he was nothing of the sort. The only time that she really knew where she was with him was when he was angry with her, when he left her in no doubt.

Strips of sunlight slashed across the walls, showing the room in its true colours—a statement of its occupant's personality. No frills, no unnecessary furniture, not even curtains. Just the clean lines of his brand-new vertical blinds, a bed, a bedside table, a chest of drawers, and a mirror. But the door of the built-in wardrobe was open, the sleeve of one of his jackets preventing it closing; several shoes, none of which seemed to match any of the others, were scattered over the plain, space-enhancing carpet; and the unfussy lines were obliterated by cast-off clothing, bottles of aftershave, piles of books everywhere, and the odd newspaper and magazine. Even a mug.

But last night, once he had realized he could scare her, there had been no such comforting, familiar images. Soft, fuzzy lines of light had inexplicably penetrated the darkness of the room, disorienting her, and Lloyd's eerie tales of ghosts walking, of apparitions appearing to foretell their own deaths, had demolished the barrier of sound common sense that she had always put between herself and such things. Her imagination had been more than receptive to Lloyd's suggestions as to what the half-lit shapes might be, as to what he might be, come to that, when the moon was full.

And she had loved every scary, exhilarating, delicious moment of it. The delight had turned to desire, and the desire to drowsy tenderness; she had finally fallen asleep in a tangle of bedclothes and Lloyd and ribbons of moonlight, undeniably, inexpressibly happy.

He must have been up since then, because the duvet was now neatly over both of them. It was the only neat thing in the room. Her common sense had returned from wherever Lloyd had sent it scurrying last night, and she resolved to tidy up his bedroom whether he wanted her to or not. The bedside phone rang, and she glared at it.

Lloyd stirred. "Whose flat are we in?" he muttered, still nine-tenths asleep.

"Yours."

"Mm. Right." Eyes closed, he reached out an accurately aimed hand, and lifted the receiver to his ear. His eyes opened, and he sat up. "Say that again," he said, and listened, fully awake. He glanced at her, then looked away again. "Right," he said. "Twenty minutes."

He hung up and still didn't look at her. "I don't know how to tell you this," he said.

"Is it bad news?" she asked, alarmed.

"No—no, not like that. Nothing personal."

She breathed a sigh of relief. "What then?" she asked.

"It's Victor Holyoak," he said, and looked at her for the first time. "He's been found dead, Judy." His voice was almost apologetic.

Judy's spine tingled again. But this time she didn't enjoy the sensation.

"I'll have to go," he said, and gave a little shrug. "It looks like your leave just got cancelled," he added. "Sorry."

She nodded.

"Right," he said, getting out of bed. "I'll have a quick

107

shower and get off." He smiled. "I expect you've got time to have breakfast before you have to face it," he said.

For once she wasn't at all sure she felt like having breakfast. "Just tell me one thing first," she said. "Was any of that stuff true?"

"About my being the Phantom of the Pithead?"

"Very funny," she said. "About Victor Holyoak."

He nodded.

"All of it? All that about you were close to him, but he was far away, and you could see him but he couldn't see you?"

He nodded again, with another apologetic little shrug. "It was as though I was standing next to him," he said. "Except that I wasn't. I couldn't touch him. I know that."

She sighed, and pushed back the duvet, swinging her legs out into the cold air. In the daylight, she knew that there had to be a rational explanation. Holyoak hadn't appeared to Lloyd in a dream, or some premonition. She pursued Lloyd out of the bedroom, into the living room.

"That's just your memory playing tricks," she said.

"Is it?"

Lloyd had seen him yesterday, and had recognized him; now the man was dead. There could be a horribly rational explanation for that, and it was that that Lloyd was shying away from; the fact that his presence at the reception may have signed Holyoak's death warrant.

"Perhaps it's . . . I don't know. Psychological. You were after him for something and couldn't prove it. And that's translated itself into your being able to see him, but not touch him. Someone there knew that you could identify him, and . . ." She shrugged the rest of the sentence.

He thought about that for a second; it was quirky enough to appeal. But then he shook his head. "I'd remember," he said. "If I'd ever been after him."

He would. She knew that.

"He's dead, Judy," he said, a little uncomfortably. "I have this strange image of him yesterday, and this morning he's dead."

"It's got nothing to do with the supernatural!" she said firmly.

"I know." He didn't sound at all convinced. He walked out into the hall, with Judy on his tail.

"Do we know how he died?" she asked, as he went into the bathroom.

"Multiple stab wounds," he said, as he turned on the shower, and pulled the curtain round. Then his face appeared again. "Norman Bates isn't around, is he?" he asked anxiously.

"Who?" said Judy.

He grinned. "Forget it," he said, and disappeared back behind the curtain.

Judy frowned a little, then forgot it, as instructed. "Could he have disturbed an intruder?" she called above the noise of the shower.

"Could have done," Lloyd called back. "There was a window open, apparently. But there's a twenty-four-hour video security system in operation—I'll get someone to check through the tapes. It'll take for ever, though."

Judy thought about the situation while Lloyd showered, but her attempts to think logically had been sabotaged by Lloyd's surreal memory of Holyoak. Though the fact of the surreal image was real enough; he had told her about it when Holyoak was still hale and hearty. But there was an explanation, and they would find it eventually. In the meantime, she forced herself to approach it as she would any other incident.

"Is there anything missing?" she asked.

"It doesn't look like it, apparently. But if there is, we might never know. His wife's on very heavy sedation, and she's not going to come out of it. I don't know who else is likely to know what was up there. Maybe Anna Worthing, if Mrs. Driver's got it right about her."

"What about his stepdaughter?"

"The Scotts are apparently not at home," said Lloyd, switching off the shower, and stepping out. "All yours," he said, towelling himself vigorously.

Judy frowned, and got into the shower. "No one knows where they are?" she asked, as she pulled the curtain round. Shower curtains. Multiple stab wounds. Norman Bates. *"Psycho!"* she shouted triumphantly as the water cascaded down.

"No need to get personal just because you aren't clairvoyant." The next few words were unintelligible as he tried to speak while brushing his teeth.

"What?" She rinsed the shampoo from her hair.

"I said it's not seven o'clock yet. I don't think we've asked anyone." There was a brief silence. "But there was something odd going on there yesterday," he said, his voice a little defiant.

"You said."

"Mm. And Anna Worthing said something about Scott," he said.

"Scott?"

Lloyd was now having to shout above the noise of his battery shaver and the shower. "People were giving him a wide berth," he explained. "It was obvious—it was meant to be obvious. When I asked her why, she seemed to think that I should know."

"Do you want me to run a check on him?" she asked.

"Er . . . yes," he said, indecisively.

"Right," said Judy. Lloyd was never indecisive, and it was his half-memory of Holyoak that was bothering him, Judy knew. Because that meant that he might have been indirectly responsible for Holyoak's death; someone knew that Lloyd might have recognized him, and that was dangerous for whoever it was. Either that or he really was a seer. And though Lloyd's capacity for belief could accommodate virtually anything and everything but ordinary, work-a-day God, even he didn't believe that. Did he? She certainly didn't. Did she?

Judy rinsed herself off, and stepped out of the shower. "You have to remember where you saw him," she said.

He *had* to.

"Where did you get it?" She looked scared.

Dave Bannister was still in bed; Jackie had come in, holding out the money, wanting to know where it had come from.

"Keep that out of it," he said, pointing to his own nose, and pulling himself out of bed. "Why were you going through my pockets?" he demanded, snatching the money out of her hand.

"I was only trying to get the washing in the machine before I went to work," she said. "I always check the pockets."

"Well, don't," he said.

"Would you rather it had all gone in the machine?" she asked.

She washed all the bloody time. The kids went through clothes like nobody's business. She could have left his jeans until tomorrow. He ignored her, and counted the money; he had forgotten all about it in his panic-stricken drive homeward. My God, that little whore had really done it this time.

Two hundred and ten pounds. He reached over to the bedside table, and picked up a packet of cigarettes and a lighter.

"Where were you last night?" Jackie asked.

"Here," he said, lighting a cigarette, closing his eyes as he exhaled the smoke, and wondered what his next move should be. "All night. I was here, with you, watching telly." He caught his wife's arm. "You got that?" he asked.

She nodded, and he let her go. For a few moments only the drone of the washing-machine could be heard, as she looked at him the way only wives knew how to look at people, and he was back in that flat, frozen into immobility by the scene in the bedroom.

"Dave—what have you done?" She broke into his thoughts.

Christ, he didn't know. He was sure no one had seen him, but they would be bound to question Annabel. He stuffed the notes into the dressing-table drawer.

"Dave?"

"You'll be late for work," he said.

She looked at him, her eyes wide with a mixture of curiosity and fear. "I'm late already," she said, distractedly. "I'm not even dressed yet—I'll miss the bus." Her eyes went to the drawer. "Where did you get it, Dave?" she asked again.

He had to tell her something; just something she would believe. "I told you I'd had an offer of a job," he said.

She groaned. "Oh, Dave—not those crooks! What did you have to do for two hundred pounds?"

He sat down on the bed. My God, if she only knew. But he'd worn gloves, and they couldn't place him there. Even if that little bitch said anything, he could deny it. He was here, watching television, and they couldn't prove any different. He hadn't clapped eyes on her for almost fifteen years; they'd laugh at her. They hadn't taken her word against his last time, and they wouldn't this time. Besides, she would be putting herself in the frame if she said anything at all, wouldn't she? But he had to be sure. Easy enough to frighten Annabel into keeping her mouth shut. And no Holyoak to exact retribution.

He smiled, when he realized that. He felt better anyway now that he had put distance between himself and Stansfield, now that he'd had some sleep, now that he had a few quid. And he

111

knew Annabel of old. She never said anything in interviews, on the grounds that that way she couldn't get caught out. She wouldn't say anything. He looked up at his wife. "Where are the kids?" he asked.

"On that school trip. Someone collected them at seven in a minibus."

Oh, yes. Her mother had paid for that; the old bat had her uses. "Well," he said. "If you're late already, don't bother going." He pulled the tie of her dressing-gown, and let it fall open. She smiled as he touched her.

"Will it be regular money?" she asked, slipping off the dressing-gown, and sitting beside him on the bed. "This job? You're not going to get knocked about, are you? Because your insides won't take any more—"

"Stop asking questions," he said, stretching over her and allowing himself the luxury of crushing out a half-smoked cigarette; he could afford it. But it wouldn't be regular money.

It could be worth more than a couple of hundred, though—it bloody well ought to be. Annabel wasn't just going to keep her mouth shut—she was going to pay for this in hard cash.

"I am biologically capable of producing a child," said Geraldine, wiping away the tears that continued to fall, inconveniencing her, making reasoned argument almost impossible. "If nature hasn't given up, why should we?"

"Because it isn't sensible to have a first child at your age," said Charles, untearful, as maddeningly reasonable as he had been last night.

"If it was sensible last week, it's sensible this week!" she shouted.

"The subject's closed, Gerry," he said, buttering the toast that he had made himself, for himself.

"Then I might as well stay in the spare room," she said, not above the Lysistrata gambit if it would help.

"Please yourself," he said. "It really makes very little difference to me what form of contraceptive we use, providing it isn't your decision whether or not to use it." He got two mugs from the cupboard. "Abstinence will be fine by me," he said.

She knew that. She had known as she had said it that withdrawal of conjugal rights was no threat at all. She had always known that he had never really wanted her physical love. Or even returned her spiritual love. The love in their marriage had flowed one way; she had known all along, she supposed, but it took until last night for her to admit it to herself. In a way, Charles hardly knew her. *Her*, not the wife he had invented for himself.

A baby wouldn't have been enough. A son or a daughter might have loved her back, but she would still have needed Charles's love as well. That was what she wanted, and had always wanted, since she had met him. She sat down as she was hit by the sudden realization that she may never really have wanted a baby at all, that the one thing that had filled her hopes and dreams and fantasies had never been real. She had wanted to make up for Charles's coldness somehow. To make their love-making mean something, because it had never been important to Charles, and she had known that, even before they were married. The baby she had tried to conceive all these years was a substitute for Charles's love.

She had even convinced herself that her brief affair had been a desperate attempt to conceive, but now she thought that perhaps all she had wanted was someone who had wanted her. She had lived a lie, and she hadn't even known that until last night. The truth now seemed to empty her of emotion, of energy, of any sort of meaning to her life.

"But . . ." She looked up at Charles. "Where do we go from here?"

"Where we go is up to you," he said.

Freddie arrived just after ten, assistant in tow, to make his *in situ* examination of the body. He was tall and thin and suitably serious looking for a forensic pathologist, until he noted the lack of close relatives in the vicinity. Then he grinned and waved cheerily into the bedroom, where the Scene of Crime Officers had just finished, and Lloyd stood surveying the aftermath of violent death, watching the SOCOs leave with their booty. Scenes of crime looked like Moon landings these days, with anonymous white-suited astronauts taking samples back to Earth.

"Morning, Lloyd!" Freddie came into the room. "Ah," he said, beaming. "A nice bloody one this time."

As long as he lived, Lloyd would never understand Freddie. "We haven't found the murder weapon," he said. "But there's

113

a block of knives in the kitchen—forensic have taken them for examination."

"Right, then, let's have a look—ah, Kathy. This is a good one for you. Probable cause of death?"

"Even I can work that out," said Lloyd, as he tried not to look at the blood-soaked, bath-robed body. But all around, there was more blood. Not the full horror-film variety; a fine spray of blood, all over everything. The chairs, the dressing table, the headboard of the bed had been dusted for prints, and the blood-spattered white wood was smudged and dirty where they had been working. The blood had gone into long, thin diagonal dashes as it had hit the floor, and the wall, and the double doors set into it.

Lloyd opened both the doors of the walk-in wardrobe, and whistled slightly. It had two rails running down either side, both empty except for padded hangars; it wasn't much smaller than his bathroom in the flat, and it wasn't even being used. But much good all that money did you when you were doing a very good impersonation of Julius Caesar on the Ides of March.

"You can work it out?" said Freddie eagerly. "Come on then. Get down. Have a good look."

He enjoyed it. The blasted man enjoyed it. Some sort of macho instinct wouldn't allow Lloyd to refuse. He got down, and had a look. "Stab wounds," he said.

"Stab wounds," agreed Freddie. "But you don't die from stab wounds, Lloyd."

"Eh?"

"What I mean is that stab wounds are not of themselves a cause of death. You can be stabbed and not die. So why is he dead?"

"Because he's lost a lot of blood," said Lloyd.

Freddie sucked in his breath. "Wouldn't necessarily kill you," he said.

Lloyd sincerely hoped that something would rescue him from this, and his prayers were answered.

"Sir?"

Lloyd got up from his brief and unwilling examination of Holyoak's body.

"Sir—they've got the video set up in security."

"Oh, what a pity," said Lloyd to Freddie. "I'm going to have to leave you to it." He looked at Kathy. "Well?" he said.

"Well," she said, looking not only at the body, but at the bed, at the headboard, at the wall behind it. "We'd have to see how deep the wounds are. An artery has been severed, but he may have died from a wound or wounds to vital organs. But the indications are that he died from haemorrhage."

"Haemorrhage," said Lloyd. "Isn't that what I said?"

"Yes," they cho; used.

My God, she was getting just like Freddie. One of Lloyd's ex-colleagues had been brave enough to marry her; Lloyd hoped she didn't take her work home. He was sure Freddie did. He probably had horrible things in jars all over the house.

He went down the steps from the penthouse, and walked across to the security building, with its bank of screens, showing different areas of the factory and office premises. The tapes ran twenty-four hours a day, showing a panoramic view from a swivelling camera on the central lighting tower; other static cameras allowed the security men to watch strategic areas of the grounds and the factory floor itself. They could zoom in on anything untoward. The output from these cameras was also recorded.

"The main camera output shows the whole area," said the security officer. "There's just one blind spot—the exit from the underground staff car park—but you're more interested in people coming in than going out, aren't you?"

"Right," said Lloyd. He really wanted to play with the video himself, but even he couldn't think of a good reason why it ought to be watched by a DCI rather than someone a little lower down the pay scale.

"Most of the cameras concentrate on the factory," the security man said. "There's millions of pounds' worth of equipment in there. And the rooftop camera's just a sweep of the area covered by the static cameras. So if you do see anything that looks interesting, give us the sector letter and the time, and we can give you it in close-up. One of the cameras takes in the ground-floor of the flat—but the one that might be of most use to you is on the other monitor—that's the camera on the main entrance. All vehicles enter there, as I said, and all pedestrians enter and leave there. The gates are opened at five thirty in the morning and closed at ten thirty at night, but some vehicles do come in outside these hours—they use a phone on the gate, which also has a camera."

"What if our man came and parked in the underground car park a week ago?" asked Lloyd gloomily.

"It was completely clear yesterday morning," said the security man. "Special Branch insisted."

Lloyd brightened. They had been useful for once, instead of just getting in everyone's way. "And you've actually got on tape every vehicle that entered the premises between then and when Mr. Holyoak was found dead?"

"We have," he said proudly.

In a corner, two detective constables sat at monitors, being given their instructions. They would be watching the two tapes from the moment Special Branch, who had of course searched the place from top to bottom, left, until they reached the time that the police arrived at the scene.

Lloyd looked at the surprisingly clear black and white image of a retreating, would-be anonymous Special Branch car, its number plate brought into close-up at the touch of button, as the constables were shown what the machine could do.

"We can get you a still photograph of anything interesting," the security man said.

Lloyd beamed at the two young men. "Good luck, lads," he said. "Only eighteen hours to go."

They could fast-search through a lot of that, but they had no idea whether they were looking for someone in a vehicle, on a bike, or on foot. The tape had to be stopped every time anything moved. It had to be hoped that the intruder, if such there was, had come reasonably early. And if something caught their eye on the sweep, and that incident had to be located on another tape . . .

Lloyd gave up working out the man hours, and went back up to the penthouse. It had been his idea to look at the tapes. He just had to hope that they came up with some evidence.

"Ah—sir."

Lloyd looked at Detective Sergeant Finch, who came out of the bedroom, quite unconcerned by Freddie's activities.

"Sir—I can't find a wallet," he said.

Lloyd's eyebrows rose. "Where have you looked?" he asked.

"Well—everywhere I can think of, now that the SOCOs have finished in the flat itself," he said.

There was something almost angelic about Finch's looks; the fair curly hair, the youthful face; he looked like an eager ten-year-old, and he was as sharp as they came.

"It's not in any of the drawers," he said. "In here or the bedroom. I've even looked in the kitchen. It's not in the jacket that was in here, or in any of his other pockets. I've got them searching for it outside."

Lloyd nodded grimly, and went back into the bedroom, looking down at the body as it lay sprawled half on, half off the bed. "Would someone do this for a wallet?" he asked.

The young man shrugged, following him in.

"Depends what was in it," Freddie said.

"Mm. We need to know if anything else is missing." Lloyd looked at Finch. "There was a young woman here yesterday. Anna Worthing—see if you can get hold of her, Tom. She was fixing everything up for Holyoak—she might know what ought to be here."

"Yes, sir."

"And there were a lot of people in and out of here yesterday—we're going to need their prints for elimination. Get hold of the collective Drs. Rule—I've already asked Mrs. Driver to come in some time."

As Finch left, Lloyd heard Judy's voice. Oh, boy. Judy was less than enthusiastic about blood; she hadn't even cared for the first-aid classes that all police officers had to attend, and had had to accept that either she learned how to dress wounds and give artificial respiration or her career stopped there. And though apart from the body itself there was no heavy blood-staining in the room, what there was seemed to Lloyd to be even more unsettling. The fine flecks of blood gave the impression of having been painted on to the surfaces; it looked like hell might look if someone got in an interior decorator with a sense of humour. She and Finch came to the bedroom door, and he could see her grow visibly pale. She had never fainted yet, but there was always a first time.

"Morning, Judy! Lovely as ever, I see," said Freddie, not actually looking at her.

Judy grunted a reply.

117

"Have you run your check already?" Lloyd asked.

She swallowed. "Yes," she said. "And there's interesting stuff on Scott. That's why I hung on to Tom."

"Good," said Lloyd. "Perhaps we could listen to it in the kitchen?"

Judy needed no second telling; he and Finch followed her back through the sitting room, past the open door where they could see the fingerprint man who was now working in the lift, shepherding her through to the little kitchen, where she leant against the washer-drier and took several deep, slow breaths before she attempted to speak again.

"Right," she said. "Scott was very strongly suspected of having murdered his first wife thirteen years ago next month."

Lloyd's eyebrows rose again. So that's what Anna Worthing had meant.

"Scott claimed that he was in London when his wife died," said Judy. "Which we know was between five forty-five and seven o'clock in the evening of the third of May."

"How did she die?" asked Finch.

"Strangled," she said. "Manually."

"Go on," said Lloyd.

"At first Scott said that he had gone back to vote—it was election day, and he had only just moved to Stansfield, so he wasn't registered here. And that while he was there he decided to go to a prostitute." She raised her eyebrows, indicating her disbelief.

"Doesn't everyone?" said Finch. "That's why I hate stable government. The more elections the better, that's what I say. Once every five years is a killer."

Judy laughed. The colour was coming back to her cheeks now that she was no longer faced with the horror of the bedroom.

"And he had no idea who, or where, I expect," said Lloyd.

"He never went through with it, he told them. So no alibi. Except that he knew the address he'd gone to—but none of the girls there were very forthcoming."

Was very forthcoming, thought Lloyd. He'd have said so, if Finch hadn't been there.

"But he has a reputation with women which made the investigating officers a touch suspicious of his sudden shyness."

She was enjoying herself now. Lloyd waited to hear what gem she was about to give them.

"Anyway," Judy went on, "he stuck to this not terribly convincing story until one Miss Barnes turned up the next morning. She was seventeen, and had worked for him in London. She said that he had been with her on business, and had been trying to keep her name out of it, not wanting to get her mixed up in a murder enquiry. She had a bedsit in that block of flats, but there was no suggestion that she was on the game herself." She smiled. "In any event, Scott married her just over six months later."

"The woman he's married to now?" said Lloyd.

Judy nodded. "No one believed her for a minute, but they were never able to get any hard evidence that he'd been at home either. Forensic couldn't place him at the scene, no one remembered seeing him when he shouldn't have been there. It was election day, so there were a lot of people about in the area, which is how come they could narrow down the time of death. Broad daylight, but none of them saw Scott. And the case was never officially closed. And something else. Zelda Driver tells me that Scott didn't even know Holyoak *was* his wife's stepfather until the day before yesterday."

"And when her stepfather turns up . . ." said Finch slowly. "Scott starts slapping his wife about."

Lloyd thought about that. A man like Holyoak, with a multi-million-pound fortune, discovering that his stepdaughter had been used to concoct some phony alibi, might have been able to dig into the matter of Mrs. Scott's death with more time and money and fewer restrictions on how he operated than the police; he might have found out too much. Scott might have thought his wife had colluded with her stepfather in some way, especially if she had kept the relationship a secret.

"A chat with Mr. and Mrs. Scott would appear to be indicated," said Lloyd. "If we can find them. But in the meantime, Tom, you have a word with Miss Worthing."

Finch went off, and Lloyd told Judy about the lack of a wallet, which was a little puzzle that didn't quite fit in, in his opinion. "I think you should get as much as you can on the first Mrs. Scott's murder," he said. "It may well have to be unofficially reopened from never having been officially closed."

"You can have the body taken to the mortuary now," said Freddie. "I can do the PM tomorrow morning."

"Good," said Lloyd. "Any chance of a time of death?"

"Thirteen minutes past eight," said Freddie.

Lloyd sighed. "All right, all right. I just want a very rough estimate."

"Very rough? All right. Over twelve hours. That's as rough as you can get."

Lloyd's face lit up. "Over twelve hours?" he repeated, and looked at his watch. "Are you saying he was dead by eleven o'clock last night?"

Freddie sighed deeply. "I'm saying that rigor mortis is complete," he said, and shrugged. "That makes it just possible—no more—that he's been dead for over twelve hours, and under twenty-four. His body temperature suggests the lower end. It could get argued out of any court in the world. I don't know what he was doing at the time of death—if he was taking exercise, that could have speeded everything up, and the indications are that he was taking very vigorous exercise indeed. And, despite your expert advice, Lloyd, I still don't know what killed him. If he bled to death, the attack could have happened some considerable time before he died. If his attacker stabbed a vital organ, he could have died there and then. All or any of these factors could cancel one another out, and bring you back to the figure you first thought of. He could have died the day before yesterday, for all that rigor tells us. Or two o'clock this morning. Take your pick."

Lloyd sighed.

"But whoever did it must have caught some blood," Freddie said. "Their clothes would be flecked with the stuff—even if they weren't wearing any at the time. Unless they had hung them up neatly in the wardrobe of course," he added cheerfully. "Holyoak didn't, though. His were on the chair."

Lloyd was almost getting to the stage where he permitted the neutral plural to denote a single person of either sex. Its use in this case said more about Freddie's refusal to make automatic assumptions than his grammar.

"Probably someone right-handed," said Freddie. "I'll get a better idea when I've got him on the table, and can measure the depth and angle and all that."

He was looking *forward* to it.

120

"Sorry to have had to bring you bad news, Miss Worthing," said the young man who had introduced himself as Detective Sergeant Finch.

Anna sat down. Her head was splitting, and her memories of yesterday evening were, to say the least, haphazard. Some things she remembered with the utmost clarity, but great pieces of the evening were missing. She remembered getting into her car outside the pub, and knowing that she had had far too much to drink to be driving, but that she had driven anyway. She remembered driving into the garages behind the flats, and deciding against trying to put the car away. She had left it out, and even that had been less than successful, the car sitting at an acute angle to her garage door.

She remembered being startled to see Max as she came upstairs; he had no business being at her flat, and Victor had told her not to see him again. And he had been disapproving about her having driven. But then, Max didn't drink; he couldn't have got the car back in one piece if he had been in her condition. She remembered, vaguely, being pleased about that, as though it had put her ahead in some sort of stakes.

She had faint, confused memories of telling Max what had happened. My God, what had she told him? How much had she told him? She didn't know. She didn't *know*. In between telling Max that she had told Victor to stuff his job and waking up with Max asleep beside her and this unforgiving hangover, there was a total blank.

"Would you like something?" the sergeant was asking. "A cup of coffee, or something? Colin—make Miss Worthing some coffee, please." He jerked his head towards the open kitchen door, and the young policeman took himself off. "Black," Finch added, making a correct assessment of Anna's state of health.

It had been the knocking on the door that had brought her to consciousness; Max had slumbered on as she had pulled on the silk dressing-gown that hung on her door, and opened the front door, on the chain, to the police telling her that Victor was dead.

"We thought that you might be able to help us," Sergeant Finch said.

She looked up at him. It hurt.

"He might have disturbed an intruder," he said. "We don't seem to be able to find Mr. Holyoak's wallet. I take it he did carry one?"

She nodded dumbly. Dear God.

"We thought you might know if anything else is missing," he said. "Well, my boss thought you might know." He smiled. "He was at the do," he said. "Chief Inspector Lloyd."

She remembered him, at any rate, if she couldn't remember much else. He had fancied her. She didn't speak.

"You were in the flat with Mr. Holyoak yesterday?" he asked.

"For a little while," she said guardedly.

"We'll need your fingerprints," he said. "Was his stepdaughter still there when you were with him?"

A shake of the head, this time. But that hurt more than speaking. "She left some time during the afternoon," she said.

"You were alone with Mr. Holyoak?"

She sighed. "Yes," she said.

"And what time did you leave?"

"About quarter-past six," said Anna.

"Did you see anyone you didn't think should be there?" he asked.

"No," she said.

"Did you see anyone at all? Security men, whatever?"

She frowned. "I don't know," she said.

"Where did you go when you left?"

She didn't answer. She couldn't. She hadn't had time to think about this.

"I'm sorry if you think it's none of my business," he said. "But I have to know where you went, in order to corroborate your story that you left at quarter-past six."

Anna looked back at him.

"It's just so that we can eliminate you from our enquiries," he said. "It's routine."

"Anna?" Max's voice called from the bedroom. "Come back to bed! What are you doing out there, for God's sake?"

Oh, hell. That was all she needed. The bedroom door opened, and Max emerged, yawning, scratching his head, and quite, quite naked. "What's going on?" he asked.

"Mr. Scott," said the young man, his face expressionless. "We meet again."

122

Max narrowed his eyes a little, "Detective Sergeant . . . don't tell me, I'll remember . . . Starling. Swallow?" The words were slurring slightly.

"Finch, sir." He remained entirely impassive.

"Finch, Finch. Of course. Knew it was some sort of brainless creature. What the hell do you want this time?"

My God, Max had got drunk too. And he was still drunk, unlike her. She was horribly, desperately, sober. No wonder he hadn't heard the knocking.

"I'm making enquiries into the death of Mr. Victor Holyoak," said Finch.

"Holyoak's dead?"

The constable reappeared from the kitchen, carrying a tray on which he had set mugs and a pot of coffee. The whole lot very nearly went when he saw Max.

Anna wished he would get dressed. She stood up, taking the tray and putting it down on the coffee table, where it rested unevenly. She pulled her keys out from underneath it.

"Don't you think you should put some clothes on?" asked Finch.

"Why?" asked Max putting his arms round Anna from behind, trying to kiss her neck. She could smell the alcohol. "Is nakedness a crime? Finch is from the Thought Police," he said.

She tried to shake him off.

"I don't want to stop you *thinking*, Mr. Scott," said Finch. "Just hitting women."

Anna twisted round to look at Max. She couldn't imagine him hitting a woman. Max had been a revelation to her; he was a truly kind, gentle man. Finch must have got that wrong. But he hadn't, as she found out when Max spoke again.

"I slapped my wife's face yesterday, and I spent last night screwing you—Sergeant Peacock doesn't approve." He gave the sergeant the benefit of his booze-laden breath. "What happened to Holyoak?" he asked.

Anna took advantage of being released from Max's embrace to sit down again, and Finch handed her a mug of black coffee without answering Max's question. "Drink it," he said. "It'll do you good." He straightened up, and looked at Max. "Perhaps you wouldn't mind getting dressed, sir," he said again.

"Perhaps I would," said Max.

"I don't think you answered my question, Miss Worthing,"

Finch said. "Where did you go when you left Victor Holyoak's flat?"

"She was here," said Max. "With me."

"And what time did you get here, Mr. Scott?" he asked.

"Half six. Anna was here when I arrived, and we've been together ever since. Couldn't have got a bus ticket between us all night, isn't that right, girl?"

Finch turned to her, then, with a questioning, and disbelieving look.

She gave a nod of confirmation. Partly because Max had left her very little choice, and partly because you never told the police anything that you didn't have to. But she much preferred not lying to them, and she much preferred Max sober.

"Thank you, Miss Worthing," said Finch. "Perhaps you wouldn't mind coming in to let us have your fingerprints some—"

"What for?" demanded Max.

"Elimination, sir. We have to know who has been in Mr. Holyoak's flat."

"Then you'd better have mine," said Max, swaying slightly. "I've been there." He leered at Anna. "We've spent a lot of time up there." He looked back at Finch. "If you know what I mean," he said, with a suggestive movement of his pelvis.

"Thank you, sir, your prints would be useful."

"So you can go now, can't you?" said Max, holding out his hand to Anna.

Bemused, she took it, and allowed herself to be hauled up from the sofa. He put his arm round her waist and pulled her towards him; she could feel the tension in his body as they touched. "And let us get back to what we were doing," he said. He squeezed her even closer to him, and his heart was beating fast.

"Yes, sir," said Finch. "But I will be making enquiries to see if anyone can confirm when Miss Worthing came home last night. I'm sure you understand, Miss Worthing."

They left, and Anna almost fell under his weight as Max's body went completely limp. He pushed her away as he ran into the hallway. He made it to the bathroom, where he was predictably sick. He closed the door when he could, and Anna heard the sounds of ablutions being performed until he emerged again, his long figure looking comic in her bathrobe.

"Sorry," he said, sitting down shakily.

She left him to recover while she too showered and cleaned her teeth, and tried to make herself feel more human. Two Veganin, she thought, might help. Three.

"You shouldn't have got drunk," she said when she came back out to him. "You're not used to it."

"I didn't," he said.

"Max—I could smell it. And you were behaving like I don't know what."

"I took a swig from your bottle before I came out," he said. "What was left of it."

"Why?" she asked, mystified. "And why did you come out naked, for God's sake?"

"Would you question a repulsive naked drunk if you didn't have to? I wanted to get rid of him, and I did."

"But what made you sick?"

He dropped his head. "Memories," he said.

She knelt down beside him, suddenly aware of Victor's no longer being in the world. It was a frightening feeling.

Max put his arm round her. "You must feel dreadful . . . I'm sorry. I know how you felt about him, but I can't . . . I'm sorry," he said again. "It's a nightmare—the whole thing's a nightmare from start to finish."

"Why did you tell him I was here when you arrived yesterday evening?" she asked.

"You needed an alibi," he said simply. "I know what that feels like. So I said you were with me."

Anna swallowed. "But . . . but how do you know I didn't kill him?" she asked.

"You were very drunk," he said. "You couldn't have told me all that without letting it slip that you'd done something awful."

Oh, dear God. Told him all what?

Victor was dead. She had to keep reminding herself of that. And what she had done. She remembered that quite clearly, and had from the moment she had opened the door to a police uniform.

"No one should have to go through what I went through." He got shakily to his feet, and put his arms round her. "No one." He made a noise, a cross between a sigh and a sob. "They don't give you time to mourn. Someone you're close to is just . . . just ripped away from you, and all they can do is ask where you were, and take your clothes away and call you a liar." He closed his eyes. "I know what it's like," he said. "If I can stop them doing it to you, I will."

"But . . . but you've no idea where I was. I could have been anywhere—how do you know they can't check up?"

"I heard him, going on at you—you couldn't prove where you were, or you'd have told him. That's why I came out."

"Don't you want to know?" she asked, still a little suspicious of such gallantry, and totally lacking his faith in the uselessness of the police. Lying got you into trouble.

"None of my business," he said. "I just wanted to get Finch off your back. So I told a lie. The rest was true, though," he said with a weak smile. "You couldn't get enough of me. You wouldn't even answer the door."

She frowned. "The door?"

"Someone rang the bell. It was late—I thought it might be important, but you didn't want to know. You said we were more important. Then you passed out." He smiled. "I didn't feel terribly important."

She had faint, faint memories of being in bed with him, of wanting him never to leave her, just like he said she had. But it was like another life, another person. She had never wanted any man. She had used them, made money out of them. She had grown very close to Victor, despite the way he was, but she had never wanted him. And she hadn't wanted Max any of the other times; she had just given him what he wanted. Last night had been different; she remembered that. She wasn't sure it was a good thing.

"I'd better go into work," she said. "I know he had a TV and a video for instance—I should have told Finch that, I suppose."

Max shook his head. "It wasn't a burglary," he said.

"No." She sighed. "Victor was . . . well . . . he had real enemies," she said. "That scar he's got? He got jumped by some business rival, who slashed him with a razor—"

"What?" said Max. "What sort of business was he in, for God's sake?"

"Drugs. Big time—heroin, cocaine. Not now, of course. But then. It's how he got started."

"Nice," said Max.

126

Drug dealing was possibly one of Victor's nicer traits, thought Anna, but then Max didn't know him. Hadn't known him. Victor was dead. She had to remember that.

"Then why bother going in?" he said.

"Because it'll look bad if I don't."

He pulled her close to him. "Don't go yet," he said. "Let's forget about all this for a while. Before they won't let us forget. We managed it last night, didn't we?"

She smiled. "Your hangover may be fake, but mine isn't," she said. "And you're not exactly on top form yourself."

"I need you," he said simply.

He had stayed with her when she needed him. Despite the way she felt, and against her better judgement, she went back to bed with Max. But she didn't forget about it. Her head still throbbed, which was more than the passion did; the earth certainly didn't move, whatever it had done last night. But Max was gentle and comforting as ever; she felt less lonely. And she felt something else that she couldn't put a name to.

She had never made love; she had had men, and they had had her, since before she had reached her teens. She had learned over the years with Victor how to make sex with her an experience that they wanted to repeat. But she had never made love until now, and they were still lying in one another's arms when the police came back. Once again, she entertained Sergeant Finch in her dressing-gown, but this time Max got dressed before he emerged from the bedroom.

"I must ask you both to come to the police station to answer further questions concerning the death of Mr. Victor Holyoak," said Finch. "You are not under arrest, and you are not obliged to answer the questions which will be put to you, but what you do say may be given in evidence." He looked at Max. "Are those the clothes you were wearing last night, Mr. Scott?"

Max nodded, and glanced at Anna.

"And you, Miss Worthing? Could I see the clothes you were wearing?"

Anna went into the bedroom, scooping up the pile of clothes that still lay by the side of the bed, and came out again, looking at Finch with loathing as she thrust them silently into his hands. Max had warned her.

He glanced at them, and handed them back to her. "Thank you," he said. "Could you get dressed now, please?"

Catherine sat in the car, where she had been waiting for Max to arrive. Zelda had arrived; she hadn't seen Catherine as she had become impatient waiting for the lift, and taken the stairs, as everyone else had done. Catherine wasn't going to go in until Max arrived.

It was much later that she realized that Max was probably already there; he would have taken a taxi to work. Anna Worthing hadn't arrived either, she noticed. But Catherine still hadn't gone up.

It wasn't really fear any more. It was a feeling of helplessness, of wanting just to sit here and never move again. But it was mid-morning; she couldn't stay here for ever. Max might be worried. She had to go up and face the music. She got out of the car, stiff and sore, and pressed the lift button, preparing herself for what was to come. She had been awake all night, the car not being the most comfortable place to sleep, even if she could have done. But she doubted that she would have slept wherever she had been. She had been trying to work out how to cope with this moment, and now that it had arrived, she still had no idea.

The lift wasn't going to come; she climbed the stairs, and pushed open the door with its oak-tree motif. She was faced with groups of people standing around; receptionists, police officers, members of staff. One of the girls on reception pointed over to her, and murmured something to a dark-haired woman who stood by the reception desk. The dark haired woman advanced.

"Mrs. Scott?" she asked.

Catherine nodded. "Is . . . is Max here?" she asked the receptionist, but she didn't answer.

"Mrs. Scott, I'm Detective Inspector Hill, Stansfield CID. Could I have a word with you?"

"Where's Max?" she asked again, but the inspector led her to the little rest room off reception, and closed the door.

"Mrs. Scott," she said. "I'm afraid I have some bad news for you about your stepfather."

CHAPTER SIX

Then: Winter, thirteen years ago . . .

ANNA WAS WITH VICTOR, FEELING SECURE, AS SHE AL-
ways did when he was there, and never did and never had all
the rest of her life. The blinds shaded the bright January sun,
and she left them drawn as they spoke.

"I dealt with Bannister," he said. "Some of the damage will
be permanent, I assure you."

Anna's eyes widened slightly at the chilling statement, but
she didn't say anything. Victor wasn't the sort of man whose
actions you queried.

She had seen a lot of him; it was his stepdaughter he really
wanted to see, but she was at work all day, and she was getting
home later and later. He hadn't found her in yet. And over the
weeks, she had heard his story.

He had been in hospital, receiving outpatient treatment for a
minor injury, and he had met Margaret who was recovering
from a stroke which had left her in delicate health. Margaret
had been widowed when Catherine was a toddler; she and Victor had married six months after that first meeting, when Catherine was thirteen. For eighteen months everything was
wonderful. But then his wife had had a second, crippling
stroke that had cut her down when she was just thirty-eight,
and she had been left almost totally paralysed, with little or no
hope of any improvement. After another eighteen months his
stepdaughter had run away from home, which had devastated
her mother, and Victor had spent huge amounts of time and
money trying to find her, to persuade her to go home. It

amounted to an obsession, in Anna's opinion, but she didn't voice it. For one thing it wouldn't help, and for another, she knew better than to criticize Victor.

"Now I want you to do something for me," he said.

"Anything." She meant it; she was pleased that there was something she could do. She had never in her life felt so secure as she did now; whatever he'd done to Bannister, whatever he wanted her to do, was fine by her. She was always pleased to see Victor, even though his heavy schedule sometimes meant mid-morning visits, because he had never once, not from the awful moment he had met her, spoken to her as if she were any different from anyone else.

You got a lot of different attitudes; some men were scared of you, some were contemptuous—though what they had to be contemptuous about, she had never worked out—most were terribly aware of who called the tune. Victor wasn't like that; he spoke to her as an equal. It always made her feel good when Victor had been to see her.

"I'm sending someone to you."

Victor had never come for sex. He seemed to be staying true to his wife, though she would never be able to do anything for him again. Anna sometimes wondered, in her more cynical moments, if the marriage had been as idyllic as he remembered it, but it didn't really make much difference. He believed it had been, and he, she had begun to realize as the weeks went by, was as crippled by his obsessive love as his wife had been by the stroke. And his wife, more than anything in the world, wanted her daughter back, which was the one thing that he, with all his money and power, couldn't provide for her.

"He'll arrive like an ordinary customer, but he won't want your services."

Even better. Two customers who didn't want her services; she would be delighted if they were all like that.

"He'll want this." Victor took from the inside of his jacket a thick envelope. "Just give it to him," he said. "Keep him here for long enough to make it look good, then get rid of him. If he asks any questions, let me know. And don't answer them."

She nodded, taking the envelope. Money. It had to be.

"I've given him the same instructions about you," said Victor. "So don't get curious." He tapped the envelope. "And don't get greedy."

"I wouldn't steal any of it," she said, stung.

He took out his wallet, pulling out notes. "That's to cover loss of earnings while he's here," he said, putting them on the table.

She didn't know what she was getting into, but she didn't care. Drugs? Probably. Victor never spoke about how he made his money, but she was pretty sure that he was into drug-running in a big way. This person who would be visiting her was probably one of the ones who carried the stuff through customs in a variety of unpleasant ways that Anna preferred not to think about. "How will I know which is him?" she asked.

"You know him," said Victor. "I've told him what he has to do, and I don't want to be seen in his company again. So all his dealings with me will be through you from now on."

He told her his name then, and her eyebrows went up. Ray Wilkes? Too true, he wouldn't want her services. He was as queer as a three-pound note. But he wasn't into drugs or anything like that, and he was far too fond of living to go swallowing packs of heroin that might burst in his stomach. So what was Victor paying him money for?

"You weren't thinking of asking a question, were you?" said Victor.

She shook her head quickly. "Except . . . " she began.

He waited, his grey eyes resting on hers, warning her not to stick her nose in where it wasn't wanted. But she wasn't about to do that. "Is this a one-off?" she asked.

"No. He'll be coming here often over the next two weeks. I'll make sure you've got his money. And your out of pocket expenses."

She smiled. "Good," she said. "That means you'll be coming here often, too."

"I don't know, Gerry. I think we should just keep trying. There's plenty of time."

"But they didn't give us much chance," Geraldine said.

"Maybe not. But if there *is* a chance, I think we should just keep trying."

A possibility. That was what the consultant had said. A possibility that Charles could father a child. He had all the necessary attributes—just not quite enough of them to make it the near certainty that it usually was.

"Charles," she said. "Why don't we make enquiries? That won't commit us to anything—"

"But we'd be . . . putting ourselves on their books." Charles switched on the television as he spoke.

"Oh, Charles! They're not going to turn up the next day with a baby!"

"All the same." He fiddled with the channels, flicking through until he found the local news, and sat down, facing the television, so that he was side-on to her.

"Can't we just find out what it entails? Charles—there are hundreds of babies born every year whose mothers can't or won't keep them! They shouldn't grow up in homes, not if there are other people who want babies!"

"There are *not* hundreds of babies," he said. "There are very few babies. These agencies try to make you adopt older children. Everyone wants babies."

" '. . . *that the election, when it came, would be, as ever, three horses in a race designed for two. First past the post was not,*' he went on, '*a system which . . .*' "

"At least let's see what they say," she said.

"Ssh—there's Mark," he said.

She looked without interest at Mark Callender, the man who was standing in Stansfield for the Conservatives. He would lose, of course. But he was a friend of Charles's from medical school, and she was supposed to hang on his every word. He had as much chance as the Liberal who had just given them his views on proportional representation, and Mark's opposing views on the matter held little interest for Geraldine.

"I think we should invite him to dinner," said Charles. "Maybe when Max and Val come. They'll be here at the end of the month." He turned to look at her. "We haven't had a housewarming," he said.

Last month they had moved into a detached ex-farmhouse that Charles had plans for. It was a lovely old house; she would like to have a dinner party. But he was changing the subject.

"That would be nice," she said.

132

"Mark, and his wife. Max and Val. Zelda . . . Zelda's always a nuisance," he said.

She couldn't help being a widow. Charles was really quite miffed about that, because she made an odd number at dinner parties.

"There's no law says that dinner parties have to consist entirely of couples," she said. "If we're having one, Zelda's coming."

Geraldine liked Zelda; she always had. Eight years older, Zelda had been rather like a big sister as Geraldine had grown up, living next door, and always prepared to let Geraldine tag along with her. She had had to get married, of course, as anyone could have told you that she would have had to do from the time she hit puberty. And then she had surprised everyone by settling down to being a wife and mother and helping Jimmy run the business for the next sixteen years, until he died.

"Good," said Charles. He smiled, and picked up his diary. "I suppose we should let Max and Val settle in first. But March is no good—I've got a dozen things on. I think it'll have to be the first week in April—let's hope the election isn't called, or Mark won't have the time to spare. If we make it a weekend, Tim might be able to come home from school—he can partner Zelda."

"Good idea," said Geraldine.

"Right—should we send out invitations, do you think, or just ring and ask them?"

She wouldn't be sidetracked like this. The bloody thing wasn't for two months. "Can we get in touch with them, at least?" asked Geraldine, a hint of desperation in her voice as the subject was changed.

He frowned. "Who? Zelda and Tim?"

"The adoption agency," she said, stubbornly. He knew perfectly well who.

"We will, if we really can't have one of our own," he said. "But it's much too soon to do anything like that now."

No adoption, then. Geraldine knew by now that Charles's "but" meant "no." And Charles was the boss.

But he couldn't give her a baby. She knew that. He knew that. A chance, a possibility. Winning the pools was a chance, a possibility. It didn't happen. A baby wouldn't happen. Oh, she

133

would go on trying, like people went on filling in coupons. But they knew, and she knew, that it would never really happen.

She didn't think she could bear that.

Holland seemed the logical place. Victor knew the country well, and he had money and contacts there; it wouldn't be difficult to set up a legitimate business. He had never so much as parked on a double-yellow line in Amsterdam; now was the time to get out of the game for good and become the respectable businessman that he appeared to be in England. The Drugs Squad knew nothing about him, and they weren't going to, but he would be coming to the attention of the police one way or the other, so Holland seemed like a good idea.

Margaret had accepted that a move was necessary as she had accepted everything else; she had asked if there was any chance of Catherine's coming with them, and he had told her he would try his best to persuade her.

He had been able to let the private investigators go; they had been a drain on the resources that he now had to husband, if he was to get the sort of start he wanted in Holland. Anna was keeping a permanent eye on Catherine now, for a fraction of what he had paid the agency. He had been unlucky on his last few visits to the flats; Catherine had been out.

She was out again this time; her window was in darkness. It could almost be a deliberate avoidance of him, he thought, as he knocked on Anna's door, which was opened on the chain, then thrown open to welcome him in.

"You didn't tell Catherine that I've been coming here, did you?" he asked Anna quietly, as she let him in. If she had, she'd be very sorry.

"No, of course not. You asked me not to."

"I told you not to."

She smiled a little. "I didn't," she said. "Honest."

He accepted that; he pulled a package from his inside pocket, and handed it to Anna. "For our mutual friend," he said. "He'll visit you tomorrow night."

She took it, and went into the other room to put it in the drawer of her dressing table. He pulled notes from his wallet, and put them on the table to cover the lost revenue that Wilkes's visits caused.

They went into a tin which she kept in a cupboard. He

watched as she carefully hid the tin, and wondered what to do with her when he went to Holland. She could, he supposed, be reasonably useful to him if he were to take her. She would have to lose the rough edges, but it might be an idea. She was still in her teens, good body, attractive face, clean. She kept herself healthy; no drugs. Anna intended doing this for just as long as it took for her to have enough money to get out of it; she wasn't hustling for a shot in the arm. And she was determined enough to succeed. He'd have to curb the independent streak.

"How well are you doing?" he asked.

She closed the cupboard door and locked it. "Not bad," she said. "I've got a lot of regulars now."

If her customers came back for more, there was potential there; he could take her in hand. She was bright; she would learn quickly how to satisfy more discerning customers. He could try her out. He took out his wallet again, and counted out notes, watching Anna's reaction as the amount grew to what she took in a week.

"I owe a friend a favour," he said. "I want you to visit him in his hotel room." He looked at what she was wearing, and sighed. "Do you own anything to wear that will get you past the doorman?"

She nodded, still looking at the money.

"It's an expensive hotel," he said. "He's got expensive tastes. You have to work for that sort of money."

She gathered up the cash. "Where and when?" she asked, going to get her tin.

He wrote down the name of the hotel, the room number, a date and time, and a pseudonymous Christian name. "Go straight up to the room," he said. "And don't let me down, Anna."

"I won't." She smiled. "Ray and I could make a good team for you," she said.

He walked over to where she knelt by the cupboard, the tin half open as she counted the money, and stood over her. "What do you know about what Wilkes is doing for me?" he asked, and took a handful of her hair in his hand. "Have you been asking questions?"

She looked up, her mouth open, the money falling from her

135

hand. "I didn't ask him anything!" she cried. "I didn't ask him anything, I swear!"

"I want to know every word that has passed between you and Wilkes." He tightened his grip on her hair.

"Don't hurt me! I never ask him anything! He just tells me—I swear to God, Victor!"

"Every word," he repeated. "You're not getting up from there until you've told me every word." He looked down at her. "And then I'll decide what to do with you."

She stared up at him, dumb with fear.

"From the first visit," he said. "Now."

It took a long, long time to get the details out of her. He had scared her too much; at first she lied, and when she finally tried to tell him the truth, she couldn't think straight for fear of what he might be going to do to her. He sighed, and took her through it all again, over and over again. He had to know what Wilkes had been saying.

Max looked across at Catherine's empty desk, then looked for the umpteenth time at the clock; it was five to twelve, and still she hadn't arrived. This was his last day; he started his new job on the fifth of February, and was giving himself a week to get settled in at the new house. He and Catherine had stayed on at the office until late into the evening the day before; it was the best he could do by way of farewells. He had thought she had understood, had seen the situation from his point of view, but she hadn't come in. He didn't want it to end like this.

She lived alone. She might be ill, unable to get help. He shook his head, trying to laugh at himself. She lived in a flat; there must be dozens of people around. But perhaps not, he thought again. Not in view of the calling of her fellow residents. Most of them shut up shop in the early morning and went off to where they actually lived. If they didn't, chances were they would be asleep at this time in the morning.

She could have had an accident. What sort of identification did she carry? Any? She might, now that her employment was on a regular footing, and her fear that someone might trace her was less marked. Perhaps she was in hospital somewhere, and there was no way of contacting him.

Or perhaps they wouldn't contact him. That thought, the realization that he wasn't the only person in her life, made him feel inexplicably lonely. That was ridiculous, he told himself. When he had picked her up on the road that night she had had clothes, and money. She obviously had a family. Perhaps they had been contacted, this family that he assumed she must have, but about whom she never spoke, and from whom she had run away. Perhaps she needed him to rescue her again. But she would have rung, if that were the case, he told himself. Not if she was ill, he argued.

He should go and see if she was all right, he thought, as the door opened, and she was there.

Relief flooded through him; she hadn't run away again, she wasn't in hospital, she wasn't lying racked with pain, unable to contact help. But there were dark circles under her eyes, and her hand shook as she brought in the second post and handed it to him.

"I'm sorry I'm so late," she said, sitting down without removing her coat. "I overslept."

She looked as though she hadn't slept at all, and he felt terrible. "Are you all right?" he asked, hovering anxiously as she sat down. "Are you cold?"

"I'm fine," she said. "Maybe a touch of flu, or something."

He felt her forehead, and turned up the electric fire, going along with the pretence that her condition had physical origins. "Perhaps you shouldn't have come in," he said.

She caught his hand in hers. "I've only got you for today," she said.

Oh, hell. Max crouched down beside her. "You'll get another job," he said. "Meet someone nice . . ."

She was shaking her head. "I don't want anyone but you," she said. She flushed, and squeezed his hand with enough intensity to hurt. "Take me with you, Max," she whispered.

"I can't," he said, standing up, removing his hand from hers. "It's impossible—I'm going to work for someone else. I've already got a secretary there."

"Leave Valerie and take me instead," she said, the words coming out in a rush.

He closed his eyes. "Catherine—you know that's crazy," he said.

"Why? Why is it crazy? You love me, you told me you did last night."

He sighed. Last night had been a mistake. "Do you really

want it spelled out?" he asked. "All right. We're selling our house here—we're buying one in Stansfield. Half of it is hers. She's my *wife*, Catherine—you can't just cast your wife off when you feel like it!"

"But you love me!"

He sat down on his desk, running his hands down his face as he looked at her. "Catherine, for God's sake," he said. "Grow up. This is real life. I have a wife, and responsibilities. I provide for her. I provide a roof, and clothes and food. What's she supposed to do if I tell her I'm taking you with me instead?"

"She could get a job!"

If he had needed proof that a relationship with a seventeen-year-old was not one to be encouraged, he had it now. He shook his head slowly. "Catherine," he said. "I am not leaving my wife. Not for you, or for anyone else. I'm a married man, and that's all there is to it. Valerie and I are going to Stansfield, and you will get on with your life. You'll meet someone—someone your own age. This . . . this was an interlude. You'll not be able to remember my name in a year."

She sat staring down at the typewriter, as all sorts of dreadful possibilities went through his head. Suicide. Following him to Stansfield. But she wouldn't, he told himself. She was really a very sensible girl, normally. She had left the office last night and gone back to that cheap little bedsit, and had realized how alone she was. He thought about suggesting that she try patching up her differences with her family, but he decided against that; she had never shown the least inclination to go home.

She had seemed perfectly all right last night. A bit tearful, a bit sad, but not like this. He allowed the thought to flit across his mind that she was somehow staging the way she looked, to shake *him* up. But it barely touched his consciousness.

"Come on," he said. "I'll take you out somewhere nice for lunch." He could risk that at least, on his last day. A perfectly natural thing to do.

But she said no.

Sunday, the eighteenth of February. Lloyd looked at his watch, and grunted. Almost Monday, the nineteenth of February, he thought, as he wrote in his notebook. Freedom. Even if he would only have had four hours' sleep.

And one day this vicious winter would be over, too. The last two operations had also taken place in subzero temperatures, the girls risking pneumonia to make a few bob. Arresting them into the bargain seemed too unfair for words. But tomorrow he started his course, and then he would move on, to take up his new appointment. This was the last time he'd have to do this thankless job.

Lloyd had got his promotion; soon, he would be off over the river to a new station, and a new house. A brand-new house, which Barbara was already having fun planning. The kids loved it. Central heating, double glazing, you name it. It was on an estate, of course, but it was better than he'd expected for the money.

Judy had been accepted for the detective course, so she might be able to join Nottingham as a detective constable. She would enjoy that. She had been taken off the task force, and was pounding the frozen beat down below his vantage point somewhere, in response to the Met's desire to get the police back on to the streets. At least she was moving around, he thought, and shivered.

But she was a great one for worrying, was Judy. Now that she didn't have to worry about not being accepted on to the course, she was worrying about not doing well. And about moving to Nottingham. And, of course, about meeting her intended's parents, something she had been putting off like mad ever since Michael had suggested that it might be expected of her. Especially since they would be living with them. Which she was also worrying about.

He wondered what Michael's parents would think about Judy's job; come to that, he wondered what Michael thought about it. Lloyd was glad his wife wasn't a police officer. That, Judy had told him, was a sexist remark. New word—sexist. Like racist. It used to be racialist in his youth, he thought. People who hated negroes were racialist. Now people who hated blacks were racist. He had never been that, at any rate. But sexist . . . well, he was glad his wife wasn't a police officer.

They had had the engagement party, but she still hadn't set the date. Maybe it wouldn't happen, he told himself. She didn't seem to go much for commitment, as far as he could see. But he had the feeling that marriage to Michael wasn't really being seen as a commitment. More as an expedient. But perhaps he was flattering himself.

Horton was watching for the punters, rubbing gloved, but none the less cold hands together while Lloyd awkwardly wrote up his notebook detailing their night's work. Lloyd had tried to get out of this duty once they'd taken Judy off it, but since he'd wangled his way on—by arguing that a fair amount of criminal intelligence was to be had where informants could be recruited—he had been stuck with it. Because it had worked, apart from anything else, and they had already stamped out a budding drugs ring, and recovered two thousand pounds' worth of stolen goods as the result of getting a couple of the girls to co-operate. It was necessary if they were ever to keep a lid on crime, but it wasn't something that made you feel good about yourself. These girls ran risks all the time; using them as informants increased those risks. And that wasn't really what the police were meant to do.

Still, this was the last night he would have to do it. Enthusiasm for the project was waning all round. They had done three in quick succession to see if that dissuaded the girls, but if the weather didn't, nothing would.

"Lloyd," Horton murmured, as the cars began to arrive, and the whole silly business of clearing the street began again.

Lloyd watched with amused interest as one of the lads made a bee-line for the Daimler driver, determined to get there first and haul in the biggest fish, and used the binoculars for a better look.

The man emerged from his car, and gave his particulars to Bannister, breathless after his short sprint. Lloyd had thought that Bannister was one of the fit ones, but his breath puffed out too fast in the night air, and he held his side, as though he had a stitch. Too much disco-dancing, Lloyd thought sourly.

He switched his attention to the kerbcrawler. He wasn't famous, so Bannister's hundred-metre sprint had been a waste of time. A tall man with a beard. He looked like the portraits of the young Edward VII, Lloyd thought, until the man turned to look over his shoulder at his fellow miscreants, and he could see the scar over which the hair wouldn't grow. The man looked up as Lloyd scrutinized him; it was as if he were looking directly back, and Lloyd instinctively turned away, then laughed at himself. He was a long way away; he didn't even know Lloyd was there.

On, to the next one. Roll on four o'clock.

* * *

The measured tread which they had actually been taught how to achieve crunched on the glittering pavement as Judy and Slocombe walked the beat.

There was a limit to how much you could talk about, condemned to spend four hours in one another's company in the middle of a freezing February night when anyone with any sense was in bed. They didn't even go for refs for another two hours. So they walked in silence past the shuttered shops, the floodlit building site where everything had been frozen into immobility by the weather, the all-night café which was closed all night, and all day as far as anyone knew. It was companionable enough; they had quite a lot in common. They both felt cold and fed up and wished they were at home in front of the fire.

So they would walk in silence, alone with their thoughts, until some member of the public needed them or deserved them. Judy was considering Michael's plus points.

He was handsome, in a thin, well-bred sort of way. He looked like the son of the big house, but his father was a fitter and his mother had worked in a shop. Sometimes she thought he was a little bit ashamed of that—that could be construed as a minus point, but she ought to reserve judgement on that until she met them. Her heart sank at the thought.

"Dead tonight," said Slocombe.

"Mm."

And Michael just took her the way she came; she couldn't remember his ever criticizing her, or patronizing her, or giving her unasked-for advice. Lloyd did that all the time. She felt comfortable with Michael; they got on well together. She always enjoyed being with him, and missed him when he was away. He was home this week, of course, when she was on nights. Tucked up in bed, where she should be. And that was more than satisfactory, too.

In addition to his other drawbacks, Lloyd complained that she drove too fast, that she had no soul, and that her literary education was sadly lacking. He just scraped past her in the height department, and he was rapidly developing a bald spot

141

in his thick dark hair. He was married, with two children, and he was making her feel guilty about Michael.

"Do you want to help me win a fiver?" Slocombe asked.

Not particularly. "Sure," she said.

"I bet one of the lads that I would find out Lloyd's first name before he left."

Oh, God. "Did you?" she said.

"Well?" he said. "He finishes tonight. If you don't tell me now, it'll cost me five quid."

Damn Dave Bannister's eyes, she thought; he had been gossiping, of course. "No, it won't," she said. "It'll cost you a tenner."

Slocombe frowned. "How do you make that out?" he asked.

"Suppose you've got two fivers. You bet him one, and you win. Then you've got three. You bet him one, and you lose. Then you've only got one. You lost a fiver, but losing as opposed to winning costs you ten quid."

Slocombe worked that out. "So it does," he said.

"So it will," she said. "I don't know his name."

"Oh, come on, Jude. Everyone knows you and him are—"

"Everyone knows wrong," she said. "I don't know his first name any more than you do."

"I believe you," he said, in a shaft of sarcastic wit.

All stick and no carrot, Lloyd had called their relationship. And she really didn't know his first name. She had never heard anyone call him anything but Lloyd, not even his wife. And, as Slocombe had said, he finished tonight, so they had finally come to the parting of the ways. Not a moment too soon, really. From now on, she was on her own as far as the job was concerned, and with Michael as far as her life was concerned; that was as it should be, she told herself firmly.

Lloyd had told her father that she would end up a detective superintendent; her father, of course, had believed him. Her father was the only man she knew who truly didn't see women as a race apart; he had no idea of the enormous prejudice against women in the force, because he had none himself.

Lloyd and her father had met at the engagement party at the flat, to which he had come with Barbara. They had got on well, both having a penchant for malt whisky and collecting donkeys' hind legs. But Judy had watched her father's quick mind put two and two together, and afterwards, when the guests had left, Michael had been driving someone home, and her mother was waiting for her father in the car, he'd asked her if she was sure she was marrying for the right reasons.

She hadn't answered; he'd given her a hug and told her that whatever she did was all right by him, and that she would always know where to come. Not, she supposed, what the father of most brides-to-be told them, but as reassuring as Ladybird pyjamas and covered hot-water bottles.

And the beat went on.

On the other side of Leyford, Bannister got back into the van, his breathing laboured, his side aching. Over two months since it had happened, and he still wasn't right. He sat back, eyes closed with sheer relief, because now, on the final raid of the night, he had at last fulfilled his obligations, and he could stop looking over his shoulder, with any luck. He hadn't a clue what the hell Holyoak was up to, and he hoped it stayed that way.

He still had another two hours of his night shift to go; he hoped he would be able to type up reports or something. Nothing strenuous. He'd done a lot of running tonight; he had even had to scuffle with one of the punters who had lashed out at another officer, and he still wasn't up to it.

But report typing was out. As soon as they got back to the station, he was put into a Panda car with Stephens.

They cruised the streets, looking for trouble which Bannister fervently hoped they wouldn't find. And it did seem as though the intense cold which had made it so difficult for him even to get out of bed that afternoon was keeping wrongdoers off the streets of the capital. Stephens was driving; Bannister was on the look-out. But he kept thinking about Holyoak, wondering what all that business had been about.

Holyoak was a nutter; Bannister had seen it in his eyes when he had taken his miserable drive with him, and become aware of a total, unnatural lack of emotion. There had been nothing there. No anger, no desire for revenge, which was what had prompted Bannister's own more obvious but much less damaging violence towards Annabel. He hadn't been going to use the truncheon on the silly little bitch; he had just been making sure she was scared out of her wits that he would.

Holyoak didn't even get the twisted thrill out of inflicting pain that some people got. He had done it because that had been the quickest way to make Bannister do what he wanted, and it had made no more impression upon him than handing him a bribe would have done. He and Holyoak had been driven round while Holyoak had given him his instructions, and told him what would happen to him if it went wrong. Then he had been dumped out of the car not far from the section house. He had collapsed on the steps; some of the lads had found him, and had put him to bed, thinking that he was drunk. He had had a week's leave for Christmas; he had spent it in circumstances that he never wanted to repeat.

He shouldn't have gone back to work when he had, but he had to be available for duty, and the normal physical demands of the job were making everything take a very long time to mend. He could go to the doctor now; he hadn't dared before, in case he had put him on the sick, and then he would have been unable to carry out Holyoak's orders.

And now he didn't even understand what the hell it had all been for. It had worked exactly the way Holyoak had wanted it to; nothing had gone wrong, for which Bannister could only thank God, but it had to have been for some reason. And he would put nothing at all past Holyoak; the man was capable of anything.

Stephens was putting his foot down through the empty streets when they saw her.

"Jesus!" he yelled, bringing the car skidding to a halt about an inch from the old woman.

Bannister was thrown against the glove compartment by the force of the emergency stop, his bruised organs protesting; he gasped with pain, but Stephens was too busy swearing to notice.

The old lady, raincoat thrown over her flannelette nightie, was by the passenger door; Bannister wound down the window.

"Quick! quick! There's a man—he's dead, I think. Oh, hurry, please—please hurry! The phone-box wouldn't work— I've come miles—you'll have to hurry!"

"If you could move, love—" Bannister tried to open the door, but she was leaning on it, imploring them to hurry. He eased it open, and got the old lady in the back before she died of pneumonia. He got in beside her. "Now, calm down, love—what's the problem?"

"A man—in a car. I'm sure he's dead, but hurry—he might not be! Hurry!"

Stephens started the engine, looking forward to a high-speed dash. "You tell me where to go, love," he said, as the car shot forward.

She did; the car swung round corners, siren blaring, giving its back-seat passengers a rough ride. "There! There!" she shouted. "There he is."

Once again the car's tyres screamed as Stephens pulled up in a quiet, middle-class residential square, and jumped out, crossing the road towards the car whose radio blared out, audible even inside the Panda.

It wasn't a carbon-monoxide job, thought Bannister, with relief. No hose from the exhaust. Probably a drunk, or someone who had overdosed.

"I had to get up to go to the toilet," the old lady was telling him, as he tried to get her name and address. "When I came back, I could hear all that music. I came out to tell him to turn it off."

Bannister smiled, despite the way he felt. She was a gutsy old girl. But she ought to be inside in this weather. "We'll get the details later, love," he said. "Which is your house? We ought to get you—"

"Dave!"

The tone of Stephens's voice made Bannister scramble out of the car, and run across the road through the rock music that blared out. Stephens was white-faced; he jerked his head towards the car.

Bannister had never seen the effects of a bullet in the brain. He stepped back, averting his eyes.

"Tango Bravo to Tango Delta, receiving?" said Stephens, his voice weak.

"Tango Delta receiving. Go ahead, Terry."

Stephens described what they had found, gave the make and registration of the car, then looked wide-eyed at Bannister, who looked back.

"The car is registered to a Raymond Arthur Wilkes," the radio informed them, after a few moments.

Bannister forced himself to look back in. Raymond Arthur

145

Wilkes. It was him; he could see that now. He had seen him less than two hours ago.

"Terry!" Their inspector's voice. "Back-up and CID are on their way. Don't touch the car—it's wanted in connection with another incident."

Bannister ran towards the low wall that lined the neat row of houses, and was violently sick over it, into someone's ornamental evergreens.

What in God's name had he got mixed up in?

Mist lay low over the fields and hedges of the farming village as Charles ran through the village streets. He was aiming for the stile today; his next target would be over the stile and down to the river. Running was wonderful exercise; it got the muscles trimmed, and the heart pumping, and it was easy to think you could do more than you should. He kept very strictly to his preplanned regime, and today was the last Saturday in February. Next week, he would move up to his new distance.

He felt good, as he left the newer part of the village behind. Running past the sandstone cottages with the thatched roofs that he and Gerry had wanted, but which no one had been selling. Still . . . time yet. Out beyond them, to where the pavement gave out, and he was running on a frosty grass verge, alongside incurious sheep and somnolent cows. Alongside cars and vans and enormous lorries with their dust-filled backdraft and their air-brakes. He liked the traffic; he knew that their exhaust fumes were polluting his lungs as he took deep breaths of sharp air, but the busy road pleased him, and one lorry driver even waved encouragement of his efforts as he passed.

He had started jogging not long after Jimmy Driver died; then it had been tiny runs in Stansfield, twenty-minute jobs. Now, his morning jog was an hour long, and his Saturday special had worked its way up to a long run in shorts and vest, not a jogging suit. He paced himself like an athlete, and allocated himself two hours. Now, the challenge was to go further within the time at his disposal.

At first, his legs had felt shaky when he had finished running, and had ached the next day. Now, he loved it all. The cold morning air on his face, his breath misting out, the birds calling to one another, the early morning people like milkmen and postmen and paper boys calling hello to him. The crows were building their sturdy nests high in the bare trees, flapping slowly across the road as he approached; spring was waiting under the frozen earth, above the white sky.

He could think out here. He had bought the farmhouse because it had grounds; grounds large enough for his clinic. A health clinic, where businessmen like Jimmy could come and find out what damage was being done before it was too late to do anything about it; cholesterol levels, blood pressure, heart, lungs ... a gymnasium, perhaps, so that they could counteract the threat to their health of their sedentary jobs. The National Health Service was slow to react to preventive medicine, so a private clinic might do some good business.

That sort of treatment should be available to everyone, of course, but if public funding couldn't always provide it, was that any reason to deny it to those who could afford it? He could think of several of his private patients who would benefit from a thorough, exhaustive medical, and the necessary dietary and exercise advice.

And he and Gerry had been looking at a private practice near Stansfield which was perfect for them to take over; Gerry liked it where she was, she said, though God only knew why, stuck in the middle of a housing estate that looked more like a penal colony, treating the sort of people who, as far as Charles could see, would be entirely at home in a penal colony. The surgery had been broken into twice by people looking for drugs.

Gerry seemed to think her National Health Service patients needed her, but he had reminded her that she wasn't *actually* in a penal colony, and they would get another doctor to replace her. Every time he had been there, which hadn't been often, there had been youths of both sexes standing around with spiked hair and black lipstick and safety pins stuck in their noses. Small wonder they needed a doctor, but it wasn't going to be Gerry for much longer.

He ran on, through the next village, as the late February sun began to burn off the mist, and householders began taking in the milk and the mail and the papers that had accumulated on their doorsteps.

Max had been here a month; it was great having him around

again, going for a beer with him on Sunday lunchtimes, having him over for supper on Valerie's evening-class nights. She was doing French and history for A-level, for some reason, and was continuing her studies at Stansfield Tech; Max had never been much of a one for fending for himself. Gerry enjoyed having him around, too; he was someone to fuss over. Charles thought that was why she was so keen on the baby idea—she liked having someone to look after.

And she was looking forward to the dinner party. Mark and Lucy had said that they would be there, and Charles was beginning to feel that his life was coming together exactly as he had planned it; he felt entirely at peace with the world as he headed along the right of way through the rolling farmland.

He made it to the stile, and sat on it for a few moments before heading back to the way he had come, to the pretty house in the country that he had always promised himself.

Catherine looked at the postcards in the Job Centre window, but the jobs were few and far between, like the postcards themselves, which were spaced out on the rack to minimize the lack of opportunity on offer.

She had had to register for employment, in order to get some money to live on; Max had given her what he could, but she had—mistakenly, as it turned out—paid three months' rent on the bedsit on the grounds that she would have a roof over her head at least.

Now she had a different roof over her head which wasn't paid in advance, and she needed a job. She was armed with a reference from Max which made her sound like the second coming; she wasn't sure that he hadn't gone over the top a bit. People would think there must be something wrong with her, or why was he trying so hard?

Because he loved her, she told herself. Because he was only sticking with Valerie out of some sense of duty, some feeling of responsibility. She hated Valerie, whom she had never met. Hated her for being dependent on Max, instead of having a job and a life of her own like other women. Hated her for being married to Max, for having first claim on his loyalty. Hated her, most of all, for talking him into going to that place. He had been gone thirty-one days, and she missed him dreadfully, knew that he would be missing her.

Poor Max, stuck in a town he didn't know, with a job he didn't want, and a wife he didn't love any more. It wasn't right. He loved her, and she loved him. It wasn't *right*.

CHAPTER SEVEN

Now: Thursday, 2 April, P.M. . . .

CATHERINE HAD ANSWERED QUESTIONS ABOUT HER STEP-
father, mostly to the effect that she didn't know the answer.
She hadn't seen him for years until three months ago; she had
seen him twice since then. She had been told that the police
had tried to contact her early that morning, and she had been
asked where she had been. She had told the inspector that she
had spent the night in the car in the lay-by on the main road
close to Garrick Drive, where she and Max lived.

She had been asked why, and she had told her that she
hadn't wanted to go home. She had been asked why she hadn't
wanted to go home, and she had told her; she had been frightened to go home.

She had been asked if Max often hit her, and she had told
the stupid woman that he had slapped her, which wasn't the
same thing, and that he had never done anything of the sort before. She had been asked why Max had slapped her, and she
had refused to answer.

"Have you been home yet?"

"No. I came here as soon as the gates opened, and waited
for Max. But then I realized that I'd got the car, and I thought
he'd be here."

"Would you mind removing your coat, Mrs. Scott?" she
asked, as she turned pages in her notebook.

"What?"

She looked up. "Your coat," she said. "Please."

The voice was authoritative, like her old headmistress telling her to pay more attention in class and then her marks would be higher at the end of term. Catherine stood up, slipped off her coat, and sat down, letting it lie on the floor.

A little frown appeared on the other woman's brow. "Your husband didn't just slap you, did he?" she said.

Catherine looked down at her bare arms to see the ugly bruises that had formed during the night. Poor Max. She looked up again. "I tried to get away from him," she said. "He grabbed hold of me, that's all. I bruise easily. He didn't hurt me."

Inspector Hill looked at her in frank disbelief. "You tell me that this behaviour was entirely out of character, and yet you won't tell me why he did it," she said.

"I don't see what it has to do with my stepfather's murder," she said.

"Your husband was suspected of having murdered his first wife," Inspector Hill said baldly.

Catherine, who had been studying the reflection of the window in the high polish of the desk, looked up slowly. "Max didn't kill Valerie," she said.

"No," said the inspector. "In fact, you told the police that he was with you, in London, at the time of the murder."

"Yes."

"But you've just told me that you were frightened to go home last night. You spent the night in the car sooner than face him. And if that's what he does to you in public, I'm not surprised you didn't want him to get you in private."

For the first time since she had entered the office, Catherine was stirred from the terrible lethargy that had taken hold of her. How dare she suggest such a thing? How dare she? "Max isn't violent!" she shouted.

"So why did he get violent yesterday?"

"Max has nothing to do with this!"

"Nothing to do with what?"

"What happened to my stepfather! That's what you're supposed to be here about!"

The inspector raised her eyebrows. "But you can't be sure about that, can you?" she said. "Not like last time. Because you weren't with him this time—you were too frightened to be with him this time. So you can't be sure. In fact, we haven't

151

been able to find your husband yet. He doesn't seem to have gone home either."

She could help her out there, she thought. "Have you tried wherever Anna Worthing lives?" she asked.

"My sergeant was on his way there about an hour ago," Inspector Hill said.

"Then I expect he's found my husband," said Catherine.

She seemed to write everything down.

"Was she what the row was about?" the inspector asked, as she wrote.

"No," said Catherine tiredly.

She was given a decidedly old-fashioned look by the inspector. "Mrs. Scott," she said. "You have been married for ten years to a man of whom you are clearly not normally afraid. So why were you afraid last night?"

Catherine looked again at the reflection of the window.

"Why the very day your stepfather is murdered does your husband become uncharacteristically violent? It's hard to believe that the two things aren't linked. Harder still to believe that Mr. Scott has inadvertently got himself involved in the murder of yet another close relative," she said.

She was trying to provoke her again, like she had before. But it wasn't going to work.

"Why was your husband hitting you, Mrs. Scott?"

Catherine didn't speak.

"Or am I attaching too much importance to what isn't all that unusual an occurrence?"

Catherine felt herself colour up just as the inspector looked up.

"Am I? Is it just that this time someone saw him?"

"Max isn't like that," she said miserably. "He's gentle, and kind."

"He wasn't being very gentle and kind when Detective Sergeant Finch saw him."

That did it. Catherine jumped to her feet. "Will you stop going *on* about that!" she cried, hitting the desk with both fists for emphasis. "He only did that because he was confused and hurt, and he didn't know what he was doing! He's never touched me before! Leave him *alone*!"

The inspector's brown eyes looked interested in her reaction; Catherine became self-conscious once more, and sat down

152

again, knowing her fair skin was still burning with indignation. She had walked into some kind of trap, she knew she had.

"All right," said the inspector, sounding like her headmistress again. "I accept that he had never done anything like that before. So what triggered it, Mrs. Scott? My DCI was there, you know. He says it was as Victor Holyoak walked in that you ran out and Mr. Scott ran after you. And my sergeant says that that's when he was hitting you. Why, Mrs. Scott? Did it have something to do with your stepfather?"

She couldn't go on not replying. The woman never lost her patience, and Catherine did. She would win in the end, so she might as well win now. But it was hard, trying to find the words.

"When I was seventeen, I came to Stansfield to see Max," she said, after long moments of agonized thought. "And I found out what had happened to his wife. The police thought he'd killed her."

Now she was speaking slowly enough for the inspector to take down what she said word for word, and she was doing just that.

"They had to let him go in the morning—that's when I got the chance to speak to him. I said that I would tell them that he'd been with me, but he didn't want me to." She sniffed away the tears. "That was when he remembered that he'd seen someone when he left the flats. He could describe him, he said. If the police could find him, that would prove that Max was where he said he was. My name wouldn't have to be mentioned."

There was a long silence then; the inspector didn't look up from her notes, but sat, pen poised, waiting for more.

"And he described my stepfather," she said. "I didn't tell him that that was who it was, and I talked him out of giving his description to the police. I said it would just be one of the girls' customers, and no one would be able to trace him. I told the police he had been with me. Max didn't know that it was my stepfather he had seen until he saw him here yesterday morning." She could feel the tears running down her face; she didn't try to wipe them away. "He hadn't met him—he didn't even know that Victor Holyoak *was* my stepfather until Tuesday. That was why he was so angry with me," she said. "My stepfather was Max's proof that he was innocent."

153

Inspector Hill put her pen down, and regarded Catherine for long moments. "All right," she said, eventually. "Let's start at the beginning. Why did you come to see Max Scott that day?"

She had been pregnant.

"Mrs. Scott?"

"I—I wanted to see him," she said.

"Was he expecting you?"

"No."

"Why did you want to see him?"

"I . . ." Catherine licked dry lips. "I just wanted to talk to him."

"But you'd seen him the evening before."

"I wanted to be with him."

Inspector Hill's brown eyes rested on hers as she spoke. "At the time, you denied any emotional involvement with Max Scott," she said. "Are you contradicting that?"

Catherine nodded.

"And is that why Mr. Scott was reluctant to let you tell the police that he'd been with you?"

"Yes." No, but it would do.

She made a note. "Why didn't you tell Mr. Scott that it was your stepfather he had seen?"

"My parents had moved to Holland. They had left the night before. My stepfather came to . . . to tell me."

"And Mr. Scott saw Mr. Holyoak enter the flats as he was leaving?"

"Yes. But if I'd told Max that it was my stepfather, they'd have brought him back, and . . . and I was frightened he'd find out about Max and me. I thought he might be able to make me go back with him."

"Are you saying that you and Max Scott were having an affair?"

"We loved one another," Catherine said. "But the police thought that I was this other woman that his wife had been going on about, so we . . . we said we had just been colleagues."

She even wrote that down. "And it *was* you," she murmured, as she wrote. It was a statement, not a question. She looked up. "He was having an affair with you," she said. "Wasn't he?"

Catherine shook her head, and saw the disbelief. "I didn't

154

say we were having an affair. I said we loved one another," she repeated defiantly. "We still do."

"And yet you tell me that you think he spent last night with another woman?"

Catherine smiled then, for the first time. Easier ground at last. "I know what Max is like about women," she said. "I've always known. I don't mind."

"Has he had many other women?" she asked.

"Probably. I don't usually find out about them."

"How did you find out about Anna Worthing?"

"My stepfather told me. He wanted me to leave Max. He said it worried my mother, my being married to someone like that."

"Did that bother you that your mother was worried?"

Catherine shrugged. "If it worried my mother, it was because he chose to let it. He knew where Max was that night. He knew Max had seen him. He knew he hadn't murdered anyone." She doubted very much that her mother had any opinion on the subject, but she didn't express that doubt to the inspector.

"You didn't care for your stepfather over much, I take it," she said.

"I loathed him. He was a liar and a cheat and a fraud, and when I think—" She felt her heart start to race again, and made another conscious effort to calm down. "When I think that he waltzed through life without the police ever knocking on his door, and someone good and kind like Max gets accused of murder, I just—"

"He was suspected of murder," said Inspector Hill. "He was never accused."

"It's the same thing! You don't know what it did to him. He'd just moved here. He'd made some friends—they vanished. It was years—*years* before he could live his normal life again. He still has nightmares! Do you *know* how many times the police questioned him? He tosses and turns and says he didn't kill Valerie, and I . . ." She closed her eyes, trying not to think of it. "I could have stopped all that," she said. "And I didn't. I didn't. I was too young, and too silly, and too selfish. I didn't realize what it would do to him, and by the time I did, it was much too late!"

She locked eyes with the inspector, who wasn't even trying to take the torrent of words down.

"So now you know," she said. "You know why he was slapping me, and you know why I was afraid to go home. I wasn't afraid of Max! I was afraid to face him, that's all."

"Why didn't you tell him sooner?" the inspector asked. "Why did you let him find out like that?"

Because that was what she had always done with anything unpleasant. Put it off, and put it off, until the very last moment. But the last moment had never arrived, and Max had been shocked into sudden violence.

"Because I didn't know how to tell him," she said.

The inspector closed her notebook. "Well," she said. "I think I've finished, for the moment."

She came down in the lift with her. "Do you still have the car?" she asked.

"Yes. It's over by the stairs." Catherine found that she was still being accompanied; her hand shook as she tried to get the key into the car door.

"Would you rather I gave you a lift home?" the inspector asked.

Catherine nodded. Her legs were shaking too much to drive.

They didn't speak in the car; Catherine had said all that she had to say, all that she had rehearsed. Come what may, the day of reckoning had been coming; she had been going to have to say it all. She had meant to say it to her husband. She had ended up saying it to the police.

"I'll see if we've turned him up," Inspector Hill said as she drew up on the small paved forecourt of the Scott house. She used a radio; she told them that Catherine had suggested that Max might be found at Anna Worthing's flat.

He had been; Catherine stared at the inspector as the radio informed them both that Max and Anna Worthing had been brought in for questioning in connection with the murder of Victor Holyoak.

"This is ridiculous," Max said.

"What's ridiculous, Mr. Scott?" asked Detective Sergeant Finch.

Max didn't know. He just hoped that if he kept saying it, Finch would believe it and let him go.

"Miss Worthing's next-door neighbor—garagewise—says that when he came home at around eight thirty, her car was not there. When he went out to get something from the car at about eleven thirty, it was there. He knows it was because he thought he wasn't going to be able to get his car out in the morning, and he tried to get it moved." He looked brightly at Max. "Conclusion. She came home some time between eight thirty and eleven thirty."

"Is that who came to the door?" asked Max.

"He didn't get a reply," said Finch. "He assumed that no one had heard him."

"I heard him—I just didn't feel like answering the door."

"Ah well," said Finch. "He was able to get his car out after all, so what really matters is when it arrived there. And he says it wasn't there at eight thirty."

"Nonsense. I wasn't waiting that long."

The schoolboy eagerness increased. "You weren't waiting at all according to your first statement," Finch said.

Max glanced at the tape as it went round. He hadn't been cautioned before, and if there was one thing he knew, it was that they couldn't quote you if they hadn't cautioned you. "This is my first statement," he said.

Finch sat back and looked at him. "You are now denying that Miss Worthing was at home when you arrived at her flat at six thirty?"

"You must have misunderstood," said Max. "I arrived at six thirty. She came a little later."

"Like two hours later?"

"I don't know."

Max had been through all this before. Over and over and over. Different questions, different answers, but the same feeling in the pit of his stomach.

"You are now saying that you were waiting outside Miss Worthing's flat for an indeterminate period of time before she came home? You must know when it was."

Max shrugged.

Finch pushed his chair back with an angry scrape. "What time is it?" he asked, standing up.

Max automatically looked at his watch. "Five past one," he said.

157

"It didn't occur to you to look at your watch when you were waiting?"

"Why should it? She wasn't expecting me—she hadn't said that she'd be there at any particular time."

"But we have established that you were there for at least two hours before Miss Worthing arrived home?"

"I must have been," said Max.

"Or were you right in the first place?"

Max looked up at him.

"Was she there when you arrived—only *you* didn't arrive until after eight thirty, by which time she had got home?"

"Zelda Driver dropped me off at about six thirty," said Max. "Ask her."

"I will," said Finch. "Don't worry. Interview suspended," he said, switching off the tape.

Lloyd was waiting to see if they had anything on Holyoak; it seemed to him that you were unlikely to have a razor scar if you had led an entirely blameless life, or that if you had, you would assuredly have reported it to the police. Finch, on the other hand, was keen to hang on to Scott and Worthing, and was trying to convince Lloyd.

"It's not much to hold them on, is it? You said yourself that Scott was drunk," Lloyd reminded Finch. "He wakes up to find you there, badgering his girlfriend—so he says she was with him. Now he's regretting his chivalry. She was somewhere she doesn't want *him* to know about. Not you."

Finch shook his head. "She knows the score, sir," he said.

"Oh?"

"She hasn't spoken a word since I cautioned her," said Finch. "Not one. Practically everybody's had a go."

Lloyd shrugged. "That's her right," he said.

"Takes a pro to exercise it that well," said Finch.

"Well," said Lloyd, "we've nothing on her."

There was a knock at the door, and the collator came in with a piece of paper in her hand. "Holyoak, Victor Andrew," she said. "Nothing too exciting, I'm afraid. One minor conviction, thirteen years ago."

One minor conviction, thirteen years ago. Unlucky for some. He frowned. He'd thought that already today, unoriginally enough. Wasn't that when Mrs. Scott the first met her maker?

158

He checked his notes. Yes indeed. Thirteen years ago. Third of May.

"He was booked for kerb-crawling, early hours of nineteenth February, nineteen seventy-nine," she said. "But I've got a friend in the Serious Crimes Squad—I'm seeing if he can find anything. Holyoak might have been mentioned in despatches."

"Good girl," said Lloyd approvingly.

She looked at him just like Judy did sometimes. They couldn't even take a compliment these days, he thought, as he watched her retreating figure through the new glass pane in his door.

Kerb-crawling. Lloyd was transported back to London, and the depression which he still felt when he thought about it. Depressing nights at home, with long, huffy silences. Even more depressing nights at work, watching little girls and lonely men being rounded up. His eyes widened. Of course. *Of course.*

"Jenny!" he yelled as she disappeared round the corner of the corridor. She didn't hear. He picked up the phone and dialled her extension, drumming his fingers impatiently until, breathless, she picked up her phone.

"Collator."

"Where was Holyoak picked up?" he demanded.

"Leyford, South London," she said.

"Bingo," said Lloyd and put the phone down.

No dreams, no premonitions. No clairvoyance. It was something of a relief.

Another figure came into view through his glass panel. "Judy!" he shouted, with more success this time, catching her just before she turned into the CID room.

She opened the door. "You wanted me?"

"Leyford," he said.

Finch might not have noticed, because he really didn't know her all that well. But Lloyd knew her very well indeed, and he saw the little flush that touched her cheekbones as he said the word. He grinned.

"Yes, sir?" she said.

She always got formal when he'd caught her not being a policeman. "Operation Kerbcrawl," he said. "That's when I saw Holyoak. Through binoculars. That's why I could see him, and he couldn't see me. That's why he was really close to me but I couldn't touch him."

She smiled. "Well, that's a relief," she said.

"My sentiments exactly," said Lloyd, and glanced at the bemused Finch. "The Inspector and I worked together before," he explained. "The Met—Kingston Road Division, Leyford. From time to time we were both drafted into a special squad they'd set up to combat kerb-crawling. We worked about a dozen streets—residential areas. Sometimes we did them two nights running, that sort of thing. No pattern, no warning. Just getting told the day before which streets to do." He smiled. "And as a result of our efforts, streetwalkers are now a thing of the past in that particular area of London."

Finch laughed.

"And I knew I'd seen Holyoak before," he said. "I just couldn't remember where, and I couldn't make sense of the memory."

But even as he said the words, he knew that he still couldn't really make sense of it. Because try as he might to fit Holyoak's features to the memory, he couldn't. He sighed, and put it to one side.

"How did you get on with Mrs. Scott?" he asked Judy.

She gave them a brief account of the interview, and Lloyd thought about it. Especially the bit about the police never knocking on Holyoak's door. Maybe Jenny's friend would come up with something.

"Did you believe her?" he asked. "About why he was hitting her?"

"Hard to say. She won't hear a word against her husband, so I wouldn't rule out her covering up for him."

"Her stepfather's murder or his wife's murder? Both?"

A shrug. "She couldn't stand her stepfather," she said. "And she's totally loyal to Max. So there would be no contest either time, I shouldn't think."

"Even if what she says *is* true," Tom said. "His reaction was a bit strong. He was threatening to beat her black and blue to get the truth out of her when I saw him."

"He had a good try," said Judy.

Finch bristled. "Not when I was there, he didn't," he said.

"Well—she says he grabbed her arms, and she bruises easily," said Judy. "I suppose that might be true. I've got them digging out the statements and interviews and so on from the

Valerie Scott murder. Perhaps they'll show Mr. Scott in a less favourable light."

"Let me see them when you've finished with them," said Lloyd. "In the meantime, I think I'll have a word with our Mr. Scott." More movement in the corridor caught Lloyd's eye. He preferred the door he'd had in the first place, through which he couldn't see. This was supposed to encourage the troops, remind them of his presence. It hadn't been his idea. "And that," he said, with a nod, "is Anna Worthing on her way back to the interview room."

Judy turned to look, and turned back, frowning slightly.

"Finch is having a bit of a problem with her," he said. "Aren't you, Tom?"

Tom nodded. "She's no stranger to police stations, if you ask me," he said. "She's saying nothing."

"Has she got a solicitor?" asked Judy.

"When I say she's saying nothing, I mean nothing. She hasn't opened her mouth, not even to ask for a solicitor. I don't know why she agreed to come in—probably thought I'd arrest her if she didn't."

"Why don't you see how they're getting on with the security tapes, Tom?" said Lloyd. "Mrs. Hill can have a go at Anna Worthing."

Tom complied with relief, and left the room.

Judy smiled. "You want me to talk to her?" she asked.

"Please."

"But the book says women are more likely to open up to men," she said, a mischievous look in her eye. "Wouldn't you be better?"

"I just think you should have a go," said Lloyd, a touch uncomfortably.

"So it's true," she said.

"What?"

"A little bird told me that you fancied her," said Judy.

"You've been talking to Zelda Driver!"

Damn the woman, thought Lloyd. Thank God Judy wasn't the jealous type. If Zelda Driver had told him that Judy fancied some bloke, he'd have been worried.

"She's right, though, isn't she?" teased Judy.

"I met Anna Worthing socially," he said, hearing the defensive tone that he was trying to disguise. "That's all. So I don't

161

think I should interview her. Not at this stage. Besides—we really haven't much to hold her on, as I just told Finch."

"She lied about where she was," said Judy.

"No," said Lloyd seriously. "Finch was very particular about that. Scott lied. She just wasn't saying. And let's face it—unless we have some reason to believe that she stabbed her boss to death, where she went after she left is her business. I've an idea where Scott was, though," he said.

"And you're keeping it to yourself?"

"Till I've spoken to him, yes. She's in interview room one—help yourself. You're the expert at getting the silent ones to talk."

She sighed. "You make it sound as though I use a bullwhip," she said.

"Now there's a nice thought," said Lloyd.

She pulled a face, then turned her no doubt professional countenance to the door. Lloyd had had time to read exactly one page of the report on his desk when she came back.

"Confessed already?" he asked.

"This is weird," she said.

Lloyd raised his eyebrows. He knew it was weird. Until now, Judy hadn't admitted that anything could be weird.

"I think whatever you've got is catching," she said.

"What's up?"

"I know her. I thought I did when I saw her in the corridor, but I didn't think I really could. I thought it was an association of ideas. But it is her. She looks different too, but it's her all right."

Whatever it was, it had unsettled Judy to the point where she was positively rambling, and interested him to the point where he didn't even attempt to correct her grammar. "Who?" he asked.

"I knew her as Annabel, not Anna. In Leyford. On Operation Kerbcrawl. She was a prostitute. She went by the name of Annabel le Sueur, would you believe?"

Lloyd smiled. "Did she now? Perhaps I will talk to her after all."

"Do you know her?"

He shook his head, smiling. "I'm just interested in anyone who uses Joan Crawford's real surname as her alias." He grinned, a little puzzled. "Have you been reading one of these *Astound Your Friends with Your Memory* books?"

Judy smiled. "Oh, I remember her," she said.

Like he remembered Holyoak. Except that nagging away at the back of his mind was the fact that he hadn't really remembered him. He couldn't rid himself of the image, and it still had the wrong face. He wondered idly if the deceased really *was* Holyoak. His stepdaughter was identifying him later; presumably she would know.

"You've got that look on your face again," Judy said.

He snapped out of it, and looked at her. "He just seemed different," he said. "Younger."

"He was younger. I'll go and get my bullwhip—there's something very odd going on here."

"I told you that," he said, as he followed her down the corridor to the interview rooms. A gap of thirteen years didn't account for it. Holyoak would have been in his early forties; the face which he could see in infuriating flashes was someone in his late twenties. He was simply mixing up two memories.

And Finch had been right; Anna Worthing did know her way around a police station. Zelda Driver was right, too, in her way, because there was something about Anna Worthing that he liked, not least her choice of soubriquet. He didn't mind that she had been a prostitute; he hoped very much that she wasn't a murderer.

He pushed open the interview-room door, and looked at Max Scott, dressed in what he had been wearing yesterday, a little crumpled now, as he sat at the table. There were moves afoot to do away with the table in between; make it all nice and cosy. And there were times when Lloyd felt that the informal approach would work better. But Scott had been through the mill of a police investigation before; he would be wary whatever they did. Lloyd met with instant hostility.

"Are you people going to drag me in here every time anyone gets murdered?"

Lloyd shrugged. "I think we'll confine ourselves to the ones that are related to you," he said, going to the tape-recorder, setting it up. At first it had irritated him, this preamble that had to be gone through before he could start asking questions, but he had, as ever, brought it into the act. Sometimes it heightened the tension, sometimes he affected not to be entirely sure of new-fangled gadgets, sometimes he produced a kind of camaraderie with the suspect, man against machine, us against them, the ones who make up the rules.

"This is what we do these days," he said, after indicating the time, the date, and those present. "We record the interviews. Better idea, really—I can't think why we didn't always do it." He sat down. "Because quite genuine mistakes were made, you know. I mean—it isn't easy, making notes while you're talking to someone—look at the tabloid papers. They get it wrong all the time. And of course, sometimes we wrote up notes of the interview hours afterwards. You can't rely on your memory like that—a case in point," he said, conspiratorially, leaning towards Scott. "My sergeant could have sworn that this morning you said that Zelda Driver dropped you off at Anna Worthing's flat at six thirty, and that she was already there."

Scott sighed loudly.

"But what you actually said, apparently, was that you waited outside her door for two hours or more before she came home." He shook his head. "Funny the tricks your memory plays on you," he said.

Scott stared down at the table. "I just didn't want her to have to go through what I went through," he muttered.

"How very gallant of you."

And yet, from what Zelda Driver had said that morning, the gallantry didn't seem so far-fetched. She professed to be no admirer of Scott, and yet the picture she had painted was pretty much along the lines of the one his wife had given Judy. Zelda held firm in her belief that he could never have hurt Valerie. Lloyd had got the impression that Zelda even had someone else in mind, but he had been unable to draw it out of her. He might get Judy and her bullwhip to call on Zelda.

But, Zelda notwithstanding, Lloyd pressed on with his theory. After all, Tom had witnessed the man hitting his wife, and threatening her. "My sergeant heard you tell your wife you'd get the truth out of her if you had to beat her black and blue," he said, employing a tone of voice more suited to asking the man if he would like another cup of tea. "Is that right?"

Scott went brick red. "I've never done anything like that in my life before," he whispered.

"The truth about what?"

"I . . . I don't know how much she's told you about that,"

Scott said, still painfully blushing. "Holyoak could have proved that I didn't kill Valerie. I saw him coming in to the flats as I was leaving. But Catherine never told me that that was who I had seen—she let me find out at the opening. I . . . I just—"

Lloyd shook his head. "But you knew the truth about that as soon as you saw him," he said. "What truth were you going to beat out of her?"

He covered his face with his hands. "Nothing. I don't know. I didn't know what I was saying. Or doing."

"Didn't you? Then how do you account for the bruises? She didn't get them at the time, not according to my sergeant. I think *your* memory's been playing you false, Mr. Scott."

Scott's hands slid down his face as he looked at Lloyd.

"I don't think you stood outside Anna Worthing's door for two hours," he said. "I don't think you ever had any intention of going to Anna Worthing. You wanted to go home, according to Mrs. Driver. She thought you might do your wife a mischief, and told you to go somewhere to cool off. But I think once she dropped you off, you went home anyway. And I think your wife went home when she left the penthouse. I think you did try to beat the truth out of her."

Scott dropped his head into his hands, covering his face.

"Sorry, Mr. Scott, but as I explained—we do have the tape-recorder to consider now. I'd like to hear your reply. Did you go home after Mrs. Driver dropped you off?"

"Yes," said Scott, from behind his hands.

"And did you continue to assault your wife?"

"I—she ran away from me," he said. "She got into the car, and drove off. I went back to Anna's, but Anna still wasn't there."

"What time *did* Anna Worthing get there?"

"A few minutes after nine."

"What truth were you seeking, Mr. Scott?"

He took some moments getting himself under control, then emerged from behind his hands. "If I'm not under arrest, I'd like to leave now," he said, with difficulty.

"I'm sure you would," said Lloyd. "What truth, Mr. Scott?"

"I want to leave," he repeated. "And unless my wife is bringing charges against me, I don't believe you can keep me here."

Lloyd tipped the chair on to its two back legs, and terminated the interview, switching off the recorder. "Your wife says she bruises easily," he said, dropping forward again.

Scott got up to leave; Lloyd waited until he had reached the door before he spoke. "Did you get the truth, Mr. Scott?" he asked.

Scott looked at him for a moment. "No," he said, and there were tears in his eyes.

Lloyd sat for a while in the interview room trying to work out what made Scott tick. He was quite prepared to believe that Scott had never done anything like that in his life before, but he had done it this time, and if Zelda and Catherine were painting a true picture of the man, then it had to have been something quite dreadful that had sparked it off. And all right, Catherine could have produced her stepfather as another witness as to Scott's whereabouts at the time of his wife's murder, but still not an entirely independent witness. And Holyoak would have had to remember seeing Scott, which there was no reason to suppose he would have done.

That uncharacteristic violence was the action of someone who felt utterly betrayed by someone he trusted. Had Catherine betrayed him? To whom? Holyoak? Hardly, according to Judy.

He had let Scott go; was he sending him back to finish what he'd started with his wife? No. He didn't think he was. Whatever had made him beside himself with rage had burnt itself out; he may not have got the truth, but he was resigned to that. Scott was no longer a threat to his wife. He was bitterly ashamed of what he had done; he had said that he was with Anna Worthing rather than admit it.

Lloyd got up. But where was Anna Worthing that evening, and why had she been so unwilling to tell Finch? Zelda said that she had been Holyoak's mistress. Freddie had come as close to advancing a theory as Lloyd had ever heard; that Holyoak had been murdered by someone with whom he had just had sexual relations.

It wasn't looking good for her, Lloyd had to admit.

A woman had joined them. Dark, well dressed. A detective inspector. God knew what they would be wheeling in next. This one hadn't been at the opening; Anna would have noticed. She sighed as she was asked the same old questions. They'd have to let her go soon, unless they had thought up something to charge her with. As it was, she was being more co-operative with the police than she had ever been in her life, simply by staying there. They could hardly expect her to speak to them as well.

"Miss Worthing—you told Detective Sergeant Finch that you left Mr. Holyoak's flat at six fifteen," she said.

Anna examined her nails. This one didn't get all hot under the collar like Finch. He'd ended up red in the face with frustration because she wouldn't answer; now he was taking a back seat as his boss had a go. DI Hill was asking the same questions as he had, as often as he had, and looked as though she would be happy to keep it up all afternoon. But Anna could counter that with the same ease; it was stalemate, and they both knew it.

"Mr. Scott said you were with him from half-past six," she said, for the third time to Anna's recollection. "But he's changed his mind. He says it was more like nine o'clock, now."

That was new. It didn't exactly come as a surprise, though. Finch had told her about the bloke thinking the car was blocking his way out of the garage—Max would have given in once he'd been told that. She still wasn't at all sure why Max had been so quick to give her an alibi in the first place.

"Where were you between six fifteen and nine o'clock?"

Anna read one of the posters.

"Don't mess me about, Annabel. We're both getting too old for games."

Jesus Christ. She'd only just given them her prints. They couldn't have found out yet. She turned back and stared at the inspector. "Who the hell are you?" she asked, her voice hoarse from disuse.

DI Hill smiled. "The last time you saw me I was WPC Russell, Kingston Road Division, Leyford," she said.

She stared at her. "You must have booked dozens of us on that patch," she said. "What have you got up there?" She tapped her own temple as she spoke. "A bloody card-index?"

She laughed. "Far from it," she said. "I've got a rotten memory. I take notes all the time, when people actually answer my questions. It's not so bad now, with the tapes. But I've got into the habit—I don't feel right without a notebook."

167

Anna had a feeling that the chatty approach was leading up to something. Finch was looking startled at the sudden change of tone, and the inspector smiled at him.

"There are maybe half a dozen things that have happened to me since I joined the police service that I can remember without having to look up files and notebooks," she said to him.

The police service. That was what they called it now, but it didn't stop them being bastards.

"And Annabel here is one of them," she said. "That's the name she used to use—isn't that right, Annabel?"

Anna tried to look bored.

"It was when I had just finished my probationary period," she said, now talking to Anna again. "You deal with all sorts of things—I mean, one minute you're chasing some handbag snatcher through the market, and the next you're giving someone directions to the library. Or assisting at an RTA. Or looking for a missing kid. You know. But you don't really know how you'd cope in a crisis. Something the books can't tell you how to deal with. Something you've just got to find out for yourself."

Anna presumed that this crisis had somehow involved her, but she was damned if she knew what it was.

"Then one night, I saw you a millimetre away from kicking my colleague's head in," she said. "I got between you and him, and I told you to sit down. You did." She smiled. "That was when I knew that I could really do this job."

Dear God. Anna went cold. She wasn't dredging that up from her memory. They'd got Bannister, and God alone knew what he had told them. The alert look on the inspector's face meant that she had seen Anna's involuntary reaction; Anna was out of practice at this game.

"Do you want to tell me what happened last night, Anna?" she asked.

If they had Bannister, he could be telling them anything; her stand-by of saying nothing was beginning to look inadequate in the face of the evidence that they would begin to gather against her, what with Max giving her unwanted alibis, and Bannister telling them what she had done.

"I left Victor's flat at six fifteen," she said. "I told him." She nodded over at Finch. "Max saw me leave—he said so."

"We're not inclined to take Mr. Scott's word for anything after this morning," the inspector said.

"He got a lift home from Mrs. Driver! She'll tell you. Or that woman doctor! She was in the car park with them!"

"Mrs. Driver is extremely busy at work, in view of what's happened," said the inspector. "We haven't been able to get hold of Dr. Rule ourselves yet. But we aren't really disputing when you left, Anna. I'd like to know why you left, though."

Anna frowned. "Someone came to the door," she said.

"Who?" asked the inspector.

"I don't know. I didn't see them."

"Was it a man or a woman?" asked Finch.

Anna sighed. "I just said I didn't see them."

"But presumably you heard a voice," he said. "They must have used the security phone to get in."

Anna frowned a little. That hadn't occurred to her.

"No," she said. "I could only hear Victor's end."

"And this was at quarter-past six?" said Finch. "When you left?"

"Yes."

"Was he expecting someone?"

"Yes."

"But you don't know who?"

"Well . . ." She didn't want to do this—it went against every principle that she had in her dealings with the police. But he had landed her here, giving her a phony alibi. "I thought it might have been Max," she said. "But he says he saw me leave, so I don't suppose it could have been."

"We can check that out," said Finch. "But I'm more interested in you, right now. What was your relationship with Holyoak?"

"I worked for him."

"Nothing more?" asked the inspector.

Anna looked from one to the other, not sure how much they knew, how much they had been told by Bannister and Max, how much they were guessing. But she was telling the truth, and they didn't believe her, that much was obvious.

"Come on, Anna," Finch said. "There was a bit more to it than just working for him, wasn't there?"

"I worked for him," she repeated.

"Where did you go when you left?"

"I went to the pub."

"Which pub?"

"The Stag."

"It would be," said Finch.

The Stag was dark and dingy and noisy and dirty, full of winos and receivers of stolen goods. It had gleefully thrown out afternoon closing as soon as the law was changed, and it was never short of customers. It was the closest pub to the factory; that was why she had gone in there. Even if the staff did remember her, they wouldn't tell the police. She knew that, and they knew that.

"Were you alone?"

They knew she hadn't been. She shook her head.

"Who was with you?"

"You already know," said Anna. "Why ask?"

The inspector raised her eyes to the ceiling. "No more games, Anna," she said. "Who was with you?"

Anna looked at her. "Dave Bannister, of course," she said.

"Bannister?" the inspector repeated incredulously. "How does he come into this?"

Anna stared at her, but Inspector Hill wasn't play acting. Dear God, they hadn't got Bannister at all. And now she had said he was there. For a second, she panicked, but her bridges were burned, and she had to tell them. "Look," she said, her stomach turning over as it always did when she thought of Bannister's long-ago visit, of what would have happened if Victor hadn't got there when he did, "if I tell you, you've got to give me protection."

"We haven't got to do anything," said Finch. "If you've got information, you'd better let us have it—without conditions."

Anna ignored him, and turned to the inspector. "You've got to listen to me! He came after me before—he'll do it again if he thinks I've said anything!"

The inspector was regarding her with some interest, if not actual belief. "Came after you?" she said. "When? Why?"

"Because of the complaint I made about him!" shouted Anna, tired of trying to get thick cops to understand what she was saying. "He came after me—nearly a year later! He beat me up for that—God knows what he'll do to me this time."

The inspector frowned. "The complaint?" she said. "Are you talking about what happened that night in *Leyford*?"

"Yes," said Anna.

"Well, I'm not," she said firmly. "I'm talking about what happened last night, right here in Stansfield. What has Bannister's beating you up years ago got to do with Victor Holyoak?"

She hadn't been promised protection, but there was no turning back. Anna swallowed, and looked down at her hands. "Victor pulled him off me, or I don't know what state he'd have left me in," she said.

"But according to you, you only met Holyoak six months ago," Finch said.

"I lied." Anna looked defiantly at him.

"Why? Because you're his mistress? Because he had to put you on the payroll to explain your coming to Stansfield with him? What happened, Anna? Did he ditch you once he'd got you here? Who was he expecting—were you jealous?"

Anna didn't answer.

"Anna," said Inspector Hill sternly. "If you didn't kill Victor Holyoak, you have to tell us the truth. Because right now, you're the best bet—you must see that."

"It is the bloody truth!" shouted Anna.

"That you were in a pub with Dave Bannister? Anna—for crying out loud, you don't seriously expect me to believe that, do you?"

"It's the *truth*. He saw me on the bloody telly! He came haring up here to the factory, but everyone had gone. So he went to the pub, and he found me there!"

Finch had finally had enough. "Who *is* Bannister?" he demanded.

"An ex-colleague of mine," said Inspector Hill.

Finch looked startled, and turned back to Anna. "Why did he beat you up?" he asked.

"Because I reported him for sexually assaulting me," said Anna.

"Oh," he said, sitting back in his chair.

"Good for him, is that what you're thinking?" said Anna. "That's what they said, the bastards." She looked back at Inspector Hill. "He came after me, and he beat me up. Victor got him off me—he didn't know me from Adam then. He didn't have to do that. He didn't have to do anything that he did for me. I didn't kill Victor—don't you understand?"

171

"And you say this Bannister turned up here last night?" asked Finch, with total disbelief.

She nodded. "Look," she said, putting her real fear into words for the first time. "I might have caused it. I didn't mean to. I swear to God, I didn't mean to. I'd had too much to drink—I just wanted to get back at both the bastards. I didn't mean that to happen, I swear I didn't!"

"Both? *Had* you had a row with Holyoak?" Inspector Hill asked.

Anna nodded. She was rusty at this, and DI Hill wasn't.

"What about?"

"Work. I—I handed in my notice," said Anna, drawing circles with her finger on the formica tabletop. "Then I went to the pub to get drunk."

"All right," she said. "Go on from there."

"I'd been there a couple of hours when Dave Bannister comes and sits beside me." She glanced up at the inspector, who still looked unconvinced. "I couldn't believe it either," she said, "but he was there! I didn't recognize him, not straight away. I'd only ever seen him in uniform. And he thought he could screw some money out of me. He's out of work."

"Money for what?" asked Finch.

"To feed his wife and kids," said Anna.

"No—I mean, why did he think you would pay him money?"

"So as he wouldn't tell what I did for a living before I shook cabinet ministers' hands," she said, and smiled, despite the position she was in. "I shook more than their hands in my time," she said. "They like them young, and they think you won't know who they are if they pick you up off the street."

They smiled too. Both of them.

"I told him to stuff it. I don't have any money and the papers were going to find out anyway, so he'd backed a loser."

Finch leant forward. "I'm sorry," he said. "The papers? Should I know who you are?"

Anna shook her head, trying not to be goaded into anger any more. "Victor," she said. "He's news in Europe. Like they'd like to find mud to throw at him except they don't know where to look. He's got money. Power. They know he's a bastard and they can't prove it. It'll get like that here," she said, and then remembered.

172

It wouldn't. Victor was dead now. She hadn't had time to take it in, and here she was denying killing him. She knew what Max meant now.

"Go on," said the inspector. Her eyes had lost the look of disbelief.

"I wanted to get my own back, that's all. He asked if there was anything worth nicking inside the plant, and I told him there was a way in past the cameras to the office block. I spun him a tale about Victor having gone home and not to worry if lights went on and off in the flat, because they were on a timeswitch. I said he kept a collection of silver up there."

"And he swallowed all that, of course," said Finch. "Just like you expect us to."

"He seemed to," she said reluctantly. She would have known, if she had been sober. She would never have told him in the first place. "I just wanted to get back at both of the sods! I was drunk—I never thought he'd do anything like that!"

"You think Bannister killed him? Why would he do that?" asked the inspector.

"Victor got him up an alley," said Anna. "Because of what he'd done to me. He hurt him—really hurt him. He told me he had. And Bannister reckons he had to leave the police in the end because of the damage Victor did."

"What did Holyoak use on him?" asked Finch, showing real interest for the first time. "A knife?"

"Victor didn't need knives," said Anna. "He knew all that ... you know. Karate, that sort of thing. He could have put him in hospital if he'd wanted to."

"But he didn't want to?" asked Inspector Hill.

"Suppose not. But Bannister reckons he got internal injuries that caught up with him later on."

Finch looked thoughtful, and Anna knew what he was thinking. He was thinking what she had been thinking ever since he'd come to tell her that Victor was dead. That Bannister hadn't swallowed her story. That he'd tricked the information about the cameras out of her. And he had gone up there to get revenge.

"*Is* there a way past the cameras?" asked the inspector.

"Yes, if you're on foot."

"How did Bannister get to Stansfield—did he drive?"

"Yeah. An old minivan. With a DIY paint job done on it."

"When did you and he part company?"

"Just before nine," said Anna, her voice growing more and more reluctant. "I left him at the pub, and I went home. Max was waiting for me."

The inspector looked at Sergeant Finch. "Where had they got to, checking the tapes?" she asked.

"About six thirty on Wednesday evening when I spoke to them last," he said.

"Tell them to do a fast search until—" She looked at Anna. "What time did he come into the pub?"

"About eight or so," said Anna. "I think."

"Until eight thirty, let's say. If he went to the factory first, it might be on tape. Tell them if there is a van answering that description, I want the registration number checked with the computer, and if it's registered to Bannister, I want him picked up on suspicion of aggravated burglary."

"Yes, ma'am." Finch got up.

"Sergeant Finch leaves interview room," Inspector Hill told the tape.

Anna had liked seeing Finch being made to jump to it. She almost liked Inspector Hill. She had almost liked her fifteen years ago; she remembered her now. She had given her some cigarettes and a pep talk.

"We need a statement, Anna," said the inspector. "I want to know exactly what your relationship was with Holyoak, I want to know what this row was about, I want to know exactly what Bannister did tonight *and* the time he beat you up, I want to know exactly what you told him to do . . . all right? If we're here all night, you're going to give me proper, truthful answers to my questions."

Anna nodded. "And you'll give me protection?" she said again. "Because if you have to let him go again, he'll come after me."

The inspector smiled. "Don't worry," she said. "If he comes after you again, he'll have Sergeant Finch to reckon with."

This didn't exactly inspire confidence.

"Don't be misled by the innocent looks," she said. "He's got two commendations for bravery."

"Yeah?" said Anna. "Well, I haven't."

174

She could still see Bannister holding that truncheon . . . She closed her eyes. She just had to trust them to protect her.

Dave Bannister had filled up the van in readiness for his journey north.

She looked as if she was making a bob or two, the little tart. Some of it might just as well come his way. Blackmail had crossed his mind, but she had him at just as much of a disadvantage as he had her. The little bitch had seen to it that she had. A large cash sum. That was what he needed, and she'd pay up.

She must have it, stashed away somewhere for when she got too decrepit to appeal to Holyoak, even if she wasn't on the streets any more. Even sex-starved businessmen had their standards, and Annabel couldn't go on for ever. Holyoak would trade her in for a younger model sooner or later, but meanwhile he was obviously paying through the nose for her. And she had no overheads, no mortgage, no car-loan repayments, no kids to feed and clothe. She had money. Cash in hand. No banks for Annabel. No tax. No dealing with the authorities.

It would be wherever she was, and a day's telephoning had finally produced her address from a gullible secretary somewhere in Amsterdam. That was where the money would be.

And by the time he'd finished with her, she would be begging him to take her money. It was almost too easy to scare Annabel. And this time she'd have good reason to be scared, because she had pulled a stroke on him that he wasn't going to forgive in a hurry.

He opened the van door, and a shadow fell across him.

"David Bannister?"

He closed the door again. Only his ex-colleagues said your name like that. The little whore was going all the way with it.

"No," said Zelda. "Sorry."

"But you were in the car park with Max Scott at six fifteen?"

Zelda nodded. "I was talking him out of going home to Catherine in that mood," she said. "I was worried. Anna may well have left—I just didn't notice, that's all. Geraldine was there—you could ask her."

"We can't seem to get hold of her," said Judy. "Does Max Scott make a habit of hitting his wife?"

Zelda looked shocked. "Of course he doesn't!" she said. "You'd go a long way before you'd find a kinder, gentler man than Max as far as women are concerned," she said. "Believe me."

"So his wife tells me," said Judy. "But my sergeant saw him, Mrs. Driver—and he thought Mr. Scott was going to start on him, come to that."

"That I could believe—he was very angry. Max is one of these people who hardly ever gets angry, and they're always very nearly out of control when they are. But hitting a woman—" She shook her head. "If Max hadn't told me himself that he'd done it, I would have called your sergeant a liar. I've seen Catherine, I know the mess she's in. But I know what Max went through when Valerie died. And it seems she could have prevented that." She gave a brittle smile. "I wonder why she didn't?" she asked.

Judy couldn't tell her, but for once she got the impression that Zelda wasn't seeking information; she was inviting Judy to enquire closely into Catherine's reasons.

"It's almost impossible for me to imagine Max hitting a woman," Zelda said. "All he has ever wanted to do is give women pleasure. Not pain."

Judy gave her a disbelieving look. "What about his first wife?" she asked. "I'm not talking about her murder—just his behaviour with other women—didn't that give her pain?"

"I don't honestly think it did," said Zelda. "Max genuinely loves women, and women adore him. Even when it's all over, they're still on his side. And Valerie was on his side, too. Because even if he did give her some pain, I'm certain he gave her more pleasure. He's a very nice man to be around."

That wasn't quite what Sergeant Finch had said after his early morning visit to Anna Worthing's. Judy picked up her tea. "You said in your statement at the time of Valerie's death that she was extremely upset about this other woman," she reminded Zelda.

"Oh, she was," said Zelda. "But only about what she called 'his latest.' Not about the others. Not about Max himself. She wanted to hang on to Max, believe me."

"And his latest was Catherine?"

176

Zelda looked a little embarrassed, and Judy's eyes widened slightly as she realized why Zelda was so certain of Max's ability to give pleasure.

"Yes, all right," said Zelda. "I was one of Max's conquests. I'm not terribly proud of it, but he caught me in a moment of weakness. And technically, I was his latest. But it was a one night stand two days before Valerie died, and Valerie's problems started long before I ever came on the scene."

"In London?"

Zelda nodded. "Max fell in love with Catherine," she said. "He's still in love with her—never mind what he did yesterday—he thinks the world of her. That's what Valerie couldn't take. She was losing him, and she knew it. You don't kick up that sort of fuss for someone who only gives you pain, do you?"

Judy thanked Zelda, and made her way back to the station, thinking about Max Scott, and the uncontrollable anger that had led him to hit his wife, shocking rigid everyone who knew him. Had he been uncontrollably angry with the first Mrs. Scott? She sighed. Domestics were always depressing. Then she smiled, as she considered her own rather off-beat domestic set-up.

At first, she had found Lloyd's quick temper alarming; he would say things that wounded when he was angry. But it was always all over almost as soon as it had started, and Lloyd's tongue was his only weapon. Much safer than the Max Scott slow burn; losing his temper was no big deal to Lloyd. Judy couldn't imagine him out of control of his actions.

It was late when she got back; she had thought that Lloyd might have gone home, but he was at his desk. She gave him what she had got from Zelda, for what it was worth, and he looked thoughtful.

"You said that there was no love lost between Mrs. Scott and her stepfather?" he said.

"Well—if he moved his set-up to be here, perhaps he thought rather more highly of her than she did of him. But she made no bones about her feelings—at one point I actually thought her reluctance to remove her coat might be because her clothes were bloodstained, but she was just hiding kind, gentle Max's handiwork." Judy raised her eyebrows.

Lloyd smiled. "Nowt so queer as folk," he observed. "I wish

177

I knew what he wanted to know." He sighed, and picked up the still photograph of Bannister's van that the security system had magically generated for them, and which had resulted in Bannister's arrest. Only then had they been able to persuade Anna Worthing to leave the station.

Judy yawned. Anna's enormous statement had taken for ever; she had revealed that she had custody of a large collection of private detectives' reports that Holyoak had received on his stepdaughter's movements. They could prove very useful on the Valerie Scott murder, but someone had to read them. She'd get them picked up and put Finch on to it in the morning, she thought tiredly, before he went to the post-mortem.

It was almost ten o'clock. She had been awake since dawn, and had had hardly any sleep before that. Lloyd thrived on that; he could stay here all night. She didn't, and she wanted to go home, but there wasn't much chance of that yet, as Lloyd still studied the photograph of Dave Bannister's van.

"Bannister's the dancer, as I recall," he said, his first indication that he knew who Dave Bannister was. The rule that their private lives shouldn't intrude on their working lives had been made by him, which apparently meant that he could break it whenever he chose.

"He's the one with a nice line in sublets," said Judy.

"All right," said Lloyd. "Back to business."

On the other hand, she might have been better off with Dave Bannister. She sighed.

"What do we know about him?" he asked.

"Precious little," said Judy. "He left the Met about three years ago. He hasn't got a record of violence or anything else."

"But you believe all that about his beating Anna up and Holyoak 'getting him up an alley,' as she puts it?"

Judy shrugged. "I don't know," she said. "But Bannister *was* in Stansfield, and he had to be here for some reason."

Lloyd sat back, tipping the chair back, rocking slowly back and forth. "Operation Kerbcrawl?" he said.

She shrugged. "It's what they've all got in common," she said. "Though I can't see how a bit of sleazy business in a car leads to murder years and years later."

"Holyoak wasn't even picked up on Anna's patch," said Lloyd. "She wasn't involved in those arrests."

178

"Why was he kerb-crawling anyway?" asked Judy. "If Anna owed him a favour, you'd think he'd have had no need."

"Mm." Lloyd laid down the photograph. "That presupposes that Anna's telling the truth," he said.

"I think she is," said Judy. "She's scared, Lloyd. And it's not of us."

"Telling the truth even about this mysterious visitor to Holyoak's flat who isn't on the video?"

"Well it wasn't Max, not if whoever it was came at six fifteen," she said. "I imagine she made that up on the spur of the moment—she just hoped that would get us off her back, I suppose. But I think I believe her that there is someone else in Holyoak's life—I expect that that's what her row with Holyoak was really about."

"Did she expand on that?" asked Lloyd.

"She says Holyoak hadn't been very impressed with her handling of the reception, and the row ended with her giving her notice." She shrugged. "Maybe she was sacked," she said. "It seems more likely."

Lloyd frowned. "It seemed to go all right to me," he said. "I thought she did a good job. I told her so."

Judy suppressed a smile. "And if Bannister did go up there, then he can at least tell us whether Holyoak was alone, or with someone. Or alive or dead, come to that. If he was dead, then Anna has a lot more explaining to do."

Lloyd still rocked. Judy looked anxiously at the chair legs. He'd had that chair ever since she had been at Stansfield; the legs has taken an awful lot of rocking. He had stuck to it through innumerable changes of offices, and of desks. It was like a security blanket, except that it didn't seem terribly secure to her. It wasn't even an office chair; they tended to be modern, and unable to be rocked. He'd had a swivel chair for a few months, but it hadn't appealed. So he rescued this one, which had been put back in the interview room it had come from in the first place. Rock on, Lloyd.

"If he'd wanted revenge, he'd have got half a dozen bruisers to jump Holyoak," Lloyd said eventually. "In my opinion."

"We need to know if he took the wallet, too. And maybe it wasn't revenge. Maybe it was self-defence—if Holyoak was as psychopathic as Anna seems to think he was, he might have gone for Bannister again."

"If Bannister took the wallet," Lloyd said, "he would take the money out and throw it away. There and then. He wouldn't risk having it found on him, not for one minute, whether Holyoak was dead or alive. And we haven't found it." He sighed. "But all right," he said, with real reluctance, and let the chair down at last. "I don't see there's much more we can do tonight that isn't being done by other people. No point in waiting for Bannister to arrive—we can't interview him tonight. He needs his beauty sleep, according to the custody sergeant."

Thank God for that, thought Judy.

Charles had stayed late at his office in the clinic, working on the book he was writing about lifestyle, diet, and good health. There were a lot of books like that, of course, but they tended to be slightly cranky. Or very particularly aimed at women, or at men. Or at certain parts of the body, even.

His was a book aimed at entirely changing people's lifestyle; it covered everything, from exercise and diet and working practices to regular medical check-ups, smoking, drinking, and safe sex. It covered the environment, the ozone layer, the rainforests, the polluted rivers and beaches. Using the world's finite resources to better effect. It was about how individuals could make a difference to themselves, to the world they lived in, to the future.

It was very nearly finished; he was playing with titles involving puns on his surname, principally to ensure that Gerry would be home and in bed by the time he walked over to the house.

It was almost midnight when he closed up his office, and strolled through the gardens. Gerry's car was there, and the house was in darkness. Thankfully, he let himself in, had the nightcap that he had assured his intended readers would do them no harm at all, and might even do some good, and went to bed.

Tomorrow would be soon enough to face Gerry again, he thought, as he lay down.

Chapter Eight

Then: Spring, thirteen years ago . . .

"ZELDA DRIVER, AND HER SON TIM—MARK AND LUCY Callender."

"So you're going to stand in Stansfield?" said Zelda. "Are they blooding you?"

Oh, God. Zelda was going to be Zelda. Charles had rather hoped that she would have come as a normal person tonight.

"Yes," said Mark, in his well-educated Scottish accent. "New boys always get unwinnable seats. But I quite fancy my chances, to tell the truth."

"Stansfield's had a Labour MP for twenty years," said Zelda.

"Ah, but he's not standing this time. Perhaps the electorate won't feel so loyal to a new man. A union man at that—and look what the unions are doing to us! Besides, there's a big Scottish contingent in Stansfield, so I might have an advantage."

"Socialists to a man," said Zelda. "You live in the town, do you, Dr. Callender?"

He smiled. "Mark, please," he said. "No, not at the moment."

"So you haven't exactly put your shirt on yourself, then?"

Charles left them to it. Mark would get some practice in with Zelda, he supposed. It wouldn't be so bad if Zelda wasn't Tory to her roots, but she was. Charles wasn't. He and Gerry had always voted Labour. "How are the preparations for the A-levels going, Tim?" he asked.

181

"I'm doing a lot of revision," said Tim. "I don't know if any of it's sticking."

"I remember only too well. What do you hope to do at university?"

"Art and literature," said Tim.

"A career in the arts isn't too easy an ambition," said Mark Callender.

"Oh, he won't be doing that for a living," said Zelda. "He's got the business, haven't you, Tim?"

Tim looked a little uncomfortable, and Charles decided that the time was right to change the subject. "Val—have you got a drink?" he asked, knowing full well that she had.

"Yes, thanks," she said, lifting her glass.

Vapid sort of woman, he always thought. Mousy hair, mousy clothes, mousy everything, really. Why Max, who had always been able to have any woman he chose, should have married Val, had always escaped Charles. It wasn't even as if she had been pregnant, which was the usual reason for men like Max marrying anyone.

"Do you know Tim? Tim, this is Max's wife, Val."

"Valerie," she said, shaking hands with Tim.

"Val's doing A-levels at night classes," said Charles.

"Oh? Which subjects?" Tim sat down, and the awkward moment passed, as Zelda turned back to badger poor Mark, and Val bored Tim.

Of course, Max wasn't faithful to her. Charles knew that he had come to Stansfield because he'd got himself involved with the girl who worked for him, and wanted out. He had even met her briefly on their most recent visit to the Scotts, when he had called in at Max's office, partly to see him, and partly to see this girl that he was trying to get away from. Once he had got Max alone, he had asked what had happened to the girl he had told him about, and Max had said that that *was* the girl.

It hadn't crossed Charles's mind that that could be the one he meant. She was no more than a child, for God's sake. Charles had told him in no uncertain terms what he thought of that; Max had mollified him a little by explaining that he wanted to leave *before* he did anything he might regret. At least he hadn't slept with her. But the idea of being tempted by a girl of barely seventeen—well, really. There was a limit. Max was over twice her age.

182

Max was in the kitchen, helping Gerry with the starters, and Tim had drifted off to join Lucy Callender, who was looking at Charles's collection of nineteenth-century political cartoons.

Charles didn't seem to have much option but to talk to Val, a pastime which could not, in his opinion, be underrated. He was heartily relieved when the starters made their appearance, and they could all sit down.

That had taken some thought; he had ended up with himself at one end of the table and Gerry at the other. Down one side, he had Lucy, Max (in the hope that he had more sense than to seduce a prospective MP's wife), and Zelda, and down the other Tim and Val and Mark. Though Mark had Val beside him, he was more likely to talk across the table, and would have Zelda's challenge tempered by his wife's support. He'd hardly have to talk to Val at all. Tim could get lumbered with that.

The food was delicious, he had pushed the boat out with the wine, and everyone did really seem to be enjoying themselves; Mark seemed to like sparking off Zelda, which was good, and while Max had rather captivated Lucy, the Callenders would be going away again at least until the election, and very probably for good, if the electorate of Stansfield ran true to form. Even Val became better company with a few glasses of wine inside her; he really had created exactly the sort of evening he had in mind.

If Mark *did* get in, Charles would have done himself a good turn, he was sure. And he was right; he did stand the ghost of a chance. He could scrape home, just. The mood was swinging right, boundary changes had brought in the farmers and the hunting set, and their solid Tory vote. Perhaps Charles would vote for him after all. He was a good man. And he had a point about the unions.

Judy pressed her cold cheek against Michael's, and asked him about Brussels as they walked through the airport car park, battling against the cold wind.

He had done pretty well, he thought. A number of people were interested. Michael sold computers, or at least that was how Judy described his job. He said it was more complex than that; he sold computer systems to offices and factories and airlines. And he believed that he might have made a sale in Brussels. He put his suitcases in the boot, and they kissed again in the car.

"You're not still nervous," he said, smiling at her as he released her.

She was petrified, and had been ever since Michael had suggested a weekend with his parents. She had put it off for months, pleading shift-work, overtime, anything she could think of. But the wedding was on the twenty-first, and she couldn't put the visit off any longer. The extension of the trip to Brussels, necessitated by his belief that he could pull off the sale if he stayed another week, had at least cut the weekend down to just some of Saturday and some of Sunday. She wasn't nervous; she was scared stiff. She said as much.

"They'll like you," he said. "They're bound to like you."

She started the car after a couple of tries, and headed for the motorway, and the north. Lloyd laughed at her car, but it could produce a fair turn of speed once its engine warmed up, and it was altogether too efficient for her liking at getting them to Nottingham. There were no hold-ups, no traffic jams, no roadworks. None of the delays you could always count on, and she enjoyed driving fast too much to pass up the opportunity on a perfect day for it.

The traffic lights in the city itself seemed positively to bow politely and turn green as she approached. Nothing was going to delay it, nothing was going to prevent it. She was going to meet Michael's parents.

The house was in a terrace on a road so steep that it nearly needed steps; Michael's father came out as soon as they drew up, and opened her door.

"You'll want to leave that in gear, ducks," he advised her. She did.

Michael's father was an older, not so slim version of Michael. He took Michael's case and her weekend bag as he shepherded them towards the door. "We'll have the introductions once we're in out of the cold, ducks," he said.

Michael stood aside to let her go in first. She wished he hadn't; she positively sidled into the small entrance hall, and a plump, dark woman came out of one of the doors.

"Mum—this is Judy Russell," said Michael.

"Nice to meet you, Judy," she said, smiling as though her life depended on it.

Judy smiled back. "How do you do . . . Mrs. Hill," she said.

"Oh, none of that! You call me mum."

Judy could never have called her mum, not in a million years. Anything less like her own city-dwelling, fashion-conscious mother wouldn't have been of the same species.

"Well, you've found yourself a lovely girl in the big city, Michael," said his father. "I'll take these upstairs—you go in and get a warm."

Judy once again had to lead the way into a small sitting room with a coal fire burning. That was nice, she told herself. Cosy. They were nice. Welcoming.

"Well, Judy. I expect you could do with a cuppa."

Judy smiled her agreement, and wondered if she could smoke. She looked round at the gleaming tables, at the hearth, at the mantelpiece. The only possible ashtray she could see had a flamenco dancer on it, and it seemed to be an ornament. No smoking. She ought to be offering to help. She did.

"Oh, no," said Mrs. Hill. "But come and talk to me."

Michael's father came back as she went into the kitchen, and all four of them found themselves in there, watching Mrs. Hill make tea.

"So, Judy," said Mr. Hill. "Michael tells us you're a police-woman."

"Well," said Judy, "they call us women police officers these days, but . . . yes, I am."

Mrs. Hill poured the tea into china cups which were laid out on a tray with biscuits on a doily-covered plate. "You must have to deal with all sorts," she said.

"Yes," said Judy. "There's a lot of variety."

"Still," said Mrs. Hill comfortably, carrying the tray through to the living room. "You won't have to do it much longer, will you? You and Michael will be married soon."

Judy followed her through, the two men having stepped aside. "Er . . . well, I'm hoping to transfer to Nottingham CID," she said. "It depends how well I do on the detective course."

They all sat down; Mr. Hill in his chair, Mrs. Hill in hers, Michael on the sofa beside her.

"Oh," said Mrs. Hill.

"So what would you be doing then, ducks?" asked Mr. Hill.

She looked at him. "Investigating crimes," she said, a little

185

weakly. What did he suppose she would be doing? Composing symphonies?

"He means would you be in an office," interpreted Mrs. Hill. "Instead of on the beat."

"I . . . well, yes. I mean, I'd be in the CID room. But mostly I'd be out. Asking questions—interviewing people. Door to door—that sort of thing." She smiled. "They call it legwork," she said. "I think detective constables do most of it."

Mr. Hill looked at her legs.

Mrs. Hill raised her eyebrows, and Mr. Hill stopped looking at her legs. "Ah," he said. "You've got yourself a career woman, Michael. Good for you, ducks," he said approvingly to her.

"Oh, I wouldn't say I was . . ." said Judy.

"At least she won't have to wear the uniform," was Michael's sole contribution to the conversation.

They had a meal at about six o'clock. It was probably the most delicious meal Judy had ever had, and she made a mental note to tell Michael that there was no way she would measure up in the cooking department. She managed not to say it in front of his mother who she was certain would have insisted on lessons. Later, Michael's father suggested the pub; Mrs. Hill wouldn't be joining them because she wanted to see something on television.

"Oh—a friend of mine at work has just bought one of these video tape-recorders," Judy said.

"Oh, yes?" said Mrs. Hill.

"You can record things when you're out," said Judy. "They're very expensive, but he thinks the price will come down. He records old films—he's very fond of . . ." She tailed off. She was talking about Lloyd, of all people. She felt herself colour slightly. Oh, God, get me out of here, she thought.

"Nice," said Mrs. Hill, encouragingly.

She had a cigarette in the pub; Mr. Hill on his own wasn't just as daunting as both of them together. When Mr. Hill excused himself to go and see a man about a dog, as he put it, Michael looked at her seriously. "You . . . you do like them, don't you?" he asked.

She nodded. In truth, there was nothing not to like, really. She just felt like a creature from Mars, that was all. And she didn't want to tell Michael that. They left the pub, arriving back at the house at ten. By half-past, Mr. Hill was making time for bed noises. Judy was heartily relieved.

"Oh, I haven't shown you your room," said Mrs. Hill.

Judy looked at Michael. Presumably he knew where his room was; surely this wasn't going to be what she thought it was going to be? They both followed Mrs. Hill upstairs, and she opened the door to a little room with pretty wallpaper and matching bedspread. "This is yours," she said pointedly. "Michael's across the landing, and Mr. Hill and I are next door."

Judy managed a smile. "It's lovely," she said.

"I think you'll have everything you need," she said, and stepped back out of the doorway. "And I expect you two will want to say goodnight," she said, starting downstairs. "We'll be up in ten minutes or so," she warned them coquettishly.

Judy waited until the downstairs door had closed. "You haven't told them we *live* together?" she said.

"Well . . . no." Michael steered her into the little room and closed the door. "They're old-fashioned," he said. "They wouldn't understand. They'd think you were no better than you should be."

"Oh, Michael! I haven't seen you for a month!"

"I know," he said, putting his arms round her. "I'm sorry."

"It's all right," she said. "Let's not waste the ten minutes." She kissed him, and smiled.

"Are you angry with me?" he asked.

She shook her head. She wouldn't have been able to tell them either, she was sure.

"Engaged couples are obviously allowed a ten-minute heavy-petting session," he said, and they both giggled.

"They will let us sleep together when we're properly married, will they?" she asked.

Too soon, they heard the Hills make their way upstairs, and drew apart.

"Goodnight," Michael said, with a final kiss, and opened the door. "Goodnight, mum—dad."

"Goodnight, Judy," called Mrs. Hill.

"Goodnight Mrs. Hill," she called back.

"Night, ducks," said Mr. Hill.

"Goodnight, Mr. Hill."

They sounded like that bloody family on the television; Judy closed the door, and looked round the room. Mrs. Hill had gone to a lot of trouble. But she wanted Michael. She wanted her mother. She wanted her teddy bear. She wanted a cigarette. She wanted to go home.

She refused to allow herself to think of what she really wanted.

Ray was dead.

Anna really hadn't asked questions on Ray's visits to her; Victor wasn't someone she had any intention of crossing. He had believed her, in the end. But Ray had told her what he was doing for Victor, and had hinted that that wouldn't be all. He had always been like that; she could have told Victor that it was a mistake to use Ray for anything that he wanted kept discreet, but she had been afraid that that might have been regarded as failing to mind her own business.

And now Ray was dead. Suicide, they said, and maybe he had killed himself. She hoped he had. Because in the end, Victor had made her tell him everything that Ray had said to her, not letting her move until she had.

That had been the night when Victor had finally caught his stepdaughter in, which hadn't been easy. Wherever Catherine had been spending her evenings for the previous couple of months, it hadn't been in her bedsit. But Victor had stayed with Anna for hours, making certain that she had dredged up every syllable that Ray Wilkes had uttered, and then he'd spent more time advising her that if she warned Ray that Victor knew he had been shooting his mouth off, she would deeply regret it. She hadn't warned Ray.

He had been in the middle of this menacing advice when they had heard Catherine going in to her bedsit, and she had been released. She could hardly stand up by that time, having been sitting for hours on her knees at the cupboard, terrified that Victor was going to do to her what he'd done to Bannister. Instead, he'd paid her for the time she'd lost, and told her that she had done the right thing. Then he had seen his stepdaughter briefly, and Catherine had moved out next day. Back home to her mother, mission accomplished. Anna hadn't seen Victor since.

It was mid-morning when she heard the knock at the door; she felt the old, familiar stab of fear, back now that it wasn't going to be Victor. It was probably a meter-reader or a Jehovah's witness come to save her, but it might not be. Her heart was beating too fast as she opened the door on the chain; she would never forget Dave Bannister's visit, and she would never again open a door incautiously, not for as long as she lived. Victor had bought her a tougher chain; hers had given way too easily when he had broken in, he'd said.

She peered out, surprised and relieved to discover that it was indeed Victor; she smiled, leading him in to the sitting room. Victor was the only man who had ever seen her sitting room, if you didn't count Bannister. She flopped down on the sofa, smiling up at him. What had happened to Bannister, and what had happened to Ray Wilkes was pushed firmly to the back of her mind; Victor was here again, and she felt safe with him now, because she hadn't let him down. She had visited his friend in his hotel room; she was certain she had given satisfaction. Perhaps he had another job for her.

But not this time. This time, she was in real trouble, worse even than the business about Ray. She had tried to give Victor's story a happy ending, but that hadn't happened; Victor had seen Catherine, but she had rejected any idea of going home. She had moved out, not to rejoin her mother, but in order to disappear again, and Anna hadn't done anything to prevent it.

"I gave you a number to ring," he said, standing over her, one hand on the arm of the sofa, the other on the back, preventing her from getting up.

"I thought she'd gone home," she said, drawing her legs up underneath her, getting as far into the corner of the sofa as she could, as far away from him as she could.

"I don't expect you to think. I expect you to do exactly what I tell you to do. I could have had someone here before she'd finished getting her stuff out of the room," he said. "Someone who could have seen where she was going. And now it's going to take more money and more time, thanks to you."

"I didn't do it on purpose!" she cried, ready to argue her case in the desperate hope that that would save her from retribution. "I thought you'd persuaded her, I thought—"

"Be quiet! I have no interest in what you thought—you've let me down badly, Annabel."

He moved one hand, and she shrank away from him, an arm automatically shielding her head as she turned her face away, burying it in the sofa. "Don't hurt me!" she cried, her eyes tight shut.

"I'm not going to hurt you," he said.

She lowered her arm and looked round slowly, fearfully, as he still stood over her.

Victor stepped back. "I have no intention of hurting you," he said. "Now or ever. You're not worth the energy."

The relief made her feel weak. And the promise made her feel safe again, despite the reason given for it. But she had to sit there miserably listening to what he thought of her, of how he should have known better than to trust a cheap whore, of what folly it had been to give money to someone with the morals of an alleycat and expect her to take responsibility in return. His quiet voice poured out all the contempt that he felt for her, all the insults that she had had to put up with from other men. She could ignore it when it came from them, but not from Victor. She began to cry.

"Tears don't work with me, Annabel," he said.

"My name's Anna," she said defiantly through the tears, almost to herself.

He sat down beside her. "Is it?" he said. "Do you have another name?"

She wiped the tears with her hand. "Worthing," she said, not looking at him.

"Well, cry if you like, but a cheap whore is what you are, Anna Worthing. And you make yourself prey to every malcontent, every sexual deviant, every social inadequate who cares to come knocking at your door. You leave yourself wide open to rape and assault and battery—but why not? It's all you're good for, isn't it?"

She shook her head.

"Isn't it? You hire out your body to men to do what they want with it. You have one talent, Anna Worthing. Just one. But that tin box isn't going to buy you out of the gutter, because that's where you belong." He stood up. "I'm going abroad very soon," he said. "I advise you to watch that temper—I won't be around to rescue you from the next Bannister who comes calling."

He was leaving. She no sooner felt safe again than he was leaving. Leaving her to the sexual deviants and Bannisters to do with as they pleased.

"You can come with me."

She turned her head and stared up at him.

"You'll have the use of a flat, a car, clothes, whatever you need—whatever you want, within reason. You will have my protection, and my word that I won't hurt you, and I won't allow anyone else to hurt you. In return you'll do exactly what I tell you to do—whatever I tell you to do, whenever and wherever I tell you to do it. You won't ask questions, you won't talk out of turn, and above all, you won't think. You will do as you are told." He bent down towards her. "And you will never, never let me down again," he said.

"What?" She was blinking at him, stupefied.

"At the moment, you rent yourself out by the hour. I'm simply offering to buy you outright. You'll still be a whore, but you won't be a cheap one. It's your decision, but you would be wise to accept."

She'd had worse offers. None stranger, but a great many worse.

"You will also do anything else I tell you to do," he said. "One of these will be to receive phone-calls and reports from private investigators—once they've found Catherine again. I want to be able to keep her mother informed of what she's doing, and I don't want her to know how I'm doing it. She thinks Catherine and I have reached a truce, and I don't want her finding out that it isn't really like that."

He really couldn't bear the idea that a seventeen-year-old girl was doing what the police and business rivals had been unable to do. Giving him the runaround. But Anna wondered what Catherine's mother had done to her that she was prepared to hurt her like that.

No longer in fear of a violent response, prepared to be given another hurtful character assessment, she asked him why Catherine had run away, and he told her. Because she had found him with someone like her, in essence. Anna couldn't imagine thinking highly enough of her own father to care what some woman was doing to him, but Catherine had left home over her stepfather. Silly bitch. But then she got a little more, and she began to realize just what Victor had been going through. If you asked Anna, he and his wife were better off without the neurotic Catherine. Victor did not, of course, ask Anna, and Anna wouldn't have said that if he had.

But he was afraid for Catherine, he said. Afraid that his enemies would use her to get at him. He had to find her again. Keep an eye on her. Her mother would never forgive him if anything happened to Catherine. That's why he had to have people watching her.

Anna felt awful. It had taken him almost a year to find her, and three months after that just to see her; now she had let her disappear again. It had been an honest mistake, but it had been a bad one. She hadn't liked hearing all those things Victor had called her, but she understood. And instead of ditching her, Victor was offering her a new life. She had to push a lot of disturbing things to the back of her mind, but she had had to do that all along with Victor. And he had befriended her when she had needed a friend more than she had done in all her life.

She would go to Holland with him.

Judy had got married today.

Lloyd tried to concentrate on the film, but in truth it was a touch boring, and his mind kept wandering. He was in the lecture-room annexe of the local College of Technology, in which the Film Society held its monthly showing of esoteric and uncommercial films.

He could see why this one was uncommercial. In truth, he wasn't a film-society type; he had joined mainly to have somewhere to go at least one evening a week that would get him out of the house. He had tried persuading Barbara to come with him, but they never went anywhere together now; it wouldn't be impossible to get a baby-sitter, but Barbara chose to pretend that it was. He'd tried volunteering to be the one who stayed in, but she didn't want to go anywhere on her own. She didn't seem to want his company either, so he was the one who went out.

The new house was a considerable improvement on the old one, but she didn't seem to have made much of an effort to get to know any of the neighbours. She didn't want to stay in London, she said. She was missing Stansfield, still, after all these years. All her friends were there. She could go out on her own in Stansfield. Not in London. The friends she had made here were all too far away now since the move. And that was true, he supposed. Perhaps he should think about going back to

Stansfield. Perhaps that was what they needed; if Barbara was happy, perhaps he would be too.

They hadn't been invited to the wedding; he had half expected that they might be, because he had met Judy's father twice since the engagement party; by accident the first time, and by arrangement the second, when John Russell, who determinedly avoided being known as Jack, had suggested that he might like to join him in a day's fishing.

Lloyd was no fisherman, but he had got on well with John Russell, and they had ended the day in a pub, sampling malt whiskies, at Lloyd's suggestion. John had told him the date of the wedding; Lloyd had hoped that that didn't mean he and Barbara were invited, and as it turned out, they hadn't been. In fact, Lloyd had the impression that her father knew the situation; perhaps Judy had confided in him, and perhaps the fishing expedition had been a gentle warning-off. Or perhaps he was just curious to see what sort of man his daughter had fallen for, that she was prepared to marry someone else altogether to avoid the temptation.

Lloyd had got tickets for the Cup Final; he returned the favour by asking Judy's father if he would like to go, and they had another date to look forward to. He sighed. He was having a great deal more success with her father than he had ever had with her. He hoped her father knew that.

The lights went up; bearded people with frameless spectacles started discussing what they had just seen. Paper cups of tea were included in the price of the membership; Lloyd went to get one, not because he wanted one, but because he didn't want to run the risk of being called upon to have an in-depth discussion on a film he really hadn't been watching.

Biscuits, too, he noticed. He reached out for the last Penguin, and his hand collided with that of someone else on a similar quest. He smiled at the girl. "You have it," he said.

"Oh, I think you saw it first," she said.

"No, no," he said. "You take it. I can't say I have any real desire for a Penguin biscuit. I was just taking it because it was there, really."

She laughed. "So was I," she said. "Shall we leave it for someone who really needs it?"

He laughed too.

"Well," she said. "What did you think?" She nodded her head towards the blank screen.

Oh, God. Lloyd had to own up. "I'm afraid I stopped watching after about half an hour," he said. "I may even have dropped off."

"Oh, good! I thought I was the only one. To be quite honest," she said, "I only joined because I thought I might get to know people." She looked round a little warily. "I'm not really sure I want to," she said.

"Oh, I hope that doesn't extend to me," he said. "Are you new to the area too?"

"Yes. Are you?"

"We moved here about three months ago," he said. "I thought I was interested in films," he added. "But I think I probably like what you might call movies, rather than films." He sipped his tea, which had achieved a tastelessness unrivalled even by water.

"What do you do?" she asked.

"Policeman," he said.

"Oh, that's interesting," she said. "Can I ask what sort?"

"Detective Inspector," he said, still quite proud of the rank. "And you?"

"I'm a violinist," she said.

Lloyd's eyebrows rose. He had expected, male chauvinist and untutored backwoods Welshman that he was, that she would say she was a secretary. "Are you really? It's my turn to ask what sort."

"Oh, I'm no virtuoso," she said. "Just a rank and file player. BBC Symphony Orchestra."

The lights flashed, and went down, and they looked at one another.

"There's no law says we have to watch the other one," Lloyd said.

"You should know."

"Would you . . . would you like to go for a drink, or a coffee or something?" he asked.

"Yes, please," she said.

Victor looked at Anna's wardrobe, and closed his eyes, shaking his head in disbelief.

"I don't want to take much of what I've got here," she said.

"Get your coat on. We're going shopping." He sighed. "I take it you have some idea of how normal people dress?"

"Yes," she said, insulted. "I've got one or two good things. I wore this to that hotel."

She reached in and took out an outfit that wasn't at all in bad taste, but it was cheap; it had market stall written all over it.

"All right," he said. "Put that on. You can choose what clothes you want, but if I don't like them, you don't get them. Understood?"

She smiled. "Fine," she said, and went into the other room.

He looked round the little flat in which she no longer entertained customers, and could see why she had taken him up on his offer. Most of the stuff was the landlord's, anyway, and what little was hers had seen much better days, doubtless in someone else's possession. He hadn't been sure, despite the inducements on offer, that she had been going to accept. Anna was a great deal brighter than most of the people he had to deal with, and he had thought that she might kick against the idea of serfdom, which was, of course, what it was.

But Anna loathed the life she had been leading. Strange men hour after hour, night after night, any one of whom might turn nasty. People like Bannister taking liberties with her, rousing the quick temper that got her into trouble if she wasn't careful, and had got her into trouble with Holyoak himself more than once. But he could subdue her quickly enough; if she was coming to Holland, she had to be put to good use, and the intelligence that produced the temper would be working for him. His business associate had been more than happy with her; Victor could teach her to look and sound expensive, which would add to her value.

"The agency has located Catherine," he told her when she came out, looking presentable at last.

"Oh, good," she said, with very real relief. She had been in real trouble about that, and she knew it. Had it been possible, Victor would have abandoned the idea of taking her with him, because of that lapse. But what had been an option had become a necessity, and Victor had always made virtues out of necessities. He would with Anna; she would be very careful not to let him down again.

Anna lived and had always lived in a world where violence lurked round every corner, and she wanted out. He was offering her a life with a veneer finish of glamour, and protection from everyone but him. All she had to do to ensure that he wasn't a threat was what she was told.

He and Anna got into the car; the driver pulled smoothly away from the kerb, and the car wound its way through the rundown streets, through more popular territory, with trees and burglar alarms, and out into the busy traffic, heading towards the sorts of shops that Anna had only ever dreamed about. Victor wanted to be certain of Anna's loyalty, and offering her a total contrast from her previous existence was the best way to be certain.

She took a cigarette from her bag; Victor plucked it from her fingers, wound down the window, and threw it out. "When you go to Holland, it will be a whole new life," he said. "For a start, no swearing—and no smoking."

"I couldn't survive without cigarettes," she said, dipping into the packet for another.

"Stop the car," he said quietly, and the car stopped immediately, in the middle of the street. Car horns sounded, a taxi driver gesticulated with one hand while pumping the horn with the other. Victor just looked at Anna, while the cacophony grew louder. He let the noise outside grow as her eyes widened with apprehension; he didn't speak.

The noise was deafening as the traffic ground to a halt for the length of the street; two policemen were crossing the road through the immobile vehicles, heading for the Daimler. Anna looked at the cigarettes, and then at him. She handed them to him, and he dropped them out of the window.

"OK," he told the driver, and the car moved off again just as the police were arriving. The taxi driver overtook them, shouting obscenities. Victor closed the window, and settled back.

He had got Bannister to do what he wanted by the use of violence, and the threat of even greater violence to come if he didn't do as he was told. But that would be no good with Anna; he had known that from the moment he had threatened her over the business about Wilkes. Bannister wasn't frightened of pain; he had a quite proper respect for it which Victor had considerably reinforced. But violence appalled Anna; it frightened her much too much, and frightened people couldn't function properly.

The threat of losing the security he was offering, the protection, the *freedom* from fear—that was what he had realized would work with her. He had given her a brief taste of that freedom over the last few weeks, and she desperately wanted to hang on to it. The alternative was known, and hated, and she would do anything to avoid it. The idea of going back to it thoroughly alarmed her; it didn't render her witless.

By the time he deposited her back at the flat, he was the possessor of several hundreds of pounds' worth of women's clothing, which would be packed up and sent ahead.

"Wear that when we travel," he said, pointing to what she was wearing.

She nodded.

"And hang on to it," he said. "Because if you ever let me down again, you'll need it."

Anna understood the position.

"That was really good," said Max, as he put his knife and fork neatly together, and picked up the ice-cold Coke that Zelda had produced for him to wash down his meal. He didn't really like fizzy soft drinks any more than he liked alcohol, but he wouldn't have dreamed of refusing.

He had been working for Zelda for almost three months now; he had never worked for a woman, and so far, he had found it just as pleasant as any of the other things he did with women. She was friendly and open, if she needed advice she asked for it, and if she thought he needed advice, she gave it. It was a close working relationship; it had been Jimmy who had done what he was doing, and they had run the business together. Now she was running it with Max instead, but the closeness was still there.

He smiled. "And it was really good of you to invite me," he said. "Or I'd have had to go hungry again."

She looked at him with not a little scepticism. "Are you really incapable of making yourself a meal, Max?" she asked.

He drank some Coke, and wiped away the froth. "Well—I could produce something," he said. "But if I sound plaintive enough other people make much nicer things for me." He grinned. "It was Geraldine who was feeding me on evening-class nights," he said. "But she's got to do all his evening surgeries now that Charles is on the campaign trail."

Zelda laughed, and got up from the table. "Charles campaigning for the Conservatives," she said. "Whatever next? I don't think Geraldine will ever forgive him." She took away the plates. "It's nice to have someone to cook for again," she said as she went into the kitchen. "Even if Charles does think I killed Jimmy," she added, her voice suddenly light and tearful.

Max got up and followed her into the kitchen. "I'm sure he thinks nothing of the sort," he said.

"He said his diet killed him," she said. "It's just food. Ordinary food. Meat and potatoes. If you've been working all day, you need something substantial—" She blinked quickly.

"Hey, come on," said Max, taking the plates from her and putting them down. "Come and sit down. You mustn't let Charles upset you—he's just got a bee in his bonnet about this fitness thing."

He led her into the sitting room, and sat with her on the sofa. "Now," he said. "Charles would be horrified if he thought he'd made you think that. You know he would."

"What else am I supposed to think? He goes on about diet and fatty foods killing Jimmy—I'm the one who gave him them!"

"No," said Max. "He just thinks that people should perhaps look at the way they treat their bodies, that's all. Lack of exercise, smoking, working too hard—it's not just diet."

"I always gave him the best of everything," she said.

"I'm sure you did. And I don't think Charles would be talking about what he ate at home," he added. "He'd be talking about grabbing hamburgers and stuff like that while he was working."

"Yes," she said, her voice small. "He did do that. He'd stay at work long after I'd left. And then he'd come home and say he'd eaten."

"Well, there you are," Max said. "That's the sort of thing he means. Poor Charles—he'd hate to think he'd made you feel responsible."

She gave him a little smile. "Oh, Max, I am sorry," she said. "Going on about Jimmy. It's just that—I suppose it was just ... well, having you here. It just ... reminded me, I suppose."

"Would you rather I went?" asked Max.

"Oh, no." Her hand covered his. "No. Please—I'd like you to stay." And she looked at him.

He knew that look. He wasn't sure what it was he did to women. It really wasn't at all calculated, though people like Charles thought it had to be, and didn't believe him when he protested his innocence. It seemed to Max that when he was between extra-marital attachments, he must have some sort of aura or something that lent him desirability. He had no idea what it was, but he was very glad of it. And perhaps he could stop thinking about Catherine.

She had phoned him at work, saying that she had to talk to him. He hadn't the heart, or the willpower, to refuse to see her, and his valiant attempts to forget her had been sabotaged. He was seeing her on Thursday, and had been thinking of nothing else since she had called. Perhaps Zelda would help; she was lonely, missing Jimmy. She needed someone too.

He was kissing her, reaching for her as naturally and as casually as other men might reach for a drink or a cigar. The kiss was returned, and, of course, it didn't stop there.

And now, at her suggestion, they were in bed. But the shift of scene from the clothed excitement of the sitting room to the clinical nakedness of the bedroom had made Zelda uncomfortable; Max could see that. She was going to go through with it, of course, but that wasn't Max's style at all. She should enjoy it as much as he did, or in his opinion it was a waste of one of the world's great pleasures, and better abandoned.

He had learned very early on that quick sexual gratification was easily come by, like Jimmy's hamburgers. Like them, it satisfied the appetite without fuss. Junk sex. And it could be fun now and again, but only with a woman who was as ready and eager as he was, or half the enjoyment was lost. Zelda had thought that she was that eager, but she had been wrong. She needed time to relax, if she was to get anything out of it. And bringing that relaxation about was all part of the sheer fun.

"There's no hurry," he said, sitting up, pulling her up into his arms, holding her close to him, talking to her as they gently explored the nakedness that had made her suddenly self-conscious.

Good sex was, he reflected, a three-course meal. The starter should be light and delicious and sharpen your appetite for the main course; it was an integral part of the meal. It shouldn't be

199

hurried, it shouldn't be skipped, and it shouldn't be snatched away from one diner because the other was ready to move on. To Max, an uninhibited partner was a prerequisite, and if that took time to achieve, it was time well and enjoyably spent. And it brought ample rewards.

"Am I the first since Jimmy died?" Max was a believer in getting awkward subjects out into the open.

"Of course you are!" she said. "He's not been dead a year. I feel so guilty, Max."

"No," he said soothingly, stroking her hair. "No. You mustn't. You have every right to live your life. You are a gorgeous woman, Zelda, and men are going to want you."

She smiled. "I'll bet you really do say that to all the girls," she said.

"I do. All women are gorgeous."

"Is that a compliment?"

"No. It's a fact."

She looked at him, shaking her head. "I can't believe I'm doing this," she said. "This is not how I intended spending the evening—if you could bottle it, you'd be a multi-millionaire, Max."

He knew that. But if he didn't know what it was he did, he could hardly pass on his secret. "I like women," he suggested.

She smiled. "So I've heard."

"Not just their anatomy," he protested. "Though that is highly pleasurable." His hands lightly caressed the anatomy that was currently giving him considerable pleasure. "But if you go into a pub full of men, they're talking about football. Or cars. Or share prices. Or politics. Go into a room full of women," he said, "and do you know what they're talking about?"

"No," she said. "I've never been in a room full of women, thank God."

"People."

"Is that a dig at me?"

"No! Women are more interested in people than they are in things. And that makes me more interested in women than men. Perhaps that's what does it." He shrugged. "It's either that or my devastating looks, my witty and urbane conversation, and the twin-hulled racing yacht at Cannes."

She smiled. "But don't you feel guilty about Valerie?" she asked.

"There's no point in my feeling guilty," he said. "I'm going to do it anyway, so I just enjoy the moment. If guilt is in order, I'll sort that out later."

"Why does someone like you marry?" she asked.

"I'm no good at being alone. Besides, Valerie's gorgeous too."

That was another thing that Charles couldn't understand, or believe. That Max found his wife every bit as pleasurable as any other woman. Valerie found Charles pretentious and boring; Charles, though he had never said so, found Valerie unglamorous and boring. Max enjoyed her cooking and her company and took considerable pleasure in her body; he was very aware of his luck in having found anyone who would put up with him, however grudgingly. But he had only ever fallen in love once, and it wasn't with Valerie; her accommodation of his failings had been under severe strain as a result. She knew that the situation to which she had grown accustomed had changed; she knew that Max had found something more than physical pleasure this time. And that was hurting her, which really did make him feel guilty. And now he'd agreed to see Catherine again, and he had to make a final break with her, once and for all.

So he concentrated on Zelda, who had relaxed enough by now to be doing her best to take his mind off Catherine, despite the guilt which she had no reason to feel.

"People always feel guilty about physical pleasure," he said. "And it's so silly. You get the worst of both worlds. You don't get to feel self-righteous, and you don't enjoy the very thing you want to enjoy."

He made her laugh. Laughter was important; no one should take this Heaven-sent pastime so seriously that they couldn't laugh about it. And with the laughter, what was left of the tension left her, and his patience was liberally rewarded.

And this was the dessert, he thought, as she laid her head drowsily on his chest, and he sneaked a practised look at his watch. He really didn't understand why all men didn't use this form of relaxation in preference to toxic substances which ruined your health or your pocket or both. It was free, it was natural, it was delightful. The foreplay was exciting, the act

201

was exhilarating, the climax was intoxicating, the afterglow was enchanting. Women were a wonderful discovery that he had made in adolescence, and he had never looked back.

"Speaking of politics," she murmured. "Are you voting for Charles's chum?"

Max remembered vaguely a reference to politics being made during the preliminaries, and he smiled broadly. That was why they were delightful. One cigar must taste very much like another, one whisky very much like another. He couldn't disagree more with Kipling. He must have been of the junk-sex persuasion.

"I'm not registered here," he said. "I'm going back to Camberwell in the hope that my vote might still cancel out Charles's, in a round-about way."

"Are you a socialist?" Her eyes were closed.

"When it comes to putting crosses on ballot papers," he said. "I'm not what you would call a crusader."

She raised her head. "Is that the only reason you're going back to London?"

Was he that transparent? He shook his head, smiling. "Zelda—what have you been hearing about me?"

She sat up. "Charles ticks me off for gossiping," she said. "But he's no slouch himself." She looked at him. "You haven't really had an affair with a seventeen-year-old girl, have you?"

"Catherine and I worked together," he said.

"Charles seemed to think—"

"Charles is shocked because I find all women desirable," he said. "Even seventeen-year-olds."

"But you didn't—"

"No."

"Good," she said, and bent her head to kiss him. "I wouldn't want to know you if you'd seduced her and abandoned her, like Sir Jasper. But don't forget you've got to be at that creditors' meeting all Thursday."

"I'm not forgetting. I'm going to London in the evening. But I'll report back to you before I go." He accepted the kiss, and sighed deeply. "And now," he said, with real regret, "you are a particularly gorgeous woman, Zelda Driver, and I hope you'll let me come back again, but I have to go."

She released him. He was home just before Valerie, as always. She wasn't speaking to him.

"I'm sorry, but he's at a meeting in Barton all day today."

Catherine had only now found a phone-box that worked; she had gone through the pile of change that she had brought with her waiting for that stupid woman to find Max, and now . . .

The pips went; the dialling tone purred in her ear, and she slammed the phone back on the rest, tears pricking the backs of her eyes. She took a moment to compose herself before she left the box.

There was a café across the road; she side-stepped the traffic, and went in, offering her last pound-note for the cup of tea she had ordered, asking for the change in tenpenny pieces. She still had a ten-pound note; she hadn't broken into it. But it cost too much to ring at this time of day. All her tens would be gone in no time. She would have to wait until the afternoon rates.

She sat at the formica-topped table on which there was a long cigarette burn, and sipped tea from a Perspex cup. All day, she had said. Did that mean he wasn't going to be in the office at all? She had better not ring until late afternoon, in that case. He might be back by then. She didn't know if she could wait that long, and she didn't want to leave the vicinity of the one phone-box that she knew was actually working. It had taken considerable courage to ring Max in the first place, and that was only when she had acknowledged to herself that there was no other explanation, and precious little time left to decide what to do.

The first month she hadn't thought anything of it—she had always had trouble, and missing a month was quite usual. The second, she knew it had to be, but she wouldn't admit it to herself. She hadn't been to the doctor; she hadn't done anything. She had still hoped that it might all be a mistake, that if she didn't get it confirmed then it wouldn't be the case.

But then came the third month, and absolute certainty. And she had to tell Max; she didn't know what else to do. It wasn't fair. It wasn't *fair*. She had finally rung him at work, but she couldn't tell him on the phone. She had asked him to come, and he had said that he would. Then followed the hours of rehearsing, of trying to guess at his reaction, which varied in her imagination from towering anger to a shrug of the shoulders. Nothing to do with him; it was her problem. Oh, but Max wasn't like that, he wasn't. He'd do something. She didn't know what, but he'd do something.

And only today had she realized that in her panic at what was happening, and her relief at simply hearing Max's voice, she hadn't told him that she had moved. She had to get hold of him, and he wasn't there. Maybe this woman would tell her where the meeting was—maybe she could ring him there. Maybe she could . . .

"Are you all right, love?" Belatedly, the man wiped her table with a cloth that had wiped many others, and seemed never to have been washed in between times.

"Yes," she said.

She made the long trek back to her digs; she couldn't camp out by the phone-box. She had had a temporary job, and had paid her landlady until the end of this week. Which was tomorrow. But the job had finished last week, and she had no money other than the precious ten-pound note until she got her next unemployment benefit payment. She was alone. She was pregnant. She needed Max more than she had ever needed him, and he didn't know where she lived.

She tried again in the afternoon. Early—she couldn't put it off until later, though she should have done. She had known he wouldn't be there. She tried later. This time the girl said that he had come back, but that he had left now, and the office was closing.

Catherine went miserably back to her digs. But she had his home address and phone number from when he'd sent out cards to his clients, in case they needed to get in touch with him. She knew she shouldn't ring him at home, but she was desperate now. She rang from her landlady's phone, because she had no more change, and told her she would pay her for the call tomorrow, when she paid her next month's rent. Max would give her some money, if only she could see him. The phone rang out; Catherine held her breath.

"Stansfield 5690."

"Mrs. Scott?"

"Speaking."

"Is Max there, please?"

"No, I'm sorry," she said briskly. "Can I give him a message?"

He might not be home yet. Catherine crossed her fingers.

"It's Catherine Barnes, Mrs. Scott—I worked for Max in London."

"Oh, yes," she said.

"The thing is—I've been for an interview, and I gave them the reference Max gave me, but they want him to ring them."

"I see."

"The thing is," she said again. "I'd like to speak to him first—could you ask him to ring me when he comes in?"

"I think he's probably out for the evening," she said. "But I'll take your number. Hang on, I'll get a pen."

Catherine listened in anguish to the noises off as Mrs. Scott looked for a pen. She heard the doorbell ring, and prayed that it was Max. She heard her open the door, heard her say crossly that she had already had one of their lot round. Then she came back to the phone. "I'm sorry," she said. "I'm busy." And she hung up.

Catherine stared at the phone. Max had already left. He was on his way, and she couldn't get in touch with him. She didn't dare go back to the flat, not now. She didn't even know what time he would be there. She looked at the piece of paper that had become crumpled and sweaty in her hand as she had lied to Mrs. Scott.

Ten pounds. It cost ten pounds to get the train from London to Stansfield. She knew; she'd checked over and over again, and that was why she had quite literally hung on to it so grimly.

She was ten pounds and an hour away from Stansfield, and Max would go back there eventually.

He was about four, at a guess. He was red in the face, tears coursing down his cheeks, mouth open as he bawled his unhappiness to the world. Bannister knew how he felt, though his own feelings of being ill done to had all but gone.

He had gone to the doctor. He had told him and his inspector that he had fallen down some steps; they had both accepted that. He had been admitted to hospital, where they had said that he should have seen them months ago, and that there was internal damage which was permanent. The doctor advised him to seek less active employment, but he felt all right now. By the time he had got back to work, the business about Raymond Arthur Wilkes was history; the Warwickshire police had taken it over. The inquest on Wilkes had in fact returned an open verdict, but popular opinion said he'd committed suicide, and there was no further investigation into his death. The new government said that the police were going to get a pay rise, and he had met a girl who didn't mind that he was a policeman. It had got serious; he was even thinking of asking her to marry him.

It was early May, and spring was in the air; even in the grey city streets birds flew from eaves and gutters where unsuspected nests had been built, daffodils and crocuses were pushing up in the parks, and the tourists were taking photographs of him again.

He got down to be on the child's level, taking off his helmet. "Hello, sonny," he said. "Have you lost your mum?"

The child nodded and bawled at the same time.

"Do you know what she looks like?"

He nodded and bawled, but he hiccuped too.

Bannister smiled. "Well—shall we look for her?" he said. "Tell you what—shall I lift you up? Then you'll be taller than me, won't you? You can look from up there. I'm too small to see that far."

He unwound his six foot plus frame, and stood up, hoisting the child on to his shoulder, where he sat hiccuping solemnly, looking round at the crowds of shoppers.

"Can you see your mum?"

Hiccup.

"Shall we walk around a bit?" He took a few strides, but the bawling in his right ear began again, increasing to a pitch which threatened his tolerance level, and he stopped and walked back. "Is she in this shop?" he asked.

Hiccup.

"Here," he said, handing the child his helmet. "You wear this. Then you'll be a policeman, like me."

It came down to the tip of his nose, and he pushed it back, hiccuped, and smiled.

"There," he said. "Now you'll see her. Policemen see everything."

"Oh, thank God!"

He turned to see a girl of about his own age; the child scrambled from his shoulder to hers, the helmet jettisoned in the process.

"Mummy—I'm a pleeceman," he announced.

Bannister bent down to retrieve his helmet; when he straightened up, they had gone. "Don't mention it," he muttered to himself, and smiled. He liked kids. Maybe he should get married and have some of his own.

Yeah. He'd like that.

"It isn't a form of contraception, you know," said Geraldine, as Catherine Barnes looked away from her, down at her lap. At her baby. The baby she wanted to destroy. Max Scott's baby.

"I know," she whispered.

"And there are alternatives to termination."

The girl shook her head.

No. Well, it certainly wouldn't be in Max's interests for the police to find out that his girlfriend was three months' pregnant. Catherine had told the police that Max had been with her when Valerie died, and no one who knew Max thought for a moment that he had had anything to do with what had happened. But the police did, and that was presenting Geraldine with even more of a dilemma than usual in these circumstances.

Catherine's alibi had been a mixed blessing for Max; on the one hand, she was an apparently impartial witness, an ex-employee on whom he had paid a courtesy call at the time of the murder. As ever, Charles believed him. On the other hand, the police were, rightly, convinced that she and Max had had an affair, suspicious of her turning up when she did, and that made her a biased witness, and gave Max a motive. So they were trying hard to prove that there was something more between them, so far without success.

It didn't show yet; it would, very soon, unless Geraldine agreed to arrange for a termination. But she had to be very certain why she agreed; it couldn't be for expediency's sake. She would never normally agree to the termination of a healthy pregnancy this late—by the time she could get her in, she would be sixteen weeks gone. And low though Max had dropped in her esteem, she couldn't see him putting this little girl through something as traumatic as an abortion just to make his own life easier.

"Have you told Max you're pregnant?" she asked.

207

"No!" The girl looked up, her cheeks pink. "He mustn't know—you mustn't tell him. Please, you mustn't."

"I'm your doctor, Catherine. I can't and won't tell anyone at all. But you should tell him."

"No. I can't. Not now. I was going to, but—no. Not now that all this has happened—he's got too much to worry about as it is. I can't tell him."

"Have you talked to anyone?"

"Mrs. Driver. I was sick yesterday morning, and she . . . well, she guessed. She's promised not to tell Max. She says I can have a job at her place if I want. And she'll tell him she's sent me on a word-processor course, if you—"

Zelda had promised not to tell Max. Had she promised not to tell anyone else, though? That was the question. But even Zelda wouldn't tell anyone, not this time. She was too shocked at Max's behaviour. More shocked than Geraldine, come to that. But if the police discovered that Catherine was pregnant, Max's motive would be exposed, as far as they were concerned. And Zelda wouldn't let that happen, not even now.

Why everyone was so concerned with the amoral Max, even the poor little girl who sat in her surgery, was beyond Geraldine, but they all were. And the facts were that he was being hauled in for questioning every day by the police, that they were looking for the slightest shred of evidence against him, that he and Valerie had had a row that evening, loud enough for the neighbours to hear, and that Valerie had finally tired of his infidelity, and had been saying so, loud and clear to anyone who would listen, for a month before her death.

Max was in deep, deep trouble. The child was seventeen years old, she didn't have family in this country, and she would clearly suffer acute mental stress if she was forced to have the baby. She had given Max an alibi; her pregnancy would make it suspect, and anything that happened to Max as a result would hurt her immeasurably.

"All right," she said. "But you must understand that it's something you have to live with. Having the baby may seem impossible to you now, but terminating the pregnancy can have considerable repercussions for the mother."

It was a speech she always made, when she was unable to see an alternative to termination. Women sometimes went into it with their eyes shut, thinking that a simple operation would end all their problems, only to find that they were just beginning. Catherine had to know about the possible psychological effects; she had to know what she was letting herself in for. But even Geraldine could see that it was probably preferable to what she would be letting herself in for if she had the baby.

It hurt her more than she could say, but there really was no alternative.

There was something irritating her, something that didn't quite make sense about Catherine's story. If she had intended telling Max about the baby, why hadn't she, if she was supposed to have been with him the night before? She pushed the thought that the alibi might be false to the back of her mind, because it made even less sense to imagine that Max had killed Valerie.

But then nothing made sense. She was about to make it possible to destroy the one thing she had used every means at her disposal to create. And where was the sense in that?

CHAPTER NINE

Now: Friday, 3 April, A.M. . . .

BANNISTER WATCHED AS JUDY HILL OPENED HER NOTE-book. He remembered what a stickler she had been for getting her notebook written up. Everyone else's had always been days behind, but not Judy's. It was eight o'clock in the morning; she was in early to deal with him. He smiled.

"You're in trouble," she said. "I should try taking it seriously if I were you."

He knew he was in trouble. His smile grew broader. He had spent a night in an uncomfortable cell, and he hadn't slept a wink for worrying about what Jackie thought, what was going to happen. There was no way he was showing Judy that he was worried.

He had told them that he was home watching television when they had asked him to account for his whereabouts on Wednesday night; they had arrested him on suspicion of aggravated burglary, so they must think they had some sort of evidence. It was clearly a holding charge, while they sorted out what had really happened.

Judy pushed a large black and white photograph across the table. "Do you still insist that you were at home with your wife?" she asked. "The date and time are along the bottom."

He looked at the computer-generated photograph of his beat-up old van, its number plate in sharp enough focus to be read, and sighed. He'd forgotten that his brief visit to the factory would have been recorded for posterity. He smiled again, and shook his head.

"So where were you?"

She hadn't changed much. The same short dark hair, the same brisk, no-nonsense approach. She was older, but she looked as good as ever. Out of his league, though. She always had been, even as a probationer. Her father had been some sort of college professor or something. A desire to see the job done properly had taken Judy Russell into police work, and she had been good at it; if she had been a man, she'd have been way past DI status by now. It had always irritated her, that one area in which she could never be superior. Bannister wasn't sure that there should be women on the force at all, but if there had to be, then she was the kind they should have.

"Where were you?" she asked again.

He inclined his head towards the photograph. "At ..." he leaned over and checked the time. "At twenty-oh-four hours, I was driving into that factory," he said.

"Don't try to be clever, Dave," she warned him.

He looked at her. "Do you still smoke, Jude?" he asked.

She reached into her bag and pushed cigarettes and matches towards him. No nonsense about calling her Inspector Hill. That was a relief.

He took one, lit it, and pushed them back. "What am I supposed to have done?" he asked. He wasn't admitting to any more than he had to; that little bitch had told them something, but he didn't know what. And they had to tell him exactly why he was under arrest.

"We are investigating the death of a Mr. Victor Holyoak which occurred in the penthouse flat of Holyoak Industries offices on Wednesday the first or Thursday the second of April," she said steadily. "We have reason to believe that Mr. Holyoak was killed in the course of a burglary."

They no more thought that than they thought the moon was made of lemon sorbet, but it did fit the facts at their disposal, and it meant that little Annabel had told them that he'd been there.

"We have a statement to the effect that you were given instructions on how to gain entry to the penthouse flat," she went on, confirming that.

He drew deeply on the cigarette, and contemplated Judy for a moment or two. "Annabel thought I could do myself some good," he said, coming down on the side of the truth, at least as far as the facts went. "She suggested it. And now we all know why."

Judy's eyebrows rose in a query.

"She'd had a bust-up with her boyfriend about some other woman," he said. "She was drinking—she said there was stuff worth nicking up there, and told me how to get in. She wanted to get her own back on him, she said. But she already had, hadn't she?" He took another drag on the cigarette. "And I walked right into it."

"Into what, exactly?"

"Into finding him dead in a bedroom that looked like a designer abattoir, exactly," he said.

She swallowed a little, and he smiled again. She had never been fond of blood, hadn't Judy. And the stuff had sprayed everywhere.

"Wasn't pretty, was it?" he said, rubbing it in. "If you felt bad—think how I felt. I'd just dodged past cameras and climbed a fire escape to get in there, and I find someone who's been stabbed to death."

"Did you steal a wallet?"

He finished off the cigarette and ground it out in the ashtray. If he got out of this, Annabel was in deep, deep trouble. He still had some faith in the forces of law and order, though. He imagined that they would get her for the murder.

"Did you steal a wallet?"

"No," he said. "I stole money *from* a wallet, but I left the wallet there."

"Where?"

"I just took the money out, and dropped the wallet on the floor. Then I went and found Annabel's redecoration job in the bedroom."

"So where exactly did you drop the wallet?"

"On the sitting-room carpet, exactly. I can't give you the coordinates." He frowned. "Didn't you find it?" he asked, not expecting an answer.

"Do you think there was anyone else in the flat while you were there?"

"I didn't hang about to find out. I left the way I'd come in as fast as I could." He remembered the dreadful frozen moment when he had seen Holyoak's body, and frowned. "Though—I did hear a noise," he said.

212

"What sort of a noise?"

He couldn't explain. "I don't know. It was sort of familiar, but—I don't know. I remember feeling as if it made everything all right." He looked at her. "I know that sounds crazy. But I was faced with this body, and there was this sound. It didn't fit—it belonged somewhere else." He shrugged. "Not much help," he said.

She had written it all down, though. She looked up at him. "Well," she said. "It might come back to you. Did you know the victim?"

"Don't even know his name," he said.

"What brought you to Stansfield?"

He had been through all these questions on the drive back to London, where he had had visions of police cars screaming up behind him, sirens blaring, assuming, as he had by then, that she had been lying about the cameras. When that hadn't happened, he had thought that the sober Annabel would just keep her mouth shut about what had gone on. But the little cow was trying to make him carry the can for her crime of passion.

"I saw little Annabel on the six o'clock news," he said. "I thought I'd renew our acquaintance."

"How did you know where to find her?"

"I didn't. That's why I went to the factory. But the offices were in darkness, so I went for a drink to the nearest pub, and there she was." He smiled. "My lucky night—eh?"

"Did you attempt to blackmail her?"

Christ. Murder, blackmail, burglary—was there anything Annabel hadn't thought of? Perhaps he'd kidnapped her and raped her while he was at it. "No," he said. "I stole some money from a wallet, and I failed to report a murder. In that order. I forgot I even had the bloody money until next morning."

She looked at him steadily, her brown eyes unblinking. "It didn't occur to you to report the murder?" she asked.

"No."

"Did you know the victim?"

"No."

The look in her eye indicated what she thought of that; Annabel had told them about that, too, the rotten little bitch. Now, too late, he realized what a sitting target he had been. Anna mustn't have been able to believe her luck when

213

he walked into the pub, complete with motive, asking her—
asking her how he could get in there undetected by security.

"Did you know the victim?" Judy was asking again, still
quietly, still patiently.

"No," he said.

Annabel might have told them, but she sure as hell couldn't
prove that he knew Holyoak, or that he had had a score to settle. He had a score to settle now, all right. And whichever of
them ended up in jail for fifteen years, he would settle it. And
this time he wouldn't let her off lightly.

"Why didn't you report what you had found?"

"I was in shock! I had entered the premises illegally and
found someone stabbed to death on the bloody floor—all I
could think of doing was getting the hell out! And when I remembered about the money it was too late—I had stolen from
him, for Christ's sake!" He looked round the interview room,
and held out his hands. "This," he said. "This was going to
happen if I reported it. I thought the little whore would keep
her mouth shut when she sobered up, but I was wrong."

She didn't speak. Didn't say a word. Bannister sat in silence
too for as long as he could bear it, but that wasn't long. He
couldn't be being done for this. He couldn't.

"*She* killed him! She saw me coming—all right? I see her
on the telly with her designer clothes on, and I can't believe
what I'm seeing! A cheap little whore like that? I wanted to go
and remind her who she was—that's all. She sent me up
there."

"Did you try to blackmail her?"

He made a scornful noise. "Look—I had three quid in my
pocket. She drives a bloody Porsche! Where's the justice?"

"Did you try to blackmail her?"

"Oh—if you want to call it that!" he shouted. "It got me nowhere! And she saw the answer to her prayers. She had just
stabbed her sugar-daddy to death, and I—"

He clamped his lips together, clasping his hands at the back
of his neck in frustration. With a supreme effort, he calmed
himself down, lifting his still clasped hands over his head,
slowly down on to the table in front of him. It looked like a
gesture of prayer. It was a slow-motion gesture of violence.
The table was Annabel's neck.

"I was the fall guy," he said, relaxing his hands, reaching over for the cigarettes that still lay on the table.

"We'll be searching your flat, Dave," she said. "Are we going to find anything?"

He nodded. "You'll find about a hundred and seventy pounds in the drawer beside my bed. Tell them not to frighten my wife and kids. Your custody sergeant's got the rest of the money, except what I spent on petrol."

"Did you know the victim?" she asked.

He closed his eyes. Was she never going to give up? Asking the same question, the same way, over and over. He looked back at her. "I won't answer any more questions," he said.

"Now—if you look *here* . . ."

Lloyd was being shown a transparency of the photographs at the scene which had got forensic excited. He looked at the viewer, at a close-up of the wardrobe doors.

"The blood has splashed," said the girl in the white lab-coat whom Lloyd had learned to his horror was called Dr. Greenfield, when he had taken her to be a sixth-former on work experience. Fortunately, his attitude to sixth-formers on work experience was indistinguishable from his attitude to people with Ph.D.s, so she would never know his mistake. He was just taking a little time adjusting, that was all.

The spray of someone's lifeblood was no easier to take in black and white—if anything, in an odd way, the starkness of the contrast made it worse. This particular transparency was of the thin streaks across the doors.

"See?" she said. "It's spattered across both doors, but if you close in on it"—she suited the action to the word, and three individual streaks came into close-up—"you can see that there's a break," she said. "It hits the right-hand door, then there's a gap on the left-hand door before it continues. And it's two millimetres out of alignment."

Lloyd nodded. "So the doors were open when the attack was going on?" he said.

"One. The right-hand door was ajar. When we looked at the photographs of the *open* door . . ."

The next slide clicked in, and she began demonstrating all the proofs of her statement. He then got shown the results of the tests they'd carried out at the scene and on a pair of mock-up doors. The inference to be drawn from their labours was clear. The wardrobe door had been almost, but not quite closed during the attack, and closed firmly after the attack. It couldn't close accidentally; it had to have been closed, quite deliberately.

The carving knife from the block of knives in the kitchen had been positively identified as the murder weapon. The sheets from the bed, and the bloodstains on the headboard indicated that that was where the attack had begun. Semen had also been found on the sheets, which came as no surprise to anyone; Holyoak's much vaunted fidelity to his wife seemed to have ceased that night, if it had ever been the case. And the wardrobe doors would appear to confirm Freddie's thoughts on where the assailant's clothes had been. The assailant had showered; traces of blood had been found in the shower basin, and on the towels. The same type as Holyoak's; the samples from the knife, the sheets and the towels had gone off for DNA analysis. The results would take a couple of weeks, but Holyoak's blood type wasn't common; it was unlikely that the body fluids were anyone's but his. So who was with him? All manner of theories went rattling through Lloyd's mind.

Anna Worthing and Holyoak had had a fight that had got out of hand. Bannister was set up, as he had insisted to Judy that he had been. And Anna had once come within an ace of doing Bannister a considerable injury, so she had the temper to lash out at someone. And if she had a knife in her hand, all right, she might even lash out with that. But whoever had stabbed Holyoak had meant business; that was not the result of a moment's frustration. And Lloyd didn't believe that Anna Worthing had killed him, not like that.

Someone had come in, found Holyoak with someone else, got a knife from the kitchen and attacked him. But not the woman? She had run away. Who was she? Anna? Was there something between her and Bannister? Bannister had attacked Holyoak . . . and what? Then Anna and Bannister had had a nice cosy heart to heart and agreed on a story that they would both tell when the police caught up with them? Then Bannister went home, got rid of the blood-stained clothes. No. He rejected that one too.

But something had made Anna go and get drunk. She said she'd had a row with him. And perhaps it was about this other woman, as Judy had said. Geraldine Rule seemed to have disappeared off the face of the earth, according to Finch, who had been waiting for the Rules to come and let him have their fingerprints.

Lloyd drove back to Stansfield, aware as ever of the great good fortune of having a forensic lab built practically on the doorstep, and a Home Office pathologist within fifty miles, and tried another theory.

Bannister, if Anna's story about what Holyoak had done to him was true, could have killed him. Anna's with Holyoak, and his lady friend comes to the door. Anna leaves, goes to the pub to drown her sorrows, sends Bannister up there in the hope of embarrassing Holyoak and getting Bannister into deep water again. She succeeds, on both counts. The girlfriend runs away when they are discovered, and Holyoak comes after Bannister, who grabs a knife from the kitchen. But how come Holyoak was back on the bed when it happened?

Bannister was always going up there to kill him. He didn't fall for that line that Anna gave him about the flat being empty; he knew Holyoak was up there with someone. He picked up the knife on his way through the kitchen. But he had no quarrel with whoever the woman was, so she fled, and he didn't try to stop her, even though she was a witness. If so, where was she? Why hadn't she come forward? Because of this reputation that she had to preserve? Was Bannister so certain that she wouldn't come forward that he could *afford* to let her go?

Besides, according to the camera that took in the outside door to the flat, Holyoak had had no visitor at all—not one that came in by that door, at any rate. And none of that explained why someone closed the wardrobe door after the murder. That surely had to be so that no one would know that it had ever been open. He couldn't really imagine someone neatly closing the door after she had just stabbed someone to death and retrieved her clothes from it. If this hypothetical person was an automatic door closer, she would have closed it in the first place, and it wouldn't have been ajar during the murder. Another little puzzle.

They had found two sets of keys to the flat in Holyoak's possession and Anna had to be tackled about that; if she had keys, her insistence that she was not Holyoak's mistress would seem a little unlikely, but Lloyd still felt that he wasn't the one to do the tackling.

It was almost ten o'clock when Lloyd arrived back in Stansfield; Tom Finch was wading through the private investigators' reports that Holyoak had received on Catherine all those years ago when she had run away from home.

"Any joy?" asked Lloyd.

"Not yet, sir. She's been traced, and they're keeping an eye on her." He looked up. "Daily," he said. "I'll let you know the next thrilling instalment when I get to it."

Clearly, the frequency of the reports was Lloyd's fault. He smiled. "Have we had an answer from Holyoak's secretary about keys to the penthouse?" he asked.

"Not yet, sir."

"You can leave these for the moment," Lloyd said. "I want you to have another word with Miss Worthing."

He told Finch the nature of the word, and went into his own office, where Judy had left him the files on the Scott murder. He flicked through the statements, door-to-door enquiry forms, progress reports, then took his glasses from their pouch and settled down to do some serious reading.

Mrs. Scott had begun to tire of her husband's excursions beyond his own bedroom, it appeared. She had told a friend that her husband was having an affair—she had been very distressed, according to the friend, who was, of course, Zelda Driver. Mrs. Scott had told Zelda that her husband had always been unfaithful, practically from the honeymoon onward, and she had grown to accept it. The variety was something that he needed, and he was, in all other respects, a model husband.

Lloyd looked up, and thought about that. He wasn't a wife-beater, then. And seemed to have been fortunate enough to find not one, but two wives who were prepared to put up with his infidelity. So why did he turn on his present wife on Wednesday? What truth had he tried to elicit from her with violence? Did he succeed?

He carried on reading Zelda's evidence, which would have been inadmissible if they had ever brought it to court anyway. This time, it seemed, things had been different. Scott's extra-marital affairs had never before altered his attitude to his wife, but this one had. She had taxed him with it, and he had denied having an affair at all. Then he had suggested the move to

Stansfield, and she had hoped everything would be all right. But it had still been going on; he had even stopped sleeping with his wife.

Lloyd felt his heart give a dip of guilt when he read that; it struck a little too close to home for comfort. Apart from the marriage-long infidelity, of which he had not been guilty, it read like the history of his own marriage, including the move to Stansfield which was supposed to make everything better. And the disinclination to share a bed with Barbara, brought about not by distaste, but the guilty knowledge that he wanted her to be someone else.

Would Scott have felt guilty, given his track record? Yes, Lloyd supposed, if he had fallen for Catherine, as opposed to amusing himself with her. And Catherine was sixteen years old when he met her, of course, which would only add to the problem. But surely divorce would have been a reasonable, if unhappy, solution? It was what Lloyd had done, in the end.

He checked back to see if religion had played any part; was divorce out of the question for one of them? Apparently not. So why kill her? Scott had married Catherine less than six months later, much to the glee of the press. A divorce wouldn't have allowed remarriage that soon, but there seemed to be no reason for their haste other than that there was nothing to stop them.

Mrs. Scott, it seemed, had been uttering threats that very evening, at the top of her voice. It had been a warm evening; people had had their windows open, and the neighbours had heard her saying she could and would make trouble.

That puzzled him a little, but for the moment, he was just familiarizing himself with the investigation.

The election campaigners had been around, ensuring that the faithful went to vote, and that those less able got a lift to the polling station. It was thanks to a mistake being made at the Conservative Party campaign headquarters that they had been able to narrow down the time of death to between five forty-five and seven o'clock, because Mrs. Scott had been alive and well when she had been canvassed at five forty-five, and the woman across the road had found her at a few minutes after seven.

But that lot of campaigners shouldn't have been there at all; the road had already been done earlier, by a team led by none

219

other than Dr. Charles Rule. No one on the first team had called on Mrs. Scott; Rule had told them not to bother, as she was a committed socialist. Two of that team heard the row as they knocked on the doors either side; it had still been going on as the team moved on to its next target area.

Everyone on both campaign teams had been questioned, especially Charles Rule, because he knew Valerie Scott, and the poor woman from the second wave who had claimed to have spoken to her—indeed, to have been given a lecture on social inequality by her. She had been interviewed three times, until it was finally accepted that she really didn't know Mrs. Scott, and unless she was a homicidal maniac in her spare time, had had no reason whatever to kill her.

The unfortunate lady who lived across the road, and who had discovered the body, had received similar treatment before being crossed off the list.

Then, the interesting statement. Catherine Barnes, aged seventeen, who said that she had been with Max Scott the evening before at six forty-five, in London. It took easily an hour and a half to drive from Stansfield to London, therefore if it was true, Max Scott could not have killed his wife. Every reason to doubt it and no reason to doubt it, Lloyd thought. Every reason because she was clearly in love with Scott and would have sworn anything if it got him off the hook, and no reason because obviously the affair had still been going on, and the chances were that that *was* where he had been, using the desire to exercise his democratic rights as an excuse. And no one had been able to come up with any reason at all why his wife should have had to die to accommodate his new love.

Mounds and mounds of paperwork, of painstaking evidence gathering; hours and hours of interviews, the ever-widening net taking in known criminals, conmen, rapists . . . but she hadn't been sexually assaulted, conmen didn't strangle their victims as a rule, and nothing had been taken or even disturbed in the house.

Back to Scott. Who was so conveniently in London at the time, whose little girlfriend had equally conveniently and apparently coincidentally turned up next morning to furnish him with an alibi. No forensic evidence worth talking about, no sightings of Scott's car, or of him himself, no mysterious visitors. And there had been, of course, many more people abroad than would be normal for a Thursday evening in that area of Stansfield as they went to vote.

Lloyd knew the area well, and it was composed of middle-income Tory voters—with the exception, it would appear, of Mrs. Scott—in a quiet street with net curtains from behind which people took a great deal of notice of their neighbours' comings and goings. On election night it would have been much much easier for a stranger to knock on someone's door unnoticed by the neighbours. But why would a stranger have killed her?

The husband was always favourite in any domestic murder, and Lloyd could see why, as the weeks had turned into months, Scott had been brought in for questioning over and over again. His statements ranged from the original one in which he had gone to London to vote and had thought about going to a prostitute to one in which he stated that he had spent the crucial time with Catherine. He had denied firmly any suggestion that he had been having an affair with her, or that she was the one about whom his wife had become so agitated, but had declined to furnish the police with any other avenue to pursue.

Lloyd took off his glasses, rubbed his eyes, and closed the files. Election night, he thought. And here they were again, with their rosettes and their beaming faces, telling the electorate what double-dyed villains the other lot were. Could the elections possibly have anything to do with it? Surely not. Still . . . leave no stone unturned.

After protracted negotiations, he secured an interview with the Conservative Party agent for midday. Lloyd had warned him that he would need to dip into his archives; the man had sounded less than enthusiastic, but had agreed that it was his duty as a supporter of the party of law and order to help the police. But if Lloyd knew how busy he was . . .

He was busy, Lloyd thought, going into the CID room, and picking up the private investigators' reports from where Finch had left off. They had, of course, searched through the files for a report of the night of the 3rd of May, but the by then weekly reports finished at the end of April and didn't begin again until November. Nothing had been removed; the interruption had been because the private investigators had mislaid Catherine, much to the wrath of their employer. But Lloyd had known that they would never get that lucky; it had come as no surprise.

Still, there might be something in amongst this lot that would give them some sort of lead. It was evidence that his colleagues hadn't had, and it had to be gone through.

God. Finch. With immeasurable reluctance, Anna pushed the door to, and undid the chain, opening it again to admit him.

"I'd like to ask you a few more questions, Anna," he said. "And I have to remind you that you are not obliged to say anything, but . . ."

She walked away from the caution, through to the sitting room where she had a mug of coffee, and he followed her in, sitting down without being asked.

"Do you have keys to Holyoak's penthouse?" he asked.

"No."

"Have you ever had keys?"

She sighed. "Yes. Victor asked for them back last night."

"Why?"

"They were his keys," she said. "He asked for them back, so I gave them to him."

"Why did you have keys in the first place?"

"I furnished it," she said. "Got it ready while Victor was in Holland."

"But that was months ago," said Finch. "Why did he ask for them back last night? Why not before?"

Anna shrugged, picking up her coffee. "He forgot, I suppose," she said.

"What made him remember, Anna? Why did he want his keys back?"

Anna looked at him. "Max Scott and I had been using it," she said, enunciating very clearly so that Finch would have no trouble catching the words, and wouldn't have to seek clarification, a favourite technique of his. "He told you that morning. Victor didn't want that to go on. All right?"

Finch looked pleased with himself. "So that's what your row was about," he said, getting up, walking round the room, looking at the ornaments and the paintings. "What did you say your relationship with Holyoak was?" he asked.

"I told you yesterday."

"You worked for him."

222

"Yes."

"Nothing more?"

"No."

"But you had keys to his penthouse. And you said he wasn't pleased when he found out what you and Scott had been doing behind his back."

Anna didn't speak.

"You went up to the penthouse with him just after five— what did you do?"

"We talked."

"What was he wearing while you had this talk?"

She swallowed. A lie could land her in deeper trouble; she had to tell the truth. "A bathrobe," she said, through her teeth.

He turned, frowning. "A what?" he asked.

"A bathrobe," she said again.

"Do you know, I don't believe I've ever seen my boss in a bathrobe," he said. "Odd that, isn't it? Because I talk to her quite a lot. She generally keeps her clothes on, though. But your boss took his off. You had sex with him, didn't you, Anna?"

"No."

He smiled, and sat down again. "Someone did," he said cheerfully. "Just before he was stabbed to death."

"Then it was whoever came to the bloody door!" she shouted.

"Oh, yes. His invisible visitor."

"Someone came to the door," she said.

Finch was still smiling. It took all her strength not to throw something at him.

"Come on, Annabel," he said, with a world-weary sigh. "No one came to the door. You know it, and I know it. You had sex with him. Don't be coy—it doesn't suit you."

"I never had sex with him in my life!" she shouted. "And don't you dare call me Annabel!"

He grinned. "That was what you were called when he took you to Holland," he said. "Why did he take you to Holland?"

"To work for him!"

"Doing what?"

"This and that. I dealt with the private investigators' stuff—I took calls for him. Personal things. Nothing to do with the business."

223

He shook his head. "No, Anna," he said. "If that was all he wanted, he could have got anyone to do it. But he took you with him. Why?"

"That was what I did. Until he gave me this new job."

"And why did he give you that?" He stood up again. "And this flat—and that car?" He looked out of the back window to where the Porsche still sat at an awkward angle to the garage. She hadn't gone into work; there had seemed very little point. Finch looked round the room again. "How much did this place set you back?" he asked. "And these aren't things you pick up in chain stores," he said, picking up one of the heavy bronze figures that adorned her shelves, weighing it in his hand before putting it back.

She watched him like a cat as he eyed up the leather furniture, the heavy wallpaper.

"You were worth a hell of a lot to him, Anna. You weren't just some personal assistant. He took you there, he brought you back, he gave you a job in the company, his wife was dying . . ." He turned to face her. "You thought you had it made, didn't you? But then he found out that you were playing around with Scott. You had blown it, and you lost your temper. No one came to the door, Anna. You tried to frame Bannister, and you invented the visitor for insurance."

"What are you doing with Bannister?" she asked, alarmed.

"I don't know. My boss is dealing with that."

"You promised me protection!"

He walked to the sitting-room door. "I promised you nothing," he said. "Did she promise? Inspector Hill?"

Anna's mind was racing as she followed him out into the hallway. She couldn't remember. Yes. Yes. She said that Finch would protect her. "You're supposed to be looking after me!" she shouted.

"Why are you so worried about Bannister? Because you sent him up there to find a dead body?"

"No!" she shouted. "No! He killed him!"

"Oh—I thought this visitor . . ."

"Look!" she yelled. "Either Bannister killed him or he found him after whoever came to the door killed him! But I didn't! I didn't go to bed with him, and I didn't kill him! He was alive when I left him—have you got that?"

Finch smiled. "Bannister's not going anywhere for the moment," he said, opening the door. "Don't worry."

She did worry, as she pushed the chain home. She was sick with worry, and she wanted Max. But Max wasn't there, so she used the remedy she had always used in times of stress. She went into the kitchen, reaching into the cupboard for a new bottle of brandy.

Catherine opened the door to Chief Inspector Lloyd. She had just come back from identifying her stepfather, and now he was going to ask her questions. It was all starting again. She could take it—she wasn't at all sure that Max could.

"Come in," she said, ushering him into the sitting room, where she had been pretending to read the paper. But it was full of her stepfather, and she had turned to the sports pages, which might as well have been written in a foreign language. In an odd way, she was almost glad of Lloyd's visit; waiting for it was worse than dealing with it.

"Is your husband here, Mrs. Scott?"

"No," she said. "He went into the office to sort some things out—he should be back for lunch."

"I'm glad you're on your own," Lloyd said. "Because a number of things have come to light today that require explanation."

Catherine motioned to him to sit down. All she had to do was stay calm, take deep breaths. Stay cool. Lloyd seemed less likely to fluster her than Inspector Hill.

"Mrs. Scott—you lied to the police at the time of the murder of the first Mrs. Scott," Lloyd said.

That was true, which did rather make it a bit difficult to defend. Catherine didn't try. "Max didn't kill his wife," she said, her voice clear and strong, belying the shivering she was trying hard to control.

"Perhaps not," said Lloyd. "But he wasn't with you either, was he?"

Catherine didn't speak.

"If Mr. Scott was where he said he was, then you weren't with him," said Lloyd. "Because you didn't live there any more, did you? The flat was still in your name because you had paid the rent in advance—when the police at the time enquired, your story seemed to check out. But you had moved out some time previously, and lived in digs, according to the private detective who finally located you there."

Catherine felt herself grow pink, despite her warnings to herself about keeping calm. She had hoped against hope that her stepfather had destroyed these reports, but she had known that they would turn up. "Max was where he said he was! He saw my stepfather—he described him! And that had to be at the same time as Valerie was killed—it wasn't Max, I *know* it wasn't!"

"But you persuaded him to lie instead of telling the truth?"

"I didn't want my stepfather brought back."

"No, I don't suppose you did," said Lloyd. "You were having an affair with a married man twice your age whose wife had just been murdered."

Catherine swallowed.

"But your stepfather came back in the end. And he found out what you had done. Didn't he?"

She didn't speak.

"And you didn't tell your husband. You didn't even tell him that Holyoak was your stepfather. And that's what was worrying him, wasn't it, Mrs. Scott? He wanted to know why the secrecy—he needed to know just what you had told your stepfather—that's why my sergeant found him hitting you, demanding to know the truth. Isn't that right, Mrs. Scott?"

No. But she said nothing.

"And isn't it convenient that this tale about his seeing your stepfather that night was only produced after your stepfather was dead? Did your husband tell you to say that? Did he realize that your stepfather was on to him?"

Judy had gone back to the station, having got nowhere at all at the Stag, whose staff could always be relied upon to have been struck with sudden and selective blindness and deafness. Short of tossing a coin, she had told Lloyd, she wasn't sure what to do. It seemed that either Bannister or Anna had killed him, or that they had acted in tandem.

Lloyd had been in the CID room, going through the PI reports on Catherine's movements before Mrs. Scott's death, more than a little interested in what he was reading. Catherine Scott had lied to the police at the time; he had proof of that now, unlike his predecessors. He didn't believe that either

Anna Worthing or Dave Bannister had had anything to do with Holyoak's murder.

He had told Judy what the lab had said about Holyoak's demise, and had even divulged his theories, since there was no one else in the room. Judy hadn't been terribly impressed with any of them, except the ones that he had dismissed as unlikely; the others seemed to her to be designed mostly to make Anna Worthing an innocent bystander. He had bristled when she had said that, and had delivered a swift counter-punch.

"I've got an interview with the Tory agent, and I want to call in on the Scotts before that," he had said, looking at her over his glasses. "Finch is having another go at Anna Worthing, so . . ."

"You want me to go to the post-mortem."

He had grinned. "Got it in one, Inspector."

He was never slow to pull rank, wasn't Lloyd. Finch could have done the post-mortem—he was only seeing Anna about these keys. Served her right for accusing Lloyd of bias, she supposed, as she drove into the hospital grounds, the familiar dread rising up at the sight of the notice-board pointing the way to the mortuary, never mind the place itself.

"See how much you can squeeze Freddie on the time of death," he had said. "Chat him up."

The day she was able to chat anyone up over a mutilated corpse was the day she would pack the job in.

"Ah, Judy!" Freddie's broad smile altered his whole face, which was long and serious in repose; he chatted to her cheerfully about nothing in particular as he went about his unspeakable business, giving her a running commentary, while directing Kathy to various parts of Holyoak's anatomy that he wanted photographed or pickled or whatever.

"Stabbed five times," he said. "Died from haemorrhage. Tell Lloyd I'll take him on any time."

Judy stood a very, very respectful distance away from the activity, and smiled weakly.

"I'll tell you this," he said. "You've never brought me a healthier specimen."

"He looks it," said Judy.

"I'm not kidding—he was in perfect shape. He was what— early to mid-fifties, at a guess?"

Judy nodded.

227

"Perfect specimen. Strong, well developed—he worked out in a gym, I'm sure of that. Shouldn't think he ever smoked, or if he did, he gave it up a long time ago. Certainly didn't drink to excess, if at all. Everything in beautiful condition—except for a broken bone in his hand which wasn't set any too well."

They were just like hairdressers, thought Judy. Who set that bone for you? Dear, oh, dear, he made a right mess of that, didn't he?

"Had a light supper of smoked-salmon sandwiches," Freddie said.

"Are we any closer to a time of death?" she asked hopefully.

"Well—his physique comes into play to some extent with regard to body temperature and how long it took him to bleed to death, but honestly, Judy, it is the most—"

"Inexact science known to man. I know. Please, please, please, Freddie," she said. "We're not going to put it in your statement—just something for us to go on."

"Well . . . I told you that what he was doing at the time could affect the rigor process. And I hazarded a guess as to what he might have been doing."

Judy nodded. "Forensic confirm that," she said. "And they say he was stabbed on the bed."

"Yes. That seems likely. In view of his physical strength, I'd say he had to have been taken completely by surprise. It looks like he was attacked by someone standing over him—the angle of the wounds suggest someone right-handed. After the first blow he was losing blood too rapidly to defend himself—I think he quite possibly died during the attack." He looked up. "That's about it," he said.

"Time of death?" asked Judy, with a smile.

Freddie sighed. "I've told you. I can't narrow it down any further."

"Freddie . . . you're not going to send me back to Lloyd with nothing, are you?" she pleaded, coming as near to flirting over a corpse as she could.

"Between eight and midnight, if you must," he said. "But be warned—in court, I will say it happened between the time he was last seen alive, and two in the morning. There are far too many variables to give anything more certain than that. But I will go so far as to say in court that it is likely to have happened between eight o'clock and midnight."

Judy smiled. "Thank you, Freddie," she said. "And you think that he was in bed with someone who attacked him when he fell asleep after an exhausting session?"

Freddie looked pained. "Judy," he said, "delightful though you are, you really are picking up bad habits from your chief inspector. I said nothing of the sort. If you inferred that from what I said, that is your business. I've told you the facts, and one opinion. That a man of his strength and fitness would, I imagine, have had to have been taken by surprise. No more."

Judy looked suitably apologetic. She listened to some more descriptions of Holyoak's innards, as Freddie continued to exclaim over the sheer perfection of his corpse, and formulated another question.

"On Thursday you described the exercise he'd been taking as 'very vigorous,' " she said. "What does that mean in Freddie-speak? Over-enthusiastic, or sheer brute force?"

Freddie shrugged. "Either of the above," he said. "It depends how willing his partner was. I imagine they'd be a bit sore—he was."

Judy looked at him. Freddie was being even more meticulous than usual in not making assumptions. "Do you think he was with a man?" she asked.

"I think nothing!" he said. "I see, I mark, I inform you of the facts, and I give you the benefit of the occasional opinion. Leave the theories to your lord and master," he warned. "As to the sex of his attacker . . ." He shrugged. "A couple of the wounds are deep," he said. "Which requires some strength. But nothing to rule out a woman."

"How come they could lay their hands on a carving knife, that's what I'd like to know," said Judy. She smiled. "There were a lot of people in and out of that flat on Wednesday—any of them could have slipped a knife under the pillow for later. But you tell me that it could be a man or a woman, that their clothes might have been hung up in the wardrobe and won't have any trace of blood on them, that you haven't the foggiest when he actually died—and they are *all* right-handed, Freddie, so as clues go, that one isn't the most helpful you've ever given me."

He grinned.

* * *

Max heard the Welsh accent as soon as he got into the house; he closed his eyes briefly, and went into the sitting room where Catherine sat with Chief Inspector Lloyd.

"Ah—Mr. Scott," he said. "I've been going through your wife's statement to the police at the time of your first wife's death. She has changed her mind about a number of things. Including that she was with you."

Max sat down wearily. "What do you want me to say?" he asked eventually.

"I want you to tell me why you allowed a seventeen-year-old girl to lie for you," said Lloyd. "And why I shouldn't assume that it was because you had murdered your wife."

"Max wasn't with his wife! I spoke to her!" Catherine cried out.

Lloyd was staring at her, as indeed Max was himself.

"You spoke to her?" Lloyd repeated.

"Yes," she said. "I tried to ring Max, but his wife said he wasn't at home."

Lloyd sat up, and Max wondered how much more he was to find out about Catherine before all this dreadful business was finished.

"What exactly did she say to you?" demanded Lloyd.

"Mr. Lloyd," said Max. "It was thirteen years ago—how do you expect anyone to remember—"

"No," said Catherine. "It's all right." She spoke to Max himself, not to Lloyd. "I remember every word of that phone call," she said. "I'd realized that you didn't know that I'd moved—I'd tried to ring you at work, but you weren't there. So I tried your home number."

Max had never heard any of this; he took a covert glance at the chief inspector, only to find that Lloyd was watching him.

"She went to get a pen," she said, "to take down my number. But someone came to the door, and she said she was too busy, and just hung up. It was a lie—it was no one important. And I'd missed you by then anyway. That's why I came that morning. I was lonely. I needed you."

Max couldn't believe he was hearing this. But she had been seventeen. Seventeen, and pregnant, and desperate. Then she had been faced with what had happened to Valerie. She hadn't been thinking straight.

"What time did you telephone Valerie Scott?" Lloyd demanded.

Catherine closed her eyes. "I had rung Driver's from a callbox—they were just closing. It would be half an hour after that. Maybe three-quarters."

Lloyd made a note. "You withheld this information, Mrs. Scott," he said. "Important information, which you had to know was important at the time. Either that, or you're making it up now—which is it?"

"It was just someone about the election!" she shouted defensively. "I heard her send them away! She said one lot had already been round, so it must have been the election!" She ran out of the room, upstairs. Max didn't go after her.

"This meeting that never actually took place," said Lloyd. "Am I now to understand that it had been arranged some time previously?"

"Yes," said Max. "Catherine rang me, said she had to see me. I was going in order to tell her that she had to accept that it was over."

"And yet you married her six months later," said Lloyd. "It doesn't sound as though it was all over, Mr. Scott."

Max sighed. "I loved Catherine," he said. "But I was married, and that did mean something, whatever people think of me. I had no intention of leaving Valerie. I told her that, I told Catherine that. I would never, ever, have hurt Valerie like that."

Lloyd raised his eyebrows.

"I know I did hurt her, because I fell for Catherine, but that wasn't deliberate. I did everything I could to forget about her," he said. "And perhaps in time I would have done, if I had been given the chance. But Valerie died, and Catherine came here. There seemed very little point in making everything even worse by denying what we felt for one another once the threat of my being charged with murder seemed to have passed."

Lloyd nodded slowly. "I can understand that," he said.

Max felt that he was being given a glimpse into the chief inspector's soul, just for a moment. But he mustn't let himself get fanciful. They were out to get a result, and they would use every trick in the book to get it. He knew that from experience.

"Is this tale about the phone-call yet another desperate attempt to get you off the hook?" Lloyd asked.

231

Max didn't know. He looked helplessly at the chief inspector, shaking his head.

Lloyd left at last; Max still didn't go to Catherine, and he didn't go back to work. He needed Anna.

Charles had known, really, from the moment he had got up. He had told himself that Gerry had gone out early; when he had seen her car still there where it had been the night before, he had told himself that she had gone for a walk. Just to avoid him, as he had avoided her last night. He had gone to work, and come back at lunchtime, but the feeling was still there.

It was hard to give a name to it, but it had been real enough. A feeling of not being alone, of the house not being empty, though it appeared to be. A bit like when he was with Victor Holyoak.

He hadn't called anyone yet; he hadn't moved. He had just sat down on the bed beside her. She was dead; he had known that from the doorway, but he had made the usual checks for any sign of life. The empty bottle which had contained the pills she had taken lay on the little cabinet beside the bed, together with the bottle of water she had used to wash them down. She had taken a lethal dose; no more, no less. A doctor's suicide. Not for her the taking of ten times as many pills as was necessary, or the accompanying bottle of Scotch. She had known exactly what would kill her with the least discomfort and the most efficacy.

He hadn't touched either of the bottles; he had only touched her enough to establish that she was dead, and had been for some time. He had to tell the police, get an ambulance, have her body taken away. He had to tell her mother and father, Zelda, Max, everyone who knew her. Knew her far, far better than he ever had, it seemed. But he couldn't move, not yet.

The note was in his hands, if you could call it a note. Four words. Four words that were causing him to question everything he had ever done, everything he had ever believed. Four words that hurt him more than any amount of name calling or blame or bitterness could ever have done.

He tried to ring Max first; Catherine said he was at work. The office said he was at home. Charles closed his eyes. My God, he was with that woman at a time like this.

"Can someone else help you?" asked the receptionist.

"Zelda Driver," he said. "Please."

He told Zelda, somehow. And soon she was there, guiding him gently but firmly away from the bedroom, making him strong tea with a dash of whisky. Zelda did all the right things, all the things he couldn't bring himself to do. The police, all that. All he did was look at what Geraldine had written. And now they were here; calm, uninvolved, official voices were talking to Zelda. He didn't want them to read it. He crushed the piece of paper, and stuffed it in his pocket. But the words were there, in his head, as he waited for the questions to start.

My name was Geraldine.

CHAPTER TEN

Then: Last year . . .

"MRS. SCOTT?"

Catherine looked at the dark-haired young woman who stood on her doorstep, and smiled in polite expectancy. Double glazing, life insurance, a clothes catalogue—whatever it was, she probably wouldn't want it, but she never liked to be rude. She always listened to the spiel, then regretfully turned down whatever was on offer.

"My name's Anna Worthing," she said.

Catherine's smile stopped being polite, and became genuine. "Oh—you work with Max," she said. "He's mentioned you."

She smiled. "May I come in?"

"Of course." Catherine stood aside, and waved her visitor in. "Max isn't here, I'm afraid," she said.

Max was off somewhere, doubtless with some girl from the office. Catherine hoped that he would be a little more circumspect when his new bosses arrived. Zelda put up with it, though she clearly didn't approve; the new people might not think it proper behaviour on the part of the chief accountant.

Anna Worthing smiled. "It's you I've come to see," she said.

She looked familiar to Catherine; of course, she'd been working at Driver's since the negotiations had reached the critical stage, but Catherine hardly ever set foot in the place. She was sure she hadn't met her there.

"Me?" she said. "Does this mysterious owner vet the staff wives?"

Anna smiled a little. "Well—it's that I've come about, really," she said. "The mystery, I mean. The deal has finally gone through, and the new owners will be making a public announcement on Monday."

Catherine realized that she hadn't asked her visitor to sit down; she did so now, but stayed standing herself, feeling suddenly that she was no longer in charge of this conversation. She *did* know her; she was sure she did. She felt more in command of the situation on her feet.

"I've been asked to tell you in advance of the public announcement," she said.

"Me, personally?" asked Catherine.

"Yes. You see—it does affect you. Personally."

For a moment, Catherine didn't have the least idea what she was talking about. But only for a moment, because then she recognized her. No. No—she was letting her mind play tricks on her. It *couldn't* be her. She wore clothes that Catherine only saw in magazines; she had style, and elegance. It couldn't—it was preposterous, it was ridiculous. Buyers kept their identity secret for all sorts of reasons—tax, strategy, whatever. Max had thought that the buyer was some super-rich multi-national, and that if Zelda knew who it was she would push up the price. It couldn't be . . . but it was. It was her. She sank down on to a chair, her legs suddenly weak.

"I know you," she said, her voice sounding as though someone else had spoken. "Don't I? It's my stepfather who's bought out Zelda—isn't it?"

"Yes," she said.

After all these years. Catherine sat there, shell-shocked into silence.

"Victor asked me to talk to you. He had to do it this way—he thinks you would have tried to talk Mrs. Driver out of it if you'd known any sooner. He really wants a reconciliation—"

"Get out," said Catherine, standing up.

Anna Worthing also stood, but she didn't make any move to leave.

"Look, Catherine—" she began.

"Don't 'Catherine' me! Get out of my house!"

"I can't," she said, her voice losing its well-modulated

tones, and producing an edge of something like desperation. "Not until I've said what he's told me to say!"

Catherine looked at her, and saw the fear that her stepfather could instil in everyone. She felt sorry for the girl. If she didn't carry out her instructions to the letter, she would be in trouble. Catherine didn't want to cause that, because being in trouble with her stepfather was something she wouldn't wish on her worst enemy.

"Say it," she said. "Then get out."

"Victor's still in Amsterdam," she said quickly. "He won't be coming over here until shortly before Christmas." She took a breath. "But your mother's coming over next week. She'll be staying in the penthouse flat on top of the new office building," she said. "Until the house is ready."

"House?" Catherine repeated dully.

"Victor's having a house built," she said. "In Stansfield—your mother wanted to be near you."

He was actually coming back to stay. But she was married now. She had Max. She didn't have to worry about Victor. Oh, but she did. Catherine sank down into the chair, and the reversal was complete. Anna Worthing, as she called herself these days, was standing looking down at her as Catherine tried to come to terms with the impossible situation she was in. What when Max met him? Oh, dear God. What then?

"It's really a courtesy flat for visiting businessmen," Anna was explaining. "But there's a lift from the basement car park, so it should be all right for your mother's wheelchair."

Catherine looked up at her, her mind a blank.

"Look—I just work for him, all right?" said Anna. "I know all the rumours that are flying about—but that flat isn't there for Victor and me to use."

No. Catherine hadn't supposed it was.

"Anyway, your mother's going to be there until Christmas. Victor wants you to go and see her. That's why he's done all this. She doesn't know how long she's got left—that's why she's coming over before the house is finished—it's not too much to ask for you to go and see her, is it?"

Catherine had wanted to see her mother every minute of every day for years after she had finally made the break. Time had healed that wound, but it had left a scar. It was being opened now and it hurt. But perhaps she could cope with it after all. Things had changed; she had Max, and she was stronger than she had once been. She was fighting on two fronts, and she could cope with only one battle at a time. She might as well direct her energies at the one she could contemplate.

"Do you swear that he won't be there?" she asked.

"Yes. He's in Holland—he's not coming over until late November. He said to tell you that he doesn't expect you to make it up with him. All he wants is for you and your mother to get back together."

Catherine felt light-headed, but her brain was still working. "He hardly needed to move his entire seat of operations to achieve that," she said.

"He wanted to come back to Britain," said Anna.

"You mean that they were beginning to get wise to him over there?"

Anna sat down again. "Look—I've known Victor a long time," she said. "I know what he's like, and I can understand your wanting to have no part of it. And I expect he is getting out before mud of some sort starts flying so that none of it sticks to him. But his feelings for your mother are genuine. And it's always torn him apart that you wouldn't see her just because of him."

It had torn *him* apart. Catherine sighed. "All right," she said. "I'll go and see my mother." She stood up, despite the fact her legs were still far from steady. "So now you can go," she said. "You've done what you were told to do, so you don't have to worry about reporting back to him."

Anna walked to the door.

"And I don't want you in my house ever again," said Catherine. "Tell him that, too."

Anna Worthing left, and Catherine dissolved into tears.

Linda had come expecting to find Lloyd; instead, she had found Judy, and that had not pleased her.

"He's only popped into the library," Judy said. "He won't be long—come in and wait."

"I'd rather not," she said stiffly.

Judy could have left it there. It was Saturday morning; she and Lloyd didn't get much time together, and Linda's company was not something she was likely to enjoy. But the animosity had gone on long enough. "This is silly," she said. "If you

237

want to talk to your dad, come in and wait for him—he'll be back in about twenty minutes. We can have a cup of coffee—I'll make myself scarce when he comes back."

Linda was her father's daughter, all right; blue eyes looked back into Judy's, and words—that great Lloyd family weapon—were rising to her lips, only to be bitten back. Lloyd had never learned how to do that. Her mother's influence, presumably, had at least curbed the instinct in Linda.

Linda came in, Judy made coffee, and they sat down and looked at one another.

"You know it upsets your dad that you won't talk to me, don't you?" Judy said.

"You broke up their marriage! What does he expect?"

Judy nodded. "I know I did," she said quietly. "Lloyd tries to tell me I didn't, that it would have happened anyway—but I know I did." She looked at the girl, so like Lloyd, with her dark hair and challenging eyes. "All I can tell you is that I did my level best not to break it up. I didn't have an affair with him, Linda. I got married—I moved away."

"The damage was done," said Linda.

"Yes."

"And you didn't end up in Stansfield by accident," she added.

"No." Judy picked up her coffee. "But your father was divorced by then."

"You knew that, of course. Because you kept in touch with him. And you were still married!"

"Yes." No point in denying it, or defending it. The situation had finally resolved itself without too much damage to any of the parties involved. "But I can't be sorry that Lloyd and I got together again," she said.

"Is that what you call it? Together? Living in separate flats?"

Judy smiled a little. "We don't really have much option about that," she said. "We're not supposed to be doing what we are doing, never mind living together. And I'm still not divorced. But it works," she said. "And at least I'm not always here when you want to see your father. We're very happy, Linda. I don't expect you to share it, but I wish you could understand it."

"Well, good for you! I'm so glad you're happy!"

238

Judy was happy. And there was a sense of security in Lloyd's little flat that even the hostile Linda couldn't chase away. She belonged here. Peter was fine; he would come and see his father from time to time, bring his friends and his girlfriends. He didn't seem to care whether Judy was there or not. Judy tried to imagine how she would have felt if her father had divorced her mother and gone off with some female colleague, and knew that she would feel very much like Linda did. Angry. But not unhappy, surely? Not after all this time.

"Aren't you happy?" she asked.

"He didn't leave me," she said. "He left my mother."

"Is she unhappy?" Judy had got the impression from Lloyd that Barbara was all right now. He didn't usually delude himself about such things.

"She's taken up with some man," said Linda. "Next thing he'll be moving in completely."

Ah. That had to be Lloyd territory. But Judy made a mild attempt to gauge the situation. "Don't you like him?" she asked.

Linda shrugged. "He's all right," she said.

"Weren't you thinking of going to work in London anyway?" Judy asked.

"He made such a song and dance about it that mum won't let me now!"

"Your mum's boyfriend?" asked Judy.

"No! My dad, of course! He seems to think I'll end up on the streets if I go to London."

Judy breathed a silent sigh of relief. At least it wasn't the new man laying down the law; it was Lloyd. This she could handle. "Would you like me to have a word with him?" she asked.

"If mum couldn't persuade him, I don't see how you can. You know what he's like."

Judy smiled. It was the first time that Linda had admitted that Judy did know her father really quite well. "A different approach," she said. "It might work, if you'd like me to try."

She knew Lloyd's objections; they were sound and sensible and doubtless had also been voiced by Barbara. But Lloyd was getting the blame, of course, because he was in the doghouse, and had been, not since the divorce, but ever since Judy had come back into his life.

"If you like," Linda said.

It was less than gracious, but it was a start.

"How much?" spluttered Bannister.

"That's what they cost, Dave," she said.

"For a pair of shoes that he'll have outgrown in six bloody months?" Bannister held the shoe in his hand and looked at it. "Christ, Jackie—what are we supposed to live on?"

"That's what they *cost*," she repeated. "It's better than getting him one of those computer games! Just be thankful that he *wants* a pair of trainers for Christmas!"

"They cost a quarter of that on the market!"

"I can't go to the market! It's always closed up by the time I've finished work—I have to go to the big shops that stay open late! If you want to buy his shoes on the market—you go!"

Bannister stared at her. "I'm not doing bloody Christmas shopping," he said.

"No. Or the bloody washing, or the ironing, or the cooking, or the cleaning. You do sod all, Dave Bannister!"

He threw down the shoe, and picked up the evening paper. "I'm trying to get a job!" he said, shaking it in her face. "There's three in this area tonight. Three. And two of them I don't even understand—they're all full of sodding initials and if you don't know what it means, you don't apply! You want to know the one I do understand? Night bloody watchman, and I've phoned up about it and it's gone!"

Jackie looked at him, her eyes sad. She felt sorry for him, and that made it even worse. He threw the paper on to the sofa, and ran his hands over his face. "I've been offered a job as a minder," he said.

"Not those crooks, Dave!"

"Yes, those crooks! It's good money." He sat down, and found he was sitting on a toy. "I'm thinking about it," he said, removing the obstruction, longing for the space of their old house, where they didn't all have to live on top of one another. It was worse than ever in here with the tree and the decorations. And God knows how much they had cost. He hadn't paid the rent on this rabbit hutch for two months. "I've got to," he said to her.

"No, Dave. What if you got into a fight?"

He knew the risks. But he needed a job. He needed regular money. He needed space, and a garden for the kids to play in. He needed to stop having rows with Jackie, and he needed his authority back. He couldn't tell her not to pay that kind of money for a pair of trainers, because it was her money.

"Don't work for them, Dave," she pleaded. "Not yet. We can manage a little while longer—promise me you won't. Not yet. Not unless you absolutely have to."

He sighed. "All right," he said. But he would have to. Sooner or later. He would have to get money from somewhere.

The door opened and his youngest appeared. "Why are you shouting?" she asked, slightly tearful.

Jackie smiled. "Your dad sat on that thing," she said, pointing. "He hurt his bum."

She made her laugh, when a moment before she had been worried, and a little afraid. Bannister wished she could do the same for him, as Jackie swept her up and took her back upstairs. She was a good girl, Jackie, and all he ever did these days was shout at her for spending her own money. Bannister felt tears of rage at the world and its injustice prick his eyes, and he reached over and picked up the paper again.

Maybe he could work out what all those initials meant. Maybe he could do the bloody job, once he knew what it was.

"This man Max Scott is a friend of yours, I believe," said Holyoak, towelling himself off, taking a breather as Rule moved the speed up on the jogging machine, and began to run.

It was a nice little set-up that Rule had, he thought. Get them fit, keep them fit. Check up on their heart, their blood pressure, their cholesterol levels, eyesight, teeth, the lot. One-stop health clinic. A healthy executive is a wealthy executive. One jump ahead of the competition; on top of stress, on top of the job. A ten-thousand-mile service for the executive's most important asset—his health. They paid through the nose for it because it gave them an edge.

"Yes," said Rule, perspiration running from his temple down the side of his face.

"What sort of man is he?"

"Honest," said Rule. "Reliable. But I'd be lying if I said hard working—Max does as much work as is necessary to get the job done. But he's straight. And likeable."

"I hear he plays around with women," said Holyoak.

He had taken full advantage of Rule's set-up at the clinic; Rule had been impressed by his physical fitness. Just because you were in your fifties was no reason to go to seed. Holyoak just worked harder than ever, and then relaxed by pushing himself to his limits in the gym. Like Scott, he neither drank nor smoked. Unlike Scott, he didn't play around with women.

Rule slowed the speed to walking pace, and mopped his brow with his sweat band. "I wonder where you heard that," he said.

"I was speaking to Mrs. Driver last night," said Holyoak. "I asked her the same question I just asked you. She said much the same things—except that she said he was reliable up to a point. The point being the opposite sex, where she seemed to believe he had very little willpower, and could easily get sidetracked."

Rule stepped off, and Holyoak got on, moving up through the speeds until he was running as fast as the machine would allow him to. "Well?" he said. "Does he play around with women?"

Rule was out of breath; Holyoak waited for his reply. "He used to," said Rule. "Not any more, I don't think."

Holyoak's feet pounded on the moving belt as he spoke. "I'm thinking of making him general manager," he said. "Mrs. Driver doesn't agree."

"No," said Rule. "She wouldn't. But I'd say he'd be the obvious choice, if Tim Driver doesn't want to carry on."

"Driver hates it. He wants to write about art, but he didn't think he could leave while his mother owned the business."

"That's what's really bugging Zelda," said Rule. "Not Max. She doesn't understand why Tim isn't more like his father."

Holyoak nodded. "I thought as much," he said, still less breathless than Rule, despite running as he spoke. "But be straight with me, Charles—are women a weakness as far as Scott's concerned?"

He could see that Rule was being torn between truth and loyalty under the guise of towelling off. He looked up at Holyoak. "I suppose I'd have to say yes," he said. "I think he would say yes, if you were to ask him himself." He sat back on the window ledge. "He doesn't chase women," he said. "He attracts them. And he . . . well, I was going to say that he found that difficult to resist, but I don't honestly think he ever tried to resist. But that was a long time ago. He's married now—he thinks the world of Catherine."

"But he was married before, wasn't he? Didn't his wife get herself—"

"Yes," said Rule quickly, cutting himself off. "But no one who knows Max believes that he had anything at all to do with that, except possibly Zelda. Max was at Catherine's flat in London when it happened—it all got sorted out."

"At her flat?" Holyoak said. "What was he doing there?"

Rule looked at him a little uncertainly. "Well—he was there about work, I think, but everyone thinks the worst, of course. She needed a reference, or something."

Holyoak frowned as he thought about that. He had said he was at Catherine's flat that night? It might be worth getting to know Scott a little better. It never hurt to know as much as possible about your employees. "All of which does rather bear Mrs. Driver out," he said, keeping his breathing strong.

Rule shrugged. "I wouldn't let it put you off making him general manager," he said. "He kept that business going for Zelda—Tim on his own would have been worse than useless. And he'll do a good job for you too."

Holyoak slowed the machine, and stepped off, manfully still controlling his breathing so that Rule would continue to feel inferior. "Thanks," he said. "You've been very helpful."

"It's ridiculous!" said Lloyd. "I told her so!"

Judy raised her eyebrows. "Lloyd—telling a seventeen-year-old girl that what she wants to do is ridiculous simply guarantees that she'll want to do it!"

"Oh, and you'd know, of course, having so many teenage children of your own!"

He was being unfair; he knew he was. Judy was trying to get everyone out of what promised to be a real mess, but they had had this conversation over and over again in the last two months, and it had got them nowhere.

"I *was* a seventeen-year-old girl, which is more than you've ever been."

Lloyd sank down into his leather armchair, acknowledging the truth of that, but failing to see where this endless argument was going to get any of them.

Judy came over to him, and knelt down, her hand on his knee. "It won't take long for it to dawn on her that she doesn't need anyone's permission," she said. "And that *is* dangerous."

"So I should just let her go off with my blessing, is that what you're saying? Let her take her chances? Hope that she doesn't end up sleeping in a shop doorway or walking the streets?"

Judy sighed. "Lloyd, take it from me. Seventeen-year-old girls do not aim to be street-walkers. They want to go to London because they think they'll get a fantastic job and be able to buy clothes and make-up and go to pop concerts all the time. It isn't like that, but you can't tell them that."

"So what do you tell them?" He got up again, and walked round the room in an effort to work off the frustration. He had seen them—so had Judy. Little girls hard-bitten before they hit their twenties. They weren't waifs and strays; they weren't some subspecies. They were ordinary young girls who had found themselves in extraordinary circumstances, and thought that they could see a way out. What they did have in common, most of them, was that they came from broken homes.

"You don't tell them it's ridiculous," Judy said.

"But it is! And this new man of Barbara's is just complicating everything!"

"Oh, Lloyd! You can't—"

"I'm not saying she shouldn't have a new man!" he said, cutting off her protests. He wasn't. He was pleased that Barbara had someone else; it took the edge off his guilt a little. "I'm saying it complicates things," he said. "Barbara's talking about marriage, you know. And I know that she'll be very careful and do everything right, but—" He broke off, and shrugged a little, because what he had been going to say wasn't strictly true. He had been going to say that Linda resented this man, and he knew that she didn't, not really. She liked him. She was using him as an excuse, that was all, but it wasn't terribly convincing.

A tiny part of him wanted to believe that she did resent him. Because Lloyd was afraid that he had already forfeited his daughter's love, and the manifestation of a possible stepfather had rattled him.

"It does complicate things," he said, this time being painfully honest with himself. "I lose my temper with her because I'm afraid I'm losing her."

Judy smiled, and came up to him, kissing him lightly on the lips. "I know all about that," she said.

He sighed. Did other people have all this trouble with women? Did it give them some sort of satisfaction to keep a man guessing? Judy liked living in two flats. He didn't. It always made him wonder if she really felt as strongly about him as he did about her.

"And you're not losing her any more than you're losing me," she said. "Just because people want independence doesn't mean they don't love you any more."

"Independence! What sort of independence is she going to have trying to make ends meet in London, for God's sake?"

"Lloyd—if you don't want your worst scenario to come true, you have to calm down and look at the problem. Because if you don't, then before you know it, she could actually have run away to London—and that's the last thing anyone wants."

"So what am I supposed to do?"

Judy's brown eyes looked frankly into his. "She wants to go to London," she said. "I think you should let her."

"Oh, sure," he said, breaking away from her. "Just let her. Let her go to London and share a flat with God knows who doing God knows what with God knows whom. Let her find out that you can't get a job for love nor money, and that you get kicked out of flats when you don't pay the rent. Let her—"

"If you could stop talking for once in your life and listen, it might help!"

She had raised her voice; the sheer surprise of it stopped Lloyd in mid-sentence. They had had rows—my God, had they had rows. Rows about one another, not about a third party. And never once, during any of them, had Judy shouted. He could yell himself hoarse, but she never yelled back. He was startled into listening to her.

"I think I have an idea," she said, her voice back to its usual even tone. "If you'd like to hear it."

For the first time in three months, Anna Worthing was doing something which she really understood, for which she was eminently qualified, and was doing it with her customary skill.

Max lay back, breathing deeply. After a few moments of silence, she told him how wonderful it had been, with considerably more conviction than she had ever felt with anyone else. After groping for weeks through an alien jungle of marketing strategies and product identification, she was finally operating in her own field of expertise; that was wonderful in itself. Her satisfaction was that of a job done well, but she had of course allowed Max to think that he had brought it about.

It had startled her when Victor had told her to get Max Scott into bed. She hadn't asked why; she knew better than to do that. But it did seem a little odd. And she had thought it might be difficult; she had been working with Max for three months, and he had never shown the slightest interest in her, not in that way. He was friendly, and helpful—he had even listened to her problems with work, and saved her from making a fool of herself more times than she cared to think about. But he'd never made a pass or anything like one; she had thought that he might not respond if she made the running.

She looked round the beige and white bedroom, wondering if Victor had put a camera in this one. His wife had been living here until Christmas, and he had said that he would be using it himself from time to time, so she had assumed that it would be fly-on-the-wall free. But presumably he wanted to have something on Max for some reason, and the guest flat in the Amsterdam office had had a camera recording the proceedings. Some of Victor's guests were still regretting their few hours of illicit pleasure with her. He had employed others now and again, when she wouldn't do, but mostly it was alimony-grabbing wives of whom the businessmen were afraid.

She hoped Max wouldn't regret it, but obviously he would, somehow, because he seemed to have nothing to offer Victor, which was the only other reason for her favours being bestowed. She liked Max; he was always there where you needed him, somehow. He didn't let people down. The words she had thought made her shiver slightly; she lived in dread of letting Victor down, of finding herself back down there on the street, hustling a living.

"Are you cold?" Max asked, putting his arm round her, drawing her into the warmth of his body.

"Goose walked over my grave," she said.

He kissed her. "You're not still worrying about the meeting, are you?" he asked. "Just tell them that you don't speak their jargon, and they had better tell you what they mean in plain English, or they're off the project." He smiled. "It's amazing what an effect that has on them," he said.

She hadn't thought about the meeting; the sheer relief of being back on familiar ground had driven all thoughts of Holyoak UK's image in the market place out of her mind.

She had devised all manner of strategies to hook Max, but as it turned out, it hadn't been difficult at all; the opportunity had presented itself. She had had a real problem with a letter from one of the firms which were competing to give Holyoak UK a corporate identity, of which she had barely understood a word, except the fact that their task was difficult, given the wide diversity of goods and services provided by Holyoak International; tomorrow, she would have to attend a meeting to discuss their proposals, and she had panicked.

It had almost been time for the offices to close up when she had gone into Max with it. He had explained it in layman's language; she had thanked him. She had told him—entirely truthfully—that she couldn't have survived without him for the past three months. Their eyes had met, their mouths had met, and in no time at all they were gliding up in the lift to the penthouse flat.

He was telling her how easy being a business executive was, once you got the hang of realizing that you simply got other people to do all the work. He was reassuring her, telling her she mustn't worry about the job. She was new to it, but all that she had to remember was that they were trying to impress her, not the other way round. She was the one who would make recomendations to the directors—all these flash young men were dependent on her goodwill, and would be only too eager to make certain that she understood their ideas.

She wished she could believe him, because Victor was determined that she should do this job, for some reason, even though she felt like a fish out of water. And she was so much better at this. But she liked Max, and it bothered her a little. She smiled up at him.

If he had to regret it, she could at least make sure that he would never forget it.

"Mark Callender?" said Charles, a little unwillingly, as he poured Victor a Perrier. "What about him?" He gave himself a dry sherry; it was the festive season, after all. They were in his office at the clinic and he had hoped that Victor had come to talk finance. He was showing some interest in expanding the operation; Charles had entertained visions of Rule Life Style Clinics springing up everywhere.

"He's PPS to a cabinet minister or something, isn't he?" said Holyoak.

"Yes," said Charles.

Mark Callender had been defeated at Stansfield by a tiny margin which had, of course, been overturned at the next election, by which time Stansfield had lost their chance. Mark had been snapped up by another constituency, and had been returned with a comfortable majority elsewhere. It had always irked Charles slightly that Stansfield had failed to see his friend's sterling qualities. Stansfield could have had Mark, and he could have had a friend at court, which was always useful.

"I was wondering if you could speak to him about the possibility of his boss opening the new factory," said Holyoak.

How did Holyoak know that a friend of his was parliamentary private secretary to anyone? Zelda, he supposed. Zelda could spread news faster than any other medium known to man. She had doubtless given Victor the lowdown on poor old Max, and what had happened during that election, in the hope of spiking his chances of promotion. How galling for Zelda that the only piece of information upon which Holyoak had seized was the one in which he saw an opportunity to push Holyoak UK into the news bulletins. All the forecasts suggested that the opening would coincide with the run-up to the election, and that could mean free publicity.

He had no desire at all to rake up old memories, but he didn't want to offend Holyoak, who was talking quite seriously about investing in the clinic, albeit not on the grand scale of Charles's daydreams.

"I'll see what I can do," he said.

"I never forget a favour," said Holyoak. "You get him to the opening, and I'll be very grateful. You have my word."

Charles thought about that. "Have you made up your mind about the general manager's job?" he asked.

"Not yet," said Holyoak.

"I'd like to think that Max hadn't been ruled out because of gossip and rumours," said Charles. "Or even his weakness."

Holyoak nodded. "Done," he said.

"Charles got him to do it," said Geraldine. "His friend Mark is his PPS. I think he jumped at the chance to show that someone had faith in Britain and the government."

"The opening's on the first of April," said Zelda, with a laugh. "Maybe Mark's got a sense of humour."

Geraldine smiled. "You met him," she said. "What do you think?"

"True. Not the practical joke sort. Well, that should make certain that the opening gets coverage. And I suppose it's a little feather in Charles's cap, too."

Geraldine nodded. Charles liked being the man with the contacts in high places. Getting Holyoak an introduction to someone who might one day have need of his sophisticated security systems on a government contract was more than a little feather in his cap. She heard nothing but Victor this and Victor that these days. It used to be Max; now it was Victor.

"I'm surprised Charles has never thought about standing for Parliament," said Zelda.

Geraldine smiled. "He was quite interested in politics once," she said. "I think it would be too rough for him—he'd be taking offence all the time. Anyway, he went off the idea."

Zelda laughed. "Another coffee?" she said.

Zelda always fed and watered her guests until they staggered out, begging for a week on bread and water. Charles could hardly bring himself to visit her, what with the cholesterol and the sugar and the saturated fats, and had manufactured a prior engagement when she had invited them to a pre-Christmas dinner. But she was a wonderful cook; Geraldine had learned the art from Zelda, modified by Charles's healthy eating regimen, but she still felt she could never hold a candle to Zelda herself. And she wouldn't dream of turning down an invitation to eat at Zelda's, so she had come on her own. It had been fun, just the two of them.

"You should do a cookery book, Zelda," she said, pushing her cup across the table for more coffee.

"Your husband would have it banned," said Zelda. "Do you fancy a brandy?"

Charles allowed alcohol, within certain strictly defined limits, which Geraldine was in no danger of meeting, never mind exceeding. "Please," she said.

"I thought Charles had taken his first step on the road to Westminster when Mark Whatsisname was here," said Zelda.

Geraldine nodded. "I think that was the idea," she said. "But he didn't pursue it. I don't know why, really. I think maybe what happened to Valerie gave the whole election bad associations. He had no heart for it next time round."

"Could be," said Zelda. "And I suppose you didn't help."

"Me? What did I do?" Zelda handed her a brandy which probably shouldn't be consumed prior to driving. Geraldine reached over for the bottle and solemnly poured half of it back in.

"You weren't exactly cock-a-hoop about him running all over the town wearing a blue rosette, were you?" said Zelda.

Geraldine smiled. "Not exactly," she said. "But I've got used to the idea that I married a turncoat."

"He just saw sense," said Zelda.

"I suppose he was always a Tory, really. He just thought he was a socialist because Max was. At least Max is still on the side of the people."

Zelda made a snort of contempt, something Geraldine had never been able to do. Zelda did it beautifully.

"He really burnt his boats with you, didn't he?" said Geraldine.

"Yes, he did," Zelda sipped her brandy.

It was the one subject on which Zelda could not be drawn; her legendary delight in gossip did not extend to talking about herself and Max. But from the moment Catherine had set foot in Stansfield, Max had become *persona non grata* with Zelda, and he had stayed that way.

"He's having a thing with Anna Worthing," she said, steering the subject away from herself. "If I'm any judge."

Geraldine looked at her blankly. "Who's Anna Worthing?" she asked.

"That woman that came over here from Holland—the one who was here to start off negotiations."

"Oh, her! But I thought she was supposed to be the big boss's girlfriend."

"So they say. Tim says it's all over the papers there—

250

Holyoak's famous everywhere but here, he says, and the papers have got hold of this story about him and Anna Worthing. They say it's been going on for years—he had set her up in Amsterdam, and he only put her officially on the payroll when he moved his head office over here. Tim says she knows nothing about the job—she hasn't even got an O-level to her name. That's who the penthouse flat's for—so they can slip up there after work. But Max has beaten him to it, if you ask me."

Geraldine gave a little shrug. "He does seem very devoted to his wife," she said. "I had to call in on her every day before they got the full-time nurse. And she wasn't that bad, not then. She's very sick now, though."

"Well, that's just it. He's famous *for* being devoted to his wife, amongst other things—he's all for family and honouring your obligations. Marriage vows are marriage vows, that sort of stuff. You don't get involved with other women just because your wife can't do anything for you. Tim says the newspaper stuff is getting quite juicy—they say Holyoak actually took Anna Worthing over there at the same time as his wife." She shrugged. "But perhaps his wife knows all about it," she said.

"For what it's worth," Geraldine said, "Charles doesn't think she is Victor's mistress, and he's got to know him quite well over the past few weeks."

"Charles doesn't think that Max screws around, and he's known him for thirty years. You'll forgive me if I don't place much faith in what Charles thinks."

Geraldine laughed. Zelda had had poor Max in bed with every woman to whom he had ever so much as said good morning, and Charles was quite convinced that he had entirely mended his ways since he had married Catherine. Somewhere about the middle of these two extremes was Geraldine's guess.

"What do you think of Holyoak?" she asked Zelda.

"I don't really know him all that well," she said. "Tim's done all the negotiation."

"What does Tim think of him?" asked Geraldine.

Zelda looked down into her coffee cup. "I haven't seen much of Tim since he got back," she said.

"Not even at work?"

"No." Zelda looked up. "He took a month's holiday once the deal went through," she said. "He's told Holyoak he doesn't want to carry on in the business."

"Oh." Geraldine wasn't sure what to say. Everyone but Zelda knew that Tim hated the business; he had gone into it when he left university as a stop-gap measure simply because of Zelda's refusal to promote Max. Max did all the work, and Tim signed the letters and contracts. Zelda had never promoted Max, and never looked for anyone else. Tim had worked very hard to sell the business, because that way he could get out. It wouldn't be his father's business any more, and the moral blackmail which had kept him there would cease to have any effect.

Not that Zelda had had any notion that that was what she had been doing; she still hadn't. She just thought that Tim was misguided.

"So—who'll be the new general manager?" asked Geraldine.

"Well it won't be Max Scott, if I have any say in the matter," said Zelda. "I've put Holyoak straight about him."

The Christmas holidays were over; the old Driver practice of closing the factory over both Christmas and New Year had been swept away by the new management, who had also instituted the heartily disliked half an hour for lunch; the office closed thirty minutes earlier in the evening, now that they were in the new building. Max didn't see what difference it made, except that he and Anna could get together half an hour sooner, so it suited him.

It was business as usual on the last day of the old year, as Max knocked on Zelda's door, and went in.

"Come in, Max," said Zelda. "Sit down."

Max looked round Zelda's new office. Her new title was Director, Personnel—it was on the door. "This is what I call executive status," he said, with a smile. "You could mark out a tennis court in here." He sat down.

She didn't smile back. But then, he couldn't honestly remember the last time Zelda had smiled at him. It was a source of some regret to him that he had never been able to develop his infant relationship with her; he still found her very attractive. And he liked her, quite apart from that; all he really wanted from Zelda was a smile. But it wasn't to be.

"Our lord and master communicates with me by phone most

252

of the time," she said. "I presume you know him rather better than that."

Max frowned. "Holyoak, do you mean?" He shook his head. "I've never clapped eyes on him," he said. "I was beginning to think that he must be a fantasy friend of Charles's. I'm relieved to hear he communicates with you at all."

It was Zelda's turn to frown. "You mean he doesn't even know you?" she said. "He's never spoken to you?"

Max shook his head, puzzled by her reaction. "No," he said. "Why should he have?"

"Because he's just made you general manager," she said.

Max stared at her. "What?" he said.

"Against my advice," she said. "But I did at least think that he'd had some discussion with you on the matter."

General manager? Just like that? Max still couldn't believe she'd said it. And he'd detailed poor old Zelda to tell him, which must be very nearly killing her.

"It's a responsible job, Max," Zelda was saying. "I think you may have to cut down on the number of young women who come into my office saying that they have to leave for personal reasons."

Max grinned. "I don't think they're all down to me," he said.

"I can only assume that he listens to the advice of his Public Relations manager when he makes senior appointments," she said, handing him his letter of appointment.

Good old Zelda. Trust her to have noticed him and Anna. Could that possibly by why he'd got the job? Surely not.

"A word of advice, Max. I think you're trespassing on his territory. You might not keep the job too long if he finds out what's going on."

Was he? Anna hadn't said anything to that effect. Max smiled. He hadn't wanted the job in the first place—he was astonished that he had been given it. The delightfully accommodating Anna, though—that was a different matter; he had never been so well-catered for in that department. No declarations of love, no demands, no hassle at all. They just took sheer pleasure in one another, and he'd sooner keep Anna and lose the job any day.

And if she was prepared to risk it, so was he.

CHAPTER ELEVEN

Now: Friday, 3 April, P.M. . . .

"VICTOR HOLYOAK," JUDY SAID.

"I said I wasn't answering any more questions."

Judy smiled at him. "You said you'd never seen him before, Dave. But you had. You booked him for kerb-crawling in Leyford, thirteen years ago."

"You expect me to remember that? *And* recognize him after he's been stabbed to death?"

"Do you expect me to believe this?" she countered, lifting up a copy of his statement. She waited for a moment, then turned a page in her notebook. "Do you knock your wife and kids about, Dave?" she asked pleasantly.

"What sort of question's that?" he demanded.

"Do you?" she repeated.

"Of course I don't!" He had never laid a hand on Jackie or the kids.

"But you hit Anna, didn't you? After she reported you?"

Bannister flushed a little. He should have known Anna would have told them that, once she had started speaking at all. "That little whore had it coming," he said.

Judy nodded. "You wanted revenge," she said. "Is it true that Holyoak gave you a severe beating in return?"

If he didn't answer, it looked more like a motive for murder than if he did. He sighed. "Yes," he said. "I passed out long before he'd finished with me."

She looked at him, her brown eyes troubled by the thought of that. "Did you want revenge again?" she asked.

Bannister smiled. "If I'd gone after him with a knife he'd have had it off me and at my throat before I could blink," he said. "I just wanted compensation."

She wrote that down. He smiled.

"There I was," he said, "watching the early evening news. And I'm looking at little Annabel, dressed up to the nines, doing some high-powered job for a security company, shaking hands with a bloody cabinet minister. Then I see who she's working for. Dressed in his Armani suit—what did they say? He was one of the richest men in Europe?" He leant forward. "You know where I was? I was in a high-rise flat which I'm going to be evicted from any day now. I couldn't keep my job because of what that bastard did to me."

"Did you leave the service on health grounds?" she asked.

"No. Because I'd been offered a job with a security firm, and if I'd done that, they wouldn't have wanted to know. So I just left. But the security firm went bust. I haven't had a proper job since. Thanks to him. So I thought about that, and the more I thought about it, the less fair it seemed. So I came here, I went to that factory. But the jamboree was all over, and I went to the first pub I saw instead. And I met little Annabel again."

"And then what?"

"I got her to tell me how to get in. She was pissed—she'd had a row with him. I thought he'd got some woman up there, and that was why she was so keen for me to call unannounced. She left, I waited until closing time, then I walked to the factory, got in the way she'd told me, and the rest you know."

"You weren't afraid to face him after what he'd done to you last time?"

"He's respectable now," said Bannister. "I didn't think he'd want to explain why he'd got scrambled ex-copper all over his carpet. And I thought he was with someone—he wouldn't do anything to me in front of a witness."

"What made you think he'd give you money? Did you think he might feel remorse for what he did to you?" Her brown eyes were amused now.

He didn't answer.

"Anna said he could have put you in hospital," she said. "How come he didn't? Why stop short? Why weren't you taken away in an ambulance, Dave?"

He smiled again. He had always known that Judy would get on. She was sharp. But he wasn't going to get done for aiding and abetting a criminal or being accessory to murder or any of the other things he had done that night.

"I admit burgling the flat," he said. "I admit failing to report a murder. Charge me, or let me go."

She terminated the interview, and sealed the tapes. Then she looked at him.

"Come on, Dave," she said. "By my reckoning, you still owe me a favour. You had something on Holyoak, hadn't you? You thought you could get money for keeping your mouth shut about whatever he involved you in. Because he didn't give a damn about Annabel, did he? He wanted a policeman in his pocket, and if I knew why, I might find out who murdered him. It had something to do with Operation Kerbcrawl, didn't it?"

Well, well, he thought, looking at the switched-off tape-recorder. She broke the rules sometimes, then. And she was half-way there with her guesswork. No tapes, so he could deny saying anything. No Holyoak, so no broken kneecaps. He did owe her a favour.

"All I had to do was contact him once we were told we were going out on Operation Kerbcrawl. Then I had to watch for his Daimler—if I ever saw it, I had to make sure that I was the one who booked the driver or else."

"And did you see it?"

"Eventually. I nearly broke my neck getting to him before anyone else. It looked like him, behind the wheel. I mean, the beard and the scar and everything."

Her eyes had widened; there was no way she was going to believe what he was about to tell her, but she had asked, so he was telling.

"But it wasn't him," he continued. "It was someone much younger. You could see that, close to. And it was a false scar—you could smell the spirit gum. That was why I had to be the one to book him. And then I realized that I knew who it was—it was a guy by the name of Wilkes. Raymond Arthur Wilkes. He was an actor, of sorts. He was always being done for gross indecency—he'd hang around the Gents looking for pick-ups. I booked him as Victor Holyoak, and my job was done."

He knew it sounded crazy. It had seemed crazy at the time, and now, actually telling someone about it, it sounded worse than ever. He couldn't look at her. "You don't believe a word, do you?" he said.

"Oh, but I do," she said.

He looked up.

She smiled. "My DCI will be very anxious to talk to Raymond Arthur Wilkes," she said.

Bannister looked bleakly at her. "That's just it," he said. "He can't talk to him. Because two hours later we found him in his car with his brains blown out. They reckon it was suicide."

"What do you remember about it?" she asked.

"Blood on the windscreen," said Bannister.

He told her what little he knew. "If this comes to anything, you get me immunity from prosecution, or you're the one in trouble," he said.

Judy nodded, and got up to go. Then she turned back. "Could it have been the shower, Dave?" she asked. "This noise you heard?"

He could hear it, like a snatch of a song that you can't catch hold of. He could hear it, but he couldn't put a name to it. It wasn't a shower.

"No," he said. "Sorry."

"Raymond Arthur Wilkes was a frequent visitor to the house of a businessman called Simon Tarrant," said the fairly hostile voice on the other end of the line. "His car was seen driving away at speed the night Tarrant got shot. Then a few hours later Wilkes is found, having blown his brains out with the same gun that was used on Tarrant—what are we supposed to have overlooked, Chief Inspector?"

Lloyd sighed. "Did you carry out enquiries into Wilkes's death?" he asked.

"No. He killed his boyfriend and he killed himself—we weren't looking for anyone else in connection with the incident," he said, switching on an official accent.

"Why did the inquest return an open verdict?"

"The pathologist came out with some stuff about that not being how people normally shot themselves in cars," said the voice. "They normally put the gun in their mouths, or whatever. He shot himself behind the ear. And he thought the radio had been turned up to mask the sound of the shot, and why would a suicide do that—that sort of thing."

"That didn't seem worth investigating to you, Chief Inspector?" asked Lloyd.

"If suicides were normal, they wouldn't be shooting themselves in sodding cars at all, would they? And he wasn't normal in the first bloody place!"

"So he wasn't worth an investigation?" asked Lloyd. "Is that it? Warwickshire were happy that they had their man, and you all knew that he hung about public lavatories, so it was easier just to put the file away and quietly forget about any doubts there were, is that it?"

"Of course it wasn't worth it! He was a poofter who lost his rag with his boyfriend. He went out of his league, and didn't like it when he was shown the door. So he shot Tarrant and he shot himself. Or are you trying to say he was murdered?"

"I'm saying you had better take another look at it," said Lloyd. "I have reason to believe that on the night in question, Wilkes was impersonating one Victor Holyoak, and getting himself booked in that name by a police officer who was working for Victor Holyoak, and who recognized him."

There was a silence, during which Lloyd shot a look at Judy. He was none too sanguine about how she had obtained the information about Raymond Arthur Wilkes, but at least he wasn't going mad.

He spoke again to the now blessedly silent chief inspector at the other end. "Holyoak was on the list of known associates of Tarrant that the Warwickshire police would have interviewed, had Wilkes not conveniently turned up dead. I suspect that he would have produced the summons to prove that he was in Leyford rather than Warwickshire that night. But Holyoak's dead too, now, so I can't very well ask him."

"Well . . . wouldn't it be easier just to let sleeping dogs lie?"

Lloyd took a deep breath. "It would be easier," he said. "Just like it was easier to forget about Wilkes than to do any proper investigation of his death. But I have no intention of forgetting about it. A young man died, Chief Inspector. I think he died at Holyoak's hands, and I believe that sheer prejudice prevented the murder investigation which should have taken place at the time."

He slammed the phone down and glared at Judy. This murder would stay forgotten if Bannister denied what he had told her. But then, he would never have told her at all if it hadn't been off the record.

"That rather brings us back to Anna, doesn't it?" she said, after a moment.

Lloyd didn't see how. He put on his glasses to read the list that Holyoak's secretary had sent over of exactly who had keys to Holyoak's penthouse. The security was tight; the man had had no intention of being murdered in his bed, but that was exactly what had happened to him. The keys had to be obtained from the locksmith who had provided the locks; three keys to the ground-floor door, and two to the flat door itself had been provided.

"She's the only other person involved in Operation Kerbcrawl," Judy said. "Unless you killed him, because I know I didn't."

He looked up, and she blurred. He moved his glasses down his nose, and she came into focus. "Why would she kill him?" he asked.

"They had some sort of row—she's admitted that."

"Over her job, according to her. Over her affair with Scott, according to Tom Finch. Over another woman, according to you at one point. It could have nothing to do with Operation KC."

Judy gave him a look. "Lloyd—why did he take her to Holland? Why did he buy her Porsches and jewellery and *objets d'art* that cost as much as I earn in a year? Why does she wear designer clothes and live in a luxury flat?"

Lloyd shrugged slightly. "Her services were worth it?" he suggested.

"But if that's the case—why does she insist that she wasn't sleeping with him?"

That was easy. "Because whoever was sleeping with him seems to have stabbed him to death," Lloyd said. "If she wasn't, then she would be quite insistent, wouldn't she?"

Judy sat back. "So—if she *was*, then she's top of the list. And if she *wasn't*—I come back to my original question. Why all the goodies?"

Lloyd took his glasses off. "You think she was blackmailing him?"

"If she knew about this elaborate alibi, she certainly could have been."

"Then I'm back to *my* original question," he said smugly, putting his glasses back on, and returning to the list of key-holders. "Why would she kill the proverbial goose?" He smiled to himself as Judy failed to come up with an answer. "And I might just have found out who this mysterious other woman is," he said.

Judy sat up, trying to read the list upside-down.

"What sort of person's reputation would have to be protected?" he asked. "*Have* to be, as opposed to its being better that way?"

"Don't know, give up."

"A doctor—her livelihood could depend on not getting caught in bed with the patients."

"Geraldine Rule?" said Judy, incredulously.

"It says here that there were three copies made of the key to the outside door to the penthouse. Holyoak had one for each door, and so did Anna Worthing. But a third key to the downstairs door was made." He looked up from the list. "For one Dr. Rule," he said.

Judy's eyebrows rose a little. "Freddie seems to think that it was as likely to be Dr. Charles Rule as Dr. Geraldine," she said.

Lloyd smiled. "Dr. G. S. Rule," he said.

"But no one went in by that door."

"She might not have had to," Lloyd said. "She was in the car with Scott and Zelda, but perhaps she didn't leave with them. Perhaps she went back up to see Holyoak."

"Isn't this just a bit shot-in-the-dark-ish?"

"Why would she have a key?" Lloyd persisted.

"I don't know—why didn't she have both keys, come to that?"

"He didn't want her going in there when he wasn't there," said Lloyd.

"Then why give her a key at all?"

"I don't know." He reached for the directory, and found her number. "But I think I'll make an appointment with the doctor," he said, with a smile. "And find out."

The phone, as they do on such occasions, rang and rang;

Lloyd was about to give up, when it was answered. "Finch?" Lloyd said, startled.

"Sir—I was just about to ring you. I gave up waiting for the Rules to come and give us their prints, and came here to get them." There was a pause. "The uniforms were already here," he said. "Geraldine Rule is dead."

Lloyd took a moment to take that in, then relayed the information to Judy. The sceptical look vanished, and she grew thoughtful.

"We'll be right there, Tom," he said.

They took Judy's car; these days she had one that actually started, and she drove faster than he did. Not that there was any real urgency; the woman was dead, and Finch was already on the scene. But Lloyd felt in his bones that things were coming together somehow, and for once he let Judy exceed speed limits without grumbling at her.

Finch met them at the door. The police surgeon had sent for the pathologist, he said, but it was only because it had happened in the middle of the murder enquiry in which she was peripherally involved, because it seemed to him to be straightforward suicide.

At least, that was Lloyd's pained interpretation; what Finch had actually said was that the doc had sent for Freddie just in case it wasn't kosher, but it looked like she had topped herself, all right.

"Husband's through there," he said. "He looks gutted."

He did, Lloyd conceded. Charles Rule sat upright on an armchair, staring at nothing. Zelda Driver, of course, was there. But she was a good person to have around in a crisis; Lloyd didn't mind her presence. She made to leave when Lloyd and Judy went in, but her attempt to do so stirred Rule from his trance, and he put out a hand, touching her arm.

"No," he said. "Stay."

Zelda looked at Lloyd, then back at Rule. "They might not want me here, Charles," she said gently.

"Please stay," he said.

Lloyd shrugged his indifference; Zelda sat down on the pouffe by Rule's chair, as he continued to hold on to her arm, like a child.

Lloyd glanced at Judy, and plunged in. There wasn't much else he could do. "Dr. Rule," he said, "I know that this is a dreadful time to have to ask you questions, but I'm afraid it's necessary."

Rule nodded. His eyes still stared ahead.

Lloyd didn't want to do this, but he had to; he had no choice. "Do you have any idea why your wife would take her own life?" he asked.

Rule nodded again, and Lloyd didn't speak. He had to let Rule take his own time.

"She . . . she wanted a baby." He blinked slowly, not speaking. "It was all she thought about. Always. But I— I couldn't . . ." His eyes slid slowly round to Lloyd. "I couldn't give her a baby. We tried, but we knew. I couldn't. She . . . she tried to have another man's baby."

Lloyd looked at Zelda, who shook her head to indicate that she knew nothing about it.

"I found out . . . I put a stop to it," Charles said. "I had to. Not again. I couldn't go through all that—not again."

"Whose baby?" asked Judy quietly.

"Holyoak's. I knew. When we took Catherine up there, and Gerry—" He paused. "Geraldine knew where everything was. Where things were kept, which room was the bedroom . . . I knew."

Lloyd had barely had time to feel smug before Zelda Driver spoke.

"But she would," she said.

Charles Rule's agonized eyes moved towards her.

"Mrs. Holyoak stayed there until the house was ready," she said. "Geraldine saw her there every day. Didn't you realize that that's where she was?"

Rule put a hand to his mouth. "But . . . I heard Holyoak. I heard Anna Worthing saying she wouldn't be a decoy—I heard her. He wanted people to think it was her so that no one would find out the truth."

Lloyd wasn't sure which question to ask first. When had he heard Holyoak and Anna Worthing? How had he heard them? What exactly had he heard? He settled on the third.

"Did Holyoak mention your wife by name?" he asked.

The bleak eyes looked back at him now, and Rule shook his head.

"When did you overhear this conversation, Dr. Rule?" Judy asked, as a middle-aged man came into the room.

"Charles—I came as soon as I heard. I don't know what to say—" He broke off and looked at Lloyd. "Are you the police?" he asked.

"Yes," said Lloyd. "And you are . . . ?"

"Brindley. I'm Dr. Rule's doctor—and I must ask you to leave. He's in no fit state to answer questions."

No. Lloyd knew that. It was the very best time to get answers, in his opinion. "We will have to talk to him as soon as possible," he said.

"Yes, of course. But if you'll please leave now—and Mrs. Driver?"

Charles made no objection this time, and all three of them found themselves firmly on the other side of a closed door.

"Zelda," said Lloyd, steering her into an empty room which turned out to be the waiting room. "A word."

Zelda waited until the door was closed, and looked at Lloyd. "He's raving," she said. "Geraldine was no more having an affair with Holyoak than I was."

Lloyd wasn't convinced. "Did you know she had a key to Holyoak's flat?" he asked.

"Yes, of course she did. The lift from the car park is closed down after six thirty."

"Why couldn't she just ring the doorbell?"

"Mrs. Holyoak found it quite difficult to reach the button on the door phone from her chair—the one that opens the outside door. Geraldine was given a key because she went there every day. Holyoak insisted. Geraldine said he was overprotective—"

Judy interrupted her, the only way of stopping the flow of words. "What about this full-time nurse?" she asked.

"They've got one again now that Mrs. Holyoak's in the house," Zelda explained briskly. "But there was no room for one in the flat—and no need, really. She's really only needed full-time care this last month, but that was why Holyoak wanted Geraldine to go every day—because there was no nurse."

Judy smiled. "Ever thought of joining the police, Mrs. Driver?" she asked.

"Zelda, please." She looked at Lloyd. "And I think I know when Charles must have overheard that conversation," she said. "He went back into the building to find a phone. His bleeper thing went. He went back up in the lift. But he's wrong, Lloyd. I *know* Geraldine—I'd have known if she had been involved with Holyoak."

She was too bright, too brisk. And she had known Geraldine Rule since they were children. Zelda was fighting tears, and winning. But she shouldn't be. Lloyd led her to a chair. "Sit down, Zelda," he said. "Don't pretend nothing's happened."

She sat, but she determinedly remained in control. "You *can't* think Geraldine was having an affair with Holyoak," she said.

Lloyd shrugged a little. "He was with someone before he died," he told her, a touch unprofessionally. He supposed that was how come Zelda knew so much about everyone's business.

"Anna Worthing, of course!"

"She denies that completely," said Lloyd.

"Well, she would! I really don't think you should let your first impressions—" She broke off. "Oh—I'm sorry," she said. "Forgive me. But—whoever he was with, it wasn't Geraldine, unless it was in the middle of the night, because she was with me from when we left the reception until midnight."

Lloyd's ears pricked up.

"We dropped Max off," she said. "But we were both convinced he would just go straight home—and . . ." She looked at Judy. "We were worried about Catherine—with Max behaving so oddly. I mean—well, I'd never seen him like that, and neither had Geraldine. Charles thought we were being very silly, but you have no idea how unlike Max it all was. Have you met Max?" she asked suddenly.

Judy shook her head.

"I know what you must think. All you know of him is that he hit Catherine and you found him at Anna Worthing's flat. But he's a lovely man. Oh, I know—he lied to me about Catherine, and I never really forgave him for that, but I had never thought for one moment that he had anything to do with what happened to Valerie, until—" The tears were bright in her eyes. "He . . . he was so odd. It was horrible thinking that maybe— maybe he really had . . ." She straightened her shoulders. "Anyway, I drove straight to their house, to get there before he did. But Catherine wasn't there." She looked up at Lloyd. "There's a pub across the road," she said. "So we went in there and watched and waited, but neither of them had come home by closing time. I took Geraldine home." She was trembling as she spoke. "I dropped her off here at about midnight—Charles was here, he'll tell you. She had nothing to do with Holyoak!"

The unnatural composure snapped, much to Lloyd's relief, and Judy led her off somewhere.

Charles Rule was going to have to answer questions whether his doctor liked it or not. The evidence pointed to a sexual encounter, and Geraldine was no longer in the running as Victor's playmate; was Judy's throwaway remark about Charles Rule being a possibility not so throwaway after all?

Judy came back then. "I've left Zelda making tea for everyone," she said.

Lloyd smiled. "Zelda never just makes tea," he said. "We'll be lucky to escape without a three-course meal. Did you speak to the doctor about when we can talk to Rule?"

"Yes," she said. "In about twenty minutes, he said."

Lloyd sat down, and picked up a *Country Life*, flicking through its genteel pages. He was waiting, in a waiting room. He might as well do the right thing.

"He said something interesting about Geraldine," said Judy.

Lloyd looked up from the magazine.

"He said he wasn't surprised at the suicide. That he'd often worried about what would happen when Geraldine realized how unhappy she was."

"Because she couldn't have a baby?"

Judy shook her head. "He said that before she married Charles Rule she thought that no one should be able to buy good health. She was a fervent believer in the National Health Service—and she was twenty-seven, not a teenager, so it was a real commitment. But she ended up helping run a private clinic for rich capitalists, and jointly running a private practice. He says she hadn't changed her opinion—she just gave in to her husband's. And if she did that about work, she must have done it about everything else. And one day she would realize that she had."

"So you don't think her suicide has anything to do with Holyoak?"

"I'm beginning to wonder," said Judy, "if Holyoak had anything to do with women at all. Anna swears her relationship with him was non-sexual . . . and Raymond Wilkes was gay."

Lloyd thought about Raymond Arthur Wilkes. Gay, according to Judy. A faggot, according to the unpleasant Bannister, a poofter according to the odious chief inspector with whom he had spoken. A homosexual in Lloyd's book, and in cahoots with Holyoak in establishing an alibi for some nefarious doings, probably the murder of this man in Warwickshire.

"It would explain why Holyoak wanted Anna to pose as his mistress, if what Rule said just now is true," said Judy. "His image was of macho man, after all."

"Were you serious when you suggested Charles Rule himself?" asked Lloyd.

"Not entirely," she said.

It was possible, he supposed. But it was just as possible that Rule had believed his wife to be having an affair with the man. Either way, it was all too possible that he ended up stabbing Holyoak to death. But where was Anna, when all this was going on? If she had left when Rule came to the door, she would have had to have seen him, and why in the world wouldn't she have said?

Lloyd thought about that. And he thought about the wardrobe doors. And about how scared Anna was, all the time.

Max had come to find comfort; the excitement of their previous meetings had gone, and his pleasure was diminished by her lack of response, but he needed to lose himself in her, all the same. And she still needed reassurance. She clung to him now as they lay together, and the afternoon darkened into evening.

"They think I killed Victor," she said miserably.

"No," he said, kissing her. "No, no. No, they don't."

"They *do*. Bannister thinks I did. And I didn't, Max—I swear, I didn't!"

"I know," he said, his lips on her neck. "I know you didn't kill him."

"You don't. No one does. But I didn't. Someone came to the door—Bannister thinks I set him up. He'll come after me, I know he will."

"Ssh," Max said, rocking her gently, like a baby. "Finch said he'd look out for you."

266

"I don't believe him."

Max still wasn't sure where this Bannister person fitted in to all of this, except that Anna had sent him up to get into the flat that night, and now she was frightened of him.

"I'll stay with you," he said. "I won't let him hurt you."

"Victor," she said. "I wish Victor was here. He'd keep him away. He'd keep them all away."

Max sighed. "I'm here," he said, but he knew that he was a poor substitute.

She suddenly pushed herself free of his arms, and sat up, reaching for the brandy that she had been about to hit when he'd arrived.

"Anna—that isn't . . ."

"No? Well, a quick screw might help you relax, but I need more than that."

He watched as she poured herself a large measure.

"I need Victor," she said, gulping some down.

"How did you meet him?" asked Max, in the hope that getting her life story might stop her drinking so fast.

"I met him when he was looking for your wife. She lived across the landing from me," Anna said.

Max's eyebrows rose. "You lived there?" he said. "I thought the tenants were all hookers apart from Catherine."

She swallowed the brandy, and looked at him through the empty glass. "You thought right," she said.

Max blinked. "You were a prostitute?" he said slowly. Then he felt silly. Positively unworldly. He really should have realized; she was rather better versed in the erotic arts than most of the women of his acquaintance.

"Oh, yes." She recharged the glass. "Taking me to Holland did seem a bit coals to Newcastle, but I wasn't about to turn it down." She gulped down half the measure. "He'd pay my fare, my rent, my food and clothes."

"He promoted you to kept woman?" he said, with an attempt at a smile.

She shook her head. "No," she said wearily. "Why will no one believe me? I'm not his mistress. I never have been."

"So what did you do for him?"

"I worked for him, that's all."

And he had sacked her. Max still felt bad about that. "Did you get into trouble because of me?" he asked.

She looked at him, shaking her head a little sadly. "He *told* me to sleep with you, Max," she said.

"What?" He must have misunderstood.

"He told me to do it," she replied. "I never stopped being a prostitute. That's what I did. What I do. What I am. My job was to make men like you think they were fantastic in bed. All right?"

No. No, it was far from all right. And it made no sense. "Why?" he asked, bewildered. "Why did he tell you to sleep with me?"

She shrugged.

Max closed his eyes for a second, then threw the sheets back, swinging his legs out of bed.

"Don't leave me," she said.

He turned to look at her. "You tell me that I was just some trick that you turned, and—"

"You're not now. Please, Max. Stay. I'm frightened."

He got back into bed; she was a damsel in distress, and he couldn't resist that. He couldn't leave her to drink away thoughts of a vengeful Bannister and whatever other demons lurked in her psyche; he couldn't abandon her, despite what she had done to him. Like Catherine at the side of the road, she would be better off with him than with the alternative. He took the glass from her. "You don't need that," he said.

Someone who had seen it all, done it all, and then some; she would take some convincing that his ministrations could beat the bottle. It was a challenge; it would concentrate his mind on something other than what was happening in the world beyond the darkened window.

And that was what he needed, because he didn't think his mind could cope with that any more.

"Are you feeling up to this, Dr. Rule?" asked Lloyd.

"Yes," he said. "You must have questions . . . I'm sorry—I probably wasn't making much sense earlier."

"Dr. Rule," said the inspector briskly. "I understand that you went back into the Holyoak office building after everyone had left on Wednesday night," she said.

Charles nodded. "I had been paged," he said. "It could have been urgent. I . . . I saw Mr. Holyoak," he said. "Perhaps I should have told you that before. I couldn't find a phone that worked downstairs because the switchboard was closed—so I went up to ask if I might use Mr. Holyoak's phone."

A silence. He didn't have to answer their questions, they had said. "But the thing is," he said, "as I came out of the lift, I could hear that he was arguing with someone. I assume it was Anna Worthing—she had left the reception with him, and that's where everyone thought they had gone. I waited for a little while—I didn't like to interrupt. But then I knocked on the door. There was a bit of a wait, and when Holyoak opened it, he was alone. At least, no one else was in evidence."

"You didn't think to tell us this before now?" asked Finch angrily, to be silenced by a look from the inspector.

"Well—no. I didn't know it was critical."

Silly answer. A disappearing trick prior to a murder, and he didn't think it was critical. But he was cross-examining himself; the inspector clearly didn't want Sergeant Finch to, and he had to content himself with looking unimpressed by Charles's reply.

"What exactly did you hear?" she asked.

Exactly. He shook his head. He didn't know, not exactly. "They were shouting," he said. "Angry—I just heard snatches." He thought about it. "She was angry," he said. "She was shouting—I could hear her more clearly. He was just talking, really."

Victor's tone of voice had actually seemed almost threatening to Charles, but in truth, it simply hadn't sounded anything in particular, and he certainly hadn't been threatening her in so many words, so he mustn't give them that impression. In fact, Holyoak hadn't evinced any emotion that Charles could put a name to. She had been angry, though. Very angry.

"She said she wouldn't be a decoy for whoever he was—" He broke off. "She was a little coarse," he said.

"And what did he say?"

"He just told her not to swear," said Charles. "Then she asked why it was better that people should think it was her rather than this other person. He said because it was vital that no one found out; he had given his word. She called him names then."

"Was he angry?"

"No. He just told her to be quiet and listen. I couldn't hear what he said to her, but then she was shouting that she didn't

269

want to work for him any more. Only she didn't put it quite like that. He told her to think about what she was giving up, and it went quiet. I knocked on the door then. I heard them speak in low voices—then he opened the door."

"And Anna Worthing was no longer in the room?" said Lloyd, removing his glasses and straightening up from the cartoons, in which he had been apparently engrossed.

"She—she didn't seem to be in the flat at all," said Charles. "In fact, he offered me a drink, and . . . well, I was there for a couple of hours."

"A couple of—?" Finch began angrily, but once again subsided under a look from his inspector.

"Couldn't Anna Worthing simply have been in another room?" she asked.

"She must have been, but I don't really understand. I felt as though someone was there, but I used his loo, so there was no one hiding in there. But she must have been there somewhere—not the kitchen, because I was in there too."

"Were you in the bedroom, Dr. Rule?" Lloyd asked.

Charles looked up at him. "No," he said. "No. Of course not."

"So . . ." Lloyd shrugged.

"No—the door was open. You can see the whole room, really. Because what you can't see through the door is reflected in the mirror—I was *looking* for her," he added. "You can't even get under the bed—it's flush to the floor."

"What was Mr. Holyoak wearing when you saw him?" Finch asked.

"Well . . . he was wearing a white bathrobe. I obviously had interrupted something. But I don't understand where she went."

"You said you could see the bed," said Finch. "Was it made or unmade?"

"Made," Charles said. "At least, the duvet was straight, if that counts as made."

"How did you get out of the building, Dr. Rule?" Lloyd asked. "You didn't use the ground-floor door to the flats."

"No—I went down in the lift," said Charles, puzzled. "To the car park—that's where my car was."

"But I understood from Mrs. Driver that the lift was closed down at six thirty," said Lloyd.

"Not entirely. You can take it down to the car park—you just can't take it back up again. It has to be called from inside the building."

"Thank you, Dr. Rule," said Inspector Hill, standing up. "Just one other thing," she asked pleasantly. "Why did you withhold this information? Because you murdered him, perhaps?"

Charles, half-way to his feet, fell back into the chair as though she had hit him. "No! I . . . I just didn't want to get involved," he said. "It's as simple as that. Victor and I were discussing his possible investment in the clinic. He was talking about expansion—setting up a clinic in another part of the country." He looked up at her. "I thought he was having an affair with my wife, and that that was in all probability why he was murdered. I didn't want the clinic's name—*my* name—linked with that."

Sergeant Finch spoke, then. "You thought he was having an affair with your wife, but you were still quite happy to go into business with him?" he said.

"Yes," said Charles. "I didn't want it to continue, that was all."

"You said you put a stop to it. How?"

"I told Gerry—Geraldine—that we were no longer going to try to have a child," he said. "That would have made the affair pointless as far as she was concerned. But Zelda says I was wrong about her and Holyoak. And she's usually right, so I . . . I caused my wife's suicide for nothing. For what it's worth, I think she did it sooner rather than later. I think she would have done it once the possibility of having a baby had gone. But I would have caused it, in any event, and I have to live with that."

"When did you indicate to your wife that the affair you suspected her of having was pointless?" asked Lloyd.

"When she came home. At about midnight. She said she had been with Zelda all evening, but I had *rung* there, so I thought she'd been with him. I told her then. She went downstairs—I could hear her crying, but I . . ." He swallowed hard. "I didn't see her again until the morning. She . . . she was still crying. Then—I heard what had happened to Victor. And I thought that . . . I thought she might have—"

271

"Are you saying you failed to come forward with this information because you thought your wife had killed Holyoak?"

Charles hadn't wanted to face this. He nodded.

"Why? What made you think she would kill him?"

"I heard the way he was with Anna Worthing. How . . . how *ruthless* he sounded. It wasn't what he was saying, it was—I don't know. He wanted something and he was going to have it. I thought if she had gone to him, told him it was over, he could have turned nasty. She might have had to . . . to defend herself."

"Mr. Holyoak was almost certainly dead by midnight, Dr. Rule," said Lloyd. "I don't think your wife had anything to do with him. Then, or at any other time. And I don't believe you murdered him in a jealous rage over your wife."

Charles felt very relieved to hear it. But not for long.

"But I understand that you and Mr. Holyoak had become quite close friends?" Lloyd said.

Charles shrugged. "Not friends, exactly."

"But you went to some trouble to get him the man he wanted to do the opening ceremony, didn't you?"

Charles looked away. "Not trouble, not really."

"You had to ask someone else to do you a favour—that's surely an act of friendship?"

"Well . . . yes and no. I mean, it wasn't because of my friendship with Victor. He did do something in return."

Three faces waited to hear exactly what.

"He gave Max the job he should have had all along," said Charles.

And they left. Zelda was still there, though. She had made him something to eat. She had taken great care to ensure that it was healthy. He thanked her. But he couldn't eat it.

Anna woke up, surprised to discover that she had been asleep. She could barely remember the last time she had slept without the anaesthetic of alcohol. Through the open bedroom door she could see Max, as he came out of the kitchen with two mugs.

"Coffee." He put the mugs down, and sat on the edge of the bed.

She smiled, and took his hand. "I've never met anyone like you," she said.

He looked unconvinced. "Were you faking it this time too?" he asked.

She smiled. "I wasn't always faking it before," she said. That was true; she had enjoyed being with Max.

"Just most of the time?"

She conceded that. "But no," she said, in answer to his anxious question. "I didn't fake it. Not this time." That *wasn't* true, but she hadn't wanted to hurt his feelings then, and she didn't now.

But she had stopped being afraid, which as far as she was concerned was much, much better, before she had slipped into her blissful, non-artificially induced sleep. She had believed every word that Max had said, in the end. She could still believe it now, with him sitting on the edge of her bed. But he couldn't stay with her forever. The future was staring her in the face, and nothing Max could do would alter that.

She drank her coffee, and had a bath with Max's active participation. Then they got dressed, laughing. Actually laughing. It was almost possible to forget that any of the nightmare was happening, until the knock, the knock that only policemen could produce.

She was taken in for questioning. Again. Not Max this time, though. She gave him permission to go home; she couldn't make him wait for her. She might be arrested for all she knew. And she felt as though Max were with her, at her elbow, telling her that she could do anything, without fear, because she had done nothing wrong. Not strictly true. But nothing like they thought she had done. Tell them the truth, Max had said. Just tell them the truth, Anna.

Chief Inspector Lloyd, this time. The one who fancied her. With Finch, who was doing the talking.

But telling the truth was one thing; being believed was quite another. And even if they believed her, Bannister never would. If only she had kept her mouth shut about him—but it was the shock of being called Annabel like that. It had taken her right back to Leyford, and the life that once again beckoned, now that she was no longer nineteen, no longer what the punters wanted.

"We've found him," said Finch. "Your visitor."

Him? Oh, that explained a lot, really. Was that why Victor

was so keen to keep it quiet? Why the hell didn't he just tell her?

"He came up in the lift to the flat door," Finch continued. "But you led us to believe that it was the ground-floor door, because you had told us you left without seeing who it was. And that isn't possible. You didn't leave at all, did you, Anna?"

"Yes," she said tiredly, knowing where the questions were leading, knowing what the answer would sound like.

"How did you manage that?" he asked. "If this person was on one side of the door and you were on the other? He didn't see you leave."

"I left by the fire escape," she muttered.

He looked like an old man, hard of hearing, as he cocked his head towards her. "I'm sorry?" he said. "What was that?"

"I left by the fire escape," she said, loudly and clearly, lifting her head, looking into his eyes.

Finch looked back at her, his eyebrows arched. "The fire escape?" he echoed.

She remembered Max doing that that night when they were in bed. She'd told him that, then. And he'd been sober, so he'd remember. Finch probably already knew all of this. Max had been talking, Bannister had been talking, Victor's bloody boyfriend had been talking. If she wasn't careful, they'd talk her into a murder charge.

"Yes. That's why the fire door was open," she said.

"Now why would you do that?" he asked, his routine questioning taking on a tone that she knew only too well.

"Victor was expecting someone, and he didn't want me to see whoever it was," she said. "He told me to leave by the fire escape, and I did."

"The fire escape's a proper staircase, is it? I mean—it is a normal means of entry and exit as well as being a fire escape?"

Anna had had enough of the cat and mouse; her temper, the quick temper that had got her into so much trouble all her life, snapped. "Your lot were crawling round there all that day!" she shouted. "You know perfectly well what sort of fucking fire escape it is!"

Finch nodded. "It's a ladder," he said, his voice hard, at odds with his choirboy looks. "Hardly a normal way to leave the building is it?"

She hated policemen.

"So ... you climbed off the balcony and down a ladder in your best party frock because Mr. Holyoak *asked* you to?"

She shook her head slightly. "Max said that," she said. "You've no idea, any of you. No—not because he asked me to. Because he told me to."

Lloyd came over and sat down, looking at her for a long time. If Finch hadn't been here, she might have tried chatting him up, offering something in return for being left alone. But Finch was here, giving him protection against predatory interviewees.

"What was your relationship with Victor Holyoak, Anna?" he asked.

"Oh, for Christ's sake, how many more times? I worked for him!"

"Doing what?"

Just tell them the truth, Anna. She could hear Max's voice, gentle, persuasive. But Max didn't know the whole truth.

"I kept his business acquaintances sweet," she said. "Or compromised them. It depended on Victor what the outcome was. I did whatever turned them on, whatever they wanted me to do, whatever Victor wanted me to do—and Victor got pretty pictures of it all."

Finch's eyes widened. "And you were prepared to do that?"

"I had no choice. I did what I was told."

"Did you sleep with him?"

She sighed heavily. Were they deaf? "No. He never wanted me to—you just said his visitor was a man. I expect that's why."

"Wouldn't you have known if Holyoak had been homosexual?" asked Lloyd.

Anna smiled. "Only if he had wanted me to know," she said. "And he obviously didn't want anyone to know."

"Does the name Raymond Arthur Wilkes mean anything to you?"

Oh, God. She had spent years trying to forget that. She nodded. "He did some work for Victor," she said.

"What sort of work?"

"Same as me."

"Compromised people?"

"No," she said, thinking about that. "Not that time, I don't

275

think. He would go to this bloke's house, and even Victor couldn't put cameras into other people's houses without their noticing. I think Ray was just payment for services rendered or something."

"He was homosexual?"

"Yes."

"How were you involved with him?"

Tell them the truth, Anna. She looked at Lloyd for a long time, then took a deep breath. "Victor needed to keep someone sweet, and got Ray to visit him. Ray would come to me to get paid. Ray told me that was what he was doing." She told Lloyd about Victor making her tell him everything Ray had said, about telling her not to warn Ray that he knew. "I don't think he did kill himself," she finished, her voice quiet. "I think Victor killed him because of what I told him."

"When did Holyoak get this information from you?"

She shrugged, then remembered. "Oh, yes. January—late January. Because that was when she left."

"She?"

"Catherine. Victor saw her that night, and next day she left. I thought she was going home!" She still defended herself. "But she had just disappeared again, and I got into trouble the next time Victor came. She always got me into trouble with Victor. But that was when he told me I could go to Holland with him. That was when he promised he'd never hurt me." She smiled. "He didn't have to do that for me," she said. "I'd let him down. I was supposed to be watching Catherine. But he took me with him. He didn't have to do that. I didn't murder him, Mr. Lloyd. Why would I?"

Lloyd sighed deeply. "But did you witness his murder, Anna?" he asked quietly.

She stared at him.

"You see," he said, as he tipped his chair on to its back legs. "There's a wardrobe in the bedroom—great big thing," he said. "Built in."

"Victor's got a thing about clothes," she said.

"But he doesn't have any clothes in it."

"Not yet." Not ever. She shivered.

"So it was an ideal place to stay out of the way for a few moments when someone came to the door. Which is what he told you to do. Except that he was angry with you—you had been calling him names, you had told him you weren't going to do what he wanted this time. So he was going to teach you a lesson, humiliate you—he invited his visitor in and entertained him while you were stuck in the wardrobe."

Anna shook her head slightly.

"The wardrobe door was open before the murder and closed after it," Lloyd said. "Why would it be open? It was empty—no one was using it. And even if someone did open it, why close it after the murder? Did you close it? In the hope that we wouldn't know that you were in the flat when his visitor was there? Did you witness the murder, Anna? Did you leave by the fire escape afterwards, so that the cameras wouldn't pick you up? Is that what made you go and get drunk? Is that why you're so scared?"

Anna smiled at him, at the flurry of questions. "You've got Victor all wrong," she said. "He wasn't into humiliating people—shutting me in a wardrobe while he had a roll in the hay with someone wasn't his style. All Victor was interested in was getting people to do what he wanted. Someone was at the door that he didn't want me to see, so he told me to go. The only way out was the fire escape, so he told me to use that."

Lloyd's eyes were slightly puzzled. "So what made you go and get drunk?" he asked.

"I drink. It's how I cope. Victor made me do things I didn't want to do, and I drink so that I can sleep at nights. But this time I sent Bannister up there to catch him with whoever this visitor was. And I realized that I'd gone too far, and I got really drunk, because I was scared."

"That you'd lose the car, and the clothes and all the rest?"

She shook her head. "That I'd lose Victor. Because I felt safe with him," she said. "And I'm scared because he's not here any more."

"Safe? With someone who blackmailed his business contacts? Someone who beat a man senseless, who made you do things you found so repellent you had to drink to live with yourself? Someone you believe murdered a young man in cold blood because he talked out of turn? You yourself called him a psychopath! Safe?"

"Yes," she said. "I felt safe with him. Because he'd given me his word he wouldn't hurt me. He was a total bastard, but you could rely on his word. He had a thing about that. But that was the only guarantee I got from him. I knew the score."

"How much of what you've got do you actually own, Anna?" he asked wearily.

"Nothing," she said. "He's got an inventory—everything's on it. Everything I use, right down to the black suspender belts. If I lost my job, everything went back to him. And if I ever let him down, I'd lose my job—he'd have taken the clothes off my back. He said he would—and he means what he says. I didn't kill him."

"We know that," said Lloyd. "His visitor was with him until eight—Bannister was with you in the pub from ten past."

"If I had killed him at least I'd know I'd got a roof over my head for the foreseeable future," she said.

"Don't you have any money put by?" asked Lloyd, looking worried.

"I didn't get any money until three months ago when he made me the public relations manager. Pocket money, that's all. For personal things. Toothpaste, that sort of thing. I've saved quite a lot of money from my salary, but not enough to live on for long. Everything else I've got belongs to whoever picks up his loot in his will. Bloody Catherine, I suppose."

Lloyd looked quite baffled. "Then what made you pick a row with him, Anna? Why did you tell him to stuff his job if it was the last thing you could afford to do?"

"I was angry," she said. "The deal was that he'd look after me as long as I didn't let him down. And I didn't! I did everything he wanted. He gave me the PR job when the deal with Driver's went through." She laughed at herself. "I believed it was a real job. But I wasn't good at it—I told him I was happier doing what I'd done before."

Lloyd watched her intently as she spoke.

"And he told me I was too old. That he'd no use for me any more, and he'd given me a job I couldn't do so that I'd be bound to let him down, and he could get rid of me without going back on his word. And I had let him down, but I was being given another chance, because things had changed."

"What had changed?"

She shrugged. "Something to do with Max, I think," she said.

"Go on."

"It was so obvious that I couldn't do the bloody job that people had jumped to conclusions, and it suited him for them to believe that I was his mistress. So I still had my uses after all. The tabloids could latch on to me instead and my background would give them plenty to get their teeth into. I told him to stuff it—but it was only because I knew he needed me, and I could get away with it. I knew how far I could go with him."

Lloyd looked at her for a little while, shaking his head slightly again. Then he terminated the interview, and switched off the tape. "Don't forget that you have still got the job with Holyoak UK," he said quietly. "That belongs to the shareholders, not Holyoak himself."

She had forgotten. "But I can't do it," she said.

"Neither can half the managers in the country. Being incompetent isn't grounds for dismissal these days—they just promote you out of the way. Play your cards wrong, and you could end up on the board of directors."

She smiled. She was in danger of liking Lloyd.

Catherine looked at the cool Inspector Hill, and wondered when she would get that grown up.

"So—what can I do for you?" Max asked, once they were all seated.

She took out a notebook. "You told my DCI that you came here after Mrs. Driver dropped you off, and continued your assault on your wife."

Max went slightly pink. "I've just spent all evening extolling the virtues of the truth," he said. "I should have taken my own advice. But it was one of those occasions when it seemed that a lie was more likely to be believed."

"You wouldn't believe me when I told you, either," said Catherine. "I bruise easily."

Catherine could see the disbelief still there in the inspector's eyes as they left hers and turned to Max. "What *did* you do?" she asked. "Between six thirty and nine?"

"I waited outside Anna's flat, but your colleagues were singularly unwilling to believe that. I didn't want to go home. I needed time to think. And I needed Anna. It's how I relax, and I badly needed to relax before I saw Catherine again."

The inspector glanced at Catherine. "Mrs. Scott, you might prefer it if I spoke to Mr. Scott alone," she said.

"Why?" said Catherine. "I know all about Anna. I told you I did."

Inspector Hill looked a little baffled.

Max smiled at her. "You think love and sex are inextricably entangled, do you, Inspector?" he said.

She was commendably unfazed by the question, winning some grudging admiration from Catherine. "No," she said. "Since you ask, I don't think I do. It's good when they are, though," she added.

Max smiled at her.

"All right," she said. "If neither of you mind, I'll go ahead. When Holyoak arrived here, he discovered that you had been suspected of murdering your first wife, and that at the time you had been having an affair with his seventeen-year-old step-daughter, whom you allowed to lie for you. It was also virtually common knowledge that you were being unfaithful to her, now that *she* was your wife. I'm not making moral judgements, Mr. Scott, but I don't suppose he thought very highly of you."

Max smiled a little. "I'm sure you're right. I'm sure my stepfather-in-law had very little time for me," he said. "I can't say that that upsets me too much now that I know the sort of man he was."

"Quite," said the inspector. "The fact is that Victor Holyoak was both ruthless and vicious, if only half of what we've been told is true. And he had no time for justice. So what did he have in mind for you, Mr. Scott? Or did you decide not to wait to find out?"

"Oh," said Max. "So that's what you think I was doing, is it? Killing my wife's stepfather?"

"His death could have considerable advantages," said Inspector Hill.

Max looked up, puzzled, as was Catherine.

"Who inherits your stepfather's wealth, Mrs. Scott?" she asked.

Max's jaw dropped, but Catherine sighed with sheer relief. "I think it goes to various charities," she said. "I disqualified myself by marrying Max, and he only provided life care for my mother, not money."

280

The inspector frowned.

"I was the beneficiary only on condition that I remained unmarried."

"Why?"

"He thought I had family obligations that marriage would interfere with. I married Max as soon as I possibly could." She looked at Max, who wasn't looking at her. He was staring down at his feet. "He nearly turned me down," she said. "He said I was too young to know my own mind—but I knew one thing if I knew nothing else. That I could get out from under—I could stop myself being sucked into his . . . his madness, like my mother had."

Inspector Hill looked at Max, and then at her. Catherine went on.

"You read about dictators," she said. "They wipe out the opposition, people disappear if they disagree with them—they use fear to control people." She glanced at Max. "Not all power-mad dictators have countries to play with," she said. "My stepfather didn't have the good fortune to be born in Latin America—but it's the same mentality. It's madness. Megalomania. Whatever. Marrying Max without his consent would put me beyond the pale as far as he was concerned, and the further beyond it I could get, the better."

"Did you know that?" the inspector asked Max, when Catherine's speech was over.

Max looked up then. "I didn't know why Catherine was so keen to marry me," he said, with a half-smile. "And I didn't know that Victor Holyoak was her stepfather until Tuesday. Believe me, how much money she was going to be worth when he died was not uppermost in my mind. I simply couldn't understand why she hadn't told me. And then when I saw him I realized why, of course. Catherine had lied to me—I got very angry, and I did something I'm very ashamed of. I just . . . flipped, I suppose."

He looked at the inspector. "But I spent that two and a half hours waiting outside Anna's flat," he said. "I didn't continue my assault on my wife, I didn't kill my stepfather-in-law—I just waited for Anna to come home. It's the truth."

They had to believe him, Catherine thought. This time they had to believe him.

* * *

Judy arrived back to discover that Bannister had been bailed, and that as a consequence, Anna had resolutely refused to leave the station, demanding that they give her protection.

Lloyd had gone, so she was lumbered. The duty inspector was adamant that he had no men to spare to sit parked outside a flat all night because of some neurotic female.

Why, Judy wondered, was the word female used as an insult? Finch was packing up his desk; she smiled at him. "Job for you, Tom," she said.

His face fell. "It's Friday night," he said. "My wife's forgotten what I look like—I promised to take her to the pictures."

Judy looked at her watch. "You'll be in time for the second house if you get a move on," she said. "We have to get Anna Worthing home."

He slammed his drawer shut. "Bannister isn't going to go anywhere near her," he said. "Ma'am," he added, hurriedly. "He's just glad he's not being charged with murder—he's on bail. He won't jeopardize that."

"And she won't go home unless she has protection," said Judy. "We can't give her that, but at least we can see that she's inside with the door firmly locked."

He muttered and grumbled, but eventually she and Anna were drawing up in the vehicle access area, with Finch's car behind them.

Finch got out, pointing over to the Porsche, which still sat at an angle to the garage. "You'd better put that away before some joyrider takes it," he said.

"It's not mine," she said. "They can take it if they like."

"It's our job to make sure they're not tempted," he said, having obviously read the directive from above that had been distributed as a result of the conference. "Put it away."

"I'm not going into that garage—he might be waiting for me."

"Give me the keys then!" Finch shouted, and she went into her bag, throwing him the keys.

Angrily, he got into the car, putting it in gear and swinging it into the garage with the same ease that Lloyd always exhibited. Judy admired those who could make cars bend to their will.

"Is that where you left it on Wednesday night?" she asked Anna.

"Yes."

Judy was glad she didn't have the garage next door to Anna's neighbour, who tried to get people out of bed to move cars that weren't blocking his garage at all. If he simply disliked bad parking, she'd never get a wink of sleep.

Finch came out, slamming the door shut, and gave Anna back the keys. "Let's get on with this," he said.

Anna led the way up to her flat; as she turned on to the top landing, with Judy and Tom Finch a few steps behind, she was suddenly pushed by an unseen hand and fell backwards against the wall, falling to the floor.

"You set me up, you little whore!" Bannister appeared, aiming a vicious kick at Anna as she scrambled beyond his reach, into the corner, where she hid her head, like a child.

Finch was at the top of the stairs in what seemed like one jump. "Do you have business here?" he enquired, making Bannister whirl round on one foot, the other poised to deliver a blow.

"And you can keep your nose out, whoever you are!" he shouted, trying to land a punch while still off balance.

Finch moved too fast for Bannister; the punch went wide, and Finch caught his outstretched arm, pushing it up behind his back, as he pinned him against the door of Anna's flat. "I understood that your innards couldn't take any more punishment," he said, taking out his card. "So don't get into fights. Finch, Detective Sergeant."

He held on to Bannister as he spoke to Anna. "Do you want this man prosecuted?" he asked.

He was choosing to regard it as a domestic; on the whole, Judy thought that might be the right approach, if they didn't want to add to Bannister's list of grievances against Anna. She tried to unwind her from the ball into which she had rolled. "Anna?" she said. "It's all right. He can't hurt you now."

She turned to look at Judy, but she was still in the foetal position.

"Do you want us to charge him?" Judy asked, her voice gentle.

Anna shook her head.

Finch let him go. "You're lucky," he said. "Go home to your wife and kids. And remember—you're still not off the

283

hook for murder. But Anna is. She didn't set you up, Bannister."

Bannister looked helplessly at Judy, and jerked his thumb at Anna. "She ruined my life," he said.

"Sergeant Finch," Judy said. "See him on to his train."

"Yes, ma'am."

Judy knew that there would be baby-sitters to cancel, and a peeved wife for him to go home to, but that was sometimes the way it went. Bannister had to be removed from Anna's vicinity, and it needed someone like Finch to do the removing. Her inadequacy in that regard would please Bannister, if nothing else did.

She finally got the distressed Anna into her flat, arranged with a now more co-operative duty inspector for an eye to be kept on her, and went home herself, pulling into the kerb in front of the fruit and veg shop. She would be glad to get in, get her shoes off, and put her feet up. A knocking made her look up; Lloyd was at the flat window, waving down to her. She wondered which discreet parking space he'd found this time, and smiled. He hardly ever came to her flat; she thought he felt as though he was sanctioning the set-up, which wasn't how he wanted it.

She was barely inside the door when he caught her in his arms and kissed her soundly. "I love you," he said.

"That's nice to know," she said, taking off her coat, and sinking down on to the sofa, kicking off her shoes, and groaning with relief. "But what's brought it on?"

He flopped down beside her. "Anna Worthing," he said. "Zelda Driver. Geraldine Rule." He kissed her again. "I'm very glad you're you." He looked at her from under his eyebrows. "You don't seriously believe that I fancy Anna Worthing, do you?" he asked.

Judy's smile grew broader. "You like her," she said.

"I like Zelda—doesn't mean I fancy her."

"It's different with Anna," she said. "She brings out the protective instinct in you."

He sat back a little. "Yes," he admitted. "I suppose she does." He patted his knee, and Judy swung her legs up for him to massage her feet. "You shouldn't wear these shoes if they hurt," he said.

"I know. But they go really well with this outfit."

284

He smiled. "You'll have to take off your tights if you want me to do it properly," he said.

She complied. "So what is it about Anna?" she asked, as he brought her feet back to life.

"Well—we know why he took her to Holland, now, don't we? Holyoak swopped cars and ID with Wilkes, and killed Tarrant, making sure the car was spotted. They switched back, and Holyoak killed Wilkes, because he couldn't be trusted to keep his mouth shut. But he thought the suicide would be investigated, and that they would be bound to wonder why a known homosexual was visiting a female prostitute, and question her. Taking her with him was simply less risky than doing away with her too." He looked at her. "And he put her to work," he said. "All the trappings were window dressing. But she still thinks he was doing her a favour."

Judy nodded.

He gave a short sigh, and thought before he spoke again. "But she's bright, Judy. Really bright. And attractive. She virtually sold herself into slavery—why would she do that? And she's terrified people are going to hurt her—why?"

"Because they have. Finch just stopped Bannister giving her what he would doubtless call a good kicking."

Lloyd looked upset. "What sort of background does she come from? How did she get like that—how did she get so that everyone could push her around? She's got spirit, if she could find it two days running without recourse to the alcoholic sort. But it got broken, didn't it? When she was a child, before she went on the game. And I've no doubt she comes from a broken home."

"Oh, Lloyd." Now she understood. She put her arms round him. "Lloyd—there are broken homes and broken homes. Parents separating doesn't equal a broken home anywhere but in statistics."

He worked on her feet, not looking at her.

Judy carried on. "Girls like Linda don't turn out like Anna," she said. "Girls like Anna do. I *do* know Anna's background. You think because she's bright and knows how to put a sentence together that she must come from a good home, with books and discussions and concerned parents, just like Linda. And that when all that fell apart she took it badly, and went running off to London as soon as she was old enough—right?"

He was listening, but he didn't answer.

"You left Barbara when Linda was almost fifteen—Anna Worthing had been on the streets for two years by then."

He turned to look at her.

"She was sent out by her mother. If she didn't go, or didn't bring back enough money, her father took a belt to her—her father, Lloyd. She isn't from a broken home, not in theory, except that she is, of course. She was in and out of care, she ran away, she was brought back, she went to four different foster homes—she ran away from them, she was brought back. She went to a young offenders' place—she absconded, she was brought back—it was endless, until she had reached an age where she could throw off her mother and her father and the social services and do the only thing she knew how to do."

Lloyd looked a little ashamed of himself. "I'm being paranoid," he said.

"Just a little. Look—I know Linda wasn't too struck on my idea, but she's thinking about it. And even if she does go it alone, she won't get into trouble. She's *not* from a broken home, Lloyd. She has not just one, but two entirely intact homes to come back to where she'll be welcome and loved. Three, if she counts mine. Anna had nowhere to go but the street."

He kissed her. "I said I was glad you were you," he said. "When did you find all that out?"

"The night she nearly kicked Bannister's head in," said Judy.

He smiled. "So she did it to you too?"

Yes. And Judy had tried to talk her into getting an ordinary job, going to night-classes, using her brain. "She told me she could earn more in a night than I could in a week," she said. "She was probably right. But she hated it, and Holyoak offered her a mink-lined escape route, so she took it. Holyoak's the one who's given her the education—not her parents."

"He gave her an education all right." Lloyd squeezed Judy's foot with more venom than finesse, making her yelp. "Sorry," he said. "I get angry when I think about Holyoak." He went back to rather gentler massage.

"And Holyoak's the one who broke her spirit," Judy added. "Even her parents couldn't do that. No wonder someone killed him."

Lloyd sighed.

Judy knew he didn't like it when she suggested that murder was ever justified, but she was beginning to think that she might have murdered him herself, given half a chance.

"Let's forget about work," he said.

But Judy couldn't. "If you ask me, everyone he had anything to do with would be too scared of him to try it," she said. "He may have been killed by someone who knew that he really *could* give Max Scott an alibi for his wife's murder, and that that would reopen the case without Max as the star turn."

"I said—let's forget about work. It's Friday night."

"Soon," she promised, and told Lloyd about her interview with Max, and Catherine's choosing to forfeit her stepfather's money by marrying Max. "She hated her stepfather," she said. "She married Max Scott to escape from him. I think she was desperate to marry him."

"Tell me in the morning," he said.

"Yes, but giving Max an alibi effectively gave her one too, don't forget. And now we know she"—she carried on, despite the fact that Lloyd was now tickling her feet while looking as though he was hanging on her every word—"wasn't with him. She got him to go to . . . London that evening, and she didn't tell him"—she got giggly, but she carried on—"that she'd *moved.* He goes to the wrong address, so . . . he doesn't know where *she* was, does he?" She finished in a rush of words, before the giggles consumed her. "I think that's why he reacted so violently when he realized who Holyoak was." Lloyd went back to the massage, and she could speak like a rational being again. "Do you believe her about someone coming to the door while she was on the phone to Valerie?"

"It tallies. Valerie Scott was interviewed by a Tory lady at about five forty-five—that's around the time that Catherine says she rang Mrs. Scott."

"She could have found that out at the time—be using it now to give herself a different alibi."

Lloyd looked thoughtful. "Now you come to mention it," he said, "I think she may have been doing just that. Because I think she gilded the lily just a little too much." He smiled.

He wasn't going to tell her; she wasn't going to ask. She ploughed on. "And I still don't think she got those bruises because her husband grabbed hold of her. We've only got her word for it about where *she* was on Wednesday night."

"Well, she wasn't committing step-patricide," said Lloyd. "No one came to the door, remember—and she couldn't get up there by the lift. And even if she knows Anna's patent method for beating the cameras, she couldn't have known the fire door had been left open."

"True," said Judy.

"But," he said, firmly putting her feet down. "That can all wait until tomorrow. There's a good film on tonight, and I'm going to make us some supper, and watch it."

Who *did* know it had been left open, she wondered. She'd check her notebook in the morning.

"We'll have another word with Mrs. Scott, I think," he said, as he got up. "Do you actually have any food in the house?"

"Some," she said, and caught his hand. "I love you too, you know," she said, in case he thought for one moment that she didn't, in view of his morose chat about broken homes.

He clutched his heart. "My God, things must be worse than I thought," he said. "So what brought *that* on?"

She smiled. "Max Scott, Charles Rule, Bannister . . ."

"You didn't fall under the Max Scott spell, then?"

Judy thought about that, and grinned. "No," she said. "But I didn't find him a . . . what was it Finch called him?"

Lloyd let go of her hand and made for the kitchen. "I can't remember," he said. "But roughly translated it meant 'a boorish, unwholesome person.' "

Judy smiled. "Yes, well—I didn't think he was that," she said, and remembered what Finch had called him.

It would get a lot of points at Scrabble.

Chapter Twelve

Then: Tuesday, 31 March, this year . . .

THE MAIL CAME NOT LONG AFTER JACKIE HAD GONE TO work; just one letter, which Bannister tore open with his thumb. If he didn't come up with the arrears of rent, an eviction order would be served.

He sat down, visions of them all living in one room of a bed and breakfast hotel rising up before him, and he felt sick. What kind of man was it that couldn't keep a roof over his head, couldn't provide for his wife and children?

It was Jackie's fault. She had never learned to economize, always carried on spending as though he was still earning good money. He'd told her and told her that she had to spend less, but she didn't. She said it was her money, when he got angry with her. And it was. But her job didn't bring in anything like enough to live the way they used to live, and he couldn't get that through to her.

Next door the washing machine's monotonous churning began again as it moved into its next cycle, and he wanted to scream. He couldn't get away from any of it. He was trapped in a downward spiral, with money flowing one way. She should do one big wash a week, not shove things in before she went to work, so that it slapped and sloshed its way through electricity that he hadn't paid for, and couldn't pay for. Somehow that machine had become the focus for his frustration, and he wanted to go in and kick it into silence.

But it wasn't Jackie's fault. She shouldn't have to pennypinch. He should have a proper job with a proper future, and proper money coming in. And he didn't. He didn't because one night he had taken liberties with a cheap little whore, and if he could recall just one moment of his life, that would be the one.

But he couldn't, and he had to get money from somewhere; whether Jackie liked it or not, he was going to have to take the minder's job before the offer was closed.

Judy had chosen the burger bar in the Square, Stansfield's main shopping centre, in preference to her own flat, where Linda might feel at a disadvantage, or Lloyd's flat, where Linda thought Judy had no right to be.

Linda had at least turned up; she sat at a table with a cup of coffee. Judy took a deep breath, got herself coffee and joined her. "Thanks for coming," she said.

"I can imagine what he'd have said if I hadn't," she said.

Judy smiled. "Are you having something to eat?" she asked.

Linda shook her head

"I hardly ever eat lunch," said Judy, but she decided that small talk was not required. "Well," she said. "I've spoken to him, and—subject to certain conditions—he's agreed."

She looked at Judy with Lloyd's eyes. "What are the conditions?" she said. "That he comes with me?"

"No," said Judy, with a laugh. "But you have to try to see it from his point of view, Linda. Lloyd and I have seen more of what can happen to young girls in London than most people—he's concerned, that's all."

"He thinks I'll end up on the streets!" she said, in a loud enough voice to make people turn and look.

That particular Lloyd trait had long since ceased to embarrass Judy. "Some girls do," she said. "I don't think for a moment that you would, but Lloyd and I spent several nights of our lives sweeping up the ones that had. And some of them were simply girls who had gone to London thinking that they'd get jobs and flats and boyfriends, and drifted into it when the money ran out and the creeps started coming out of the woodwork."

Linda raised her eyes to heaven. "I'm not that stupid," she said. "What makes him think that I am? Why doesn't he give Peter a hard time about what he wants to do?"

"He doesn't think you're stupid. It's just that fathers of teenage girls tend to be over-protective." She smiled. "And Peter wants to be a plumber."

Linda very nearly laughed. But not quite.

"Anyway," said Judy. "My parents have a spare room, and they've said that they'd be more than happy to put you up while you look for a job. If you get a job, then obviously you'd be able to look for somewhere else to live, but you'd have a base to do it from. And if you can't find a job straight away, it won't be the end of the world. It'll give you a chance to see if you do really want to live there, as well."

Linda looked very unimpressed. "But your parents must be ancient," she said.

"Thanks," said Judy, and smiled. "My mother has just celebrated her sixtieth birthday, and my father retired last year. Pretty ancient, I suppose, by your standards—but they're anything but old-fashioned. I think you'd like them—obviously, you'll want to meet each other first before any decision is taken, but—"

"They'd always want to know where I'd been and who I'd been with," said Linda.

Judy thought about that. "No," she said. "I think they'd mind their own business. But they'd be there if you needed them," she said. "Until you found your feet, as my mother would say. That's the whole point."

"I don't have to put up with any of this," said Linda. "I could just go, right now. And he couldn't stop me. I'll be eighteen in August anyway—he's behaving as if I was a child."

They had quite a captive audience at the next table, all of whom now looked at Judy to see what counter she had for that.

"I know," she said. "Of course you could just go, and worry your mother and father to death. If you do it this way, you might only have to put up with my ancient parents for a few weeks before you get a job, and find somewhere to share, or whatever. But you wouldn't have to take the first thing that came along."

Linda stared into her coffee.

"Your mum and dad know they can trust you, Linda. They just don't want to have to worry about you. It would set their minds at rest if they knew you were in good hands while you were looking around, that's all."

Judy was rather proud of it as an off-the-cuff speech; she half expected a round of applause.

Linda frowned. "Does my mother know about this, then?" she asked.

"Yes, of course she does."

"And she doesn't mind? I mean—my being with your parents?"

"No," said Judy. "It's the late-twentieth-century equivalent of the extended family, I suppose. Your father and mine are pretty good friends, you know—Barbara's met my parents, and I think she likes them. And they won't crowd you, I promise. They were enlightened even when I was seventeen."

"I don't know," said Linda.

"Will you think about it?"

"I suppose so."

Judy had expected no more.

"I know it's short notice, Lloyd—I'm sorry. But apparently the Chief's getting hot under the collar about joy-riding, and both the chief super and I have got to go to this conference."

Lloyd was never too upset when his detective superintendent had to leave the office. But joy-riding? "It's not really much of a problem in Stansfield," he said. "Even if it was—it's not really a CID problem at all."

"Quite. But he thinks that it will reach Stansfield unless something's done to nip it in the bud," said Andrews. "And he thinks that CID should be aware of it. In some places, it's practically organized crime—he thinks it can't be left to the uniforms to sort out once it's in full spate."

"I suppose he's got a point, sir."

"Yes. So—you'll have to stand and smile, shake hands, eat some lunch, mingle with the councillors, that sort of thing."

"It is my day off, sir," said Lloyd.

Andrews shrugged. "Can't be helped," he said.

Lloyd had been looking forward to his day off; Judy was on leave this week, and he had thought that they could perhaps go somewhere for the day. He really didn't fancy putting on his best bib and tucker to represent the police at some factory.

"It's a bit hush-hush because of security problems, but some cabinet minister's doing the honours," said Andrews. "They haven't officially said which."

Lloyd groaned. "Special Branch will be involved?" he said.

"Involved—my God, Lloyd, they'll search your underwear for bombs. They've already got Driver's—sorry, Holyoak UK—jumping through hoops. It's got enough security to satisfy anyone, but not Special Branch. It's a bloody security systems factory, for God's sake."

"Oh—it's Zelda Driver's firm, is it? I didn't realize—I knew she'd sold the business, but I didn't make the connection." He sighed. "It's an all-day do, is it, sir?"

"Probably. Holyoak's pushing the boat out, apparently. They say he's twice as rich as Croesus and we should all be on our knees thanking him for choosing Stansfield as his base, so be on your best behaviour."

He really couldn't think of a more boring way to spend his time. Lloyd thought hard for who he might convince Andrews would be an infinitely better choice. Finch was already going to be on duty outside the factory, and Judy, who would have been ideal, in Lloyd's opinion, was on leave, which was why he really didn't want to go, so it was a vicious circle.

"And of course the press and TV will be there."

Lloyd remained unimpressed. Outwardly. "Well, if I'm it, I'm it," he said. "What time do I have to be there?"

"I take it you and Charles are invited to this do tomorrow?" asked Zelda.

"Oh, yes," said Geraldine, unenthusiastically. "Have you come all the way out here just to ask me that?"

"No," said Zelda. "I've come all the way out here to see if you know what's going on."

Geraldine frowned, and picked up the coffeepot. "Do you want a biscuit or anything?" she asked.

"No," said Zelda. "Not if it's one of Charles's awful muesli things."

It was one of Charles's awful muesli things. Geraldine poured the coffee, and sat down at the kitchen table. "What's going on about what?" she asked.

"Catherine and Max," said Zelda.

"Is something going on?"

"You mean apart from the fact that I saw him sneaking up to the penthouse flat as I was leaving?" asked Zelda.

"Well, you have told me about him and Anna Worthing already, haven't you? You didn't come hotfoot from work to tell me again."

"Catherine says she isn't going to be there tomorrow," said Zelda.

"Whyever not?"

Zelda shrugged. "She says it's nothing to do with Max," she said. "But I thought Max might have confided in Charles, or something."

Geraldine smiled. "If he had, you're the last person I'd tell," she said.

"I know," Zelda sighed. "You're no fun, Geraldine."

"Anyway, as far as I know, he hasn't. Didn't Catherine give you any reason?"

Zelda sipped her coffee and shivered. "This is decaffeinated," she said, and looked round for sugar, but Charles had banned it as unnecessary. Geraldine indicated the sweeteners, and Zelda raised her eyes to heaven, dropping two into her cup. "She just said she didn't like that sort of thing," she said, stirring the coffee. "I said she'd have to get used to that sort of thing now that Max is being crowned general manager, thanks to his winning ways with the new management."

Geraldine shook her head. "You'll go too far one day, Zelda," she warned her. "What in the world did poor Max do to you?"

"I just don't think much of the way he behaved with Catherine—then or now," said Zelda.

"With Catherine?" said Geraldine, wickedly. "Or you?"

Zelda had become involved with Max, Geraldine was certain, because whatever Max had done, it was much more personal to Zelda than his treatment of a third party, however young. And yet she had taken Catherine entirely under her wing, so presumably she hadn't been that jealous of Max's affair with the girl. Zelda had seen Catherine as a wronged innocent, but Geraldine hadn't then, and didn't now.

It took two to tango, after all, and Catherine had known what she was doing. That story about having come to tell Max that she was pregnant, while insisting that Max had been with her the evening before . . . Geraldine had never believed that. One or the other. If Max *had* been with her, then she had already decided to terminate the pregnancy without Max's knowledge. The more likely scenario was that he hadn't been

294

with her at all, and that Catherine had seen the chance to put poor old Max for ever in her debt by giving him a much-needed alibi.

Geraldine had never felt that Catherine's performance had been entirely convincing. If you were to ask Geraldine, Max hadn't been the first, though that was the impression Catherine had tried to give. She had been desperate to hook Max; becoming pregnant was an old ploy, and Catherine had used it. But when she had arrived to drop her bombshell, she had realized what a desperate mess it would put Max in, and had deliberately destroyed her baby. Geraldine could never forgive her for that.

Zelda, of course, hadn't responded to her question, and was now looking at her, eyebrows raised. "Penny for them," she said.

Geraldine smiled. "Nothing," she said. "It's just . . . well, everyone being together again like that—it's bringing back unpleasant memories, I suppose. And it'll bring them back to everyone else. I don't blame Catherine for not wanting to go. I'm not exactly looking forward to it either."

"Well," said Zelda. "I don't know how Max will feel about it—he could do with some moral support, if moral isn't too much a contradiction in terms when we're talking about Max."

"She hasn't told him?"

"She's telling him tonight. A great one for leaving things to the very last minute, our Catherine."

Wasn't she, though, thought Geraldine.

"I didn't think we'd get the flat," he said. "I thought Holyoak would want it, with the big day tomorrow."

She sat on her knees between his drawn-up legs, his arms round her, his smooth chest touching her back. She had been right in the first place; there was no hidden eye watching them, for Max had obviously not been presented with evidence of his folly. They had been meeting like this every week for months; she could only conclude that Max had done Victor some sort of favour on the promise of the sex that he was enjoying even now as Anna did all the right things, murmured all the right things, and produced all the right reactions while thinking of something else altogether.

Tomorrow was all about Catherine, and it had been worrying Anna, as she had remembered to thrill to Max's touch. It was so important to Victor, and he had left all the arrangements for the lunch and the cocktail party to her. She had never done anything like that in her life. And she had been praying that she wouldn't let him down, as she had moaned her appreciation of Max's technique. Letting Victor down was something that she could never afford to do. She had been mentally ticking off everything that had to be done first thing in the morning as she had writhed with pleasure. Poor Victor. Catherine had always run rings round him. He could make captains of industry, policemen, politicians, street-wise crooks, and money-wise financiers jump to his tune, but not his step-daughter. And Anna had so much on her mind, what with the lunch and the cocktail party, that it really was inconvenient having to do this as well, she had thought, as she had gasped with excitement in their simultaneous orgasmic ecstasy.

She rested her elbows on his knees. "He's not coming until the morning," she said. "But he said he'd be using the flat tomorrow night. Don't let me forget to change the sheets."

"Are you and Victor Holyoak lovers?" he asked suddenly, for the first time.

"No," she said firmly. "But I still think he'd rather have clean sheets."

He laughed, and nuzzled her neck. "So how long have we got?"

"Until about nine, or so." She laid her head back on Max's shoulder, and wondered if that menu would be all right for lunch. She had never had to do a menu before.

"Are you worrying about tomorrow?" he asked, his lips close to her ear. "You don't have to. Everything will go swimmingly, I promise."

She smiled, as he held her very close, telling her what he'd told her a dozen times already, and she still didn't believe.

"He wouldn't have given you the job if he didn't think you could do it," he said. "You're worth a dozen university graduates, Anna. What would Holyoak want with them? You believe in him. He couldn't buy that belief."

She believed in him, all right. Because whatever it took, Victor got what he set out to get, even if he no longer wanted it. And it was true that only someone who knew him as well as she did, or who had been at the receiving end of his ruthlessness, could have that belief. But Max was wrong. Victor could, and did, buy it; Max had clearly capitulated before he had found that out.

He drew her into a long, reassuring kiss. It was nice; she liked Max.

"Tell me something," he said. "Did you put in a good word for me with Holyoak? Zelda thinks you did."

Anna frowned. "What do you mean?" she asked.

"Well—he's given me this job, and he's never even met me."

Anna wasn't sure what to say. She had naturally assumed that Max and Victor had met. But it wasn't necessary to come face to face with Victor to find yourself dancing to his tune; he had never met Zelda Driver, and yet he had finally wrested her business from her. She didn't realize that she had been manipulated; Anna presumed that Max didn't either. Perhaps Victor was just grateful to him for taking his stepdaughter off his hands, she thought, a little less than charitably.

"Did you?" he asked again.

"No," she said. "I suppose he just felt Catherine's husband should have a more senior position."

"Catherine?" he said. "What on earth's Catherine got to do with it?"

Oh, God, she'd offended him. "Oh—I didn't mean that you wouldn't have got the job anyway," she said. "Everyone thinks you should have got it years ago."

"Never mind that," Max said. "What has Catherine got to do with anything?"

Anna's mouth went dry. He didn't know. He really didn't know.

"Anna?" His elbow touched her ribs. "Tell me."

Oh, Christ, what had she done? She licked her lips before she spoke. "Max—" Now she really was breathing hard, with sheer fear. If Victor hadn't meant Max to know . . .

"Anna?" he said again, his voice anxious.

She couldn't not tell him; she had said too much for that. "Catherine is Victor Holyoak's stepdaughter," she said.

There was total silence for a moment as he stared at her, his eyes quite blank.

"You mustn't tell Victor I told you," she said, twisting round between his legs so that she was facing him. "I thought you

297

knew, Max—please, you mustn't tell Victor. You must promise. Promise me, Max!"

He was staring into space, not taking in what she was saying.

"Max!" she said desperately. "Promise me!"

His eyes focused, and he blinked. "What? No . . . no, I won't tell him." He put his hand to his forehead, rubbing it. "Are you sure?" he asked, with a sort of laugh.

She nodded.

"But . . . why in God's name wouldn't she tell me?"

"I don't know," said Anna miserably. "She . . . she hates him, as far as I can see. She ran away from home when she was sixteen."

"I know," he said, nodding, still bewildered. "But why wouldn't she tell me who he was?"

Anna felt sick. "I don't know why they didn't tell you, but I shouldn't have, and I wish to God I hadn't."

"Are you afraid of Holyoak?" he asked.

Anna smiled nervously. "I'm . . . I'm afraid I'll lose my job if he finds out," she said.

"About us?" He shook his head. "He won't find out," he said.

She allowed him to believe that that was what she meant, and breathed a small sigh of relief at his assurances, but there was only one man whose word she relied on, and he had given her his word that she would be back on the streets if she ever let him down. She had let him down now, all right. Bloody Catherine. She had got into more trouble over that little bitch . . .

"Were they ever going to tell me?" he asked.

"Victor's announcing it tomorrow," Anna said. "I think he assumed you knew."

"Announcing what, exactly?"

"That that was why he came here. Why he chose Stansfield. Why he chose Driver's."

"Do you know why she ran away from home?" he asked.

Oh, God. "Yes," she said.

"Why? She's never told me."

He ought to know, she thought. He bloody well ought to know just what sort of a selfish bitch he'd married. And he would either tell Victor of this conversation or he wouldn't;

298

she was in trouble anyway if he did, because she had promised never to discuss Victor's business with anyone, and now she had. She had talked out of turn.

In for a penny, she thought, leaning her elbows on Max's knees as she began her story. "Victor met Catherine's mother when Catherine was about twelve," she said. "They were very close—her mother had had a mild stroke, but she was doing all right."

"Catherine resented the intrusion?"

"No, I don't think she did. But about eighteen months later her mother had another stroke—the one that paralysed her. Catherine blamed Victor."

"Why?"

"She said he'd made demands on her," said Anna.

"What sort of demands?"

She indicated their own entwined bodies with a wave of the hand.

"Oh," said Max.

"Then one weekend when she was about sixteen, her mother had to go into hospital. Victor was going to be away, so Catherine was supposed to go to friends. But Victor had a spot of bother, and couldn't go."

"A spot of bother?" Max repeated.

"Victor didn't make all that money by opening a post-office savings account," said Anna.

"He was a crook?"

"Of course he was," she said, impatient to get on with her story, now she'd started. "Anyway, he didn't go away. He arranged some company for himself. And there they were, on the sheepskin rug in the sitting room, with her doing the business on him, when in comes Catherine."

"Ah," said Max.

"She yelled at him that that was proof that his excesses had all but killed her mother, and by the time Victor had got rid of the woman and made himself decent, she'd packed her little bag, whipped some money from the safe, and gone."

"Oh," said Max.

"Victor spent hundreds of pounds looking for her," Anna went on. "And as soon as he found her, she skipped again. And he found her again, but—I know she's your wife, Max,

299

but she is so ungrateful. She wouldn't even come to the ferry with us to say goodbye to her mother."

Max was still looking stunned. "I know there are a lot of questions I should be asking," he said. "But most of them I have to ask Catherine, and I don't want to think about them." He smiled. "But you said you only met Holyoak six months ago. So how come you were going to a ferry with him before Catherine and I were even married?"

"All right," said Anna. She had known she could never keep up the lie about working for him for six months. "I've known Victor a long time," she said. "He took me to Holland with him."

"You *and* his wife?"

"We didn't travel as a party," said Anna. "But we were on the same ferry, yes."

Max smiled. "So Zelda was right," he said.

"He's done everything he could think of to make it up to Catherine," Anna said. "And he swore off women completely—he blames himself, thanks to Catherine."

Max frowned. "You mean, you really *aren't* his mistress?"

"No I'm not!" she said. "Max, I swear to you—he's given her and her mother everything they could ever want or need, he's tried everything he can think of to make her see sense. I mean—all right, she was only a kid when it happened—but my God, Max, if you knew the trouble he's gone to! She is a selfish—" She broke off. "I'm sorry," she said. "She's your wife. I shouldn't be saying these things. I'm sorry."

Max still looked bewildered. "Are you sure she knows it's him?" he asked. "I mean—if he wasn't legit—he hasn't changed his name, or something?"

"Of course she knows," Anna said. "I told her. Before the takeover was made public—Victor sent me to tell her that it was him, to ask her to see her mother. At least she did that. Once. But I don't know what else the man is supposed to do, Max—he moved his entire operation here because of her! And she won't give an inch."

"No," said Max. "I know what she's like. She's got a—a horror, I suppose—of sex. She always has had. I can imagine her jumping to that conclusion when her mother had the stroke. And it wouldn't help if she walked in on him and a woman. But she must realize now, surely, that—"

Anna wasn't listening. "You mean you and she don't . . ."

"No," he said. "We never have. That's why I don't have to explain where I've been."

Anna was appalled at the idea of a man like Max finding himself in such a predicament. Bloody Catherine. She had messed up more people's lives than Victor's.

Max lay back, arms outstretched. "And I'm with you now," he said. "So let's not waste it."

Anna still sat as she had, elbows on his knees, hands loosely clasped in front of her. She smiled at Max, and hoped to God she could trust him.

Because now she really had something to worry about.

Catherine took things from the wardrobe, stuffing them into a suitcase. She didn't know what she was taking, she was simply packing. That's what you did when you were running away. This time there was no money to take from the safe. This time there was no safe, because Max wouldn't know what to put in one, thank God. There was no one in the world like Victor Holyoak, but Max was as unlike as it was possible to be.

She had a joint account with Max, but it wouldn't be fair to use that. She would just have to get a job. Unlike Valerie, she could at least do that; she had worked for Max, and at Driver's for a little while. She could type—she could file. She looked round the bedroom; Max had bought this house before they were married, and this room had seen a lot of painful tears, a lot of laughter, and a great deal of love.

No one could have been kinder than Max, more understanding. And she had tried. She had gone to all the people that Max had asked her to see. All she had got out of it was the trick of deep breathing at moments of panic. She still couldn't let poor Max touch her. And then he'd tried all sorts of things himself; he had been so patient, so good. She had told him that he could have other women, but for a long time no one really wanted to know him. Then that had passed, and Max had got his hobby back. She smiled. She was glad about that.

Then the smile went as she thought of the nightmares the bedroom had witnessed, when Max would shout his innocence, and cry in his sleep. She could have stopped that. It was way, way too late by the time the nightmares started for her to tell him what she had done. And tomorrow he would find out. But

301

she wouldn't be there, because she was running away again. She closed the suitcase, and carried it downstairs, just as some-one came to the door.

She put it down behind the door, and opened it, expecting Zelda, come to tell her that she must give Max moral support tomorrow.

"Hello, Catherine," he said, walking in, and closing the door. He looked at the suitcase. "Running away again?" he asked.

"It's got nothing to do with you!"

"Oh, but it has," he said. "You're frightened of what your husband's going to say when he sees me." He smiled. "I told you the solution to that," he said. "Don't come—then you won't have to see him realize what you did to him. Of course you could tell him, but that is something that I'm sure you'll put off until it's too late."

"You said you wouldn't come here again," Catherine persisted. The only thing that Victor Holyoak had principles about was keeping his word, and that was just another aspect of his obsessiveness. But you could rely on it, she had thought.

"Things have changed," he said. "So you can unpack the suitcase, Catherine."

She shook her head.

"I think you will," he said. "When you hear what I have to say."

"Everything's fixed. He'll be there at about ten thirty in the morning, he hopes, but he's got two ports of call before that, and things often get very bogged down, so don't think he's let you down if he's late."

Charles smiled weakly at the telephone. "Thanks, Mark," he said. "It was good of you."

"He's delighted to do it. Not too many people building big-ger factories these days. And you'll have the press pack, and the TV, so your friend Holyoak should be pleased."

"Good."

"Sorry I can't be there—it would be nice to see you and Geraldine again." A pause, during which Charles was sup-posed to issue an invitation, but didn't. "It's been too long," he said. "In fact—I don't believe we've seen each other since I stood for Stansfield."

"No," said Charles. "I don't believe we have."

"We must make a date soon. 'Bye."

Charles put the receiver on the rest, and looked round his sitting room. It was a long, low room, with exposed beams painted black, and the original fireplace, a huge stone-built affair that had once had seats right inside it for the farmhands to get warm in winter. He had put shelves in; they had taken out the old grate and replaced it with a gas fire that looked like a real fire. It hadn't looked like this when they had bought it; the clinic had paid for the modernization of the interior, and the restoration of the exterior. Charles would really have liked to add on a wing, but they had told him he couldn't. He had had to fight to build the clinic; in the end they had agreed, providing it was made of the same materials.

Gerry didn't really approve of private clinics, but then she had never grown out of sixties optimism about the way of the world, when everyone was going to be equal: black, white, upper class, working class. Everyone was going to heaven on pot and free love with flowers in their hair. He had never liked all that. Gerry had got him to take a puff of a joint once, and he'd expected the Drugs Squad to come bursting in to ruin his career before he'd even qualified.

He had been shocked, the first time she had suggested that they went away for the weekend together, once he'd realized what she meant. She had laughed at him. The pill had revolutionized all that, she had said. She needn't have bothered with the pill, as things had turned out.

She would have been better off with Max, really. Someone who shared her belief in socialism, who was a believer in free love if ever there was one, who could probably have given her children, though he had never wanted any himself. But Max had been lumbered with Valerie, and Gerry, for some reason, loved him. He wasn't sure why; he had never been sure why. Charles wasn't at all sure that he loved her; she had been the only girl he'd ever felt at ease with, that was all.

But she was his wife, and he had given her everything that could be expected of him. Except a baby. He had done everything in his power to get their standard of living to the heights that it had reached, and keep it there, and there were still further heights to scale. Victor Holyoak was a good person to know; he might never have met him if it hadn't been for the clinic. He was a fitness fanatic; he had started using the gym at the clinic as soon as he had heard about it. He overdid it, in Charles's opinion. He was almost obsessed with keeping fit.

But he had been as good as his word, and Max had been confirmed as a general manager the day that Charles had confirmed that the minister would do the opening ceremony. There might be other favours Charles could do him that would be repaid as promptly.

This one had been done at a price; Charles hadn't really wanted to renew his acquaintance with Mark. That election held terrible memories, and all he had ever wanted to do was to forget it. Week after week of the police taking Max in for questioning, even having to answer questions himself more than once. Gerry looking ill for months, Zelda becoming totally hostile to Max, because she believed Max had murdered Valerie, whatever she said. Horrible days, and making the arrangements with Mark had brought them all back.

And tomorrow, they would all be there. Him, Gerry, Max, Zelda . . . all together in one room for the first time since the dinner party. With Catherine instead of Valerie. It was going to be very difficult for everyone.

But at least Max had a proper job at last, he thought, snapping out of his brown study as he heard the surgery door close. Gerry had finished her late appointment with the colonel who would do well to study Charles's lifestyle book.

She came in, and took off her white coat, throwing it down on the sofa. "There's nothing wrong with the old fool," she said.

"Would you like a drink?" Charles asked.

"No. I'd love a cup of coffee—oh, that reminds me. I had Zelda over earlier. Wanting to know why Catherine is refusing to go to the opening tomorrow." She looked at him. "Do you know anything about that?" she asked.

No. It was news to him. "I don't think Max knows, which is more to the point," Charles said. "I'm sure he'd much rather she was there."

"Well, Zelda thinks it has to do with Max being over friendly with this Anna Worthing woman," she said, going out into the hall, and down to the kitchen.

"Nonsense!" said Charles. "Zelda's imagining things. Max and Catherine are as happy as any couple I know. If she

304

doesn't want to go . . . maybe she isn't feeling well, or something."

"For a doctor, you're very coy about menstruation," Gerry shouted back down the hall to him. "And she isn't that bad with it, anyway."

Charles shrugged, and poured himself a drink.

Holyoak looked at his watch. "I'll go now," he said, looking at his stepdaughter, who stared back, the defiance gone. "I'm sure you would rather your husband didn't find me here when he gets back from his whoring."

She didn't speak.

"You really should have told him, Catherine. You can't blame him if he's angry."

Still nothing.

"You always did leave everything until the last minute, didn't you? It isn't a good idea."

Her eyes were wide with resentment now that she knew she had no way out this time. She should be grateful; he had been prepared to accommodate certain conditions, when she was in no position to impose them. But she had never been grateful.

Anna would be. He had intended terminating her employment, but she had elicited information that he would otherwise not have had, and he still had a use for her after all. He would tell her that, except that he would let her think it was a reprieve, rather than a stay of execution, or she would have no incentive to do what he required of her. And he would tell the little whore what he thought of her. She liked to imagine that his opinion of her had altered over the years, but it never had, and he would make certain that she understood that.

Once he had no more need of her, that little episode with Scott that he had just witnessed would seal her fate. She knew the terms of their bargain; she had brought it on herself.

And his stepdaughter knew the terms of their bargain. "A bargain is a bargain, Catherine," he said. "I'm glad you didn't let me down after all."

He left, and drove to the factory, parking at the rear of the building, getting security to let him in to the building, where he went up to his office, and sat at his desk. He took out his keyring, and unlocked the door to the cupboard behind his head, where a tape silently recorded the images on the screen.

He had no desire to watch their couplings; he just wanted to listen to what they had to say to one another.

He picked up headphones, and turned away from the scene that the overhead camera was watching.

Above her head Max could see the superfine mesh that subdued the hidden lighting, and lent her glowing body a soft golden sheen. He always wanted light; he liked to see his partner. Her upper lip was touched with perspiration as she held her head back, eyes closed, quite still.

Then she looked down at him, frowning slightly. "How can someone like you put up with a sexless marriage?" she asked. "Didn't you find out what she was like before you married her?"

Max smiled again. Even Anna couldn't see that sex was simply a matter of animal instinct improved by human ingenuity—which Anna possessed in abundance—and nothing whatever to do with love.

"No," he said. "I wanted her to feel she could change her mind right up until the last minute. She was very young."

"What did you do when you found out?" she asked.

"Persuaded her to see psychiatrists and psychologists—we even found a sex therapist. Nothing worked. She's never let me near her."

"What—nothing?"

"Nothing," he said.

Anna stripped the bed as he showered and dressed, and showered and dressed herself as he shoved the sheets into the machine, and set it going. Then they would make up the bed together. It was routine now, and even that was good, with the desire gone, for the moment, to jump between the sheets they were spreading on the bed; he liked the company of women, with or without physical contact. Anna couldn't understand.

"Separate rooms, all that?" she asked.

"Same room, separate beds," he said.

Her eyes widened. "But how can someone like you bear that?" she asked.

"Because I've got someone like you," he said. He tucked in the sheet, and straightened up. "I love her, Anna. I love her very much—she's the only woman I've ever loved. And noth-

306

ing would please me more than to make love to her, but I can live without it, and I don't want to live without her."

She looked at him, her head to one side. "You're a really nice man, aren't you?" she said. "I don't believe I've ever met one before."

But he couldn't let her believe that he was some self-sacrificing hero. "I'd have been here anyway," he said. "I couldn't forsake all others. I couldn't the first time, and I wouldn't have with Catherine—I don't kid myself. This time round, I don't have to feel guilty."

They stuffed pillows into pillowcases.

"You *like* having a sexless marriage?" she asked.

"It's no big deal," he said.

The reason for her phobia was a big deal. These people might have helped, if she had explained what she had believed about her mother's stroke. What she had done to her mother was a big deal, running away like that. But he could forgive all that; she had had a lot to cope with, and she had failed; there was no shame in that. But not telling him that Victor Holyoak was her stepfather; that he was finding hard to forgive.

They persuaded the cover to go on the duvet, and they had run out of chores. He had to go home.

He found Catherine sitting at the dining table; all the way home he had told himself that he mustn't get angry, but all his good intentions evaporated, like the euphoria of being with Anna had done.

"When was I supposed to find out?" he demanded, as he walked in. "Tomorrow? When he made his announcement?"

Catherine sat, her head on her hand, not responding. It was as though he hadn't spoken.

"Look at me, for God's sake! I want to know. What were you going to do tomorrow? What did you imagine you'd achieve? Does he know you haven't told me? What was he supposed to do?"

"I'm not going to be there," she said. "I don't care what he does."

He came over to her, pulling out a chair, sitting down. "You are going to be there," he said.

She looked at him then, shaking her head.

"Yes, Catherine. You have to face him. You have to look at him and accept that he isn't the monster you've created. Whatever he did, you can't go on blaming him for what happened to your mother!"

"Can't I?" she said, almost inaudibly.

"No, damn it, you can't!" He banged the table with his fist. "It's cruel, Catherine, can't you see that? It's cruel, and unfair!"

She closed her eyes.

"Catherine, I can't believe this is happening—I can't believe you did that. You didn't just walk out on him—you walked out on your mother! Because you found him with some woman? What did that prove, for God's sake?"

"Some woman?" she repeated, dully. "Is that the story?"

Max sat back, frowning, then realized. "Is *that* what this is all about? It was a man? A boy? All right, it frightened you, and you got it all mixed up with what had happened to your mother—that was all right when you were sixteen, Catherine, but you're not sixteen any more. You can't let something like that blight your whole life!"

She turned away, and he put his hands on her shoulders, firmly turning her towards him again.

"For God's sake, Catherine, I'm not telling you anything you don't know yourself! Whether or not you like him is up to you. Whether or not you want to speak to him is up to you. But why didn't you *tell* me who he was? Why didn't he? Is that why he's been keeping out of sight? Did you ask him to? What did you hope to achieve? Did you think he'd melt away?"

"I'm going to bed," she said, getting up.

"You never tried to get help, did you?" he said. "You never told these people anything that they could work with." He shook his head. "I'm sorry about what happened to your mother. And I'm sorry that you had some traumatic experience. But cutting yourself off completely from your family was no answer. All you've done is hurt your mother and me as well as him."

She walked away.

"And you've got to come tomorrow," he said. "I am the general manager—albeit owing to nepotism I knew nothing about—but I am, and my wife should be there."

She turned. "But I'm not your wife, am I?" she said.

Max jumped up. "Oh, yes you are," he said. "I love you.

You *are* my wife. And you must know what it's going to be like for me—half the people there are still convinced I'm a murderer! I need you, Catherine."

She left the room, and went upstairs. Max sank down again at the table, wondering just what would have happened tomorrow if Anna hadn't told him. Why would she have preferred him to find out that way? What reason could she have had for not telling him, when he was going to find out anyway?

He didn't understand.

CHAPTER THIRTEEN

Now: Saturday, 4 April . . .

MAX LOOKED AT THEM, AND THEN AT CATHERINE. SHE was, she had been reminded, still under caution. They wanted to ask her some more questions concerning Valerie's death.

But they knew all the answers to the questions that had been asked then. And they knew that Catherine's alibi had been false, that he hadn't been with her at all. He had told them this time round that he had been having an affair with Catherine; he had had to, once he had discovered about the abortion, because they would find out, eventually. So surely he was even more suspect than before?

But it wasn't him they had come to see. It was Catherine. They had told her she could have a solicitor, but she had said she didn't want a solicitor; she wanted Max. They had agreed that he could stay. Because they knew that he knew what it was all about; that what would come out of the interview would come as no shock to him, because that shock had already rocked his system once, and it could do no more harm.

They were all in the sitting room; him, Catherine, Lloyd, and Hill. All seated. Max sat on the arm of Catherine's chair, his arm round her, because now he understood. They hadn't discussed it; there had been no need.

Inspector Hill spoke first. "Mrs. Scott, you told me last night how determined you were to marry anyone in order to get away from what you called your stepfather's megalomania," she said.

Catherine shook her head firmly. "No," she said. "Not any-one. Max. I loved him. I wouldn't have married anyone else."

No. He knew that; he knew a great many things now that he had never known.

"But he was already married."

"Yes."

"Had you asked him to seek a divorce?"

She took a deep breath and let it out, the way she had learned to do when they were still trying to conquer her pho-bia, and then looked up at him. Max patted her. He mustn't an-swer for her, he had been told. Same questions, different answers. Truthful answers, now, from Catherine, as far as pos-sible. But they all knew that the moment would come, and Max could only hope that they could prove nothing, like be-fore.

"Yes. He said he couldn't possibly do that."

"Did that upset you?"

"Yes."

"And you told DCI Lloyd that on the third of May that year you telephoned and spoke to Valerie Scott?"

"Yes."

Lloyd took over then. "You said that you heard her answer the door to an election campaigner, and complain that she had already had one of 'their lot,' " he said.

Max stiffened, but Catherine still felt almost relaxed under his protective arm; her shoulder muscles no longer tying them-selves in knots, as they had been for weeks.

"Thus placing yourself firmly in London at the time Mrs. Scott died." He sat back, and regarded her. "But it wasn't true, was it, Mrs. Scott?" he said.

Catherine frowned, but still no reaction, still no tensing up. Max could feel his legs, his neck growing stiff from tension.

"Two lots of campaigners did go round from one party—you had got that right. And there was a campaigner with Mrs. Scott at approximately the time that you stated you had made this call." He leant towards her. "Unfortunately," he said, "that was the only one who visited Valerie Scott. The first team was organized by Dr. Rule, who knew only too well that there was no point in calling on the Scotts, who he knew always voted Labour. So no one from the first lot called on Valerie Scott at all."

"But that's what she said," said Catherine, frowning.

"No," he said. "I don't think so, Mrs. Scott. I think you came to Stansfield that evening, having got Mr. Scott to go on a wild-goose chase to London, or at the very best realized that he was on one, because he didn't know your new address. I think you wanted to see Valerie Scott. Alone."

Catherine shook her head, and Max prayed that they were shadow-boxing, like they had with him.

"Perhaps you took matters into your own hands. Told her you were having an affair with her husband, had a row with her that ended in violence. Or perhaps you were desperate enough to have Max Scott for yourself that you went with the sole intention of ridding yourself of your rival."

Catherine went pale, and twisted round to look at Max, her eyes wide. "Oh, my God," she said. "That's what you thought. That's what you thought when you saw him—you thought I'd ... you thought—" She stared at him. "You still think it. You still think I killed her!"

Max held her close, no longer capable of thinking anything. If Catherine hadn't ... who? Why? He had always forced the questions away, because at the back of his mind, at the very back, he had always wondered about Catherine's overwhelming insistence that she would tell the police that he had been with her when he hadn't, her turning up exactly when she did, asking him to go and see her, not telling him she'd moved. And when he had seen Holyoak, seen the man he had seen that night, known that Catherine could have proved his innocence, and had insisted on that lie ... He had felt the rage and horror well up, and found himself slapping her, demanding to know the truth. But he had believed, he had believed inside that he did know it, that he had known it all along. And then, later, he had believed that he knew why, and he had finally understood, and had forgiven her.

Now he didn't understand, and he held the sobbing Catherine, and looked helplessly at Lloyd and the inspector. It made no sense. Who else could have wanted Valerie dead?

"I was in London," Catherine was protesting through the sobs, looking up at him. "I was at my digs. I did ring Valerie, she did say what I said, I swear to you, Max, she did!" She turned back then, to the police. "My stepfather and Annabel ... Anna Worthing—whatever she calls herself—they

312

came to my digs! They saw me! About an hour after I called Mrs. Scott! They saw me—he was going to Holland that night—he wanted me to go to the ferry with them and say goodbye to my mother. I wouldn't go, and they stayed for about twenty minutes trying to persuade me!" She turned back to Max. "It's the truth!" she said "Oh, Max—I didn't . . . I would never have done such a thing to you!"

"And Anna Worthing will confirm this?" asked Lloyd.

"Yes," said Catherine. "Yes! Ask her. Just ask her. I wasn't here, I was in London. I didn't kill Valerie."

No. The subject had remained undiscussed, even when everything else was being unlocked, that first night they had had together after Holyoak had died; the idea that had consumed him with rage, then haunted him for hours, persisting even when a new and equally appalling truth had dawned on him, was that Catherine had killed Valerie, and he had accepted that, in the end. But now he knew he hadn't just been uncontrollably, unprecedentedly angry with his fragile and precious wife; he had wronged her.

They left; he and Catherine stayed locked together, not speaking, not moving, for a long, long time.

Anna had retired with the brandy bottle, but she hadn't drunk any. She hadn't slept either, but she did feel that it was a step in the right direction.

She answered the door, opening it on the chain. It was Inspector Hill, this time. She had never entertained so many police officers since her Leyford days, when the two-faced bastards would come looking for freebies. But she and the inspector had had a long talk last night; Anna had told her everything she was scared of, from Bannister to corporate image-makers to trying to hustle a living, without Victor to protect her.

"How are you?" asked the inspector.

Anna shrugged. "OK, I suppose," she said. "I saw the patrol car a few times last night." She had spent a long time looking out of the window at the darkness, at the town, at the future.

"Good. They'll keep an eye on you over the weekend," Inspector Hill said briskly. "Bannister will be back to appear before the magistrates—we'll oppose bail if we have any reason to think he'd come here again. But I don't really think he will," she added. "Not now he knows you didn't set him up."

Anna could never be that sure of any man, except Victor, and Victor was dead. "Would you like a cup of tea?" she said. She, AnnaBelle le Sueur, was asking a cop if she would like a cup of tea.

"Thanks," she said. "But first—the night you went to Holland with Holyoak. Was that election night?"

"Yes."

"Did you and Victor Holyoak call on Catherine?"

"Yes. She was in her digs by then, and he'd just found her in time before he left. I don't know why he wanted me to be there, but he did, and I knew by then not to ask questions. She wouldn't come with us, though, and he only wanted her to—"

"Say goodbye to her mother," finished Inspector Hill.

"Yes. Take a seat." Anna went into the kitchen, and set about making the tea, still thinking of her future. "I'll have to get out of this place, won't I?" she called through.

"Not yet," said the inspector. "It'll probably take them months to sort out his financial affairs—I'd sit tight if I were you. Whoever ends up owning it might let you rent."

Anna laughed. "What do you suppose the rent is on a place like this?" she asked.

"You've got a good job."

Anna went back in to look at her. "I know Mr. Lloyd says everyone's incompetent," she said. "But at least they know what they're supposed to be doing. Victor gave me that job because he *knew* I couldn't do it."

Inspector Hill gave her a disbelieving look. "The Anna he knew might not have been able to do it," she said. "But that's because he degraded her year after year until she thought she couldn't survive without him. But you did, Anna, before you met him. The Anna I knew could have done it standing on her head."

Anna thought about that, as the kettle boiled. She would have jumped at it in the old days. Swanning about, organizing parties, chatting up the local bigwigs, putting on exhibitions, selling the company, selling herself.

"You have to build a new life, Anna," the inspector called through. "Victor Holyoak stole it from you."

Anna made the tea. "But I'm scared, she said. "I only know

314

one job." She got two mugs. "How do you take your tea?" she asked.

"Milk, no sugar. Anna—you've been in public relations all your life."

"I think that must have been a misprint on the charge sheet," said Anna as she brought the tea through.

The inspector smiled. "They're not called charge sheets any more," she said. "And girls like you are regarded as victims, which is what you are."

"Hasn't made much difference, though, has it? I mean, there are still girls like me—you haven't changed anything by changing the system."

"No," the inspector conceded. "But that's your past, Anna. This is your future. All you have to do is make people feel special," she said. "That's what public relations is all about. How they see you is how they'll see the company. Be yourself. Leave logos and letterheads to people who understand that sort of thing—you're the boss. Delegate. You do what you're best at—deal with the public. Make sure that whoever you're dealing with thinks that he's the most important person in your life. You must be good at that, or Holyoak wouldn't have hung on to you this long."

"Oh, yes," said Anna, handing the inspector her tea, and sitting down. "I can do that, even if I am in my dotage. I had Max fooled."

"Max?" Inspector Hill put down her mug, at once interested and alert. "Are you saying that Holyoak arranged that?"

Anna smiled. "Max didn't know it was arranged," she said. "It's not difficult to trap Max."

"But why did he want him trapped?"

"I don't know. But whatever it was, it worked, I think."

"Trap him how?"

"The bedroom in the penthouse has got a camera in the ceiling," said Anne, a little reluctantly. "I didn't know—I thought Max was getting some sort of payoff for something he'd done for Victor. I'd never have talked to him about Victor's business if I had known—that's why Victor was going to get rid of me, because I'd talked out of turn. He told me on Wednesday. But he said that what I'd done had changed things—that's why I was being kept on after all—I didn't know what he meant."

315

Inspector Hill was staring at her. "There's a camera in that room and you didn't tell us?"

Anna realized what she thought. "Oh! No, don't get excited. He was expecting someone, and he wasn't about to record that. You don't have the murder on video, if that's what you're hoping."

"Where's the recording equipment?" she asked.

Anna shrugged. "There's a cupboard in Victor's office that no one else has the key to," she said. "It might be there."

"Right." The inspector abandoned her tea, and stood up.

"But all you'll find is Max and me," she said. "I don't know if that sort of thing turns you on."

Inspector Hill smiled. "Neither do I," she said. "But you said it had changed things—so I think I'm going to have to find out. Sorry."

Another shrug. More people than the inspector had watched Anna in action, on video and in the flesh. One more wouldn't hurt any worse than all the others had.

But she still didn't see how it had changed anything.

Jackie was at work; she hadn't wanted to go, but they couldn't afford to lose the money. Normally, he would have the kids on a Saturday, take them to the park maybe, or one of the big shopping areas. Not to buy anything, of course. Just somewhere he could let them run about without worrying about traffic. But their gran had taken them last night so that he and Jackie could have the place to themselves.

Jackie had cried last night. He had very nearly cried; it was so good to be home again after a night on the other side of a cell door. There had been some considerable time when he had thought he was really going to get done for knifing the bastard. The sergeant had said that he wasn't out of the woods yet, but they would never have let him go if they hadn't believed him.

And the good news was that *someone* had knifed him; not before time. But not little Annabel, it seemed. Well, now that he had time to think about it rationally, it wouldn't have been. That little whore had always known which side her bread was buttered.

Next door in the kitchen, the ever-present washing-machine churned, and the sound that had got him near to screaming point sounded so good to him now. It was home. It was Jackie.

It was the kids, with their football shorts and muddy jeans. It was just a nice, familiar, comforting . . .

His eyes grew a little wider, and then he smiled, and reached for the phone. Why not? It would be nice to have Judy Russell owing him a favour for once.

She was out, but he left a message with Sergeant Finch.

Lloyd came into Holyoak's office, smiling at Judy as she sat behind Holyoak's huge power desk. "It suits you," he said, and sat on the edge of it, immediately cutting it down to size. "I got a message from Finch to say that you wanted me to watch a blue video with you," he said.

"Very funny."

"It'll be better fun than the security videos," Lloyd said darkly. "God knows how many manhours spent apprehending a sneak thief. Not another vehicle came into the plant from then until the cleaners arrived in the morning. Thank God Andrews is away."

Judy gave him a sympathetic smile, and opened the cupboard behind her head, pressing the play button on the video recorder. "This bit isn't very blue," she said. "But listen." She handed Lloyd the headphones as the unintentionally artistic image from the overhead camera came on the screen. Two people talking; naked, but their closeness rendered them entirely modest from above, as though the scene had been arranged by a clever television director. The fine mesh through which it had been shot gave the whole thing a misty, romantic look.

Lloyd listened, frowning slightly, the way he did when he thought that his time might be being wasted, until he got to the really important part. He took off the headphones. "Their marriage is *unconsummated*?" he said.

Judy nodded, and switched off the video, shutting and locking the cupboard door, not so much to preserve evidence as to lock in Holyoak's evil. Because she was beginning to feel that that was what they were dealing with, as she told Lloyd what other conversation had passed between Anna and Max Scott.

He got off the desk, and pulled up a chair as he thought about something. Then looked at Judy. "Do you remember you once asked me if I'd ever been unfaithful to Barbara?" he said.

Judy was startled; Lloyd broke the rule about leaving their private lives at home all the time, but not usually quite this blatantly. "Yes," she said. "You said you had. Just once. She was a foot soldier with the London Philharmonic, or something."

Lloyd laughed. "A rank and file violinist with the BBC Symphony Orchestra," he said. "I met her the day you married Michael."

Oh God. Why was it Make Judy Feel Guilty week? She'd had enough of that from Linda.

"I . . . I had an affair with her because—not to put too fine a point on it—I was frustrated."

Judy smiled. "That is putting too fine a point on it," she said. "Finch would say you weren't getting any, if he was being polite."

Lloyd looked round the opulent office. "I hope Holyoak didn't have this place bugged," he said. "Anyway—yes, that was why. You steadfastly refused to go to bed with me, but Barbara thought you had been doing, so she wasn't over keen on me either."

Judy looked at him uncertainly. "What am I supposed to do?" she asked. "Tell you to say three Hail Marys?"

He raised his eyes heavenward. "I'm not confessing," he said. "I'm applying my own solitary experience of marital infidelity to Scott's predicament."

"Oh."

"Well, if it drove me into another woman's arms—what do you suppose Scott would do? He would find someone to give him some consolation as soon as he could, wouldn't he? He did it all the time anyway."

"Well, he did, didn't he? Zelda."

Lloyd shook his head. "Valerie Scott was heard shouting that she would make trouble for this woman," he said. "That's bothered me all along—how could she make trouble for Catherine? As far as anyone knew, Catherine had no family, she had no husband—what trouble could she make for her? Or Zelda? Zelda was a widow, she was Max's boss—Valerie couldn't make trouble for her either, could she?"

Judy nodded slowly. "We're back to the doctor, aren't we?" she said. "Having an affair with a patient. She could make trouble for her, all right."

"I think so. Max Scott came here to try to forget about Catherine, so I don't think he would hang about. He already

318

knew Geraldine, and Rule said that he couldn't go through all that again, when he thought Geraldine had been having an affair with Holyoak. Because Geraldine had done it before—that's why he jumped to conclusions. I think Geraldine was Max's latest, as far as Valerie was concerned."

He got up. "Come on," he said. "Let's call on Zelda. She might be a bit more forthcoming now that Geraldine is beyond scandal."

Zelda, pressing elevenses on them, was more forthcoming.

"Well, Valerie was upset. She said he'd got someone, and he was in love with her, and she didn't know how to cope with that because he'd never done that to her before, he had always just had women on the side who didn't mean anything . . . but he'd actually moved to Stansfield to be with this one." She shrugged. "I didn't know what to say. I knew Max had been going to see Geraldine at the surgery on Valerie's evening-class nights, but he wasn't in love with her. Anyway—it only lasted a couple of months before Geraldine came to her senses. It was over by the time Valerie cottoned on."

Judy took a tiny sandwich. They did look particularly good. Lloyd, however, was not eating, and his face held a dark look. Judy knew the look well, but for once she wasn't the one who had made him angry.

"Have you any more to tell us, Zelda?" he asked, sounding very, very Welsh.

"She was threatening to tell Charles, the BMA, anyone and everyone. She was fighting for Max. Anyway, that day she told Max that she would report Geraldine. He told her that the affair was over, but she didn't believe him. Because of course he wasn't in love with Geraldine at all—it was Catherine. And that affair wasn't over, was it? So, in a way, Valerie was right."

Make Judy Feel Guilty time again. She took another sandwich. All right, her existence had broken up Lloyd's marriage, but she hadn't done it deliberately, and she hadn't done it for fun, and she hadn't even *had* an affair with him. And Catherine certainly hadn't had one with Max. She thought about that, as she ate. And she wondered again.

"Are you seriously telling me that you knew that the dead woman had uttered threats? That she had been intending very seriously damaging the career of a local doctor, and had actually informed her husband of this intention?"

"Max didn't kill her."

"I know Max didn't kill her," said Lloyd, his voice low and dangerous. "Max, in all probability, was where he said he was. Max thought until about two hours ago that Catherine had killed her—but you and I, Zelda, we know differently, don't we?"

Zelda looked at him, totally puzzled. Then her face cleared. "Oh—no! No. Of course I wouldn't have kept quiet if there had been the slightest chance of Geraldine's having done it!"

Sure, thought Judy. But there wasn't the slightest chance of Geraldine's having done it, as Zelda went on to prove.

"Geraldine was doing all Charles's evening surgeries," Zelda said. "Charles was campaigning for his friend Mark, so Geraldine had to work. From five to seven. Every weekday evening. Geraldine had about twenty witnesses as to where she was for the whole two hours—what was the point in making a scandal for her? But poor Max left the office at five thirty and as far as the police were concerned, he went home and killed his wife. I wasn't going to make that worse for him by telling them about Geraldine."

Lloyd took a sandwich and ate it whole. "Bloody hell, Zelda," he said, when he had swallowed it. "Do you know how much trouble you would be in if he *had* killed his wife?"

"Zelda," said Judy, hardly aware of what Lloyd was saying, so keen was she to ask the question. "You said Max Scott lied to you about Catherine?"

"He swore to me that he hadn't had an affair with her—he knew I'd have nothing more to do with him if he'd seduced a little girl and then just left her when it suited him. I believed him."

"What makes you think he was lying?" she asked, not wanting to hear the answer, not really.

Zelda looked at her, and sighed. "I suppose you really ought to know," she said. "Since you seem to have stopped suspecting Max at last. Catherine was pregnant when she came here," she said. "Max didn't know—he wouldn't ever have known, but I thought Charles knew, and Charles thought Max knew, and . . . he found out on Wednesday," she said. And gave a Zelda shrug.

Lloyd and Judy looked at one another. Zelda wasn't slow to notice.

"What? It's the truth—ask Charles. Ask Catherine—I don't suppose she wants it kept secret now. But she thought at the time that it would make things look so bad for Max that the police would never leave him alone, so she had an abortion. I knew about it at the time," she said defiantly to Lloyd. "So you charge me with whatever you like. Yes—I was withholding evidence. Because Max Scott didn't kill Valerie, and I was quite prepared to cover up the fact that he'd got Catherine pregnant before he left. I just wasn't prepared to forgive it."

Lloyd stood up. "Er . . . no," he said. "No, I don't think I'll be charging you, Zelda."

They left Zelda agog with curiosity and sat in Lloyd's car. Every now and then the curtain would twitch as Zelda checked to see if they were still there.

"Pregnant," said Lloyd.

Judy took out her notebook, in which every fact she had been given, every opinion anyone had held, every hint anyone had dropped, had been noted. It had crossed her mind, when she had seen that video, and she had shied away from it. But she couldn't any more. She had to be right. And if she was right . . .

Lloyd glanced at her. "How long has Driver's been closing at five o'clock?" he asked.

"Only since it was Holyoak's," she said absently, as she checked the notes she had taken directly from the tape of Anna Worthing's interview. "About three months or so."

"I am a fool," he said, putting the car in gear.

"Mm." Judy found the note she was looking for.

Late January, because that's when she (Catherine) moved. And it had to have been when she (Catherine) conceived, thought Judy as she turned the pages.

But how could she have got into the flat? Could she have known Anna Worthing's patent method for dodging the cameras? It seemed very unlikely, and even if she did, she couldn't have known that the fire door was open. She had had no contact with Anna or Max, and they were the only two who knew apart from Bannister.

And no one had come in the main gate after five o'clock, which was when Holyoak was last seen alive by a number of people—not on foot, nor in a car; they had checked eighteen hours of tape to no avail. She closed her eyes, as she realized what that meant.

No one had come in. No one, until the cleaners who had found Holyoak's body. No one at all. And they had checked the tape beyond that, right up to when the first police car came. No other car or vehicle. None.

But that still didn't explain how she had got up to the flat. The lift couldn't be taken up from the car park; she would still have had to use the front door, and she hadn't.

Unless she had been in the flat all along. But no—Zelda went up before Holyoak did. She checked back through her notes, to Rule's interview.

I felt as though someone was there.

Lloyd's wardrobe doors. Judy shivered. She must have left her clothes in there.

But she had to be sure, she thought, as Lloyd drove back to the station. She would check through everything again before she even advanced the theory to Lloyd. And she'd get Holyoak security to fast-forward through that tape right up to the last possible moment. They would find nothing. She knew that now.

In Lloyd's office, she began her painstaking check again while Lloyd phoned the Tory agent, tapping his foot impatiently while someone went to get him.

"Can you confirm that no member of your campaigning team called on Mrs. Valerie Scott after six P.M. on Thursday the third of May?" he asked. He waited, no more patiently, for the answer, thanked him, hung up, then phoned the agents of both the other parties with the same request. The others, more concerned with the current election and without the Conservative agent's advantage of having already been asked questions about a thirteen-year-old murder, took rather longer, but the intense police questioning at the time had meant that memories remained sharp, and records had been kept.

"No one," Lloyd said to her, as he finished the final phone-call. "Come on."

"You wouldn't like to tell me where we're going?" Judy asked, practically having to run along the corridor to keep up with him.

"Ma'am," called Tom Finch as she whizzed past the CID room. She skidded to a halt, and looked in.

"I've got an urgent message for you. From Bannister."

Judy silently dared Finch to be making some sort of joke. She wasn't in the mood for fun and games, and she had had plenty of experience of rank-pulling. She was sure she could carry it off with just as much panache as Lloyd if she felt it was warranted. This had better be good.

"He said just to say washing-machine, and you owe him one," said Finch. "He said you'd know what he meant."

No joke. A genuine message. A genuine message that made no sense at all, because why would she use the washing-machine? She hadn't washed the towels, so why wash anything else? Nothing else would have needed washing, if Judy's careful gathering of the facts meant anything at all.

"Right, Tom," she said absently. "Yes. Yes—thanks."

Lloyd appeared at her elbow. "I thought you were behind me," he said. "Come *on*."

"Yes," she said. "Where did you say we were going?"

"We're going to bring Dr. Charles Rule in for questioning," he said.

She ran after him once again, catching him up as he stepped out into the overcrowded car park.

"Someone's boxed me in!" he roared. "Get whoever it is down here to move that bloody thing!"

Judy complied, by dint of issuing the same order to a passing probationary constable, and finally, finally, she knew she had the answer.

"Phone," she said, dashing back in, along to the collator's office. "Phone," she said to the girl, who pushed it across to her. She rang Finch's extension.

"CID, Sergeant Finch."

"Were your knees jammed under the steering wheel when you put Anna Worthing's car away?" she asked.

There was a silence. "No," he said quietly. "I'm sorry, ma'am. I was . . . well, you know. A bit miffed. What with . . . the pictures and everything. Sorry."

"Forget it."

She hung up as the British Telecom engineer, shepherded by the anxious constable, went past the door on his way to get an earful from Lloyd. But God bless him, she thought, for jogging her memory.

Not that she was anxious to bring the crime home to anyone, if she were honest with herself. But now, at last, everything fitted, as she went through her notes for a third and final time. Including the washing-machine, and Anna Worthing's over-anxious neighbour. Including Finch's unprintable opinion of Max Scott, so at odds with the mild-mannered, polite, likeable man she had met. Including the disappearing wallet. Even including Anna's first thought when there had been a knock at Holyoak's door.

I thought it might have been Max, but he says he saw me leave.

But she hadn't seen *Max*, or she would have known that it couldn't have been him. And now Judy knew what she had seen, what had led Anna to that opinion.

Proof would be found in the filter of the machine, she had no doubt; she would go to Holyoak's, get the filter sent off to the lab, receive confirmation that she was right about the security tape, and then ... and then, she would really much rather tip the whole lot down a hole and bury it. But they would have to make an arrest instead. Sadly, she closed her notebook.

"Right," said Lloyd. "Now that you've finished, can I tell you *why* we're taking Dr. Rule in for questioning?"

Charles had gone back to work on his book. There seemed very little point in sitting round the house feeling guilty about Gerry; it wasn't going to bring her back, and it was doing him no good.

He addressed the grey screen of the word processor, and tried out a few options on the preface. He wanted to explain about Jimmy Driver, about how helpless and angry Jimmy's untimely death had made him feel. About how the plans for the clinic had been conceived at Jimmy's graveside. How he had felt compelled, driven, to do something to cut out such waste of human life. How poor diets weren't confined to poor countries. Rich diets were poor diets, too.

Poor Diet, Rich Country, he typed in capital letters. *Rich Country, Poor Diet. Rich Diet, Poor Diet.* They were all right. But really only for a book that confined itself to diet, and of course his ranged much, much further than that. It wasn't some miracle slimming diet that he was trying to sell. It was health. The health of the body, of the planet. It covered everything from what you ate to what you ate it out of. Eating properly would give you a better body, but you had to keep it that way. Eating, drinking, smoking, sex, CFCs, exhaust poisons, stress, salt, sugar—

Smoking, sex, stress, salt, sugar—he played with that for a moment or two. Supping, sipping, smoking, sex, stress, salt, sugar, saturates . . . suicide.

He would have thought of that anyway, he told himself. It would be foolish not to use it just because of Gerry. She had always been heading for disaster when the hope of a baby was taken away, whenever and however that had happened. It hadn't been healthy.

He hadn't got a section on mental health, he thought, with the exception of the chapter on stress, and that was more about the physical aspects. He perhaps ought to have a therapist at the clinic, now he came to think of it.

Perhaps he should have got Gerry to see someone.

He turned as someone knocked at the door. "Two police officers are here, Dr. Rule," said the girl, a little embarrassed. "Shall I show them in?"

"Yes, do," he said, swivelling round to face the door as Chief Inspector Lloyd and Inspector Hill came in. He stood up. "Take a seat," he said. "Coffee?"

"No thank you," Lloyd said, clearly answering for both of them.

Charles dismissed the girl. "I . . . I find it more therapeutic to work," he said.

"I can understand that," Lloyd said. "But I must ask you to come with us to the station, Dr. Rule. We have some questions to put to you concerning the murder of Mrs. Valerie Scott . . ."

Charles listened to himself being cautioned. They had done that at the time, he thought. They had questioned him several times, because he had known Valerie. And now that they had reopened the case, they were having to do it all again. They hadn't taken him to the station before. Just questioned him at home.

He looked at the word processor. At the certificates on the wall, his own and those of the people he employed. He had almost made it. Once the book had been published, he would have made it. People would have beaten a path to his door. If Holyoak had been around, pumping money into it, it couldn't have failed. But Holyoak was gone. Gerry was gone, and that was who he had been doing it for. No it wasn't. He had been doing it for himself. Rule Clinics everywhere. *Living By Rule* That would have been a good title.

He went with them, got into the car, got to the station, was taken to an interview room, and after a moment or two, they came in, told him that the interview would be recorded, did the preliminaries, and then faced him across a table.

"Dr. Rule—did Valerie Scott tell you that her husband was having an affair with your wife?" asked Inspector Hill.

No one had asked that last time. Was he having an affair with Valerie—oh, boy, he'd got asked that over and over again. The very idea. They were working on some desperate theory that Valerie had indulged in a tit-for-tat affair, and the boyfriend had become violent when she had tried to end it before she began divorce proceedings or whatever against Max over this other woman.

But they had never asked if Max had been having an affair with Gerry. Because they had been convinced that his other woman had been Catherine, and they didn't really appreciate Max Scott's appetite. God knew how many women he'd laid since getting Catherine pregnant. The business with Gerry had been over for weeks by the time Valerie had managed to work out what her husband had been doing on her evening-class nights. My God, in the bloody surgery, according to Valerie. Someone had asked her if Max was all right, because she'd seen him coming out of the doctor's three times in as many weeks.

"Yes," he said. "She did."

"And did she threaten to tell the British Medical Association?"

Wrong lot. He'd told her that. Complaints should be made to the General Medical Council, he'd told her. Forget it, Valerie, he'd told her. I have. It's over—you and I both know what Max is like.

"Yes, she did."

"Did she speak to you about this before or after the general election was called?" asked Lloyd.

"Odd question."

"Could I have an answer?"

They knew. He had got away with his one antisocial act for

all these years, but they knew, or they would never have asked that question.

"Before."

"And you hastily joined the Conservative Club, and signed up as a member of the campaign team to support the Conservative candidate?"

"He was a friend of mine." But he shouldn't capitulate too soon. There was still a chance. They hadn't charged him, hadn't even arrested him. He had been taken in for questioning. They presumably didn't actually have evidence—how could they have, thirteen years later?

"And you were doing him a favour," said Lloyd.

"Yes."

"And then a few months ago, you asked him to return the favour. Not for yourself, for Victor Holyoak. And not so that he would invest money in your clinic, but so that he would make Max Scott general manager."

"Yes."

"You're very loyal to Mr. Scott."

"He's my oldest friend."

"You never once, for instance, doubted—not even for an instant—that he was innocent of the murder of his wife, did you?"

"Of course I didn't."

Lloyd nodded. "Of course not," he said. "Even though you knew that just once in a blue moon, Max Scott could be roused to anger, and that he found that anger very difficult to control."

"Not that difficult—not where women were concerned. To him, it would be like defacing the Mona Lisa, or dropping a Ming vase."

"You didn't even let the tiniest doubt creep in on Wednesday, when you knew that he had followed his wife out of the office and started slapping her very hard—hard enough to leave marks?"

"No," said Charles.

"Everyone else did. People who had believed in him enough to cover up his indiscretions at the time of his wife's death were frightened that perhaps he really had murdered Valerie after all. But not you, Dr. Rule."

"No, not me! I know him. He slapped her, for God's sake! He didn't punch her, or kick her. He slapped her, when he was ablaze with anger at what she had done to him. Because that had to be the ultimate in violence towards a woman as far as Max was concerned. Of course he didn't murder Valerie!"

"Of course not," said Lloyd again.

"Your interest in politics didn't last, Dr. Rule," said the inspector, looking up from the notes she was taking of the interview, her brown eyes looking frankly into his.

"No."

"When you went out—on the knocker—is that the expression?" she asked.

"Doorstepping, sometimes," said Charles. "Probably not back then. Canvassing. Campaigning, I call it."

"Do you?" said Lloyd. "I call it murder, Dr. Rule."

Right. Keep cool. They have no proof. They don't have a shred of evidence. "I'm afraid I don't follow," he said.

This was the first time he had ever been in a police interview room. Mean little places, with notices about AIDS and your rights. A tattered copy of the Police and Criminal Evidence Act guidelines hung from a drawing pin on the wall. He had been told he could read it at any time.

"Let me explain," said Lloyd. "You became a campaigner for your friend, the candidate. You got yourself on to the team that was doing the road where the Scotts lived. You told the others not to bother calling on the Scotts—they were Labour voters, so it would be a waste of precious time. Right so far?"

Charles nodded. "It was quite usual—no point in trying to change hearts and minds that are committed to another party."

"Quite. I understand that the Labour party didn't campaign there at all—solid Tory vote. Anyone who wasn't Tory would be voting for them anyway. No point in wasting time. So the Conservatives had a clear field—just urging the faithful to vote in a town where they believed they stood a chance."

Charles indicated that that was what he had just told him, with an inclination of his head.

"But a second team went to the same street," Lloyd said. "Hot on your heels."

"Yes. Some sort of cock-up."

"Possibly caused by your switching your team from one area to the other?"

Think. Think. This has to be guesswork.

"Did you, Dr. Rule?" asked the inspector.

He had made it perfectly clear to the fool in the office that they were swapping areas with the other team. But the team originally designated had come huffing and puffing round behind them. In a way, that would work to his advantage now.

"Did you switch your team, Dr. Rule?" she asked again.

"Yes. I wanted to ... I hoped I would get the chance to speak to Valerie."

She gave him an old-fashioned look. "You and her husband were best friends," she said. "You could have spoken to her any time at all."

"I ... I didn't want to go there specially about Gerry. Valerie and I weren't on the sort of terms that meant we called in on one another, and I didn't want Valerie to think that I regarded the affair as that important. The only reason Max didn't bed Gerry sooner was that there was ninety miles between them—girls left me in droves to go with Max. I was used to it, to be perfectly honest—and so was Valerie. She was making a ridiculous fuss about nothing. So I thought if I could ... just be there on some other pretext, she would realize how unimportant the whole episode was."

"Are you saying that you didn't mind your wife having an affair with your best friend?" asked Lloyd.

"I didn't know it was happening, until Valerie told me." Charles ran his hand down his face, and tried to explain. "But when she did, I knew it would have meant nothing at all to Max. He had slept with Gerry just as he'd slept with countless women before her. Valerie was saying that he was in love with Gerry, but that was nonsense." He had been embarrassed, annoyed. No more. "And ... we had just been told that the chances of my fathering a child were extremely slight," he said. "Gerry was shattered—she was immediately trying to make me ring adoption agencies, and clinics—she even talked about artificial insemination with donor sperm! I told her I would countenance none of these things, and she was very upset. Vulnerable. Women turn to Max with their problems, and Max invariably turns that to his advantage."

"And that made it all right?" asked the inspector, genuinely puzzled.

"No. Well, yes—yes, in a way. Because I think all that really happened was that Gerry hoped that Max would give her a baby, and that I would never know it wasn't mine. Because there was this infinitesimal chance." He unconsciously indicated just how infinitesimal with his thumb and forefinger. "I told Valerie that. Max was just a means to an end. And it didn't even work."

"So you did go to see Mrs. Scott?"

"Yes. I told the others not to bother, and when we moved on to the next street, I went back to call on Valerie, as though I was just canvassing her. And I told her that she had nothing to worry about. It was over—I knew it was, as soon as she told me that it had been going on in the surgery. Gerry had been staying late after surgery to sort out some system for periodical checks on blood pressure and weight—until she wasn't any more. He had obviously stopped seeing her. I told Valerie that too, but the woman was mad with jealousy. Max had moved to Stansfield to be with Gerry, according to her. I told her that he'd moved away from the girl who worked for him in London, but she just laughed, and said that Max didn't go in for teenage girls."

"When did it turn violent, Dr. Rule?" asked Lloyd.

"It didn't. I persuaded her not to make a complaint about Gerry, and I left."

Lloyd's eyebrows shot up. "How?" he asked. "According to you, she was mad with jealousy, wouldn't believe you that the affair was over, wouldn't believe you about Catherine . . . how did you persuade her, Dr. Rule?"

"I just kept going until I did. If you check, you'll find that she was alive and well when the second lot of canvassers went round at five forty-five." God bless the cock-up.

Lloyd shook his head. "Max Scott left the office at five thirty, and went home. He had a brief but voluble row with his wife which a couple of your fellow campaigners heard—they pointed out that they would have been unlikely to call on them anyway. He didn't leave until after the campaigners had moved on. So you didn't call on Valerie until after *he* had left, obviously."

Charles frowned. "No," he said. "I don't think that anything I've said contradicts that."

"And you persuaded her to give up this ridiculous notion, and left her alive and well, and resigned to the situation?"

Charles wanted a cigarette. He hadn't smoked for twenty years, and he wanted a cigarette. He had dedicated his career

330

to healthy living, and now he wanted nothing more than to draw nicotine and tar into his lungs, and poison himself.

"Yes," he said. "You can check—I've just told you."

"The next team came round almost immediately after Max Scott had left the house," said Lloyd. "Naturally, they discovered their mistake as soon as the householders told them, and left straight away—no point in wasting time on people who had already been doorstepped. Except one, who spoke to Mrs. Scott."

"I—I'm sorry. What has this to do with me?"

"You had ensured that no one called at the Scott house from your team—so it must have been a bit of a shock when Valerie Scott told you she had already had one of your lot round."

How did they know that? That was precisely what she had said, and then walked away, back into the sitting room, leaving him standing there. Then she'd come back, and said that he had better come in, because they had things to discuss.

"No other campaigner from any party standing in Stansfield was in that street at that time on election day," said Lloyd. "But someone called on Mrs. Scott, sporting a blue rosette, some time after six o'clock. It was the second such person she had seen. The first was the lady from the second, erroneous team. And the second was you, Dr. Rule."

Charles stared at them. "No. No—someone posing as a campaigner, perhaps—"

"You. You've just told us it was you. If not, then, she would have been even more cross—and would have pointed out that this person was the third such that she had seen. And she would not have immediately terminated her phone call in order to speak to him. We have a witness, Dr. Rule. The person who was on the phone to Mrs. Scott that day has made a statement."

Charles didn't speak. He had known, from the moment Valerie had telephoned him about Max and Gerry, that she would ruin everything unless he stopped her. If he could have stopped her any other way, he would have; he had tried. But she had been determined to bring Gerry down, and he couldn't have allowed that to happen. Everything would have gone; everything he and Gerry had worked so hard for, everything they had saved for, all their dreams.

All his dreams. For they had never been Gerry's dreams, he

knew that now. And yes, he had killed Valerie Scott for them, but he had killed Gerry too. No. Not Gerry. Geraldine. He had killed Geraldine a long, long time ago, and she had been the real victim of his dreams. Valerie Scott had merely been a threat to them that he had removed, and now, at last, he had been found out. In a way, it was a relief.

"She . . . she was going to destroy everything before it even got started," he said.

"So you destroyed her?"

"The clinic. I'd dreamed about it. I'd worked so hard for it. It was beginning to happen. We were just about to buy the private practice—I was building up the private patient lists. I'd bought the farmhouse, and the land for the clinic. Mark Callender was my friend, and he might be going to be our MP! She was going to ruin all that. Sex in the surgery, for God's sake! You *know* what the tabloids are like about these cases! And she was going to do it—make no mistake, she was going to do it!"

Lloyd just looked back at him. The inspector was writing everything down.

"I told her! I said even if Max was in love with Gerry, which he wasn't, making a complaint about her wasn't going to cure him of it! And she said she didn't pay her NHS subscriptions to provide facilities for doctors to have sex with the patients, and she meant it—she was going to do it! I tried to reason with her, I swear to you, I tried! She wouldn't see reason, she—I . . . I found my hands round her throat . . . I just . . ." He bowed his head. "I didn't go there to murder her," he said.

"It looks planned to me," said Lloyd.

"It . . . it wasn't. It was a last resort. I . . . didn't go there to do that, but I did it because there was no other way." He looked up. "But, I never, never, meant Max to be suspected. That was dreadful. I put him through all that—I had to prescribe tranquillizers and sleeping pills for Max, of all people. And people who didn't know him thought he'd done it. Zelda thought he had—she had only known him a few months, or she would have known that he couldn't . . . she always said she believed him, but she didn't. That's why she wouldn't promote him. And it was all my fault. All my fault. I tried . . . I tried to put that right, at least."

Lloyd stood up. "Charles Rule, I am arresting you for the murder of Valerie Anne Scott on the . . ."

Yes, yes, yes. He'd been waiting for that. For almost thirteen years.

Catherine looked round the interview room. She was under arrest. That was different from last time. But she was in an interview room, waiting to be interviewed. Again.

She came in then, and set up the recorder. "This interview is being tape-recorded," she said, as she opened new tapes and put them in. "Interview with Catherine Elizabeth Scott," she said, then her name, and the date. "Interview commences . . ." She glanced at the big clock with the sweep second-hand.

That had been there last time, Catherine realized; it had a V-shaped scratch on the plastic. She must be in the same interview room.

"Ten twelve A.M. on Saturday, fourth of April." She looked across the table at Catherine. "Mrs. Scott, you understand that you are not obliged to say anything, but anything you do say may be given in evidence. We wish to put questions to you concerning the murder of Victor Holyoak on Wednesday, first of April . . ."

A lot of things had changed. They hadn't taped the interviews then. The caution was different. There had been a silent uniformed policewoman, there to protect the male detective against any allegations, but there hadn't been a woman actually asking the questions. But that clock was the same, with its second-hand crawling round while they had asked her question after question.

The inspector looked up from her notebook. "Mrs. Scott," she said, "I have to put some questions to you about the events of Wednesday night which you may find distressing. Is there someone—other than your husband—whom you would like to have present? You may also have a solicitor present if you wish."

"No," said Catherine. "No."

"You told me on Thursday morning that you had spent the night in your car, in a lay-by, and that you had come directly to Holyoak's as soon as the gates opened, in order to wait for your husband." She looked at Catherine, her face serious, a little sad.

"That wasn't true, was it?" she said. "No vehicle entered Holyoak's gate before the cleaners arrived at six in the morning. And I now know that your car didn't enter at any time on Thursday, up to the time that you spoke to me. Because it had never left the day before. You had never left. Had you?"

"No," said Catherine. "Charles and Geraldine took me up to the penthouse after I fainted. I went down to the car park, hid the car behind the stair wall, and went back up."

"You wanted people to believe you had left?"

"Yes," she said. "I want to make a statement." They had agreed, she and Max.

"I think I understand why," said Inspector Hill. "You can give us a written statement if you prefer."

Catherine shook her head. She and Max had known that this would happen, that they couldn't keep fending off the inevitable, and he would have preferred it if they had just told the police; she had begged him not to. But it would get easier with each telling, and telling was much more likely to make them understand than words on paper. And they had to understand.

"Your stepfather abused you when you were a child, didn't he?" the inspector said, her voice gentle.

Catherine smiled a little. "My stepfather abused everyone he ever came into contact with," she said. "He sexually abused me, yes."

"Was it after your mother became paralysed?"

"No," Catherine said, with a sigh, looking down at her hands, consciously keeping them loose in her lap. "You think you understand, but you don't, because you never knew Victor Holyoak."

"Help me to understand," she said.

Catherine looked up at her; she did want to understand. That was something. The truth, Max had said. When they do talk to you, tell them the truth, Catherine.

"Holyoak married my mother to get me," said Catherine, simply. "He met us when I was visiting my mother in hospital. She had had a stroke, but she was recovering. He couldn't have been nicer. He came every day, he brought presents, he made her feel good. When she was allowed out, he took us to all sorts of places. He always made sure my mother was warm

334

and comfortable and not too tired. And he'd think of things that would entertain me, and it was all wonderful."

Inspector Hill wasn't taking notes this time. The machine was doing that; she was listening. It had been so hard, telling Max. But it was easier now. Better though, if she didn't look at her. She looked back down at her hands. Loose. Keep them loose.

"I was staying with friends of my mother until she left hospital. And one day Holyoak came and told me that he would like to marry my mother, and did I have any objections. Of course I hadn't. It was a lovely idea. But things would be different when my mother got home, he said. She wouldn't be able to do all the things that mothers usually did. That would be my job."

Now she looked up, her face reddening. "I thought he meant cooking and cleaning! I was twelve years old!" She looked back at her hands, clenched into fists, and carefully, deliberately, relaxed them. "But he paid people to do that for him."

"It's all right, Catherine," said the inspector. "You don't have to justify yourself."

"And he said that I would have to do what he told me to do. Of course, I said. Homework, washing the dishes, that's what I thought." She took several deep breaths. "And he said that we had a bargain. He'd look after my mother to the very best of his ability, give her the very best that he could afford, and I would do what I was told. It started right after they got married."

The inspector reached into her bag, and took out a little packet of tissues, tearing it open, handing it to Catherine. That was when she realized that she was crying.

"He came into my bedroom. I asked what he was doing there, and he said, 'We have a bargain, Catherine.'" She closed her eyes. "I can't tell you how many times I've heard those words. We have a bargain, Catherine. He had married my mother because he wanted me, he said, but people wouldn't understand. He didn't want my mother—she had had another man, and he wanted to be sure—" She broke off as the tears became too much.

"We don't have to go on right now," said Inspector Hill. "You can have a break."

She used a tissue, and took a deep breath. She didn't want

a break. "I tried to shout, but he told me I mustn't make a sound, or my mother would hear, and she would come and find us. She wouldn't understand either, and the shock could kill her. You don't want to kill your mother, Catherine, do you? So ... so I didn't make a sound, and I didn't tell anyone.

"It went on for eighteen months; once, he told me he'd made a will. That he had provided for my mother—the very best of care until the day she died, and I got everything else that he owned, providing I remained unmarried, and was not cohabiting with anyone. Because I must never let any other man do what he did to me." She shuddered. "Then one night, he really hurt me, and I screamed. My mother did hear, she did come, and she did have another stroke."

There was silence. Catherine looked at her hands, clasped so tightly that white marks showed when she pulled them apart.

"But she didn't leave him," she said, her voice light with tears. "She didn't take me away from him."

"But wasn't she in hospital again?" said Inspector Hill, gently.

Catherine nodded. "And he didn't touch me, not then. I was fourteen and a half. I had read books about it, since it had started. I thought—I thought he was one of those men who wanted really young girls. I thought it was over. My mother came home—she was almost completely paralysed, but her mind was all right. I asked her why she hadn't taken me away. And she told me it was over. That he hadn't meant to do it, it was her fault—all that. I was unhappy, but at least he was leaving me alone."

Inspector Hill gave a little sigh before she spoke. "When did it start again?" she asked.

"Just after my sixteenth birthday. My mother had had to go into hospital again, and he was supposed to have gone to some business meeting. I thought I was alone in the house. I was taking a shower, when he came in. He said he'd waited until I'd reached the age of consent out of deference to my mother." She closed her eyes. "But I wouldn't give my consent, not any more, so he—I tried to fight him off, and I couldn't, of course. But he always used to use one of those cut-throat razors, and it was on the bath, open. I could reach it. So I did. And I slashed his face with it. He had to go to hospital himself then. And I packed clothes, took money from the safe, and ran to the main road to hitch a lift to anywhere. Max picked me up." She closed her eyes. "Thank God," she said.

"But he found you again," said Inspector Hill, quietly.

"Yes. It was the day before Max closed up the office. We stayed late, talking, like we'd been doing for weeks." She looked up at the inspector. "I don't know what we talked about now, but we did. And we loved one another, but Max had never done anything—he'd never made a pass, or anything. I thought . . . I thought I could make myself—but I never had to, because Max never asked me to. But he was going away, and I didn't want him to. I begged him to stay, and he spent hours explaining why he couldn't. Then I went home, and about five minutes after I got in, someone knocked at the door. I thought—it was silly—I thought it was Max. I thought he'd changed his mind, he was going to stay. But it was him, and I didn't have a cut-throat razor that time."

She took a long, long time composing herself. Dabbing her eyes with the tissue, taking deep, deep breaths, laying her hands, loose, on her lap.

"After he left, I spent all night packing everything I possessed into bags and boxes and anything else I could lay my hands on. I spent all morning finding digs, where there would be other people, and I wouldn't have to see him alone, because I knew he'd find me again. It's what I should have done in the first place, but I wanted so desperately to be on my own."

"And then you discovered that you were pregnant," came another gentle prompt.

Zelda must have told her. Well, she'd been going to tell the whole truth anyway.

"I was frantic with fear and worry and—in the end, I rang Max and said I had to talk to him. I was going to tell him everything, then I realized that he didn't know where I *lived*." She could feel again the panic that had gripped her. "I phoned Driver's, but he wasn't there, and I rang his wife, but she hung up on me. And then they came to try to make me go to the ferry with them. He'd brought her so that I would think it was safe. But I knew she'd be told to look the other way. I wouldn't go." She looked up then, at the inspector. "When they'd gone, I went to the flat and waited, but I'd missed Max. And next morning, I got the train here, and I went to the factory. Zelda told me what had happened to Valerie."

"And then Max described your stepfather as a possible witness to where he had been?"

"Yes. It was like a nightmare. I couldn't let them bring him back. He'd gone. He'd really gone. So I said that Max had been with me. But then Max had to endure all that suspicion, and questioning and ... and when we married, I found that I couldn't ... couldn't let him touch me. I just couldn't. I couldn't bear the thought of Max doing these things to me. And poor Max was having nightmares and he needed someone—he's always needed someone. I told him—go to Zelda. I didn't mind. But Zelda didn't want to know him, because she thought he'd got me pregnant, and I couldn't tell her any different."

"But things resolved themselves eventually?"

"Yes. People forgot. Max still has nightmares—maybe not now, now that you know he didn't kill his wife. But not so often, and not so dreadful. And we were happy. We really were. Until I found out who had bought Driver's."

"Why didn't you tell your husband?"

"I was going to," Catherine said. "I kept putting it off, and off—I know what I'm like. I couldn't see how he could forgive me for putting him through all that. Because I could never tell him *why* I'd done it. I was too ashamed. I didn't want to tell him until the last minute, so that I could hang on to him as long as possible. But I went to see my mother. I told her what I thought of her."

And now she was dying. Catherine had had to face that too, in the middle of the night with Max, when souls had been bared. But that was private guilt, private grief. Not to be seen by anyone but Max, not to be shared with anyone but Max.

"I still thought he was a paedophile," she said. "I thought I would be of no interest to him. But it wasn't that. It was an obsession—he couldn't control me like he did everyone else. He came and told me I had gone back on my bargain by marrying Max, but he had looked after my mother because she hadn't made a fuss about what had happened. Another bargain. And he had brought photographs of Max and Anna Worthing—I wouldn't look at them. He was trying to punish me for going back on our bargain by giving me proof of Max's infidelity. He told me he knew I'd lied to the police—wasn't I worried about being married to a murderer? And I told him

338

that Max had seen him picking up Annabel to go to Holland, and that I had lied so that he wouldn't come back. He said he wouldn't want to be in my shoes when Max found out."

The inspector had been writing it all down. She looked up now.

"And he'd made me believe that I couldn't face Max. So I was going to run away again. But he came back on Tuesday night because he'd found out that my marriage wasn't consummated. He said he still wanted me, and if I didn't honour my obligations, he would tell the police that my alibi was fake, and that he could prove it with his private investigators' report. He said he would deny ever being at the flats that night."

"But he'd picked up Anna Worthing," said Inspector Hill. "She knew that he'd been there."

Catherine nodded. "That's what I said. But he said that Anna would say whatever he told her to say."

The inspector nodded her head slightly.

"Within a month, he said, there would be a witness to say that Max left his own house at six forty-five that evening. There were any number of people he could pay or force to do that," she said. "I knew he would do it. And that even if Max was found not guilty, he would have had to go through it all again, and I couldn't make him do that. Not twice. I knew I had to do what he wanted. I said I would do it but he had to make certain that no one ever found out."

"So you came to the opening, and then pretended you had left the building?"

"Yes. I heard the lift, but I could hear Zelda's high heels, so I hid in the big wardrobe. Then it came up again, and it was him that time, but he'd brought Anna Worthing with him—he was going on about what a bad job she'd made of the reception, so I hid again. She was there for over an hour, and then someone came to the door. He thought it was me, so he got rid of her. It was Charles, and he stayed for almost two hours. Then I heard Charles leave, and—and . . . I got ready for him. I wanted to get it over with. I sat on the bed, and I told him I was there. And I did what he wanted."

"What went wrong?"

"I thought it was over, because he got up and put on his bathrobe. But when I tried to get away, he forced me back. That's when I got the bruises. I thought it would never stop. But then

339

I saw . . . I couldn't believe it . . . it was like a dream, like an hallucination. I saw Max."

Max. Towering above them like an avenging angel, a halo of golden light behind his head.

"I could see from the kitchen right into the bedroom. The light was on, and I could see what that vicious bastard was doing to her. I just grabbed one of the knives, to stop him doing it any more. He moved, when I brought the knife down. It caught his arm—an artery. I just kept going until he sort of slid half off the bed, and didn't move."

Scott sat with his head in his hands, not looking up at Lloyd.

"Catherine was . . . calm. As if it wasn't happening. I got her into the shower before she realized the state she was in, and I looked at my clothes. Then I remembered the washing-machine. I took my clothes off and ran cold water from the shower on to them—a lot of blood came out then. It was just thin streaks, like rain. Like red rain. I got as much as I could out, and then I put them in the machine. Catherine's clothes were all right—I found them in the wardrobe."

And closed the door, thought Lloyd. So no one would know that she had been there.

"And I got her dried, and dressed, and we worked out what we were going to do."

Phoning the police would have been a very good idea, thought Lloyd. But he supposed one didn't come up with one's very best ideas under these particular circumstances.

"I told her to stay in the car, in the car park. Not to draw attention to herself by driving out. I told her I would go back to Anna's. We would do what we had been going to do. She hadn't intended going home, because of how I'd reacted when I saw Holyoak—she had been going to come to the office to talk to me there. So that's what she did. But . . ."

But he wasn't there, because he had been taken in for questioning by Finch. And Catherine had had no support when she faced Judy's questions. Nothing but her wits to tell her what to do. And she had very nearly succeeded.

Scott spoke again. "I washed the knife, and put it back. Then I had a shower. I was getting myself dry when I heard

340

a noise, and I almost died with fright. I thought he wasn't dead. But I came out, and he hadn't moved."

"But there was an empty wallet lying on the floor," said Lloyd.

Max nodded. "I picked it up before I thought. It was his. His credit cards were still in it. I had no idea how it had got there, but I realized that I had to take it with me. My fingerprints could be found anywhere at all in that flat without suspicion, but not on Holyoak's wallet, and I didn't know if I could get them off leather. I took my clothes out of the machine, and got dressed."

"But they were still damp," said Lloyd, and Scott looked impressed.

Lloyd was getting the credit for this bit of deduction, but it was Judy's. Because she had been looking at Max Scott with the appraising eye of a woman, and what she had seen had been at odds with what she had heard from Tom Finch about a drunken, naked, lewd yob. Or words to that effect.

"I got out the way I had come in, and drove the Porsche back, and parked it the way Anna had."

Not quite, thought Lloyd. Judy had wondered about this man who tried to get people out of bed to move cars that weren't blocking his garage. But it had been, of course. It just wasn't still blocking it by the morning. And Finch had got in and driven into the garage without the least trouble, despite being ten inches taller than Anna Worthing.

"You forgot to put the seat forward again," he told Scott.

Scott nodded. "I remembered, next day. But at that moment I was just praying that Anna would still be asleep, and she was. I pulled off my clothes as I went into the room in case she woke. Then I hung them over the chair. I thought they'd be properly dry by morning, but they weren't."

So Scott had had to do his naked drunk act to get rid of Finch for long enough. No point in interviewing a drunk; you had to wait until they'd sobered up, and Scott had spent enough hours in a police station to know that. He had persuaded Anna back to bed, where Finch had interrupted them. The clothes had been dry by then.

"How did you know to go to the penthouse?" Lloyd asked.

At first, when he had seen Holyoak at the reception, Max Scott had thought that Catherine had killed his wife. Then

Charles Rule had told him about Catherine's abortion. Scott had thought his story was crazy, until Geraldine Rule confirmed it.

"And I knew," he told Lloyd. "I knew that she had had a horror of sex since she was fourteen years old—I didn't know why, not then. But I knew that if someone had got her pregnant, then he had to have forced her. And I thought ... I thought it must have happened after I left. Some drunk, some customer who'd been thrown out of a whore's flat. And I knew how desperate, how lonely she must have felt. I could see that she might have been driven to take desperate ..." He didn't end the sentence. "But it wasn't Catherine," he said.

"No." Lloyd hadn't told him who was being charged with his wife's murder.

"Anyway—that's what I thought at the time."

"At the time you were waiting for Anna Worthing?"

"Yes. I couldn't go home, not until I'd sorted it all out. It seemed to make no sense. But when Anna came she was stoned out of her mind, and telling me some rambling story about Holyoak wanting her to decoy gossips and reporters ... I thought he was just queer, at that point, and didn't want people knowing. But he wasn't queer."

Holyoak seemed queer enough to Lloyd, but that was another perfectly good word that had been hijacked. And another strange turnabout. Once, it had been an insult, like black had been, if you were talking about someone who was pale tan or very dark brown. Now, black was right, and queer was what homosexuals called themselves.

"But later, I began to think about it all calmly. About Catherine running away from him as soon as he had found her, about how she had been that last morning in the office. It had to have happened then, if she was three months gone by the time she came here. And if she had been raped by one of the girls' customers, or someone in the street, she would have told me—she would have told the police. And I realized what must have happened to her. What must have been happening to her since she was a little girl—why she had a horror of sex. What she had been running away from when I picked her up that night."

He looked up then. "And then I remembered that Anna had thought that it was me at Holyoak's door," he said. "She knew

342

I hadn't left, but she hadn't seen me. And she had asked me why I hadn't taken my car. That meant she had seen the car. It had been there all the time. *Catherine* had been there all the time—she hadn't gone home at all.

"I took Anna's keys, and drove over there. I got in the way Anna had said—I couldn't risk being stopped by security, because I had no business there at that time of night. I had to stop whatever was going on up there—I had to."

He dropped his head again.

"Thank you for your co-operation, Mr. Scott," Lloyd said.

It wasn't something he often said before charging someone, though others had been much more readily co-operative than the Scotts, who had tried very hard to get away with it.

Scott looked drained, but he summoned up a smile. "I knew when I saw the inspector coming up the path," he said. "She looked like a foxhound who had just caught the scent, and Catherine and I were too tired to keep running. We'd already agreed we'd make statements."

Later, Lloyd sat with a ploughman's lunch at which he had nibbled, listening to Judy and Finch.

"What do you think'll happen to them?" Finch asked.

Judy shrugged. "Depends on the judge, I suppose," she said. "But Anna Worthing's prepared to give evidence for the defence about his obsession with Catherine, and how she herself was treated by him."

"And the Tarrant murder case has been reopened," said Finch. "I think Bannister will give evidence when he realizes how much inside stories about Holyoak are worth to German news magazines. He was acting under duress too, after all."

Judy nodded. "So with any luck, the defence will be able to make it clear what sort of man the Scotts were up against," she said.

"If I saw anyone raping my wife, never mind her bloody stepfather, I'd—"

Lloyd smiled. So would he, but he mustn't say so. Finch could, though. He hadn't been in charge of the investigation. He picked up his beer. "Do you want to know what I think?" he said.

Two reasonably interested faces turned to him.

"I think that if ex-PC Bannister had acted like a professional

343

officer of the law, and kept his hands to himself fifteen years ago, none of this would have happened," said Lloyd.

A slight frown came over Finch's face. "How do you make that out, sir?" he asked.

"Have you ever heard the rhyme about the horseshoe nail?" asked Lloyd.

Predictably, Finch had not.

"For want of a nail the shoe was lost," said Lloyd. *"For want of a shoe, the horse was lost. For want of a horse, the rider was lost."*

Finch's face held the faint look of alarm that it always did when Lloyd began quoting at him.

"For want of a rider, the battle was lost," Lloyd went on. *"For want of a battle, the kingdom was lost."* He sat back and contemplated Finch. *"And all for the want of a horseshoe nail,"* he finished, and leant forward again. "Think about it," he said. "If Bannister hadn't assaulted Anna Worthing, she wouldn't have made a complaint. And if she hadn't made a complaint, Bannister wouldn't have gone there to remonstrate with her."

Finch's brow cleared a little. "So Holyoak wouldn't have rescued her," he said. "He would never even have met her, and he would never have known that Bannister existed."

Judy was nodding agreement. "So he couldn't have used Operation Kerbcrawl to establish his alibi for Tarrant's murder," she said.

"Tarrant would still have been topped, though," said Finch.

Lloyd looked pained. "It is probable," he said, "that Tarrant would have been murdered before he could give whatever information he had to the Drugs Squad. But it wouldn't have involved Raymond Arthur Wilkes, who wouldn't have boasted to Anna, and wouldn't have died the way he did."

"No," said Finch.

"And Anna would never have gone to Holland," Lloyd went on. "So Max Scott wouldn't have seen Holyoak that evening." He was rather proud of his assessment of what had happened, but Finch still wasn't convinced.

"I don't see that that would have made much difference," he said. "To what happened here, I mean."

Lloyd lifted his eyebrows in a little shrug. "Perhaps not," he said. "But Catherine gave Max Scott a false alibi to replace

344

the real one, as it were. The one she was desperate that he shouldn't use. He didn't need an alibi—there was no evidence against him. It was the fact that she was obviously lying that made him the main suspect."

"That's true," said Judy.

"And it was a lie that she would have had no need to tell if the threat of Holyoak's return as a witness hadn't been hanging over her. If she hadn't lied, Holyoak couldn't have blackmailed her into going to his penthouse, she wouldn't have been with him, and Max Scott wouldn't have stabbed him to death."

Finch was nodding slowly, but he still had another round to fire. "Valerie Scott would still be dead," he said.

"Would she?" said Lloyd. "I wonder. Take Bannister and Anna Worthing and Operation Kerbcrawl away, and what have you got? Holyoak discovering where Catherine was living, which is what he'd spent a great deal of time and money trying to do. Operation Kerbcrawl took priority because it was coming to an end, and he had to set everything up—but without that to think about, I don't think he'd have hung about for three months before visiting himself on her, do you?"

"No," said Finch.

"So what would have happened?"

Finch blew out his cheeks. "What did happen," he said. "The bastard would have raped her."

"Quite. But it would have happened in October, when he found her. Before Max Scott had even told Catherine that he was thinking of leaving London. So what then? What when she came into the office in an evidently distressed condition? He wouldn't have put it down to the fact that he was going anywhere, would he?"

"And she'd have told him, in the end," said Judy. "She wanted to tell him anyway—that was why she came here. The only reason she didn't was because his wife had been murdered." She looked at Lloyd. "And he would never have left her alone in London to cope with that nutcase on her own," she said.

"No. So my guess is that he would never have come to Stansfield," said Lloyd. "And Charles Rule would never have had any reason to murder Valerie Scott."

Finch smiled a little sadly. "So it's all down to Bannister, is that what you're saying, sir?"

Lloyd shook his head. "I'm saying that Bannister unwittingly set in motion a train of events that culminated in Victor Holyoak's being stabbed to death on Wednesday night," he said.

"Good for him," said Finch.

It was difficult, Lloyd reluctantly admitted, to regard Holyoak's death as anything other than a merciful release for those whose lives he had so brutally manipulated for his own ends. He stood up. "It's all down," he said, "to Victor Holyoak himself. And he got his just deserts. But justice and the law don't always go hand in hand. Holyoak was the victim, and we can't forget that." He picked up the empty glasses. "Same again?" he asked.

"Please," said Judy.

"Yes, sir," said Finch. "Thanks."

"Call me Lloyd, for God's sake, Tom," he said. "It's ridiculous to sit in a pub with a man and be called 'sir' like some feudal lord."

"Lloyd?" said Finch, a little diffidently. "But that's your surname, sir."

"Have you ever heard anyone call me anything else?"

"No, sir. Lloyd. Sir Lloyd." He grinned.

"That's a thought, Lloyd," said Judy, her eyes dancing with mischief as she looked up at him. "What if you get knighted for your services to the English language or something?"

Lloyd glared at her.

"Well? Maybe it's against the law to call yourself Sir Something Else. You might have to use it."

Finch grinned at her. "Do you know what it is, then?"

"Oh, I've been given little clues here and there," she said, looking up at Lloyd again. "And I've worked it out."

"No, she hasn't," said Lloyd.

"Yes, I have," she said, and smiled at him.

There was no mistaking that smile. It came right after the gundog look—or the foxhound look, as Max Scott had said. It hadn't come with the solution of the case, which had distressed her as much as it had its victims, but it was there now.

Judy knew his name. Oh, calamity.